THE WOLF SEA

ROBERT LOW

The Wolf Sea

HarperCollins*Publishers*

HarperCollins*Publishers*
77–85 Fulham Palace Road,
Hammersmith, London W6 8JB

www.harpercollins.co.uk

Published by HarperCollins*Publishers* 2008
1

A catalogue record for this book
is available from the British Library

ISBN 13 978 0 00 721531 7

Typeset in Sabon by Palimpsest Book Production Limited,
Grangemouth, Stirlingshire

Printed by Clays Ltd, St Ives plc

This novel is entirely a work of fiction.
The names, characters and incidents portrayed in it are
the work of the author's imagination. Any resemblance to
actual persons, living or dead, events or localities is
entirely coincidental.

Mixed Sources
Product group from well-managed
forests and other controlled sources
www.fsc.org Cert no. SW-COC-1806
© 1996 Forest Stewardship Council
FSC

FSC is a non-profit international organisation established to promote the
responsible management of the world's forests. Products carrying the FSC
label are independently certified to assure consumers that they come
from forests that are managed to meet the social, economic and
ecological needs of present and future generations.

Find out more about HarperCollins and the environment at
www.harpercollins.co.uk/green

To Lewis and Harris, two islands in a sea of troubles. I hope, one day, they enjoy what their grandfather has made for them.

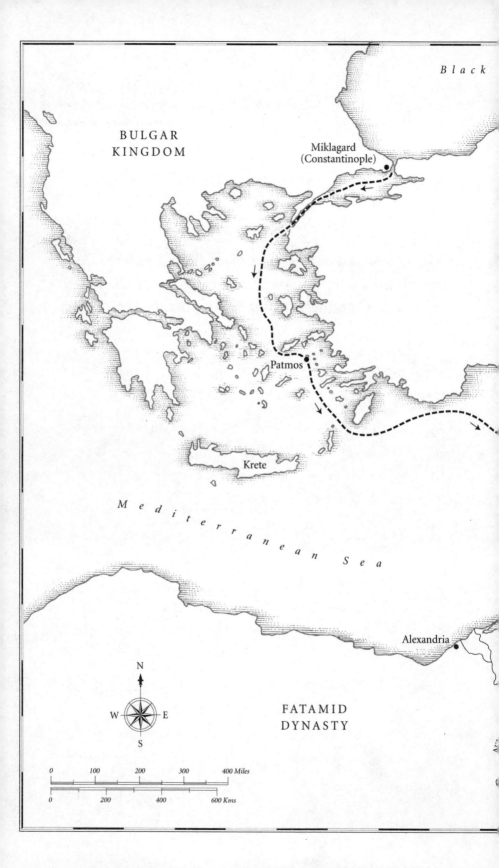

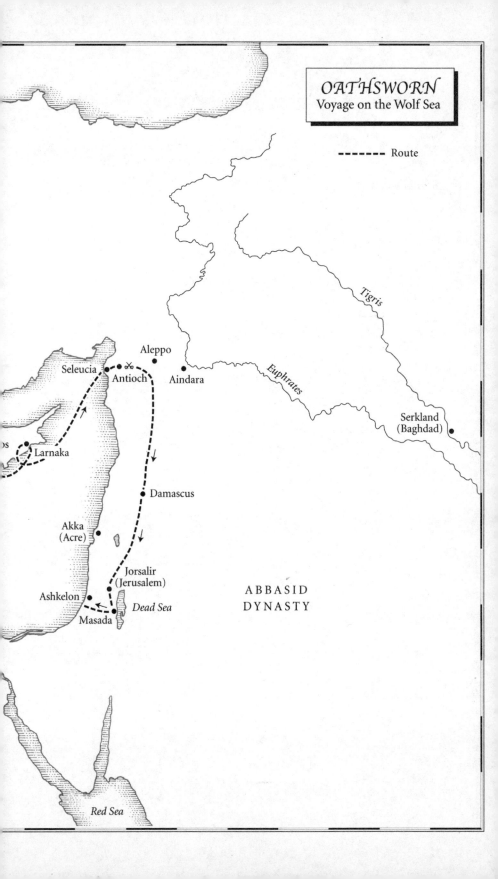

Only the hunting hungry

Set sail on the wolf sea

Old Norse proverb

ONE

MIKLAGARD, the Great City, AD 965

His eyes flicked to the bundle in my hand, then settled on my gape-mouthed face like flies on blood. They were clouded to the colour of flint, those eyes, and his snake moustaches writhed as he sneered at me, the blow I had given him having done nothing except annoy him.

'Big mistake,' he snarled in bad Greek and moved up the alley towards me, hauling a seax the length of my forearm out from under his cloak.

I hefted the wrapped sabre, swung it and revealed how clumsy the weapon was in that single moment. He grinned; I backed up, slithering through black-rotted rubbish, wishing I had just gone my way and ignored him.

He was quick, too, darting in fast and low, but I had been watching his feet not his eyes and swung the bundle so that it smacked him sideways into the wall. I followed it with a big overarm hack, but missed. The bundled sword cut through the wrappings and struck sparks from the wall.

Showered with brick and plaster chips, he was alarmed, both at the near miss and the fact that there was now a sharp edge involved. I saw it in his eyes.

'Didn't expect this, did you?' I taunted as we shifted and

eyed each other. 'Tell you what – you tell me why you are following me all over Miklagard and I will let you go.'

He blinked astonishment, then chuckled like a wolf who has found a crippled chicken. 'You'll let me go? I don't think you realise who you are facing, *swina fretr*. I am a Falstermann and not one to take such insults from a boy.'

So I had been clever about him being a Dane, I thought. It was a pity I had not been so clever about taking him on. His feet shifted and I had been watching for that, so that when he swung I caught the seax on the shredded bundle, wincing at the blow. I turned my wrist to try and tangle his blade in cloth and almost managed to twist the seax free of his grasp. He was too old a hand for that, though, and I was too clumsy with the sword wrapped as it was.

Worse than that – even now I sweat with the shame of it – his oarmate came up behind me, elbowed the breath out of me and slammed me to the clotted filth of the alley. Then he plucked the wool-coddled sword from my fluttering hands, easy as lifting an egg from a nest and, dimly, I realised that's what they had wanted all along. I was gasping and boking too much to do anything about it.

'Time to row hard for it,' this unseen one growled and I heard his steps squelching through the alley filth.

I was sure death had not been in the plan of this, but the man from Falster had blood in his eye and I had rain in mine, blurring the world. The cliff walls of the alley stretched up to frame a patch of indifferent grey sky and it came to me then that this would be the last sight I would see.

I did not want to die in a filthy alley of the Great City with the rain in my eyes. Not that last, especially, for the vision of the first man – the boy – I had killed came back to me, lying on a heath with his bloodless face and his eyes open and startled under little pools of rainwater.

The Falstermann loomed over me, breathing hard, the seax reversed for a downward thrust straight at my belt loop, rain

2

pearling mistily on the pitted steel, sliding carelessly along the edge . . .

The rain, says Sighvat, will tell you all about a place if you know how to read it. The rain in a Norway pine wood is good enough to wash your hair in but, if a city is really old, it drips from the eaves with the grue of ages, black as pitch, harsh as a curse.

Miklagard, the Great City, was ancient and her pools and gutters spat and hissed like an evil snake. Even the sea here was corroded, heaving in slow, fat swells, black and slick and greasy as a wet hog's back, glittering with scum and studded with flotsam.

I did not even want to be in this city and the gawping wonder of it had long since palled. Stumbling from the ruined dream of Attila's silver hoard, those of the Oathsworn who survived the Grass Sea of the steppe had washed up here, after a Greek captain had been persuaded to take us. Since then, my great plan had been to load and unload cargo on the docks, husband what little real money we had, waiting for the rest of the Oathsworn to join us from far-off Holmgard and make a crew worth hiring for something better.

At the end of it all, distant as a pale horizon, was a new ship and a chance to go back for all that silver, a thought we hugged for warmth as winter closed in on Miklagard, drenching the Navel of the World in misery.

That black rain should have been warning enough, but the day the runesword was stolen from me I was wet and arrogant and angry at being followed all along in the lee of Severus's dripping walls by someone who was either bad at it, or did not care if he was seen. Either way, it was not a little insulting.

On a clear day in Constantinople you could almost see Galata across the Horn. That day I could hardly see the man following me in the polished bronze tray I held up and pretended to study, as if I would buy it.

A face twisted and writhed in the beaten, rain-leprous surface, a stranger with a long chin, a thin, straggled beard, a moustache still a shadow and long, brown-red-coloured hair that hung in braids round the brow, some of them tied back to keep the hair from the blue eyes. My face. Beyond it, trembling and distorted, was my shadower.

'What do you see?' demanded the surly Greek owner of the tray and all its cousins laid out on a worn strip of carpet under an awning, heavy with damp. 'A lover, perhaps?'

'Tell you what I don't see,' I said with as sweet a smile as I could muster, 'you *gleidr gaugbrojotr*. I don't see a sale.'

He snorted and snatched the tray from me, his sallow face flushed where it wasn't covered with perfumed beard. 'In that case, fix your hair somewhere else, *meyla*,' he snapped, which I had to admit was a good reply, since it let me know that he understood Norse and that I had called him a bowlegged grave-robber. He had called me little girl in return. From this sort of experience, I learned that the merchants of Miklagard were as sharp as their manners and beards were oiled.

I smiled sweetly at him and strolled off. I had learned what I needed: the bronze tray had revealed, beyond my face and watching me, the same man I had seen three different times before, following me through the city.

I wondered what to do, clutching the wrapped bundle of the runesword and chewing *scripilita*, the chickpea-flour bread, thin and crusty on top, glistening with oil on the bottom, wrapped in broadleaves and – wonder of wonders – thickly peppered. This treat, which was never seen further north than Novgorod, was so expensive beyond the Great City, thanks to the pepper, that it would have been cheaper to dust it with gold. The seductive taste of it and the cold was what made me blind and stupid, I swear.

The street led to a little square where the windows were already comfort-yellow with light as the early winter dark closed in. I had, even in so short a time, lost the wonder that

4

had once locked my feet to the street at the sight of houses put one on top of the other and had eyes only for my tracker. I paused at a knife-grinder's squeaking wheel, glanced back; the man was still there.

He was from the North, for sure, for he was taller than any others and clean-shaven but for the long snake moustaches, a Svear fashion that was much fancied by dandies then. He had long hair, too, which he had failed to hide well under a leather cap, and wore a cloak, under which could lurk anything sharp.

I moved on, past a stand where a woman sold chickpea flour and dried figs. Next to her, a man in a sleeveless fleece sold cheeses out of a single basket and, leaning against the wall and trying not to let their teeth chatter in the cold, a pair of girls tried to look alluring and show breasts that were red-blue.

The Great City is a miserable place in winter. It has the Sea of Darkness at its back and behind that the Grass Sea of the Rus; and it is a place of gloom and penetrating damp. There may be a flicker of late summer and even pleasant days at the start of the year, but you cannot count on sun, only rain, between the last days of harvest and the first ones of the festival of Ostara, which the Miklagard priests call Paschal.

'Come and warm me,' one of the girls said. 'I can teach you how to make a beast with two backs if you do.'

I knew that trick and moved on, trying to keep the man in sight by turning and exchanging some good insults, then bumped into a carder of wool coming up the other way, demanding that people buy his mattress stuffings or risk freezing their babies by their carelessness.

The street slithered wetly down to the docks, grew crowded, sprouted alleyways and spawned people: bakers, sellers of honey, vendors of tanned leather for making cords, those selling the skins of small animals. This was not the fashionable end of Miklagard, this collection of lumpen faces and

5

beggar hands. They were the halt, the lame and the poxed, most of whom would die in the cold of this winter unless they got lucky.

It was already cold in the Great City, cold enough to numb my senses into thinking to find out who this man was and why he followed me.

So I slid up one of the alleys and hefted the bundle that was the runesword, it being the only weapon I had besides an eating knife. My plan was to tap him with the cushioned blade of it as he passed, drag him in the alley and then threaten him with the sharp end until he babbled all he knew.

He duly obliged, even pausing at the mouth of the alley, having lost me and wondering where I had gone. If I had stayed in the shadows, I would have shaken him off, for sure – but I stepped out and rapped him hard on the head.

There was a clatter; he staggered and yelled: '*Oskilgetinn!*', which at least let me know I had been right about him being from the North – though you could tell by his roar that it meant 'bastard' even if you couldn't speak any Norse. The curse let me know he was at least prime-signed, if not fully baptised, since only Christ-followers worried about children born out of wedlock. A Dane, then, and one of King Harald Bluetooth's new Christ-converts. I did not like what that promised.

The third thing I found out was that his cap was a metal helmet covered in leather and most of the blow had been taken on it. The fourth was that he was from Falster and I had made him angry.

That was what I learned. I missed many things, but the worst miss of all was his oarmate, coming up behind me and leaving me gasping in the alley, the sword gone and pearled rain dripping off the Falstermann's blade, raised to finish me.

'Starkad won't be pleased,' I gasped and the big Dane hesitated for long enough to let me know I had it right and he was a chosen man of an old enemy we had blooded before.

Then I lashed out with my right leg, aiming for his groin, but he was too clever for that and whacked my knee hard with the flat of the blade, which he then pointed at me.

He wanted to kill me so bad he could taste it, but we both knew Starkad wanted me alive. He would want to gloat and wave the stolen runesword in my face, the one now long vanished up the alley. The Falstermann, wanting to be away himself, started to say a final farewell, which would have included how lucky I was and that the next time we met he would gut me like a fish.

Except that all that came out was 'guh-guh-guh' because a knife hilt had somehow appeared beneath his right ear and the blade was all the way into his throat.

A hand pulled it out as casually as if it were plucking a thorn and the hiss of escaping blood was loud, the splatter of it everywhere as the Dane collapsed like an empty water-skin.

Blinking, I looked up to what had replaced him against the yellow lantern glow of the window lights beyond the alley: a big man, shave-headed save for two silver-banded braids over each ear, wearing the checked breeks of the Irish and a tunic and cloak that was Greek. He also had a long knife and a tattooed whorl between his eyes, which I knew was the *Ægishjalm*, the Helm of Awe, a runesign supposed to send your enemies away screaming in terror with the right words spoken. I wished he would turn it off, for it was working well on me.

'I heard him call you pig fart,' he said in good East Norse, his eyes and teeth bright in the alley's twilight. 'So I reasoned he bore you no goodwill. And, since you are Orm the Trader, who has a crew and no ship, and I am Radoslav Schchuka, who has a ship and no crew, I was thinking my need for you was greater than his.'

He helped me up with a wrist-to-wrist grip and I saw that his bared forearm had several thick-welted white scars. I looked at the dead Dane as this Radoslav bent and rifled his purse, finding a few coins, which he took, along with the seax. Then it came to me that I should be dead in the alley and my legs trembled, so that I had to hold on to the wall. I looked up to see the big man – a Slav, for sure – cutting his own arm with the seax and realised the significance of the scars.

He saw my look and showed me his teeth in a sharp grin. 'One for every man you kill. It is the mark of my clan, where I come from,' he explained, then helped me roll the Dane in his cloak and back into the shadows of the alley. I was shaking now, but not at my narrow escape – it had come to me that the Dane would have gone his way and left me lying in the muck, alive – but at what had been lost. I could have wept for the shame of losing it, too.

'Who were they?' asked my rescuer, binding up his new scar.

I hesitated; but since he had painted the wall with a man's blood, I thought it right that he knew. 'A chosen warrior of one Starkad, who is King Harald Bluetooth's man and anxious that he get something from me.'

For Choniates, I suddenly thought, the Greek merchant who had coveted that runed sword when he'd seen it. It was clear the Greek had sent Starkad to get it and would be unhappy about the death. The Great City had laws, which they took seriously, and a dead Dane in an alley could be tracked back to Starkad and then to Choniates.

Radoslav shrugged and grinned as we checked no one could see us, then left the alley, striding casually along as if we were old friends heading for a drink-shop. My legs shook, which made the mummery difficult.

'You can judge a man by his enemies, my father always said,' Radoslav offered cheerfully, 'and so you are a great man for one so young. King Harald Bluetooth of the Danes, no less.'

'And young Prince Yaropolk of the Rus also,' I added grimly to see his reaction, since he was from that part of the world. Beyond a widening of his eyes at this mention of the Rus King's eldest son there was silence, which lasted for a few footsteps, long enough for my racing heart to settle.

I was trying desperately to think, panicked at what had been lost, but I kept seeing that little knife come out of the Dane's neck under his ear and the blood hiss like spray under a keel. Someone who could do that to a man is someone you must walk cautiously alongside.

'What did he steal?' Radoslav asked suddenly, the rain glistening on his face, turning it to a mask of planes and shadows.

What did he steal? A good question and, in the end, I answered it truthfully.

'The rune serpent,' I told him. 'The roofbeam of our world.'

I brought him to our hov in a ruined warehouse by the docks, as you would a guest who has saved your life, but I did this Radoslav no favours. Sighvat and Kvasir and Short Eldgrim and the rest of the Oathsworn were huddled damply round a badly smoking brazier, talking about this and that and, always, about Orm's plan to get them back to sea in a fine ship, so that they could be proper men again.

Except Orm didn't have a plan. I had used up all my plans getting the dozen of us away from the ruin of Attila's howe months before, paying the steppe tribes with what little I had ripped from that flooding burial mound – and had nearly drowned to get, the weight of it stuffed in my boots almost dragging me down.

I could not get rid of the Oathsworn after we had all been dumped on the quayside. Like a pack of bewildered dogs they had looked to me. Me. Young enough for any to call me son and yet they called me 'jarl' instead and boasted to any they met that Orm was the deepest thinker they had ever shared an ale horn with, even as I spun and hung my mouth open

9

at the sheer size and wealth and wonder of the Great City of the Romans.

Here, the people ate free bread and spent their time howling at the chariot and horse races in the Hippodrome, fighting mad over their Blue or Green favourites and worse than any who went on a vik, so that city-wide riots were common.

The char-black scars from the previous year still marked where one had spread out, incited by opponents of Nikephoras Phocas, who ruled here. It had failed and no one knew who had fed the flames of it, though Leo Balantes was a name whispered here and there – but he and other faces were wisely absent from the Great City.

A black-hearted city right enough, which turned the slither from the gutters crow-dark so that we knew, even if the story of it curled on itself like a carved snake-knot, that cruelty squatted in Miklagard. Blood-feuds we knew well enough, but Miklagard's treachery we did not understand any better than the city's screaming passion for chariots and horses that raced instead of fought.

We were wide-eyed bairns on this new ship and had to learn how to sail it, fast. We learned that calling them Greek was an insult, since they considered themselves Romans, the only true ones left. But they all spoke and wrote in Greek and most of them knew only a little Latin – though that did not stop them muddying the waters of their tongue with it.

We learned that they lived in New Rome, not Constantinople, nor Miklagard, nor Omphalos, Navel of the World, nor the Great City. We learned that the Emperor was not an Emperor, he was the Basileus. Now and then he was the Basileus Autocrator.

We learned that they were civilised and we could not be trusted in a decent home, where we would either steal the silver or hump the daughters – or both – and leave dirty marks on the floors. We learned all this, not from kindly teachers, but from curled lips and scorn.

The slaves were better off than us, for they were fed and sheltered free, while we took miserable pay every day from a fat half-Greek, which would not let us afford either decent mead – even if we could find it here – or a decent hump. My stock of Atil's silver was all but exhausted and still no plan had come to me yet and I wondered how long the Oathsworn would stomach this.

Singly and in pairs like half-ashamed conspirators all of them had approached me at one time or another since we had been here, all with the same question: what had I seen inside Attila's howe?

I told them: a mountain of age-blackened silver and a gifthrone, where Einar the Black, who had led us all there, now sat for ever as the richest dead man in the world.

All of them had been there – though none but me inside it – yet none could find the way back to it, navigating themselves like a ship across the Grass Sea. I knew they also felt the fish-hook jerk of it, despite all that they had suffered, no matter that they had watched oarmates die there and had felt the dangerous, sick magic of that place for themselves.

Above all, they knew the curse that came from breaking the oath they had sworn to each other. Einar had broken it and they all saw what had become of that, so none slipped away in the night, abandoning his oarmates to follow the lure of silver. I was not sure whether this was from fear of the curse, or because they did not know the way, but they were Norsemen. They knew a mountain of riches lay out on the steppe and they knew it was cursed. The wrench between fear and silver-desire ate them, night and day.

Almost every night, in the quiet of that false hov, they wanted to look at the sword, that sinuous curve of sabre wrenched from Atil's howe by my hand. A master smith had made that, a half-blood dwarf or a dragon-prince, surely no man. It could cut the steel of the anvil it was made on and was worked along the blade length with a rune serpent, a snake-knot whose meaning no one could quite unravel.

The Oathsworn came to marvel at that steel curve, the sheen of it – and the new runes I had carved into the wooden hilt. I had come late to the skill and needed help with them, but those were simple enough, so that any one of the Oathsworn could read them, even those who needed fingers to trace them and mumbled aloud.

Only I knew they marked the way back to Atil's howe in the Grass Sea, sure as a chart.

A chart I had now managed to lose.

All of this swilled round in my head, dark as the water from Miklagard's gutters, as I hunched through the rain towards our ratty warehouse hall, dragging the big Slav with me. The wind blasted and grumbled and, out across the black water, whitecaps danced like stars in a night sky.

'You look like you woke up with the ugly one, having gone to bed with golden-haired Sif,' Kvasir growled as I stumbled in, shaking rain off, slapping the piece of sacking that was my cloak and hood. His good eye was bright, the other white as a dead fish, with no pupil. He looked the big Slav up and down and said nothing.

'Thor's golden wife wouldn't look at him,' said a lilting voice. 'Though half the Greek man-lover crews here would. Maybe that is the way ahead for us, eh, Orm?'

'The way behind, you mean,' jeered Finn Horsehead, jerking lewd hips and roaring at his own jest. Brother John's look was withering and Finn subsided into mock humility, nudging his neighbour to make sure he had caught his fine wit.

'Never be minding,' Brother John went on, taking my elbow. 'Come away here and sit you down. There's a fine cauldron of . . . something . . . with vegetables in it that Sighvat lifted and Finn made with pigeons. And a griddle of flatbread. Enough for our guest, too.'

The men made room round the brazier and Brother John ushered us to a place, gave us bowls, bread and a wink. Radoslav looked at the food and it was clear a stew made of the Great City's pigeons was not the finest meal he had eaten, nor – with the wind hissing through the warehouse, flaring the brazier embers – was this the best hall he had been in. But he grinned and chewed and gave every indication of being well treated. I took a bowl, but my mouth was full of ashes.

I introduced Radoslav. I told them why he was here and that what we had feared had happened – the rune-serpent sword was gone. The silence was crushing, broken only by the sigh of wind ruffling the curls on Brother John's half-grown forehead. You could hear the sky of our world falling in that silence.

Brother John had been on the boat when we had boarded it on the Sea of Darkness. The Greek and his crew thought he was one of us, we thought he was one of them and neither found out until after we were ashore. We had taken to Brother John at once for that Loki trick and afterwards he had astounded us all by telling us he was a Christ priest.

Not one like Martin, the devious monk from Hammaburg, the one I should have killed when I had the chance. Brother John was from Dyfflin and an altogether different breed of horse. He did not shave his head in the middle like the usual priests, he shaved it at the front – when he could be bothered. 'Like the druids did in times of old,' he offered cheerfully when asked.

He did not wear robes either and he liked to drink and hump and fight, too, even though he was hardly the height of a pony's arse. He was on his second attempt to get to Serkland, trying to reach his Christ's holy city, having failed the first time and, as he said himself, sore in need of salvation.

I was sore in need of the same and dare not look anyone in the eye.

13

'Starkad,' muttered Kvasir. 'Fuck his mother.' His head drooped. There were grunts and growls and sniffs, but it was a perfect summing up and the worst sound of all was the despairing silence that followed.

Sighvat broke it. 'We have to get it back,' he declared and Kvasir snorted derisively at this self-evident truth.

'I will tear his head off and piss down his neck,' growled Finn and I was not so sure that he was talking about Starkad and not me. Radoslav, food halfway to his mouth, had stopped chewing and looked from one to the other, only now realising that something truly valuable had been taken.

'Starkad,' said Finn in a voice like a turning quernstone. He stood and dragged the seax out, looking meaningfully at me. The others growled approval and their own hidden knives flashed.

Despair closed on me like dark wolves. 'He works for the Greek, Choniates,' I said.

'Aye, right enough, we saw him there,' agreed Sighvat and if there is a colour blacker than his voice was then, the gods have not seen fit to show us it yet.

Finn blinked, for he knew what that meant. Choniates had power and money and that permitted him armed guards and the law. We were Norse, with all that stood for in the Great City. Bitter experience had taught the people of Miklagard just what the Norse did in their halls during the long, dark winters, especially men with no wives to stay their hands. The Great City's *tabernae* and streets did not want feasting Northmen getting drunk and killing each other – or worse, the good citizens – so the city had made a law of it, which they called the Svear Law. We could carry no weapons and would be arrested for the ones gleaming in the firelight here. We had only a limited time in the Great City and soon we would be rounded up and pitched out beyond the frontier if we did not get a ship in time to leave ourselves.

Finn wolfed it all out in a great howl of frustration that

bounced echoes round the warehouse and started up local dogs to reply, his head thrown back and the cords of his neck standing out like ship's cables. But even he knew we would not profit from charging up to Choniates' marbled hov, kicking in the door and dangling him by the heel until he coughed up the runesword. All we would get was dead.

'Choniates is a merchant of some respectability,' Radoslav said, quiet and cautious about the smouldering rage round him. 'Are you sure he has done this thing? What is this rune serpent anyway?'

Glares answered that. Choniates had it, for sure. Architos Choniates had seen the sword weeks ago and I had been expecting something since then – only to ease my guard at the last and lose it.

When we had first staggered on to the docks of the Great City, it was made clear we would remain unmolested provided we could pay our way. I had half a boot of coins and trinkets left, the last cull from Atil's howe, but they were not seen as currency, so had to be sold for their worth in real silver – and Architos Choniates was the name that kept surfacing like a turd in a drain.

It took two days to arrange, because the likes of Choniates wasn't someone you could walk up to, a ragged-breeks boy like me. He had no shopfront, but was known as a *linaropuli*, a cloth merchant – which was like calling Thor a bit of a hammer-thrower.

Choniates dealt in everything, but cloth especially and silk in particular, though it was well known that he hated the Christ church's monopoly on making that fabric. Brother John found a *tapetas*, a rug dealer, who knew a friend who knew Choniates' chief *spadone* and, two days later, this one turned up in the Dolphin.

Outside it, to be exact, for he wouldn't set foot inside such a place, despite the rain. He sat in a hired carrying-chair, surrounded by hired men from the guild of the racing Blues, wearing their neckcloths to prove it. They were all scowling toughs sporting the latest in Great City fashion: tunics cinched tight at the waist and stiffened at the shoulders to make them look muscle-wide. They had decorated trousers and boots and their hair was cut right back on the front and grown long and tangled behind.

It was all meant to make them look like some steppe tribe come to town, but when one came into the Dolphin and asked for Orm the Trader, he was almost weeping with rage and frustration at the hoots and jeers of men who had fought the real thing.

We all went out, for the others were anxious to see what a *spadone*, a man with no balls, looked like, but were in for a disappointment, since he looked like us, only cleaner and better groomed. He was swathed in a thick cloak, drawn up over his head so that he looked like an old Roman statue, and he inclined his head graciously in the direction of the gawping mob of pirates who confronted him.

'Greetings from Architos Choniates,' he said in Greek. 'My name is Niketas. My master bids me tell you that he will see you tomorrow. Someone will come and bring you to him.'

He paused, looking round at us all. I had followed his talk well enough, as had Brother John, but the others knew just enough Greek to get their faces slapped and order another drink, so they were engaged in peering at him. Finn Horsehead was practically on his knees, trying to squint into the carrying-chair, and I could see he was set on lifting clothing to get a better look at what wasn't there.

'We will be ready,' I said, cuffing Finn's ear. 'Convey my thanks to your master.'

He nodded at me politely, then hesitated. Finn, scowling and rubbing his ear, was glaring at one of the smirking thugs who formed the bodyguard.

'You may bring no more than three others,' Niketas said as they left. 'Suitably comported.'

'"Suitably comported",' chuckled Brother John as we watched them go. 'How are we to do that at all?'

In the end, I decided Sighvat and Brother John were best and left it at that, ignoring Finn's demands to be included.

'He may just decide to lift it,' he argued. 'Or send men to ambush you on the way.'

'He is a merchant,' I said wearily. 'He depends on his reputation. He won't get far by waving a blade and robbing everyone.'

How wrong that turned out to be.

The next day we were escorted by another of Choniates' household to the expensive end of the city and were greeted by Niketas in the immaculate atrium of a large house. He eyed us with one brow raised, taking in our stained, worn clothes, flapping soles and long beards and hair. I felt like a grease stain in this marbled hov.

Sighvat, who took considerable pride in his appearance – we all did, for we were Norsemen and, compared to others in the world, a byword for cleanliness – scowled back at Niketas and hissed, 'If you had balls left, I would tear them off.'

Niketas, who must have heard it all before, simply bowed politely and then left. It may be that Choniates was then busy for two hours, or that Niketas was vengeful.

But it gave us a chance to watch and learn in a part of the city where life seemed careless. People came and went in Choniates' lavish hall with no apparent purpose other than to lean against polished balustrades and laugh and talk and bask in the perfect sun of their lives, warmed, on this chilly, damp day, by heat that came under the floor.

They drank wine from bowls, spilled it, laughingly daring, as an offering to older gods and chided each other for getting it on their expensive sleeves, patting their clothes with sticky-ringed hands. Sighvat and I spent some time wondering if you could get those sticky rings off without cutting their fingers

17

and even more wondering how the heat came up from the floor without the place burning down.

Choniates, when we were finally ushered into his presence, was tall, dressed in gold and white and with perfect silver hair. He conducted affairs in a chair at first, surrounded by men who softened his face with hot cloths, slathered him with cream and then, to our amazement, started painting it with cosmetics, like a woman. They even used brown ash on his eyelids.

He was offhand, dismissive – I was a badly dressed *varangii* boy, after all, clutching a bundle wrapped in rags, accompanied by a big, hairy, fox-faced man and a tiny, bead-eyed heretic monk who spoke Latin and Greek with a thick accent.

After he had seen the coins, though, he grew thoughtful and that did not surprise me. They were Volsung-minted and the only ones in the world not in Atil's dark tomb were the ones he turned over and over in his fat, manicured fingers. He knew their worth in silver – and, more than that, he knew what they meant and that the rumours about the Oathsworn were true.

He asked to see the sword and, made bold and anxious to please, I unwrapped that bundle and everything changed. He could scarcely bring himself to touch it, knew then who this Orm was and saw the beauty and the worth of that sabre-curve, even if he did not know what the runes meant, on hilt or blade.

'Will you sell this, too?' he asked and I shook my head and wrapped it up again. I saw in his eyes the look I was fast getting used to: the greed-sick, calculating stare of those wondering how to find out if the rumours of a marvellous silver hoard were true and, if so, where it was. The sword, as it was bundled up again, was like the dying sun to a flower as Choniates stood and watched it vanish into filthy wrappings. I knew then that showing it to him had been a mistake, that he would try something.

The barbers and prinkers were waved away; he offered wine and I accepted and sipped it – it was unwatered and I laughed aloud at his presumption. By the end of a long afternoon, Choniates reluctantly discovered that he would get no bargain for the coins, nor any clue as to other treasures.

He bought the coins and trinkets, paying some cash then, the bulk by promise – and extra for trying a cheap trick like getting me drunk.

'That went well,' beamed Brother John when we were out on the rain-glistening street.

'Best we watch our backs,' muttered Sighvat who had seen the same signs as I had.

Then, as we turned for a last look at the marble hov, we both saw Starkad, quiet and unfussed, hirpling through the gate like an old friend, not exactly fox-sleekit about it, but looking this way and that quickly, to see if he was observed. Even without the limp, which Einar had given him, both Sighvat and I knew this old enemy when we saw him – but, just then, the Watch tramped round a corner and we slid away before they spotted us and started asking awkward questions.

That had been weeks ago and Choniates, it had to be said, had been patient and cunning, waiting just long enough for us – me – to relax a little, to grow careless.

Oh, aye. We knew who had the runesword, right enough, but that only made things worse.

Finn grew redder and finally hacked the pigeon he had been plucking into bloody shreds and flying feathers until his rage went and he sat down with a thump. Radoslav, clearly impressed, picked some feathers from his own bowl and carried on eating slowly, spitting out the smaller bones. No one spoke and the gloom sidled up to the fire and curled there like a dog.

Brother John winked at me from that round face with its fringe of silly beard and jingled a handful of silver in one fist. 'I have enough here for at least one mug of what passes for

drink in the Dolphin,' he announced. 'To take away the taste
of Finn's stew.'

Finn scowled. 'When you find more of that silver, you dwarf,
perhaps we can afford better than those rats with wings that
I catch. Get used to it. Unless we get that blade back, we will
eat worse.'

Everyone chuckled, though the loss of the runesword drove
the mirth from it. The pigeons in the city were fat and bold
as sea-raiders, but easily lured with a pinch of bread, though
no one liked eating them much. So the thought of drink cheered
everyone except me, who had to ask where he had got a fistful
of silver. Brother John shrugged.

'The church, lad. God provides.'

'What church?'

The little priest waved a hand vaguely in the general direction of Iceland. 'It was a well-established place,' he added,
'well patronised. By the well-off. A well of infinite sub-
stance . . .'

'You've been cutting purses again, holy man,' growled
Kvasir.

Brother John caught my eye and shrugged. 'One only. A
truly upholstered worshipper, who could afford it. *Radix
omnium malorum est cupiditas*, after all.'

'I wish you'd stop chewing in that Latin,' growled Kvasir,
'as if we all knew what you say. Orm, what's he say?'

'He says sense,' I said. 'Love of money is the root of all
evil.'

Kvasir grunted, shaking his head disapprovingly, but smiling
all the same. Brother John had no mirth in him at all when
he met my eyes.

'We need it, lad,' he said quietly and I felt the annoyance
and anger drain from me. He was right: warmth and drink
and a chance to plan, that was what we needed, but cutting
purses was bad enough without doing it in a church. And
him being a heretic to the Great City's Christ-men was

20

buttering the stockfish too thick all round. All of which I mentioned in passing as we headed for the Dolphin.

'It isn't a church to me, Orm lad,' he chuckled, his curls plastered to his forehead. 'It's an eggshell of stone, no more, a fragile thing built to look strong. There is no hinge of the Lord here. God will sweep it away in His own good time but, until then, *per scelus semper tutum est sceleribus iter.*'

Crime's safest course is through more crime. I laughed, for all the sick bitterness in me. He reminded me of Illugi, the Oathsworn's Odin godi, but that Aesir priest had gone mad and died in Atil's howe along with Einar and others, leaving me as jarl and godi both, with neither wit nor wisdom for either.

But, because of Brother John, we were all declared Christmen now, dipped in holy water and sworn such – prime-signed, as they say – though the crucifixes hung round our necks all looked like Thor hammers and I did not feel that the power of our Odin-oath had diminished any, which had been my reasoning for embracing the Christ in the first place.

The Dolphin nestled in the lee of Septimus Severus's wall and looked as old. It had a floor of tiles, fine as any palace, but the walls were roughly plastered and the smoking iron lanterns hung so low you had to duck between them.

It was noisy and dim with fug and crowded with people, rank with sweat and grease and cooking and, just for one blade-bright moment, I was back in Bjornshafen, hugging the hearthfire's red-gold warmth, listening to the wind whistle its way into the Snaefel forests, pausing only to judder the beams and flap the partition hangings, so that they sounded like wings in the dark.

Heimthra, the longing for home, for the way things had been.

But this was a hall where strangers did not rise to greet you, as was proper and polite, but carried on eating and ignoring you. This was a hall where folk ate reclining and sitting upright at a bench marked you at once as inferior, yet another strangeness in a city full of wonders, like the ornate basins which existed for no other reason than to throw water into the air for the spectator's enjoyment.

The reason I liked the *taberna* was because it was full of familiar voices: Greeks and Slavs and traders from further north all talking in a maelstrom of different tongues, all with one subject: how the river trade was a dangerous business now that Sviatoslav, Great Prince of the Rus, had decided to fight both the Khazars and the Volga Bulgars.

It seemed that the Prince of the Rus had gone mad after the fall of the Khazar city of Sarkel, down on the Dark Sea – which event the Oathsworn had attended, after a fashion. He was now headed off to the Khazar capital, Itil on the Caspian, to finish them off, but hadn't even waited for that before sending men further north to annoy the Volga Bulgars.

'He's like a drunk in a hall, stumbling over feet and wanting to fight all those he falls on. What was he thinking?' demanded Drozd, a Slav trader we knew slightly and a man fitted perfectly to his name – Thrush – being beady-eyed and quick in his head movements.

'He wasn't thinking at all, it seems to me,' another said. 'Next you know, he will think he can take on the Great City.'

'Pity on him if he does, right enough,' Radoslav agreed, 'for that means hard war and the Miklagard Handshake.'

That I had never heard of and said as much. Radoslav's mouth widened in a grin like a steel trap and he laughed, causing his brow-braid to dip in his leather mug.

'They offer a wrist-grasp of peace, but that is only to hold you close, by the sword-arm,' he told us, sucking ale off the wet end of his hair. 'The dagger is in the other.'

'Let's hope he does and dies for his foolishness. Maybe then we can go back north,' Finn said, blowing froth off his straggling moustache.

I said nothing. The truth was that we could never go north,

even if Sviatoslav turned his face to the wall tomorrow. He had three sons who would squabble over their inheritance and we had annoyed them all in the hunt for Attila's hoard out on the steppe – the secret of which now lurked under Starkad's fingertips.

He did not know, I was sure. Almost sure. He took the sword from me because Choniates the merchant had valued it and had probably offered highly for it. Even Choniates did not know what the scratches on the handle meant, but he knew how fine the blade was and where it had come from. Even if Starkad read runes well, he would make no sense of the ones on the sword's grip.

Perhaps they even thought the rune serpent, carved into the steel when it was made, held the secret of the way to Atil's tomb – and perhaps it did, for no one could read that spell in full, not even Illugi Godi when he was alive and he was a man who knew his runes. I had my own idea about what those runes did, all the same, and felt a chill of fear at not having the sword. Would all my hurts and ills come back in a rush now, no longer held at bay by that snake-knot spell?

Finn only nodded when I whispered all this out, eyeing me scornfully when I came to the last part, for he and Kvasir were the only ones I had shared this with and neither of them believed my good health and wound-luck was anything other than youth and Odin's favour.

For a while Finn sat moodily stroking the beard he had plaited into what looked like black leather straps, trying to ignore the woman yelling at him from the other side of the hall.

'She wants you, does Elli,' Kvasir pointed out. 'The gods know why – sorry, Brother John, God knows why.'

'You'll be well in there, with no silver changing hands at all,' Sighvat added moodily.

Finn stirred uncomfortably. 'I know. I have no joy in me for it this night.'

'It's the name,' declared Sighvat and that, together with Finn's half-ashamed scowl, managed a laugh from us. Elli, according to the old saga tales – and we had no reason to disbelieve them, Christ-sworn or no – was the giant crone who had wrestled with Thor, the one who was really Old Age.

I could see where that could be . . . diminishing to a man of sensitive nature. I said as much and Finn drained his mug, slapped it angrily on the table and lurched off to the whore, looking to soak his black rage in the white light of sweaty humping.

I sat back, easing. Brother John was right; we had all needed this. Now . . . it was clear Starkad was working for Architos Choniates, the merchant. We needed to—

Then, of course, Odin's curse kicked in the door.

Well, Short Eldgrim did, slamming through in a hiss of damp wind and curses from those nearest as it washed them, swirling the lantern smoke. He spotted me, bustled his way through and sat, breathing heavily, the network of scars on his face made whiter by its weather-red. 'Starkad,' he growled. 'He's coming up the street with men at his back.'

'That's useful,' muttered Kvasir. 'I want to see his face when he finds out he has picked the last drinking place in the world he wants to be in.'

'One!' roared the crowd behind us. Elli was showing how many silver coins she could stick on the sweat of her bared breasts. Kvasir grinned. 'She cheats – she uses honey. I tasted it once.'

'Pass the word,' I said softly. Odin's hand, for sure – I knew One Eye would not let that sword fly from us so lightly, that he had walked the thief right into our clutches.

'Three!' Elli was doing well behind us.

Short Eldgrim nodded and slid away. Behind us, a coin slid from Elli's ample, sweaty charms and the crowd roared. Brother John swallowed ale and narrowed his eyes.

24

'A dangerous place to confront him,' he said, looking round at the crowd.

'Odin chooses,' I said flatly and he glanced at me, who was now, supposedly, a prime-signed Christ-follower.

'*Amare et sapere vix deo conciditur*' he said wryly and I had felt my face flush. Even a god finds it hard to love and be wise at the same time; I wondered, after, if our little Christ priest had the power of scrying.

'I hope that is Roman for "kill them all and let Christ Jesus sort them out", little man,' Finn growled, for he hated folk talking in tongues he did not understand. Since he did not understand any other than west Norse, he was frequently red in the face. Someone bumped him and he rounded savagely, slamming the man with an elbow. For a moment, it looked like trouble, but the man saw who it was and backed off, hands held up, aghast at having offended the Oathsworn. Skythians, they called us, or Franks – those who knew a little more used *Varangi* – and they knew if you took on one, you took on all.

Then the man himself came in, shoving through the door, pausing in a way that let me know, at once, that it was no accident, his arrival in the Dolphin. Heads turned to look; conversation died and silence drifted in with the cold rain-wind at the sight of him and the two behind him, openly armed, wearing mail and helms. That only revealed that Starkad and his crew had a powerful new friend in the Great City.

'Starkad,' I said and it was like the slap of a blade on the table. Silence fell, voices ceased one by one when they heard their own echo and heads turned as people sensed the hackle-rise tension that had crept into the fug and lantern smoke. Finn's scowl threatened to split his brow and he growled. Radoslav looked quizzically from one to the other and, even in that moment, I saw the merchant in him, setting us in scales and balancing our enemies on the other pan to see who was worth more.

Starkad was splendid, I had to allow. He was still hand-some, but pared away, as if some fire had melted the sleek from him, leaving him wolf-lean, with eyes sunk deep and cheekbones that threatened to break through the skin.

Wound fever, I thought, seeing how bad his limp was – Einar had given him a sore mark, right enough, that day on a hill in the Finns' land. The Norns' weave is a strange pattern: Einar was now dead and Starkad was standing there in a red tunic, blue wool breeks, a fine, fur-lined cloak fastened with an expensive pin and a silver jarl torc round his neck. He was, it seemed, making sure I knew his worth.

'So, Orm Ruriksson,' he said. There was a shifting round me, the little sucking-kiss sound of eating knives coming out of sheaths. I placed my hands flat on the table. He had two others at his back – one with squint eyes – but I knew there would be more outside, ready to rush to his aid.

'Starkad Ragnarsson,' I acknowledged – then froze, for he was wearing a sword at his side and he and his men had dared swagger through Miklagard with weapons openly, which fact had to be considered.

Not just any sword. My sword. The rune-serpent blade he had stolen.

He saw that I had spotted it. He had a smile like the curve of that blade and, behind me, I felt the heat and the stir and heard the low rumble of a growl. Finn.

'I have heard of the death of Einar,' Starkad said, making no effort to come closer. 'A pity, for I owed him a blow.'

'Consider it Odin luck, since he would have balanced you up with a stroke to the other leg if you had met again,' I replied evenly, the blood thundering in my ears, ringing out the question of how he came to be wearing that sword. Had he stolen it from Choniates, too? Had the Greek given it to him – if so, why?

Starkad flushed. 'You yap well for a small pup. But you are running with bigger hounds now.'

'Just so,' I answered. This was easy work, for Starkad was not the sharpest adze in the shipyard for wordplay. 'Since we are speaking of dogs – have you been back to sniff Bluetooth's arse? Does that King know that you have lost both the fine ships he gave you? No, I didn't think so. I am thinking he may not stroke your belly, no matter how well you roll on your back at his feet.'

The flush deepened and he laid one hand casually on the hilt of the sabre by way of reply. He saw me stiffen and thought it recognition of the blade and smiled again, recovering. In truth, it was the sight of his pale fingers, like the legs of a spider, sliding along the marks I had made on the hilt, watching them unconsciously trace the scratches, all unknowing.

'Look . . .' began the tavern-owner, his hands trembling as he wiped them over and over on his apron. 'I want no trouble here . . .'

'Then fasten yer hole shut,' growled the squint-eyed man, his affliction adding to the savagery of his tongue. The tavern-owner winced and backed off. I saw little Drozd sidle away from us, as though we had plague.

'King Harald can spare two such ships,' Starkad went on dismissively. 'I have been tasked with something and will travel to the edge of the world to obey my King.'

I mock-sighed and waved an airy jarl hand at a seat, as if in invitation to discuss this matter that troubled him. I hoped to get him closer, away from the door and the men at his back and the ones I was sure were outside. There would be a fight and blood, since they had weapons and we did not and that would bring the authority of the Great City down on us, but still . . .

He was polished as a marble step and no fool. 'You are not what I seek, boy,' he said with a sneer that refused my invitation. 'Nor any of these who treat you like a ring-giver on a gifthrone, for all that you have neither seat, nor neck ring, nor even ship to mark you. No sword, either, since I took it.'

He drew back a little from his hate then and forced a smile into my face, which I knew was pale and stricken. I felt the Oathsworn behind me, trembling like ale at an over-full brim and Finn, quivering, barely leashed, finally snapped his bonds.

A bench went over with a clatter and he howled himself forward at Starkad, who whipped that sabre out with a hiss of sound, fast as the flick of an adder's tongue. Finn, with nothing but his fists, came up two foot short of Starkad's face, with the point of the rune-serpent sword at his neck. Someone squealed; Elli, I thought dully.

I held up my hand and leashed the others, which act gave me a measure of stone-smoothness, for Starkad noted that and was impressed, despite himself. I could hardly breathe; I wondered if he knew how deadly that blade against Finn's neck truly was. Even just resting it left a thin, red line. For his part, Finn had froth at the edges of his mouth and I knew that one more comment and he would run his neck up the blade, just to get his hands round Starkad's own.

'I have heard tales of this blade,' Starkad said softly. 'It cut an anvil, I hear.'

'Just so,' I agreed, dry-mouthed. 'Perhaps, Finn, you should come and sit by me. Your head is hard, but not harder than the anvil that blade was forged on.'

The rigid line of Finn softened a little and he took a step backward, away from the blade. Each step laboured, he unreeled from the hook of that runesword. I breathed. Starkad, smirking, waited until Finn was seated, then sheathed the weapon; life flooded back to the room with a breathy sigh.

'You have the look of a jarl,' I said into Starkad's smirk, my chest still tight with the fear of what might just have happened, 'but you should beware the jarl's torc.'

'You should only beware it when you do not have it,'

Starkad spat back. 'The mark of ringmoney is the mark of a gift-giver, whom men follow.'

I said nothing to that, for Gunnar Raudi – my true father – had often told me that you should never interrupt an enemy who was making a mistake. I already knew the secret of the jarl torc Starkad was so proud of wearing. It was just a neck ring of silver, which we still call ringmoney, whose dragon-head ends snarl at one another on your chest.

The secret was that the real one was made of steel, carried by the men who wielded it for you. It hung round your neck, another kind of rune serpent, at once an ornament of great-ness and a cursed weight that could drag you to your knees and which you could not take off in life.

I knew that from Einar, who had warned me of it as he died by my hand, sitting on Attila's throne. Now I felt the weight of it myself – even though I could not, as Starkad had seen, afford a real one.

'I seek the priest, one Martin, the monk from Hammaburg,' Starkad went on. 'You know where he is, I am thinking.'

I was silent, knowing exactly what it was Starkad sought. Not a silver hoard at all, but Martin's treasure, the remains of his Christ spear, the one stuck in the side of the White Christ as he hung on the cross and whose iron head had helped make the sabre Starkad now wore. He did not know that and I leached a little comfort from the secret.

Now that King Harald Bluetooth was a Christ-man himself, he fancied this god spear to help make everyone in his kingdom stronger in the Christ faith – no matter that the Basileus of the Romans claimed such a spear already resided in the Great City. Like me, Bluetooth believed Martin had the real one.

'He fled,' Starkad added, when my silence stretched too far. 'The monk fled. To here, I am thinking, and to you, since you are the only ones he knows.'

It was a good thought, for Martin had been with us for long enough, but Starkad did not know that it was not as a friend. My tongue was already forming the words to tell him this when the thought came to me that we could not – dare not – take him here. It was certain that the Watch had already been called and Starkad was measuring his time like a ship-master tallies his distances, down to the last eyeflick.

Miklagard was a haven for Starkad; he had to be lured out of it.

'East,' I said. 'To Serkland and Jorsalir, his holy city.'

I have my own thoughts on who made me gold-browed at that moment, to come up with a lie and the wit to speak it with such shrugging smoothness. Like all Odin's gifts it was double-edged.

He blinked at the ease with which I had given up the infor-mation and you could see him weigh it like a new coin and wonder if it rang true when you dropped it on a table. I felt the others twitch, though, those who knew it to be a lie, or suspected the same. I hoped Starkad did not look in their bewildered eyes.

In the end, he bit the coin of it and decided it was gold. 'Let this be an end of things between us, then. Einar is dead and I have no more quarrel with the Oathsworn.'

'Return the sword you stole and I will consider it,' I told him. 'I once thought you a wolf, Starkad, but it turns out you are no more than an alley dog.'

He had the grace to redden at that. 'I took the sword the same way you took my *drakkar* – because I could and it was needful,' he replied, narrow-eyed with hate. 'It stays with me because you and your Oathsworn pack cost me dear and I will count it bloodprice for the losses.'

'Not the last losses you will have,' Kvasir interrupted angrily. 'We are not finished with you – take care to keep beyond reach of my blade, Starkad Ragnarsson.'

'What blade?' sneered Starkad and slapped his side. 'I have the only true blade you nithings owned.'

The door opened in a blast of wind and rain and a head

hissed urgently at Starkad's back. It did not take much to know the Watch was coming up the street. Starkad leaned forward at the hip a little and his lip curled.

'I know you, Kvasir, and you, Finn Horsehead. You also, boy Bear Slayer. I will find out the truth of what you say. If you spoke me false here, or if you get in my way, I will make you all unwind your guts round a pole until you die.'

He backed out of the door while I was still blinking at the picture he had placed in my head with that last one, for I had heard of this cruel trick.

There was a surge, like a wave breaking on a skerry, and I hammered the table to bring the Oathsworn up short, while the others in the tavern scrambled to be out and away. Finn hurled one luckless chariot-racing fan sideways, then stopped, sullen as winter haar.

'We have to kill Starkad,' he growled, sitting. 'Slowly.'

'Is this sword so valuable, then?' asked Radoslav. 'And who is this priest?'

I told him.

'What holy icon?' demanded Brother John when he heard my brief tale of Martin and his spear.

'A spear, like Odin's Gungnir, only a Roman one,' I answered. 'The one they stuck in the Christ when he hung on the cross. Only the metal end is missing from it.'

Brother John's mouth hung open like the hood of a cloak, so I did not mention that the metal end had been used in the making of the runed sabre Starkad had stolen to feed the greed-fire of Architos Choniates. I did not understand why Starkad had the sword, all the same.

'Another Holy Lance?' Brother John was a flail of scorn. 'The Greeks-who-are-Romans here swear they have one, tucked up in a special palace with Christ's bed linen and sandals.'

I shrugged. Brother John snorted his disgust and added, scornfully, '*Mundus vult decipi.*'

31

The world wants to be deceived . . . I wasn't sure if it was a judgement on Martin's desires or on just how genuine the spear was. But Brother John was silent after that, deep in thought.

'Concerning this sword . . .' Radoslav began, but the Watch piled in then and the tavern-owner went off into an arm-wave of Greek. There were looks at us, then back again, then at us.

Eventually, the Watch commander, black-bearded and banded in leather, peeled off his dripping helmet, tucked it in the crook of his arm, sighed and came towards us. His men eyed us warily, their iron-tipped staffs ready.

'Who leads?' he asked, which let me know he was no stranger to our kind. When I stood up, he blinked a bit, for he had been looking expectantly at Finn, who now showed him a deal of sarcastic teeth.

'Right,' said the Watch commander and jerked a thumb back at the tavern-owner. 'Not your fault, Ziphas says, but he still thinks you brought armed men to his place. Scared off his custom. Neither am I happy with the idea of you lot blood-feuding on my patch. So beat it. Consider it lucky you have no weapons yourselves, else I would have you in the Stinking Dark.'

We knew of that prison and it was as bad as it sounded. Finn growled but the Watch commander was grizzled enough to have seen it all and simply shook his head wearily and wandered off, wiping the rain from his face. Ziphas, the tavern-owner, still smearing his hands on his apron, finally left it alone and spread them, shrugging.

'Maybe a week, eh?' he said apologetically. 'Let folk forget. If they see you here tomorrow, they will not stay – and you don't spend enough to make up the difference.'

We left, meek as lambs, though Finn was growling about how shaming it was for a good man from the North to be sent packing by a Greek in an apron.

'We should follow Starkad now,' Short Eldgrim growled. 'Take him.'

Finn Horsehead growled his agreement, but Kvasir, as we shrugged and shook the rain off back in our warehouse, pointed out the obvious.

'I am thinking Starkad's crew are now hired men and so permitted weapons,' he observed. 'Choniates will stand surety for them here like a jarl.'

Radoslav cleared his throat, cautious about adding his weight to what was, after all, not much of his business. 'You should be aware that this Starkad, if he is Choniates' hired man, has the right of it under law. We will have warriors from the city on us, too, if blood is shed and not just the Watch with their sticks. Real soldiers.'

'We?' I asked and he grinned that bear-trap grin.

'It is a mark of my clan that when you save a man's life you are bound to keep helping him,' he declared. 'Anyway, I want to see this wonderful sword called Rune Serpent.'

I thought to correct him, then shrugged. It was as good a name for that marked sabre as any – and it was how we got it back that mattered.

'Which brings up another question,' said Gizur Gydasson. 'What was all that cow guff about the monk going to Serkland? Has he really gone there?'

That hung in the air like a waiting hawk.

'If force will not do it, then cunning must,' Brother John said before I could answer, and I saw he had worked it out. '*Magister artis ingeniique largitor venter.*'

'*Dofni bacraut,*' Finn growled. 'What does that mean?'

'It means, you ignorant sow's ear, that ingenuity triumphs in the face of adversity.'

Finn grinned. 'Why didn't you say that, then?'

'Because I am a man of learning,' Brother John gave back amiably. 'And if you call me a stupid arsehole again – in any language – I will make your head ring.'

Everyone laughed as Finn scowled at the fierce little Christ priest, but no one was much the wiser until I turned to Short Eldgrim and told him to find Starkad and watch him. Then I turned to Radoslav and asked him about his ship. Eyes brightened and shoulders went back, for then they saw it: Starkad would set off after Martin and we would follow, trusting in skill and the gods, as we had done so many times before.

Anything can happen on the whale road.

TWO

After Starkad's visit to the Dolphin, we moved to Radoslav's *knarr*, the *Volchok*, partly to keep out of the way of the Watch, partly to be ready when Short Eldgrim warned us that Starkad was away.

There was a deal to be done with the *Volchok* to make it seaworthy. Radoslav was a half-Slav on his mother's side, but his father was a Gotland trader, which should have given him some wit about handling a trading *knarr* the length of ten men. Instead, it was snugged up in the Julian harbour with no crew and costing him more than he could afford in berthing fees – until he had heard that a famous band of *varjazi* were shipless and, as he put it when we handseled the deal, we were wyrded for each other.

But he was no deep-water sailor and every time he made some lofty observation about boats, Sighvat would grin and say: 'Tell us again how you came to have such a sweet sail as the *Volchok* and no crew.'

Radoslav, no doubt wishing he had never told the tale in the first place, would then recount how he had fallen foul of his Christ-worshipping crew, by drinking blood-tainted water in the heat of a hard fight and refusing, as a good Perun man, to be suitably cleansed by monks.

'The *Volchok* means "little wolf", or "wolf cub" in the Slav tongue,' he would add. 'It is rightly named, for it can bite when needs be. My name, *schchuka*, means "pike" for I am like that fish and once my teeth are in, you have to cut my head off to get me to let go.'

Then he would sigh and shake his head sorrowfully, adding: 'But those Christ-loving Greeks loosened my teeth and left me stranded.'

That would set the Oathsworn roaring and slapping their legs, sweetening the back-breaking work of shifting ballast stones to adjust the trim on his little wolf of a boat.

Trim. The *knarr* depends on it to sail directly, for it is no sleek fjord-slider, easily rowed when the wind drops. Trim is the key to a *knarr* as any sailing-master of one will tell you. They are as gripped by it as any dwarf is with gold and the secret of trim is held as a magical thing that every sailing-master swears he alone possesses. They paw the round, smooth ballast stones as if they were gems.

Knowing how to sail is easy, but reading hen-scratch Greek is easier than trying to fathom the language of shipmasters and I was glad when Brother John tore me from a scowling Gizur, while we waited for Short Eldgrim.

The little Irisher monk was also the one man I seemed able to talk to about the wyrd-doom of the whole thing, who understood why I almost wished we had no ship. Because a Thor-man had drunk blood and offended Christmen, I had a gift, almost as if the Thunderer himself had reached down and made it happen. And Thor was Odin's son.

Brother John nodded, though he had a different idea on it. 'Strange, the ways of the Lord, right enough,' he declared thoughtfully, nodding at Radoslav as that man moved back and forth with ballast stones. 'A man commits a sin and another is granted a miracle by it.'

I smiled at him. I liked the little priest, so I said what was on my mind. 'You took no oath with us, Brother John. You need not make this journey.'

He cocked his head to one side and grinned. 'And how would you be after making things work without me?' he demanded. 'Am I not known as a traveller, a *Jorsalafari*? I have pilgrimed in Serkland before and still want to get to the Holy City, to stand where Christ was crucified. You will need my knowledge.'

I was pleased, it has to be said, for he would be useful in more ways, this little Irski-mann and I was almost happy, even if he would not celebrate *jul* with us, but went off in search of a Christ ceremony, the one they call Mass.

Still – blood in the water. Not the best wyrd to carry on to the whale road chasing a serpent of runes. Nor were the three ravens Sighvat brought on board, with the best of intent – to check for land when none was in sight – and the sight of them perched all over him was unnerving.

We tried to celebrate *jul* in our own way, but it was a poor echo of ones we had known and, into the middle of it, like a mouse tumbling from rafter into ale horn, came Short Eldgrim, sloping out of the shadows to say that two Greek *knarr* were quitting the Julian, heading south, filled with Starkad's war-dogs and the man himself in the biggest and fastest of them.

We hauled Brother John off his worshipping knees, scrambled for ropes and canvas and, as we hauled out of the harbour, I was thinking bitterly that Odin could not have picked a better night for this chase – it was the night he whipped up the Wild Hunt hounds and started out with the restless dead for the remainder of the year.

Yet nothing moved in the dark before dawn and a mist clung to the wharves and warehouses, drifting like smoke on the greasy water, like the remnants of a dream. The city slept in the still of what they called Christ's Mass Day and no-one saw or heard us as the sail went up and we edged slowly out of the harbour, on to a grey chop of water.

37

Wolf sea, we called it, where the water was grizzled-grey and fanged with white, awkward, slapping waves that made rowing hard and even the strongest stomachs rebel. Only the desperate put out on such a sea.

But we were Norse and had Gizur, the sailing-master. While there were stars to be seen, he stood by the rail with a length of knotted string in his teeth attached to a small square of walrus ivory and set course by it.

He also had the way of reading water and winds and, when he strode to the bow, chin jutting like a scenting hound, turning his head this way and that to find the wind with wettened cheeks, everyone was eased and cheerful.

Him it was who had spotted the *knarr* ahead, not long after we had quit the Great City, on a morning when the frost had crackled in our beards. For two days we kept it in sight, just far enough behind to keep it in view. Only one, all the same – and, if we saw it, it could see us.

'What do think, Orm Ruriksson?' he asked me. 'I say she knows we are tracking her wake, but then I am well known for being a man who looks over one shoulder going up a dark alley.'

Then a haar came down and we lost her – or so we thought. Finn was on watch while the rest of us hunkered down to keep warm. The sail was practically on the spar and yet we swirled along, for we were caught in the gout that spilled through the narrow way the Greeks call Hellespont and only us and fish dared run it in the dark. I had resigned myself to casting runes to find Starkad when Finn suddenly bawled out at the top of his voice, bringing us all leaping to our feet.

By the time I reached the side, there was only a grey shape sliding away into the fog. Finn, scowling, rubbed the crackling ice from his beard.

'It was a *knarr*, right enough – we nearly ran up the steerboard of it, but when I hailed it, it sheered off and vanished south.'

'As would I have done,' Brother John chuckled, 'if you had hailed me in your heathen tongue. Did you try Greek at all?'

Finn admitted he had not mainly because, as he said loudly and at length, he could not speak more than a few words as Brother John knew well and if he had forgotten he, Finn, would be glad to jog his memory with a good kick up the arse.

'Next time, try your few words first,' advised Brother John. '"*Et tremulo metui pavidum junxere timorem*" as the Old Roman skald has it. "And I feared to add dreadful alarm to a trembling man" – bear it in mind.'

Everyone chuckled at a shipload of Greeks being scared off by a single Norse voice, while Finn, spilling ale down his beard and trying to stuff bread in his mouth as he drank, grumbled back at them.

Sighvat pointed out that if Finn did hail another ship as Brother John wished, it would turn round and vanish as well, for who wants to hear someone wanting to know how much it costs to have your balls licked?

'Either that,' added Kvasir, 'or they will be confused by a demand for two more ales and a dish of mutton.'

But Radoslav looked at me and both of us knew, because we were more traders than the others, that the ship had held Starkad, or at least some of his men. Traders thrived on gossip: what cargo was going where, what prices for what goods in what ports. They sucked it up like mother's milk and, to get it, they talked to every other trader they saw coming up against them or sailing down a route with them. Unless you looked like a warship, or a sleek *hafskip*, which could be more wolf than sheep, you hailed them all for news; you didn't sheer away like a nervous maiden goosed behind her mother's back.

Nor, if you were anyone but the Norse, did you run the Hellespont at night.

But it had vanished south and we followed. In the morning,

39

Sighvat cast his bone runes on the wet aft-deck and tried to make sense of it, Short Eldgrim peering over his shoulder. In the end, Sighvat made his pronouncement and Gizur leaned on the steering oar as the sail cranked up; I saw we were taking the most likely trade route and wondered if that course had truly been god-picked or was Sighvat's common sense.

What nagged me more was where the second boatload was – and if the one we had seen had had Starkad in it. For days I wondered where either had gone and whether we had passed them.

As always, Odin showed the truth, with a finger-nail trace of smoke against the sky.

The smoking boat was a Greek *knarr*, listing and down at the stern. It had been on fire, but the waves had soaked out the flames, leaving a smouldering hulk. Two bodies rolled and bobbed among the ash and spars nearby, reluctant to leave even in death.

Up in our bow, Arnor used his harpoon to gaff one of the bodies and drag it closer. He was an Icelander and everyone had mocked at him for seeking out a whaling harpoon instead of a spear – but Arnor knew the weapon and it had certainly been of use now.

The bodies were gashed and torn, bled white so that the wounds were now pale, lipless mouths. They had been stripped of everything and made a sorry sight on the deck of the *Volchok*, leaking into the bilges.

'Stabbed and cut,' remarked Brother John, examining them. 'That's an arrow wound, for sure, but they recovered it. Barbed, too – look where it hooked out heart-meat when it was pulled.'

'I know this one,' said Finn suddenly.

'Which one?' I asked.

'That one with the heart-wound and the squint. He was in

the Dolphin guarding Starkad's back. I remember thinking that he was an ugly troll and that if I had the chance I would knock his eyes straight for him.'

Anything can happen on the whale road . . .

I had that proved as the *knarr* gurgled and sank. Brother John fell to his knees and offered up prayers to his god and the Christ, which seemed a little harsh to me, for he was congratulating this Jesus on having led these men to this doom rather than us. I had not thought the Christ, white-livered godlet of peace, was so harsh – but I had much to learn; as Finn said, even as he followed me, the horn-moss was barely rubbed off me.

Of course, the rest of us joined in piously and those, like me, who thought no harm in getting all the help we could offered silent thanks to Odin, whose hand was in this for sure.

Now we knew.

We sat and worked out what had happened as the remains of the *knarr* hissed away to nothing, leaving only the stink of wet char. A ship, perhaps more than one, had come on it and there had been a fight, though Finn reckoned the attackers had sat back and shot arrows until the defenders had given in.

It seemed to him that the others had been taken, probably as slaves, because there were only two bodies, but the defenders had given in when the ship had been fired. This showed that the attackers were skilled, not just for having fire aboard for arrows, but because they would have to have worked swiftly to secure cargo and prisoners in little time before the ship burned and sank.

'It is a blade path we are on and no mistake,' Sighvat offered mournfully, which got him some hard looks; a blade path was what steersmen call a hard pull into a gale, where the only progress was by the oarblade.

It also meant the road walked by those who had died as

41

oathbreakers, a trail studded with sharp edges, so that those who cared enough howed such wyrd-doomed up with thick-soled ox-hide shoes, to help them walk their way to Hel's hall.

While they were shaking their heads and making warding signs, I considered matters. It seemed to me that these Arabs would not go far from home, though that was the arrogance of being Norse and believing that only we dared the far seas. I learned later that the Arabs are good seamen – but I had the right of here, for these Arabs were bandits with a boat, no more.

Radoslav fished out a square of fine sealskin from his purse and unfolded it to reveal another of walrus hide; we all peered curiously, mainly because it was clear he did not like revealing it. Gizur growled when he saw it, for it was a fair chart that he could have used.

'Well, a sailor's chart is a precious thing,' Radoslav argued, scowling, 'and not to be handed out lightly.'

Gizur hawked and spat meaningfully, then scowled at the lines and marks on the walrus hide. Like most of us, he only half trusted maps for how, as I had been told by better men, can you mark down with little scratches and pictures where the waves change with the mood of Ran? Experience had already taught me that maps were more fancy than fact – like all of the monk-made ones, this had Jorsalir at the centre and a guddle everywhere else – and a man at sea was better off using the knowledge of those who had sailed before, or trusting to the gods when he was on the whale road.

Still, using this one, we worked out that an island called Patmos was not so far from us, at which Brother John brightened considerably.

'St John the Evangelist was there,' he informed us. 'He was one of the twelve disciples and was exiled to Patmos by the Romans for preaching the word of God.'

'Those Romans are stupid,' growled Finn. 'They should

42

have slit his throat. Instead, they stick him on an island with a bunch of goat-humping sea-raiders.'

Brother John hesitated, then decided against throwing light on Finn's hazy grasp of the Christ sagas. Instead, he told us all about this saint and his revelations.

'What revelations?' demanded Short Eldgrim.

'*The* Revelations,' answered Brother John. 'A holy gospel.'

We knew what a gospel was – a sort of saga tale for Christ-men – and someone asked the obvious question.

'It concerns the end of the world,' Brother John answered him.

'Ah, *Ragna Rok*,' Finn said dismissively, 'but that's no revelation to anyone.'

Brother John was set to argue the point, but I gripped his shoulder and stopped him. 'Is there anything you know about this island that is of any use?'

He blinked. 'There's a town, Skala. A harbour. A church. The cave where the saint lived . . .'

'A nice little pirate haven,' Short Eldgrim said. 'Ah well, no ship-luck for Starkad, then.'

'I trust we are not going after them,' demanded Radoslav.

That is exactly what I planned to do.

Radoslav shrugged and rubbed one hand across his shaved scalp. 'I was thinking on it,' he went on, 'and it came to me that we do not know how many camel-eating Arabs there are, or that Starkad is there, or this wonderful sword.'

'I don't care to know how many goat-botherers there are,' growled Finn. 'I just need to know where they are – and, if Starkad is there, the rune-serpent sword is there.'

Gizur grunted and hemmed, a sure sign he did not agree. 'There are a deal too many goat-humpers being talked of for my comfort.'

Sighvat nodded soberly, stroking the glossy head of one of his ravens and spoke, quiet and thoughtful and smack

43

on the mark. 'Well, what if Starkad is there? And our sword?'

Our sword, I noted. There was silence, save for Radoslav, who rubbed his head in a fury of frustration. 'What is so special about this sword?' he demanded. 'Apart from cutting anvils. Why is it called Rune Serpent?'

'What do we do with Starkad and his men if we free them?' demanded Gizur, ignoring him. 'The *Volchok* is too small for all of us.'

'We could leave Starkad and his men on the island once the goat-humpers have been beaten,' Brother John said firmly. 'Alive.'

Finn grunted, which made Brother John frown, but none of us voiced what the rest of us knew; no one could be left alive to follow us once we had the runesword back.

Still, there were heads shaking over it, but I had seen another possibility.

'What were Starkad's men wearing when they stood at his back in the Dolphin, Horsehead?' I asked and Finn frowned, thinking.

'Well, I saw one had a good cloak and a silver pin that I liked. And there was a bulge under the other one's armpit that spoke of a fat purse . . .'

I sighed, for Finn's eyes saw only what he fancied. 'A byrnie?' I prompted and the frown lifted when the idea dawned on him. He nodded, creasing his face in a grin. They had come helmed and armoured.

'Coats of rings. And no doubt good swords and helms and shields,' I pointed out. 'Even on a scabby Greek *knarr* Starkad's men would go well equipped. And even if he is not there, that loot would be worth the risk.'

Brother John clasped his hands together and looked piously at the sky. '*Et vanum stolidae proditionis opus,*' he intoned.

Vain is the work of senseless treachery – and Sighvat nodded

44

as if he understood it and released the raven in the direction we knew Patmos lay. Screeching raucously, the bird wheeled off over the white-caps and Sighvat offered his own translation of Brother John's Latin.

'Shame to leave all that battle-gear to men who treat goats so badly,' he said.

The raven did not come back.

THREE

From the brow of the ridge we could look down on the remains of Skala, a small town where lanterns bobbed in a night wind that sighed over the barren scrub and rocks. A huge fire burned in what appeared to be the central square, flattening now and then in the breeze, and I counted a good dozen round it, laughing, talking, eating from the one dish. All the good citizens of the town had long since fled to the wilderness, or been sold to slavery.

These raiders were not so much different from us, I saw. They'd had a good day, gained plunder and were enjoying the fact so much it never crossed their minds that anyone would be here. It was something I remembered after and always set men on watch.

I also remember wondering if this was how it had been with Einar, always noting little things, always having to deep-think until your head hurt, always having the others there, at one and the same time a comfort and a curse.

We had come up to it in a fever of constant watches, tacking, gybing and working the sail furiously against a hissing wind, mirr-sodden and fretful, which swung this way and that. We had to lower the sail for a while and rock there, licking dry lips and squinting at the faded horizon for the first sight of a sail that would be pirates, for sure.

Then the wind came right, smack on the starboard quarter, and we hauled up the sail again, which it was my turn to do. It is no easy task and was a mark of how strong I had become that Gizur left it to me and Short Eldgrim – me to haul, he to tail the line, making it fast round a pin.

I was so lost in the act I didn't notice anything, for it was not a simple pulling, more of a falling to the deck with your whole bodyweight cranking the *rakki* – the yoke that held the sail – up the mast to where it should be.

The line slipped, as it always does, and made a fresh welt on my hand – all of the crew had cuts and welts, slow to heal in the constant damp, filled with pus and stinging. Except me. Mine healed quickly and left no scars, which had been a hackle-raising thing for me, convinced as I was that the rune-serpent sword was the cause.

Yet it had gone and that seemed to make no difference; I healed just as well. I was cheered by that and was starting to think that perhaps I should believe what Finn and Kvasir said, that I was just young, healthy and Odin-lucky.

I was examining the fresh welt when Kvasir yelled out: 'Land ahead.'

We all craned to see. Sure enough, there it was, a sliver of dark against the damp pewter sky. Gizur looked at me questioningly and I looked at the sky in reply. We had, perhaps, four hours of good daylight and would be on the land in one. I signalled to him and we slipped the sail up a knot, so that the *Volchok* surged a little harder.

'What do you think, Trader?' asked Sighvat.

'Your Odin pet was a strong flier,' I told him, then turned to the rest of the crew who were off-watch and told them to break out weapons and shields. Sighvat crooned softly to one of the two birds he had left and stroked its glossy black head.

It looked at me with a cold, hard eye, showing me the black cave of its mouth in an ugly hiss.

Men checked straps and edges, faces like stones. Twelve of us, all that was left of the Oathsworn here, which was just enough to crowd the *knarr* and not enough for a shieldwall. I wondered how many Arab sea-raiders there were and must have said it aloud.

'Pirates,' growled Radoslav and spat over the side. 'Nikephoras Phokas drove the burnous-wearing shits out of Crete about five years ago, but the survivors took to the other islands and are now like ticks on an old bitch. Sooner or later, the Great City will have to do something, for attacks on merchants are becoming too frequent.'

'They might scare Greeks,' growled Finn, 'but they haven't met us yet. Now *we* are raiders of the sea, not just some goat-worriers in a boat.'

Radoslav nodded thoughtfully. 'Those goat-worriers forced the Basileus to use hundreds of ships and Greek Fire to stamp them out of Crete. Took him a year.'

Finn grinned and wiped his mouth. 'There's too much Slav in you and not enough good Norse blood. Eh, Spittle?'

Kvasir growled something which no one heard clearly, but Finn beamed. 'The Basileus should have used us,' he boasted, slapping his chest. 'Our steel and Orm's thinking.'

My thinking was simple enough, arrived at after a Thing held on board as we reached the island, saw the lights and moved round to the other side of it, where we land-fastened the *Volchok*.

No one was left aboard, for we needed every man, but I had explained a plan to them that they thought cunning enough to agree on. Everyone was eager as hunting dogs for this, sure that we had Starkad cornered and that the secret of Atil's silver howe would be back in our grasp before long.

Save me. I knew Starkad was not here. No pack of Arab dogs would have had such an easy time of it if he had been aboard the *knarr*. They were his men, right enough – but where he was remained a mystery, though I was sure he was heading in the right direction in another fat *knarr*. He could even be lurking somewhere close, out on the black, moon-glittered sea.

Short Eldgrim and Arnor and two others circled round to the left, carrying the dead men we had fished out of that sea. Brother John had insisted on this, to give them a decent burial rather than leave them to Ran, wife of Aegir the sea god and mother to the drowned. I had agreed, but not because of his Christ sensibilities; I had thought of a better task for them.

The men came back, all save Arnor. Short Eldgrim was still chuckling.

'All is ready,' he grunted. 'When we see the camel-humpers move, Trader, we should rush them.'

The low wailing started almost as soon as he had finished speaking. Heads came up; mouths stopped chewing.

It was a good howl, one of Arnor's finest: he was noted for being the very man you needed in a northern fog up a Hordaland fjord, with a voice to bounce off cliffs. I settled my shield and hefted my axe, good weapons and cheap enough for us all to afford from my vanishing store of silver. I checked a strap and tried not to let the dry-spear in my throat choke me; no matter how often I did this, my guts turned to water, yet everything else dried up and shrank.

A man stood up, shouted and two more gathered up weapons – swords curved like a half-moon and short bows like those of the steppe tribes, only smaller – and moved off. I marked the shouter, with his black, flowing robes and curling locks, as the leader.

There was a pause. Another wolf-howl wail split the night.

'Get ready,' I said.

The men came running back, shouting and waving. I knew what they had found: the naked bodies of the two they had left far behind in the water, dead, were now at the edge of

49

town, seemingly wailing. I learned later that Short Eldgrim had come upon two tethered donkeys and had added a touch of his own, by strapping the men to their backs using tunic belts. Now the donkeys were braying, not at all happy with their loads, and trailing the fleeing men down the street, hoping to be unloaded of the stinking, leaking burdens.

The effect was better than I could have hoped. I had thought only to create some unease and confusion, but the sight of dead men, seemingly charging them on horseback, set all the Arabs shouting and screaming.

At which point I rose up and broke into a dead run towards the fire, yelling.

'*Fram! Fram!* Odinsmenn, Kristmenn!' bawled Brother John, and the whole pack of us, lumbering like bulls, roaring into the face of our fear, hurtled in a stumbling run down the slope, through the huddle of ramshackle houses and into the confusion of those milling round the fire.

Radoslav, who had crashed his way into the lead, suddenly leaped in the air and it was only when my knees hit something that pitched me face-first to the ground that I realised he had hurdled a rickety fence I hadn't spotted.

I sprawled, skidding along on the shield and wrenching that arm. Cursing, my knees burning, I scrambled up and saw Finn and Short Eldgrim, axe and spear together, stab and cut their way into the pack, with the others howling in behind.

Kol Fish-hook took a rushing Arab on his shield and casually shouldered him sideways into the spear-path of his oarmate, Bergthor, whose point caught the Arab under the breastbone. Kol then slammed another one into the fire and his robes caught, so that he stumbled around, shrieking and flailing, spraying flames and panic.

The Arabs broke and scattered, Black Robe shouting at them. A few heard him and followed, back across the square to the white-painted church, a solid, domed affair that glowed pink in the firelight.

About six of them got in and thundered the wooden double doors shut before anyone could stop them and I cursed, for everyone was too busy killing and looting the others to bother with that.

I limped into the firelight, saw that the knees of my breeks were tattered and bloodstained. Sighvat came up, saw me looking and peered closely.

'Wounded, Trader?' he asked and grinned as I scowled back. Some jarl, looking at his skinned knees like some bare-legged, snot-nosed toddler.

'We have to get them out of there,' I said, pointing to the church.

He considered it, seeing the stout timbers and the studded nail-heads, then said: 'It will burn, I am thinking.'

'It will also burn everything inside it, including what we want,' I replied. 'I will be pleased to find that all the battle-gear and plunder is somewhere else – but that's where I would put it.'

'Just so,' mused Sighvat, peeling off his leather helm and scrubbing his head. Screams and groans came from the darkness beyond the fire.

'You should know, Orm,' said Brother John, panting up like an overworked sheepdog, 'that we need not worry about what to do with Starkad's men.'

He jerked his head at a building behind him, a place with solid walls and one door, which looked to have once been the hov of a leather-worker, judging by the litter around it.

Inside, all of Starkad's men were naked and dead, eleven fish-belly white corpses buzzing with flies and dark with blood, which had soaked everywhere.

'They brought them all this way just to kill them?' muttered Sighvat, bewildered.

'No, indeed,' Brother John pointed out. 'They gelded them to be sold as slaves, but they were not clever about it. Two died because the blood poured out and would not stop and,

51

once the thing was done, the men were untied – I think to help themselves and the others with the wounds. The others, it seems, died of strangling and this one here has had his brains bashed out.'

He straightened, wiping his hands on his tunic. 'If I was asked,' he said grimly, 'I would say the ones who survived gelding strangled each other with the thongs that had once bound them and the last one ran at the wall until his head broke.'

'Is Starkad there?' demanded Radoslav and the silence gave him as good an answer as he would get. We stared, the sick, iron smell of blood and the drone of flies filling the space as we considered the horror of it.

Doomed, they had chosen a death that did not lead to Valholl and, because they had no weapons in their hands, led straight to Helheim, especially for the last man, who had slain himself. No man who was not whole could cross Bifrost to be Einherjar in the hall of the gods, waiting for Ragnarok. That was something I knew to my cost, for I had already lost fingers off my own hand and it was my wyrd that they were lost for ever and that I would never see the rainbow bridge.

I made a warding sign against the possibility of a fetch lurking in the fetid dark here, for I had had experience of such a thing before, with Hild in Attila's grave-mound. Then I added the sign of the cross, but Brother John was too busy offering prayers, kneeling without a thought in the gory slush of the floor.

I wondered if the dead men were followers of Christ or Odin, for it seemed the Christ-god had a more forgiving nature and would accept them into his hov whether they had balls or no. Or fingers. Then I shook the thought away; Valaskjalf, Odin's own hall, was open to me and that was enough. There were many halls in Asgard who would welcome the hero-dead, whole or no.

Finn and the others arrived, speckled and slathered with blood, to be told of the tragedy. That sealed the fate of the ones in the church, for even if they had been enemies, Starkad's men were good Northmen and should not have been handled so badly.

'There is too much of this ball-cutting for my liking,' muttered Kol. 'Like that greasy thrall of the Greek merchant – what was his name?'

'Niketas,' growled Kvasir and spat.

'He was a *spadone*,' answered Brother John. 'The kindest treated.'

'Eh? What's kind about gelding?' demanded Finn. 'Fine for horses, but men? We do it to shame them.'

'It is done sometimes to men for the same reason it is done to horses,' Sighvat pointed out, 'but I did not know there were different names for it.'

'Different types,' corrected Brother John. 'A *spadone* has been gelded – the testicles removed neatly with a sharp blade.' He paused, gave a little gesture and a *sschikk* then grinned as Finn and others shifted uncomfortably, drawing their knees tighter together.

'They do that even to some high-borns, when they are babes,' he went on as we gawped with disbelief. 'Only whole men may become the Basileus, and some of these princes get it done so they can then hold high office and yet be no threat.'

'There are also *thlassiae*, ones whose testicles have simply been crushed between stones.' He slapped his hands together so that men jumped and Finn groaned.

'And the third kind?' I asked, curious now.

Brother John shrugged and frowned, waving a hand at the clotted corpses. 'You do not get these in Miklagard much these days but further east, where men are permitted many wives and concubines and the women are kept apart in a place of their own. They have slaves attend them and, if they are male, they have to be . . . made harmless.'

'Ah . . . so they can't hump the big bull's heifers,' chortled Finn with considerable insight.

53

'How?' I persisted.

'They remove everything, leave you a straw to piss through,' answered Brother John, to be greeted with a chorus of disbelief. 'The Greek-Romans of Miklagard call them *castrati*.'

There was silence where gorged flies buzzed.

'This is what happened here?' I asked.

Brother John nodded sombrely. 'Yes. It is a Mussulman thing.'

Men grunted, as if dug in the ribs, for Northmen were no strangers to cutting balls, though it was rare – so rare, I had not seen it myself. Along with cutting a man on the buttocks, it was a *klammhog*, a shame-stroke that told everyone how unmanned this enemy had been and was done when we considered the defeated warrior's fighting had been cowardly.

There was silence while we chewed over this; then Finn spat on his hands and took up a brace of hand axes and led us all back to the door. Even as the chips flew like snow, it was clear it was too stout for even his strength and fierce anger.

'They built it well,' Sighvat said, 'as a fortress in time of trouble, I am thinking.'

'Burn the door,' I said and men dragged parts of the huge fire in the square over to the door, while others hauled anything that would burn out of the long-abandoned houses of the village.

Then we sat down and waited, while the smoke rose up and the door charred and the dawn fingered a way up into the night sky. I had two men stand watch, got Kvasir and two others to break down one of the mud-brick hovels for the frame-wood and stack it in the house with Starkad's dead.

The two who had served us well on the donkeys were beginning to turn green-black, so they too were added and then it was fired. It was as close to a decent funeral as I could think of and, though the Oathsworn were tired and Kvasir had taken a cut to his side, they raised no protest at it.

The others and myself sat and watched the burning door of the church and put an edge back on blunted axes. I had others collect up the spilled weapons of the dead; though it was generally agreed that those half-moon swords were poor weapons, being single-edged and sharp-pointed for stabbing and little use to a slashing man.

Behind us, the funeral pyre for Starkad's men growled in the wind, for the baked-mud bricks of the house acted like an oven and it would not catch fire, but seemed to glow in the intense heat. Bits of it ran like water.

Radoslav went off, poking about in the houses on his own and came back with a double-handful of something that was a puzzle to him. He held them out, a handful of sharp points. 'I found a barrel of these iron things,' he said, bemused.

All of us knew what they were, for we had laboured to load similar barrels for Sviatoslav's army when it headed for Sarkel.

'Raven feet,' I said to him, taking one. 'You use them to keep horsemen away from you – like so.' I tossed one and it bounced and rolled and landed, one point upward. Radoslav saw the possibility at once: a carpet of these, scattered like sown seed in front of you. No matter how they landed, one point was always up and just right for piercing the soft flesh under a hoof.

'*Calcetrippae*,' Brother John said. 'That's what the Romans called them.'

'Whatever the name,' I declared, 'we can take them, too, since we are headed for a land where men fight on horses.'

'A good spear, well braced, would do it,' growled Finn. 'Or a Dane axe. A Dane axe is best against horsemen.'

The others nodded and growled their assent and told stories of men they had heard of who cleaved horse and rider in two with one stroke using a long-handled axe. The fire crackled against the door and the night wind breathed down the street; somewhere, the donkeys brayed.

I leaned back, having picked all the bits of dirt, stone and splinters out of my knees that I could find and remembered big-bellied Skapti Halftroll, who could make a Dane axe dance and whirr like a bird wing and would have been one of those one-stroke horse cleavers.

I remembered, too, the inch of throwing spear jutting from his mouth after it had caught him in the back of the neck as we jogged away from the three-handed fight with Starkad and the local villagers – close to two years ago, though it seemed longer. All that skill, that strength, all that Skapti had been or would be, snuffed out by a badly made javelin hurled by a Karelian sheep farmer with his arse hanging out of his breeks.

That was the day Einar had fought Starkad and given him his limp. Starkad. He had gods' luck, that one, to have survived the wound, the vengeful locals and the battle with the Khazars at Sarkel – which we had missed by running off in search of treasure.

Gods' luck, too, to have plucked the Rune Serpent from me, easy as whipping a toy from a squalling baby and even more to have been on the other boat, the one which did not sail into a pack of Arab pirates. Where was he, with all his gods' luck? Where was he, with my sword?

I had luck of my own, all the same, I thought, feeling my eyelids droop. Odin luck, that gave Starkad the prize, but not the knowledge of what he truly had . . .

'Trader . . . wake . . . Trader.'

I jerked back out of an already shredding dream, blinking into the firelight and the burning-pork stink of the funeral pyre.

Kvasir watched me for a moment longer, expressionless. Had I been calling out? What had I said? I shook the trailing smoke of the dream away.

'It is dawn.'

I struggled up, wiping my dry mouth, and he handed me

a skin of water, which I took gratefully, squinting at the brightness. It was the promise of a cold, brilliant day, of blue sky, whitecap sea and one of those brass-bright suns that never seemed to get warm. The men were nearby, watching and waiting, while the fire at the church door was out, though the blackened timbers still stood firm, smouldering in the morning air. The funeral-pyre house was out, too, but greasy smoke drifted from it and the building had melted like tallow.

Finn stepped forward, an axe in either hand. He tapped the door, pretended to listen, then turned to the rest of us. 'Perhaps they are not home. Should we wait?'

The men chuckled, but I knew there was no way out of the church that could be seen, for I had studied it from all sides. Finn spat on his hands, hefted and swung, settling into the rhythm that boomed like a bell to us and must have sounded like the knell of death to those inside.

In five strokes the blackened wood caved in, exposing the equally blackened bar beyond. In four more strokes, that fell to pieces and the doors crashed open left and right, revealing the gaping maw of blackness inside, doubly dark because of the brightness outside.

Kol yelled, 'Ha!' and rushed forward before anyone could speak; there was a sound like thrumming bees and he shrieked and flew backwards, five arrows in him. A sixth hissed over his head and just missed Finn, who dragged the writhing Kol away from the door by one arm, but by the time he had done that and we had reached him, Kol's shrieks had stopped. His eyes were already glazed, though his heels kicked for a bit longer.

I blinked and squatted beside him. I remembered Kol at the siege of Sarkel, huddled behind his shield as the arrows from the walls shunked into it, as if he was sheltering from rain. And on the steppe at my back, prepared to rush in and fight if I failed to persuade the Pecheneg horsemen to accept silver to let us pass without hindrance.

Gone. Another. I had wanted rid of the Oathsworn so much I had once begged Thor and Loki to intercede and let me loose from the Odin-oath, had then sworn to the Christ to try and be rid of it. But you should be wary of involving the gods in such affairs, for they are cold and cruel and it seemed their way of answering was to get them all killed, one by one. I could almost hear bound Loki laugh.

Kol's death gave us thought on what to do next and Finn came up with a sound plan. With Kvasir and Short Eldgrim, I formed a shieldwall of three, all that would fit abreast in the space, and we lunged forward, knowing what would happen.

The arrows whirred from somewhere unseen, for the step from light to dark lost us our eyesight and, until we gained it back, we simply had to stand and brace. The first flight smacked the shields and we huddled, grunting and sweating, with Finn, Arnor and others sheltering behind, shieldless and double-armed with axes and spears.

The next thrumming sound brought arrows lower, aiming for feet and legs, but we saw them now, seven men behind a barricade of a thick table. Kvasir yelped as an arrow stung his ankle, but the angle was awkward and they bounced and skittered everywhere.

We waited, sweating and breathing in jagged rasps. I could see nothing behind the shield, but Finn, hefting a spear, watched and calculated and, suddenly, yelled, 'Now!'

A slew of axes and spears smashed across the space, just as the archers popped up for another salvo. At the same time, we three hurled forward, roaring out our challenge.

Finn's spear took one full in the chest and hurled him backwards. An axe took another in the shoulder, blade on, a second axe slammed into the head of a third, shaft first.

Then we were on them and Black Robe, spitting curses, hurled himself at me.

We fought across the upturned table and he had clearly

done sword-work before, for he knew the moves. He stabbed out, that serpent's tongue curve of blade darting swiftly, so that my axe swings looked even more clumsy by comparison. I shield-parried, axe-parried, swung, roared and nothing made any difference while, around me, men panted and grunted and shrieked and died.

He had battled shielded men before, but ones of his own sort, with metalled shields, which was his undoing. His breath was ragged and he knew he was done for anyway, but he fought with the savage-grinned panic of a rat in a barrel – and stabbed at the lower half of my shield, which would force it forward and expose my neck.

That tactic worked only on a wooden shield like mine if the point of the sword was rounded and almost blunt, like a good Norse sword. When his sharp point stuck in mine, the alarm showed briefly in those olive-dark eyes and he made another mistake – he tried to pull it out instead of letting go at once and finding another weapon.

When I back-cut, under his outstretched sword-arm, the axe blade went in on the upstroke under his armpit and only the shoulder blade stopped it. He screeched, high and thin like a woman in childbirth, and jerked away, freeing the axe for a downstroke that, because I was clumsy and hasty with panic, did not take him neatly between neck and shoulder, but carved away his bearded jaw on the left side.

Blood and teeth sprayed. One hit me in the eye, making me duck and turn away, which would have been fatal save that he was already gone, backwards and keening, on to the blood-slick flagstones.

Then there was that moment of rasp-breathing, broken by moans of those who hurt so much they wished they were dead, the gurgles of those so near death they can no longer feel the pain. This time, there was also a deal of cursing from Arnor, who had had his nose split by a cut and was bleeding

59

badly. Others moved purposefully among the whimpering Arabs, cutting throats and not being kind about it – the treatment of Starkad's men saw to that.

Finn rolled his shoulders, as if he had just done some gentle exercise, and strolled over to look at the fallen leader, who was still gasping and gurgling, drowning in his own blood. 'Messy,' he declared, shaking his head. 'I must show you some points of axe fighting, Orm Trader, for you seem to think you are chopping wood with it.'

'You might be better with a good sword,' Brother John said and indicated the area beyond the litter of bodies. Finn's eyes grew as wide as his grin. Plunder.

It was, too. I had expected the weapons and battle-gear of Starkad's men, perhaps some of the provisions from their vessel, and that would have been worth the death of Kol, even by his reckoning. I had not thought, of course, that these were seasoned pirates, who had been taking easy pickings for some time from merchants unlucky enough not to sail wider around Patmos.

There were ells of cloth, from fine linen to wadmal, barrels and boxes packed with little packets of what appeared to be dust and earth.

There was the yellow one called turmeric and the fine crimson crescents of the fire-plants that could raise blisters on the mouth of the unwary but, if cooked properly with meat, made dishes the Oathsworn could not get enough of.

There were golden mountains of almonds, black, pungent spikes of cloves, great heaps of brown dust which we knew to be cumin and coriander and barrels of instantly recognisable chickpeas.

We stared at it all open-mouthed for, in one moment, we had all become as rich as we had previously been poor, such a change as to leave us stunned – until the realisation of it struck home and we delighted in each fresh discovery.

We laughed when Short Eldgrim unwrapped a packet from

a barrel of them and sneezed so that it flew everywhere, filling the room with a golden dust that made everyone sneeze and weep.

Cinnamon, Brother John told us sternly and Short Eldgrim had just sneezed away a fortune of it.

That sobered us, so that we took more care and uncovered carefully packed and almost fresh produce – capsicums and the like and small golden-yellow fruits which made your jaws ache, and Brother John said were called *limon*.

The treasures went on and on: barrels filled with all different kinds of olives, when we had never seen more than one sort in our lives and only since we had come to Miklagard. And pepper both light and dark, as well as leather from the Nile lands.

There were weapons, too – a consignment of spearheads and knives and Greek blades needing hilt-finishing – and three beautiful swords, all clearly made in our homeland so that it made you almost weep to see them.

They were worth more than everything else put together and those blades I took, for they were well smithed and had their story written there, like water, just below the surface of the metal. *Vaegir*, they were called – wave swords – and that marked them as superior, even though they had little or no decoration on hilt or handle, just good leather grips.

One I took for myself, the other two I gave to Finn and Kvasir, marking them as chosen men, and that pair could not have been happier if I had been handing them out from a giftthrone in a huge hall, like a proper jarl. My first raid had brought them all riches and I felt the power of the jarl torc then.

So we spent the whole day moving all this to the *Volchok*, pausing only to give Kol a proper burial, with some of the spearheads and his weapons, in a decent boat-grave marked with white stones. Brother John said his chants and I, as godi, spoke some words of praise to Odin for Kol.

Later, Brother John showed Finn how to cook with the golden *limon*-fruits, so that we had minted lamb meat soaked in that juice, chopped and rolled with lentils and barley. We put it in a communal bowl – the same one the Arabs had been using – and ate it with some fresh-made flatbread. It was, by far, better than the ship's provisions – coarse bran bread, pickled mutton, salt fish, and some dried fruit – but I still ate last, after I made sure men were on watch.

We chewed, grinning greasily at each other, fat-cheeked as winter squirrels and our bellies were full of that *limon*-flavoured lamb when we lolled by a fire near the slow-rolling *Volchok*, watching the Arabs' ship burn to the waterline; we could not crew it and did not want any we had missed coming after us, full of revenge.

The men were admiring the helms and mail and swords they had, swapping mail shirts that did not fit for ones that did, when Sighvat came up, clutching a leather bag. Men stared; he had his two ravens free of their cages, one perched on either shoulder and there were wary and uncertain looks at that, the mark of a seidr man.

'I found this in the gear when we were sorting it out, Trader,' he said, ignoring their glances and handed out a bound parchment. 'It is in that Latin you read. What does it say?'

I did not know and said so, but Brother John did, for it was Greek and he knew that language well. As he read it, his brow furrowed.

'This is from Choniates, to the Archbishop Honorius of Larnaca, saying that the men who have this message are acting on behalf of one Starkad, who is acting for Choniates and should be given all help . . . and so on and so on. It seems they were to collect something and carry it back to Choniates.'

'Does it say what it is?' I asked as everyone gathered round to listen.

Brother John examined the parchment further, then shook

his head and shrugged. 'No, not a word – but it must be expensive if Choniates handed him that sword for it.'

Aye, he had the right of it – Starkad had stolen the runesword for the Greek and then been given it back as payment for a service. If he was paid that richly, it was no small service.

'What is so special about this sword?' Radoslav demanded, scrubbing his head in fury.

There were shrugs. Eyes flicked to me and I smiled at the big Slav – then told him the truth of it, watching him closely as I did so. His eyes went large and round and he licked lips suddenly dry, a lizard look I did not care for much.

'Small wonder, then, that they wanted to avoid us,' he offered, passing it all off as casually as he could, though his fevered eyes spoiled the stone-smoothness he tried for. 'Why was Starkad not here?' he asked, recovering, and it was a good question.

Because he was on a second ship and still looking for Martin. It seemed to me that he had sent his men racing ahead, armed and prepared to undertake this quest for Choniates, but it was my bet Starkad couldn't give the steam off his piss about it, did not want to waste time sailing all the way back to the Great City. He did it for the payment, but he wanted Martin the monk – no, not even that. He wanted that stupid Holy Lance, so he could go home. He had sailed on to Serkland, as rune-bound in his way as we were in ours.

I just had to say that little monk's name, though, and everyone understood.

Kvasir spat pointedly. 'We were no threat to those men of Starkad, if they were armed with all this,' he noted with a grunt. 'Loki played a bad trick on them when he made them sheer away from us, right into the path of wolves with better fangs.'

A Loki trick that had won us a rich cargo. Finn beamed when I said this, his beard slick with lamb grease.

'Just so, Trader, and a fine price it will pull down for us.'

'True enough,' mused Radoslav, running that dagger blade over his head again, his circle of runes puckered on his forehead as he frowned. 'North-made blades sell well in Serkland – those watered blades especially.'

Finn scowled. 'I will not sell the Godi.'

'The what?' demanded Radoslav. 'Is this another marvellous sword that demands a name, like this Rune Serpent?'

Finn grinned and explained about the snake-knot of runes, adding, 'But my blade has been named. The Godi.'

'In honour of me, no doubt,' said Brother John drily.

'In a way,' Finn answered. 'Since I seem to be killing more Christ-followers these days, it seems the name to give my blade – because it's the last thing they see before they die. A priest.'

'Of course,' I went on casually into the laughter that followed, 'there is always the other matter.'

Finn looked at me quizzically and the others sat up, interested.

'We also have a secret message, about something to be picked up in Larnaca – where is Larnaca anyway?'

'The island of Cyprus,' Radoslav said. 'Orm has the right of it. Whatever they were to get for Choniates is worth much more than what we have.'

'Gold, perhaps,' I said. 'Pearls, silver . . . who knows? Choniates is a rich man.'

'Gold,' repeated Finn.

'Hmearls,' breathed Arnor through his ruined nose. He fretted about it, for a slit nose was the mark given by lawmakers to a habitual thief and he did not like having such a sign. That and the pain, though, was forgotten in the bright balm of promised riches.

'What of Starkad?' growled Finn like a loud fart at a funeral. There was silence and shame as everyone worked out what the cost of delaying on a hunt for gold and pearls in Cyprus would do to letting Starkad escape with an even greater treasure.

Then I told them what I had thought out; Einar would have been proud of me. 'Trapping is better than hunting. Instead of chasing Starkad all over the sea, let us have Starkad come to us. This treasure Choniates desires might be worth the price of a runesword to Starkad. He cannot afford to fail two masters. We have this letter, to be carried to an Archbishop who has never seen Starkad or his men. At most he may have been told Norsemen are coming.'

Radoslav grinned. 'We are Norsemen.'

'Just so,' I replied and turned into Finn's grin.

'You are a man for clever, right enough,' he growled. 'Where, on this chart of Radoslav's, is this Cyprus?'

FOUR

The *Volchock* was no sleek *drakkar*, or even *hafskip*, as I have said. It bounced on the waves rather than slicing them, and fought us, as a little bear might. But you could see why the people of the Middle Sea called ships 'she' – that was how you sailed a *knarr*, teasing her into the wind rather than using force, persuading her until you found one she liked.

Finn spat derisively when I started that, saying that you did the same with bulls and stallions and old boar pigs if you were sensible, adding that a ship was a ship and no good would come of dressing it in skirts. Especially skirts, for a woman was a useless thing at sea. There was good reason, he finished, that the word for ship in Norse is neither woman nor man.

Sighvat said it was a good thing. 'After all,' he added, 'there is always expense with a ship as with a woman. And always a gang of men around. And a ship has a waist, shows off a top and hides a bottom.'

'It takes an experienced man to get the best out of a ship and a woman,' added Kvasir into the roars of laughter. They went on with it, finding new comparisons while they cursed it in equal measure. If you could gybe or tack, a *knarr* was a good vessel, but when the wind failed, you hauled down

66

the sail and waited, rolling and wallowing, until another came up from the right quarter – or just sailed in the wrong direction.

Gizur had his own views on Radoslav's ship. 'The rigging needs to be served, seized or whipped properly,' he declared to me with disgust. 'The *beitiass* should be shortened, the cleats moved and blocks rigged to tighten it.' He raised a hand, as if presenting a jewel of great value, though his face was twisted with disgust. When he opened his fist, there was a handful of what looked like oatmeal. 'Look at this. Just look at it.'

'What is it?' demanded Radoslav fearfully and I was close behind him. Some wood-rotting disease? A rune curse?

'Shavings, from the *rakki* lines,' Gizur said with a snort. I looked up at the *rakki*, the yoke which snugged round the mast and took all the strain of hauling the sail up and down.

'The lines are rubbing the mast away,' Gizur went on, frowning. 'It is falling like snow!'

Radoslav rubbed his chin and tugged his brow-braids, then shrugged shamefacedly and said, 'The truth of it is that this is only the second sea voyage I have ever done. I am a riverman, a born and bred oarsman. I traded happily up and down from Kiev, furs for silver, and made a good living at it until the troubles started with the Khazars and Bulgars. So I bought this, thinking to change my luck.'

Gizur at once changed, clapping the mournful man on one shoulder and all sympathy, for that was his way – which the others said came from being named for his mother, Gyda. His father, it was believed, had sailed off west following tales of a land there and had never come back.

We were rarely out of sight of land in this scattering of islands, so that we could put ashore each night. I preferred not to sleep there all the same, lying at anchor instead, since I was never sure of what lurked beyond the beach.

When it suited us, we sailed into the night, which was a dangerous business that no other seamen dared try – but we were Norsemen and had Gizur. The days turned warmer, but it still rained and we needed the sail as a tent on most nights, even though we slung it under a great wheel of stars in a seemingly cloudless sky. The last filling of waterskins was before the long, deep-water run to Cyprus and a succession of days followed one on the other, with a steady wind that let the ship run on blue-green water.

We never saw another ship but, on the last night before Cyprus, as the sun sank like blood-mist, Finn split and sizzled fresh-caught fish on the firebox atop the ballast and we settled cross-legged and ate them with thick gruel and watered ale flavoured with the *limon*-fruits, something we had all taken to doing to take away the stale taste of the drink, which had been too long casked. It was also as good as cloudberries at taking away the journey-sickness that brought out sores and loosened teeth in your gums.

We missed the taste of the cloudberries, all the same, and Arnor started singing mournful songs full of haar mists and the milk-white sea of the North, where the grit is ground out of the rocks by the ice.

Then talk turned to Cyprus and Serkland and the runesword and our oarmates and, in the end, always came down to that last, turned over and over like some strange coin, in the hope that handling and looking would suddenly reveal what the true worth of it was.

Only Radoslav knew much about Cyprus, for the Romans had only just recovered it from the Arabs. For some years, it seemed, both had tried to live shoulder to shoulder on the island, but then the Basileus had ordered the Arabs out two years before and any who stayed were warred against.

'Just our Loki luck,' mourned Finn moodily. 'More heads to pound.'

As for Serkland, the only one who had been there was

Brother John. Amund and Oski were two of the most far-travelled of us – with Einar, they had once raided down the coast of the Ummayads and through the Pillars of Hercules, which we called Norvasund, into the Middle Sea.

But Serkland, which we also called Jorsaland, was an unknown place to most of us. I only knew that they called it Serkland because the people there wore only serks – white underkirtles – instead of decent clothing.

Others had heard tales from freshly made Norse Christ-men, who had gone there and swum across a river called Jordan, tying a knot in the bushes on the far side to prove they were true travellers for the White Christ. The tales were of carpets that flew and how the White Christ turned water into wine, or made a flatbread and a herring feed an army.

Brother John told us of the incredible number of snakes there, the heat and how the people who ruled it, the Abbasid Arabs, were now the very worst of infidel pagans.

'Worse than us, eh?' grinned Kvasir.

'Just so,' answered Brother John soberly. 'For you at least can be called to see the error and embrace the true God, while these believe in their Mahomet and will kill rather than convert to the true faith.'

'Kill rather than die,' Sighvat pointed out and Brother John nodded sadly.

'It is to the eternal shame of good Christians that these heathens are in control of the holiest of places.'

'Yet,' Radoslav pointed out, 'they have no quarrel with Christ-men, I have heard, even though the soldiers of Miklagard are making war on them. They even tolerate the Jewish-men, though that is less trouble-free, for they were ever a hard people to rule. Even the Old Romans never managed it completely.'

'True,' admitted Brother John and sighed. '*Omnia mutantor, nos et mutamur in illis* – times change and so must we.'

Finn grunted appreciatively. 'The Old Romans never ruled

us, either. Maybe we can get together with these Jewish-men and give Starkad a smack. If they are like the Jew-men of the Khazars, I know they can fight well enough. They did at Sarkel.'

'Easier to get one of those flying rugs, I am thinking,' Sighvat said, stroking the head of one of the two remaining ravens, both of which had become almost too tame to be of use. It was unnerving to see Sighvat with one on either shoulder, like some Odin fetch.

'I am hoping we run into Starkad without having to sail to Serkland,' I pointed out and Amund agreed, saying it was the snakes there that bothered him most. Brother John patted his shoulder.

'That is not a worry at all,' he declared, 'for am I not come from the land where all snakes were banished by the blessed Patrick? No snake will bother us, for it knows where my feet have trod.'

'In any case,' Sighvat added, 'I have deer antler to hand.'

Now Brother John looked bemused, so Sighvat told him how a deer cannot get with young until it has eaten a snake and so rush to hunt them whenever they see one. Which is why snakes, in their turn, will run from deer, so that deer horn is a talisman against them and even burning the shavings in a fire will kill serpents with the very smell.

Brother John nodded and I could see him tuck that away, like the find of a new and strange feather, or shell on the beach. Other Christ priests – Martin, for sure – would have made the sign of the cross to ward off evil and called Sighvat a heathen devil.

The next day we sweated against a bad wind, so that it took a long, hard sail to finally snug up in the harbour at Larnaca. I approached warily, tacking in almost against an unfavourable wind, so that it could be used to sweep us out if there was any sign that Starkad was there.

The town was a sprawl of white buildings, Christ churches

and a considerable fortress on a hill, while the crescent curve of the sanded bay was studded with tiny fishing boats, all brightly painted and with eyes on the prow, which we had come to note was a Greek warding sign. Behind was what we now realised was the look of all the islands here: grey rock and dust, spattered with grey-green shrubs.

'Pleasant spot,' Kvasir noted, rubbing his hand and scenting the air, which was laced with the subtle wafts of cooking. 'I smell drink,' he added.

'I would curb your thirst,' Finn growled and nodded to where people were gathering, at once curious and afraid. From the fortress, winding down the short road to the quayside, came a snake of armed men, spears glittering, led by a man on a horse.

Men muttered and looked to their weapons, but I smiled and pointed to the curled-up cat sleeping under a strung fishing net on the beach.

'There will be no battle here today,' I said and Sighvat chuckled and nodded. The rest just looked bemused, but Sighvat had remembered. *See many strange things in battle. But you never see a cat on a battlefield.*

I had a brief flash of Skarti's fever-racked face as he shivered in the shieldwall before the pocked-walls of Sarkel, telling me this in ague-stammers after we had both seen, like an Odin sign, a bird fly into that dusty hell of arrows and blood, perching on a siege tower to sing.

Minutes later, Skarti had an arrow in his throat and never spoke again, so it had been a bad omen for him and maybe he had known it.

Now I hoped he read the omens true. I had considered the chances of Starkad putting in here and discounted them; he had sent a boatload of men with a letter and would want to avoid being sucked into the quest, would want to sail hard and fast for Serkland and find his monk. I offered prayers to Odin that it would take him time to find out the lie I had

71

told him, time I needed to rob him of this prize that would bring him rushing to us on ground we chose.

Yet here were soldiers, snaking their way down to the quay-side, people parting to let them through. They formed up neatly in two ranks with their studded leather coats and metal helmets, round shields and spears.

The officer was splendid, in that armour of little metal leaves over leather that they call lamellar and a splendid helmet made to look like it was fashioned from the tusks of a boar, surmounted by a falling wash of horsehair plume.

'You could beat them all with an empty waterskin,' growled Finn and spat over the side. 'These are half-soldiers.'

He was right: half-soldiers, called-out men who were tradesmen most of the time, but issued battle-gear when need or ceremony demanded. I felt easier, until I saw another group, this time a huddle of servants and one of the carrying-seats we knew well from the Great City. I realised, suddenly, that the knees were out of my breeks, my tunic salt-streaked and stained.

The carrying chair halted and a figure got out, rearranging the folds of his white robes. He was bald save for tufts of grey hair sticking from the sides of his head and clean-shaven but for a wispy lick of beard. That and his flap of ears made him look like a goat, but the officer saluted him smartly enough.

I had ordered Finn and others into what battle-gear we had, so that they made some appearance, grim being better than ragged. I slid into mail, greasy against almost-bare skin and borrowed a pair of better breeks from Amund, who then had mine, which were shorter in the leg on him. He stood behind the others on deck to hide his shame.

So I stepped ashore, flanked by mailed men, trying to look like a jarl while the bright sun beat down and the waves slapped. Goat Face stepped forward, glanced around and gave a slight nod.

I nodded back and he rattled off in Greek. I knew the tongue, though could not write it then, but he spoke so fast that I had to hold up a hand, to slow him down. That stunned him a little, for it seemed an imperious gesture, though I had meant no such thing. Even as he blinked, I realised that he had been asking which one was the leader here, never imagining it could be the most boyish of them all. By cutting him off in mid-flow, I had announced myself and with some force.

'Speak slowly, please. I am Orm Ruriksson, trader out of the Great City, and this is my ship, *Volchok*.'

He raised an eyebrow, cleared his throat and said – slowly – that he was Constantine, the Kephale of Larnaca, which title I knew meant something like a governor.

The officer removed his helmet, revealing a moon-face and sweat-plastered thinning hair, to present himself, with a nod of the head, as Nikos Tagardis. He was *kentarchos* here, a chief of several hundred men – though if they were all like the ones sweating and shifting behind him, it wasn't much of a command.

They were, it turned out, delighted and relieved to have us, for it seemed that the last time they had been visited by *Varangi* there had been more trouble about it. Constantine remounted his carrying chair and led a little procession of us away from the sea and into the town.

Behind, I could hear the noise change as the people surged forward and the Oathsworn clattered off the boat, Finn already booming out his few words of Greek. I hoped Radoslav and Brother John did as I had requested and sold only enough cargo to pay what we would owe.

The town was a deceit from the shore, since most of it lurked, sleepy and hidden, in a hollow between the scrub-covered hills and the sea. But it had a huddle of white houses and crooked alleys, a score of wells and several Christ temples, at least one of which had been a temple to a goddess of the Greeks before that. It even had a theatre, though I did not know what that was then.

There was also an area I knew was called a forum, which seemed to be a big square surrounded by columns, like a row of trees. It had a big, white building on one side of it, which turned out to be a bath-house.

We marched up to it and went in – the rich Greeks liked to trade in a bath-house and I came to enjoy it more than I did then. Inside, wine was served and my 'guards' scowled outside, given only watered ale. Then we spoke of this and that – and previous visitors.

'It was five years ago now,' said Tagardis, telling of the last visit of my 'countrymen'. 'They raided along the coast, but always managed to escape before I arrived with my troops.'

An escape for you, I thought as I smiled and nodded, for if they had decided to stand and fight, you would not be looking so plump and pleased now.

'In the end,' he said, looking at me levelly, 'they got themselves so drunk on pilfered wine that they ran aground and could not easily escape. Those we did not kill languish in our prison to this day.'

Hitting me on the side of the head would have been a more subtle threat. I lost my smile at that and the Kephale cleared his throat as he saw my face.

'Of course,' he smoothed, 'Trader . . . Ruriksson, is it? Yes. Ruriksson. Yes. He has much more peaceful and profitable reasons for visiting our island, I am certain. What cargo do you carry?'

He was pleased with the cloth, less so with the spices, which I had suspected would be the case – the best prices for them came the further away from their origin and Cyprus was just this side of too close.

Then I announced my intention of visiting the Archbishop Honorius and the ears went up like questing hounds, for I had made it sound like I was dropping in on an old friend.

'You know our Archbishop?' the Kephale asked smoothly, lifting his cold-sweating cup.

74

'I am paying my respects to him, from Choniates in the Great City,' I answered casually. 'I have a letter for him.'

'Archios Choniates?' asked Tagardis, pausing with cup to lip.

I nodded, pretended to savour the wine with my eyes closed. Under my lashes, I saw the pair of them exchange knowing looks.

'My commander will no doubt wish to have you presented to him, if you will. Later this evening?' said Tagardis. 'The Archbishop will also be there.'

This was new. I thought he was the commander and said as much.

He smiled and shook his head. 'A compliment which I accept gratefully, my friend,' he said, all teeth and smiles and lies. 'But I am garrison commander in Larnaca only. The commander of the island's forces is a general, Leo Balantes.'

That smacked me in the forehead, though I tried to cover it by coughing on the wine, which was one of those deep-thinking moments my men praised me for; all Greeks think barbarians like us cannot drink wine, or appreciate it when we do. They smiled indulgently.

Leo Balantes, the one rumoured to have tried to riot the Basileus out of his throne the year before. So this was what had happened to him: a threadbare command at the arse-edge of what a Greek would consider civilisation, surrounded by sea-raiders and infidels.

I remembered that he was a sword-brother of John Tzimisces, the general they called Red Boots and the one currently commanding the Basileus's armies at Antioch. That favour had at least prevented Leo from being blinded, the Great City's preferred method of dealing with awkward commanders.

We met in a simple room at the top of that solid-square fortress, dining on what seemed to be soldier's fare – fine for me, though the Kephale and the Archbishop hardly ate.

75

Balantes was square-faced and running to jowl, with forearms like hams and iron-grey hair and eyebrows, the latter as long as spider's legs.

He requested the letter, even though it was addressed to Honorius. It seemed, even to me, that we were conspirators, confirmed as Archbishop Honorius, a dried-up stick of a man with too many rings and a face like a ravaged hawk, started to explain the situation and began by looking right and left for hidden listeners. It was almost comical, but the implications of it made me sweat.

'The . . . package . . . that you have to deliver to Choniates,' the Archbishop said, while insects looped through the open shutters and died in a blaze of glory on the sconces, 'is in the church of the Archangel Michael in Kato Lefkara. It was left in the charge of monks there, to be delivered here.'

'What is it?' I asked.

Balantes wiped his mouth with the back of one hand and said, 'No business of yours. Yours is simply to get it and take it to your master who will take it to Choniates. Where is this Starkad I was told of anyway?'

'Delayed,' I replied. 'He has other business.'

'I have heard of his other business – some renegade apostate monk,' growled Balantes, scowling. 'I also know you wolves were paid enough for him to put that aside until this task was done.'

'I am here to do it,' I replied with as mead-honey a grin as I could pour out, spreading my hands to embrace them all. 'Simply get me the package and I will set sail at once.'

Now Balantes looked embarrassed.

'Not quite so simple,' Tagardis said, hesitantly, looking to his chief and back to me. 'There was . . . a problem.'

And he saga-told it all out, like a bad drunk hoiking up too much mead over his neighbours.

The island had been once jointly ruled by the Great City and the Arabs, which arrangement Nikephoras Phocas had ended by making it clear if the Arabs didn't pack up their tents and leave, he would kick their burnous-covered arses into the sea. Most had gone. Some had not and one, who called himself Farouk, had taken to raiding from the inland hills.

'Unfortunately, he has grown quite strong,' Tagardis said. 'Now he has actually captured the town of Lefkara – Kato Lefkara is a village a little way beyond it and we have had no news from that quarter for several months.'

'How strong has he grown?' I asked, seeing from which quarter the wind was blowing.

'A hundred or so Saracens,' Balantes grunted, using the Greek word for them, *Sarakenoi*. I learned later that this properly referred to the Arabs of the deserts in Serkland, but had come to be used for them all.

Tearing more mutton on to his plate, he added: 'The troops I have here outnumber him three to one, so he will not attack. However, he can't get off, nor can he get help, for my ships are better.'

'I have seen your men,' I replied, 'and your ships would only need to stay afloat to be better against a man who has none at all.'

I watched Tagardis' lips tighten, then went on, 'What do you expect from me? I have less than a dozen men.'

'I thought you *Varangii* counted yourself worth ten of any enemy,' snapped Tagardis.

'*Romanoi*, for sure,' I answered, which was foolish, since there is never anything to be gained from insulting your hosts – but I was young then and enjoyed such things.

There was a sliding sound as Tagardis pushed his chair back and half rose, face flaming. The Archbishop fanned the air; the Kephale started to bluster.

Balantes slapped the table with a hand hard as the flat of a blade. There was silence. The General spat gristle and scowled at me. 'I do not know you and though you look like

77

a boy barely into chin hair, I do you the courtesy of allowing that this Starkad gave you command because you have talent for one so young. You seem witted enough. If you had more men, could you gain this church and the prize in it?'

'Not if they are the men I have seen,' I replied. 'And how do you know this Farouk does not already have your prize?'

'It is well hidden and small,' the Archbishop declared. 'It is a leather cylinder, the length of your forearm and slightly fatter than a scroll-case. I will tell you where it is when all is decided.'

I had no idea what a scroll-case looked like, but still had a fair idea of what to look for. 'And the men?'

'What say you to fifty Danes?'

I gaped like a fresh-stunned fish, recovered and managed to grin. 'If they are the ones who have been in your prison for the last five years, I would say "farewell fifty Danes" and run like wolves were chewing at my backside. They are as likely to rip both of us a second bung hole as fight a Serklander called Farouk.'

Balantes chuckled. 'That is your problem.'

'No,' I said, 'for fifty angry and armed Danes, I am thinking, are worse to you than all the Farouks on this island.'

Balantes leaned both meaty arms on the table. 'For the last five years they have been breaking stones to repair the fortress,' he said flatly. 'There is no hope for them, no chance to get off this island other than the one they take now. If they decide to turn renegade, they will have the *Sarakenoi* and me to fight and there will be no place for them to go.

'They can rampage all they like, steal what they can, but they will be opposed at every turn and die for every mouthful of bread. They may gain riches, but will have nowhere to spend it. There is no way off this island.'

This last he almost spat at me and I saw then that he was as much a prisoner here as they – which, it seemed to me, made them more Odin-lucky than he.

I considered it and the more I did the more it seemed as attractive as Loki's daughter, Hel, her whose bedhangings were Glimmering Misfortune.

'How do they get off the island when we have recovered this prize?' I asked. 'My own crew is about all the *Volchok* will take. It is a simple trading *knarr* and, even allowing that some will die, those left will be too many for that boat.'

'Your problem,' snarled Tagardis sullenly.

'No, for I am thinking these Danes will see that clear enough when this is put to them,' I answered. 'It is not a gold-gift, this offer of yours.'

Balantes stirred slightly. 'Their ship will be returned to them,' he said and I blinked at that, for Tagardis had given me to understand that it had been sunk.

'Foundered, I said,' he corrected with a smirk. 'Holed and driven ashore. We took her and repaired her, but have found no use for her yet.'

More likely the Greeks did not know how to sail it and they would not trust the Danes back on the deck of their own ship.

'I will give them their ship and arms,' Balantes said, 'and the promise that they will be unmolested for two leagues beyond the harbour. After that, if I see that ship or the crew again, I will sink one and blind everything else.

'You will go quickly to the place, get this container and return it to me unopened. I will seal it, then you will take it back to Choniates, into his hands and no other. Time is against us here, so move swiftly. I do not care about Farouk's destruction, only what is in the container. Understand?'

I was hardly listening. A *hafskip*. Even allowing for the fact that Greeks did not know bollock from rowlock when it came to Norse ships, they could hardly have botched repairs so as to make her unseaworthy.

A *hafskip* was within my grasp and all I had to do was persuade fifty Danes not to kill their captors, to trust me, a barely shaved boy, and to take on an Arab and all his men. After that, I would have to think up some way of keeping the *hafskip* – and them if possible.

All of which made the Thing we held on board later that night a lively one.

Brother John thought we should find out how many were Christ-sworn and then convert those who were not, so that we all had that faith in common. Sighvat said it did not much matter what gods men believed in, only what men they believed in.

Finn said we should get them to swear the Oath, at which my heart sank. That Odin-oath never seemed to weaken – indeed, it grew stronger with every warrior who joined.

Kvasir, of course, slashed his way to the nub of it and, for a man with only one good eye, saw clearer than anyone, save me. I had already seen what had to happen, but just did not want to have to face it.

'These Danes will already have a leader, whether the jarl they sailed with, or one they look to if he has gone,' he said and looked at me. 'Orm will have to fight him and defeat him, otherwise all of them will be patient enemies for us, not sword-brothers to trust at our backs.'

There was silence – even the incessant chirrup of the night insects had stopped – so that my sigh seemed like the curl of wave on a beach.

'You almost have the right of it, Kvasir,' I replied. 'I will not have to defeat him, I am thinking – I will have to kill him stone dead.' It was an effort to make it sound like I was asking for the mutton dish to be passed, but I carried it off.

'Just so,' agreed Kvasir sombrely, nodding.

'What if he kills you?' asked Amund.

I shrugged. 'Then you will have to think that one out for yourselves.'

It was as offhand a hero-gesture as I could make it, but I was swallowing a thistle in my throat at the very idea of a fight and my bowels were melted.

Sighvat nodded and shifted so he could fart, a long sound, like a horn call in a fog, which broke the tension into fragments of chuckles.

'Still,' mused Brother John, 'five years breaking stones will have dulled this leader's fighting skills, surely.'

A fact I was grasping at while drowning in fear.

Kvasir grunted agreement, then said thoughtfully: 'Just don't choose to fight with hammers.'

The next day, with Kvasir, Brother John and Finn on either side, I stood in front of the sorry Danes, as husked-out a crew of worn specimens as any seen on a slave coffle in Dyfflin. They were honed by rough work and too little food into men made of braided hawsers, with muscles like knots.

Burned leather-dark, their hair made white by rock dust and sun-scorch, they stood and looked at us in the remains of their tunics and breeks, torn and bleached to a uniform drab pale, like the stuff they hewed. Stone men, with stone hearts.

Yet there was a flicker when I spoke to them and told them of what would happen, the chances for plunder on the way, which they could also keep – this last my own invention, for I knew my kind well.

'How do we know these Greeks will honour such a promise?' demanded one.

There he was. Taller than the rest, with bigger bones at elbow and knees to show that, if he'd had more food, the work would have slabbed real muscle on him. A glimmer of genuine red-gold showed in the quartz-sparkled stone dust shrouding his hair and beard and his eyes were so pale a blue that they seemed to have no colour at all.

'Because I say so,' I said. 'I, Orm Ruriksson of the Oathsworn, give you my own word on it.'

He shifted, squinted at me, then spat pointedly. 'A boy? You claim to be a jarl, but if you need us you are short on followers, ring-giver.'

'You are?'

'I am Thrain, who says you should go away, little boy. Come back when you are grown.'

'You may say that,' growled someone from the back, to a muttered chorus of agreement, 'but I would like to listen more. Five years is a long time and I am sick of stone-carving.'

Thrain whirled, spraying dust from himself. 'Fasten that bag, Halfred. We agreed that I lead here. I speak, not you.'

'Did you speak when Hrolf took the steering oar when he was fog-brained with mead?' came the counter. 'Did you speak when Bardi ordered him to steer between two shoals, he who was seeing four at the time? No. I am remembering the only noise you made was the same one as we all did – the sound of a man drowning.'

I liked this Halfred. Thrain scowled, but I had the bridle of this horse now, since I had heard the dissent.

'Here's the way of it,' I said. 'You will be free, with arms and your ship, but only if I am your jarl and you take our Oath.'

We swear to be brothers to each other, bone, blood and steel. On Gungnir, Odin's spear, we swear, may he curse us to the Nine Realms and beyond if we break this faith, one to another.

They blinked at the ferocity of it, as everyone did, for it was a hard oath and one made on Odin's spear, the Shaking One, and so could not be broken. It lasted for life unless you found someone to take your place – or fought to the death to keep it against someone who wanted it, which had not happened while I had been with the Oathsworn. That, I suddenly realised, was because so many tended to die and there were always places.

For all that, these stone Danes sucked it in like a parched man falling in an ale vat. They wanted what was offered and I could see them tasting the salt on their lips and finding it spray rather than sweat.

82

'Those who do not wish to become Oathsworn can remain and dig stones,' I went on. 'Of course, anyone can become leader here if the others want him enough and, since it is clear that there will be more of you than my own men, I am supposing you will want this Thrain to take over. So I will save him all the trouble of calling for a Thing and talking round it until our heads hurt, for it will all come out the same way.'

I looked at him. 'We fight,' I said, trying to sound as if I had just asked someone to pass the bread.

There was a brief silence, where even the sun seemed loud as it beat down.

'Do you so challenge? Or are you afraid?' I asked and Thrain scowled, for he had been stunned by the speed of all this.

'I am not afraid of you,' he managed to growl, adding a wolf-grin.

'I can change that,' I told him and the grin faded. He licked dry lips and wondered about me now, this steel-smooth, cock-sure boy. If he had known the effort it took to breathe normally, keep my voice from squeaking and my legs from shaking, he might have been less uneasy when he finally issued his challenge.

I had never fought a *holmgang* before, though I had seen it once, when two of the old Oathsworn, long gone to Valholl, had stepped into the marked-off square to fight. Hring had lasted no more than the time it took Pinleg to froth at the mouth and Hring to see that he had ended up in a fight with a berserker. There had been barely enough time for him to widen his eyes with the horror of it before Pinleg charged and hacked him to bloody shreds.

Pinleg, last seen surrounded by enemies on a beach far north in the Baltic, saving us even as we sailed away and left him.

We went to a sheltered, level spot, away from prying eyes,

when the Danes were unshackled. The others, especially Finn, were full of good advice, for they knew I had never fought *holmgang*. Come to that, no one else had either – it was a rare thing, most fights being unofficial and settled without such formal fuss and seldom ending in death.

I remembered what my father, Gunnar Raudi, had told me: see what weapon your opponent has and if he has more than one, which is permitted. Make your own second one a good short seax, held in the shield-hand and, if you get a chance, drop the shield and surprise him with it – if you can let go of the shield and still hold the seax, which is a cunning trick.

Keep your feet moving always, don't lead with the leg too far forward and attack legs and feet where possible, a sea-raiders' battle trick, for a man with a leg wound is out of the fight and can be left.

But the best piece of advice I hugged to myself, turning it over and over and over in my mind like a prayer to Tyr, god of battles.

Finn and Short Eldgrim marked out the five ells, which was supposed to be a hide, secured at each corner by long nails called *tjosnur*, which we didn't have. Finn managed to get four old Roman nails from the garrison stores, almost eight inches long and square-headed, which he then put in with the proper ritual. That meant making sure sky could be seen through his legs, holding the lobe of an ear and speaking the ritual words.

Brother John scowled at all this, though the nails interested him, for it was with such as these, he told us, that Christ Jesus had been nailed to the cross.

Each of us had two weapons and three shields and the challenged – I – struck the first blow. I had made sure to craft that part carefully enough.

If one foot went out – going on the heel, as we called it – the fight went on. If both feet went out, or blood fell, the whole thing was finished.

Thrain had not been in a *holmgang* either, had not been in a fight with weapons for five years, so he was nervous. He was grinning the same way a dog wags his tail – not because he is friendly, but because he is afraid. His top lip had dried and stuck to his teeth and he was trying to boost the fire in his belly by chaffering with his Danes about how this boy would not take long.

He had a shield and a sword and a leather helmet, same as me, but you could see the sword hilt was awkward in a hand that had held only a pick and hammer for five years and he knew it, was fighting the fear and needed to bolster himself as Kvasir shouted: 'Fight.'

He half turned his head, to seek the reassurance of his men once more, before bracing for the first stroke – but I was fighting with Gunnar's best advice ringing in my head.

Be fast. Be first.

I was already across the space between us, that perfect, water-flowing blade whirring like a bird startled into flight.

It was as near perfect a stroke as I have ever done: it took him right on the strap of the helm and cut the knot of it, sliced into the soft flesh under his chin and kept going, even after it hit the bones at the back of his neck.

I almost took his head in that one stroke, but not quite. He must have seen the flicker of the blade at the last, was trying to duck and draw back in panic, but far too slow, for the blade was through him and he dragged it out by staggering back.

Then his body fell forward and his head fell down his back, held by a scrap of skin. Blood fountained straight out of his neck, pulsing out of him in great gouts, turning the dust to bloody mud as he clattered to the ground, spattering my boots.

There was a stunned silence, followed by a brief: 'Heya,' from Finn.

One stroke. My crew cheered, but I felt nothing, heard nothing but the drumming of Thrain's heels, the slush-slush of his life ebbing away and the thunder of my own breathing, made louder under the helm.

'He should have talked less and looked more,' Kvasir noted, then nudged me. 'Now is the time to swear the Oath. A *holm-gang* death – this is the best sacrifice Odin will get from us this year.'

So, as jarl and godi both, bloody blade still in my hand, I called on the Danes to swear the Oath and they did it, still stunned. Then I had Thrain taken and buried in a good boat-grave and, because he had been Thor's man, they told me, spoke words over him to the Thunderer and put a decent silver armring in it – my last – which everyone noted. Brother John wisely kept tight-lipped.

'It was well struck,' Finn growled later, coming with food to where I sat apart from the others at the fire. He thrust the food at me, but it tasted of nothing in my mouth and I could not stop the shaking that rippled me, despite a cloak against the night chill.

'The Danes are annoyed,' Finn went on, 'but only because Thrain lost so easily. They all agree you struck an excellent stroke.'

'And?'

Finn shrugged. 'And no one disputes that you are jarl, which is what was wanted. By the time we have defeated these goat-humpers, they will be one crew and not sitting on opposite sides of the fire.'

I came to the fire later, into the quiet talk about home and where the Danes had been and boasting of our own exploits. Though no one spoke of Thrain, I could feel him lying cold under his stones, weapons on his breast. Five years breaking stones, to end like this.

I could not get warm all that night.

FIVE

The rain spattered on the loop of cloak over my head, washing down from the mountains the Goat Boy said were called Troodos. We had climbed out of sight of the sea now, away from the olive and carob trees, into the limestone crags and their scatterings of pines, stunted oaks and fine trees Sighvat thought were cedars. It was cool and clean and wet here as we waited for the scouts to come back.

'Monastery fall down,' the Goat Boy had said, proud of the Norse he had put together, pointing ahead and shivering in his ragged tunic, even though Finn had given him a spare cloak which he had wrapped himself in until he was nearly lost. To us, though, the day was mild and Finn came stumping up to us booming: 'Almost like home,' and ruffling the Goat Boy's mass of black curls.

He had presented the Goat Boy and his brother to us, twin prows from the same boat it appeared, both dark-haired, olive-skinned and black-eyed. One was older, he told us proudly, being nine while his brother was merely eight.

Their mother, a plump woman swathed in black and grinning behind a hand to hide her lack of teeth, had carried water and food to the Danes for five years and was now, with others in the town, taking in our clothing to be washed and repaired. The Danes went in ones and twos to the bath-house and came back clean and combed. Then they had their hair and beards trimmed from five years of tangle – the most vain of all the Norse were the Danes.

Finn had taken a liking to the Goat Boys, white-toothed grinning little dogs who followed him around since they had come begging for washing work, their father being dead from fever some years now.

'They have some Arab in them, then,' I grunted to Brother John, when he told me they were rattling away in that tongue.

'Their mother certainly had,' chuckled Finn and curled his own moustaches, for he had an interest there, I was thinking, and her lack of teeth was a small matter to a man long at sea.

The *hafskip* was brought round under the stern eye of Balantes and duly turned over – though I saw he had stationed two *dromon* ships, light galleys with catapults on them, out at the harbour mouth, just in case we did something stupid, like try to run.

Gizur went aboard, with a Dane called Hrolf who had some skill with ship-wood and the rest of the Danes gathered in a huddle on the beach, looking and breathing in the distant pine and tar scent of her.

One, called Svarvar, told me its name was *Aifur*, *Ferocious*, and I asked if the Danes would care if we called it the *Fjord Elk*, which was the name the Oathsworn gave every ship they sailed on – even though, it seemed to me, we did not tend to have them long.

Svarvar said he would talk to them and I said I would call a Thing for it and we could all decide. Svarvar I liked, for he had come round to the new way of things swiftly and laughed a lot, even at his own misfortunes and the delight people took in them.

He had worked for a moneyer in Jorvik when he was a lad, ten years or so ago, apprentice die-maker to one Frothric, who minted coins for the young King Eadwig.

'But I never had the skill of it,' he confessed to his delighted audience. 'And then I made a good die, by my way of thinking, a skilled bit of work, with *Eadwig Rex* and the cross on one side and the name of Frothric on the other. But while the King's name was perfect, Frothric's side was upside down and able to be read only in a polished surface.'

Everyone chuckled at that and howled and slapped their legs when he added that Frothric had stamped the die on lead to test it, then thrown it out into the street in a fury – and Svarvar himself shortly after.

'So I decided skilled work was not for me and went viking that summer. Never stopped,' he added.

The new *Fjord Elk* was declared fit enough to take to sea, though its sail, having been flake-stowed on the yard for five years, needed considerable work and much of the tackle and lines needed replacing.

So I said that Radoslav, Kvasir, Gizur, Short Eldgrim and six of the Danes should stay behind, to guard and fix both ships, then showed the Goat Boys two silver pieces, minted in the Great City, one for each. One would come with us as guide and the other would stay. If there was trouble, he would bring news of it and Short Eldgrim would carve the runes of it on a stick, so that only Northmen could read it.

'I will go,' declared the eldest, striking his chest proudly with a hand red-scarred by harsh work. 'But I will need a sword and a shield. And possibly a helmet.'

Finn chuckled, gave him all three items from his own person and watched him wilt under the weight. 'A good coat of rings as well, brave Baldur?' He smiled, then tapped the top of the helmet which was swallowing the boy's head and asked if there was anyone in there. He took it off, ruffled the boy's hair and said: 'Stick to your sling, I am thinking.'

The Goat Boy laughed and handed the battle-gear back, glad to be rid of it. I realised I could not keep calling him the Goat Boy and asked his name.

Finn groaned. 'You should not have done that, Trader,' he said, shaking his head in mock sorrow. 'We may as well all take a seat.'

The boy took a deep breath and threw out a proud little chest. 'John Doukas Angelos Palaiologos Raoul Laskaris Tornikes Philanthropenos Asanes,' he intoned and beamed. No one spoke and Finn was grinning.

'His name is bigger than he is,' I noted. 'I think I preferred Goat Boy. I will not make the mistake of asking your brother the same question.'

'His name is Vlasios,' answered the boy, then stared, bemused and angry, as everyone roared with laughter.

Then, with spears and round shields and leather helmets sent out by Tagardis, the rest of the Danes lined up with my old crew and we headed off, laden with waterskins and dried meat and bread, into the depths of the island, on the day it started to rain.

Three days later, neither it nor the cold wind that brought it showed signs of stopping and we were high in the hills, having circled round to the east. We were now close to Kato Lefkara and the bigger town of Lefkara, which was said to be Farouk's stronghold, and the rain was a mirr that you had to wipe off your face and eyelashes. Yet the day was warm enough to make us all sweat in our battle-gear.

Those whose turn it was to carry the heavy sacks I had ordered brought along grumbled twice as much, but no one was happy about being soaked inside and out.

The scouts came in from three different directions. They were all Danes, for none of the original dozen Oathsworn had the skill of hunting or tracking much. These three did and the best of them was Halfred, who had spoken up against Thrain. Hookeye, they called him, since his left one was hooked tight to his nose – yet, squint or no, he read signs and tracks as easily as monks scan Latin.

He came in with the easy, ground-breaking lope of a

seasoned tracker, which he had been for Knud, whose hov was in Limfjord. Knud was known the length of Denmark as a greedy man and made his wealth dealing in slaves, Ests and Livs from further up the Baltic, which he sold to traders bound for Dyfflin and Jorvik.

It had been his job, Halfred Hookeye told us, to track down the runaways and, since Knud skimped on proper securing, Halfred had been kept busy until he grew restless for other things. That set him apart from the others, since no one liked a hunter of runaway men, even thralls.

I was glad of Knud's stinginess now, for Halfred Hookeye could read ground like my father once read wind and current – like those old, Oathsworn scout-hounds, Bagnose and Steinthor, once did, before Odin gathered them to Valholl.

'One of those domed Christ places, Trader,' Hookeye said, addressing me as he had heard Finn and others do – which was a good sign. 'Ruined, like the Goat Boy says.'

'It is called a church,' sighed Brother John. 'How many times must I tell you?'

Two Danish trackers, Gardi and Hedin Flayer, kneeling and blowing snot through their fingers, reported that they had seen nothing else but rain and stones and distant hills.

'There is not a living creature here,' Hedin Flayer said morosely, 'though I saw goat droppings, so something lives in this Christ-cursed country.' And, like the good Christ-man he was, he said sorry to a bedraggled Brother John and crossed himself while making a good Odin-ward against evil at the same time.

We moved up warily to the domed church, as silently as nearly three-score Norse could move with battle-gear, which wasn't very.

We crested a bald hillock, descended a scrub slope, then crossed a swollen stream and climbed up the other side to where the church stood – or three blackened walls of it and the dome, partially collapsed on one side. The sun was white and distant and threw no shadows; there was the faint stink of charred wood over the smell of damp earth – and something else, faint and sweet as mead-sick.

'Heya,' grunted Arnor, pinching the scabbed cleft of his nose. 'The dead are here.'

They were, too, and now that I was looking for them, it was as if a doe in a dappled wood had suddenly moved and showed all.

The dead lay everywhere, slumped and sunken like empty waterskins, the grass grown up through them. I saw the tattered remains of worn robes, the yellow of bone and, when Gardi pulled at what he thought was a brown stick, he dragged out a bone, attached to a maggot-crusted brown mass that released a waft of stinging stink to make eyes water.

Cautiously, we wandered through the place, which had been gutted and burned. I posted watchers at once, even though the signs were months old. Brother John knelt and prayed, while the others poked and prodded in the ruins. The rain slid down again: a delicate offering, like tears.

'Strange place,' muttered Sighvat, 'even allowing for it being a Christ house. I have seen those – so have you, Trader – but this is different. Why have they all these wheels?'

Now that he had spoken of it, I saw what he meant. There were the remains of shattered and burned wood, bits of metal and, everywhere, charred wheels and bits of spoke. As he said, even allowing for the strangeness of the Greek Christ-men, this was new.

'Perhaps the Goat Boy knows,' I said, but Sighvat wasn't listening. He was staring at the sky and, when I looked up, I saw the small, circling black shapes.

'Crows?' I asked, for his eyes were sharp as needles and I couldn't see which way they were wheeling – crows were left-handed, as Sighvat constantly told us.

He shook his head. 'Kites. Loki birds and treacherous. They will tell our enemies where we are, for they have smelled the old death unearthed here and think they can make new ones to scavenge.'

He shivered and that raised my hackles, for Sighvat was always sure with animals and birds. When I said so, he turned a grim face on me and shrugged. 'My mother said I would find my doom when the kite spoke to me. She had that off a *volva* from the next valley,' he said.

'Can kites talk, then?' I asked. 'I have been told crows can.'

'Neither has a voice,' Sighvat corrected morosely and shrugged again. 'There are many ways of speaking.'

'Getting darker, Bear Slayer,' announced Hookeye. 'We should move.'

Bear Slayer. He had been listening to the campfire tales and clearly liked how I had been found beside the body of a great white bear from the North, a spear up through its chin. I had not killed it, though no one knew that save me, but it was not a name I preferred. It was one of those names that made fame-starved warriors with scarred faces scowl, as if you'd just challenged them to a pissing contest.

I looked again at the sky, which was pearl-grey and empty save for the distant kites. I knew we had water and shelter here, but the violent dead made it an uncomfortable place to be near at night.

Turning, I signalled to move on, indicating that the scouts should move out ahead. Then I saw Brother John, his arm round the Goat Boy, crooning soothingly. The Goat Boy shuddered in spasms and turned his snot-smeared face to me, twisted in a grief so hard on him that he could barely make a noise with his weeping.

'His friends,' Brother John said and swept a hand at a litter of corpses.

I looked closer. They were all small, ruined little rag bundles of bone and weather-wrecked cloth. Children. Scores of them.

'This is a silk factory,' Brother John said. 'John Asanes here

93

once laboured for them on these wheels, teasing silk from cocoons – all the silk-teasers are boys – but fled because his hands hurt too much from the boiling water they use. He has never been back until now, but had heard the monastery had been attacked by this Farouk. That's why he wanted to come.' He paused and patted the boy's shoulder. 'He thought he would be coming with an army to rescue them all, like some hero. He wasn't expecting this, I am after thinking. All dead. Ah well, lad – *consumpsit vires fortuna nocendo.*'

I doubted whether the Norns had exhausted their power of hurting. Those three sisters, I had found, were infinite in their capacity to inflict pain on the world of men. The Goat Boy certainly didn't believe it, for he was blubbering on his knees, then sank full length, shoulders heaving.

'*Qui jacet in terra, non habet unde cadat,*' intoned Brother John.

If one lies on the ground, one can fall no further. There was truth in it but no help for the lad.

'Get him up, we are moving,' I said, harder than I intended, the stink of all those little deaths sharp in my nose. Brother John bent and tugged at the heaving shoulders, teasing the Goat Boy upright with soothings and croons and we moved away from that dead place.

An hour later, Gardi trotted back to us with news of a farm ahead and another stream beside it, just as the wind grew colder and the dark slid in like black water. 'There are dead there, too,' he added, which made my heart sink, for we could go no further now and had, it seemed, changed one field of corpses for another.

The farm was a huddle of ruins, but the outbuildings had suffered most, being almost all made of gnarled wood culled from the stunted pines. The main building had lost its roof, but the thick walls were intact, though blackened. Surrounding it were smoothed fields and what I had taken at first to be olive groves, but these were different trees, skeletal in the dusk. There were also the remains of splintered and burned wooden frames, like racks used to smoke herring in quantity, except that these were not slatted, but solid trays.

Finn turned a dry corpse over with a foot, a hissing rustle ending in a cracking sound as the shafts of two rotted arrows crumbled. 'Two dead here, no more. I think the others probably fled to the church, thinking it safer,' he muttered. He made a sign against any lurking fetch and I told Brother John to lay their Christ fetches to rest, just in case, for we had no choice but to spend the night here.

We had a fire, though I did not like the idea of it and weighed it against the hunched, pinch-faced fears of the crew, who did not like the idea of sitting in the dark beside strange dead and wandering fetches.

The flames chased out the dark and the fear. Hot food helped; after an hour there was even banter.

I moved to one side, staring out at the trees and trying to work out what this place had farmed, but could not. I wanted to ask the Goat Boy, but he was sleeping, exhausted by grief, and I had not the heart to wake him.

Finn appeared beside me, picking his teeth. He jerked his head back at the fire and grinned. 'We are almost one crew now, Trader,' he said, 'and a good fight will caulk the seams of it, I am thinking.'

'There won't be a long wait for such a caulking,' I replied and after that we were silent, gloomy – until Arnor started a riddle contest with one about mead which every child learns before they can walk.

'That had moss on it when I was a boy,' thundered Finn, heading towards the fire. 'You gowk, you incompetent. How dare you sit there with a nose shaped like your arse and present us with riddles so poor.'

Arnor, shamefaced and blinking, had no reply, but Vagn, a Dane they called Kleggi – Horsefly – for his stinging wit, had one ready.

'What cuts but does not kill?' he demanded, which set everyone looking at his neighbour and scratching.

'Finn's tongue,' said Kleggi triumphantly and everyone roared appreciation.

'Better, better,' said Finn amiably, shoving someone up to get a seat by the fire. 'Any more like that, little arse-biter?'

I listened to them, remembering how Einar had sat in silence, part and yet apart. Did he feel as I felt now? I slid down the wall and leaned my head back, feeling the faint heat of the flames, hearing the voices and laughter round the fire. The sword burned the back of my eyelids when I closed them. The Rune Serpent, dancing just out of reach.

A wind touched my cheek, a tendril of salt in it from a dream sea, and I lay back on the tussocked grass of Bjornshafen, where the gulls wheeled and the wrack blistered in a summer sun on sand and shingle. Somewhere, a horse whinnied and I could see it, a grey with a flea-bitten back, curling back its top lip to taste the scent of a mare . . .

In the dark, a rhythmic clanging and a blaze of sparks, each one flaring, for that brief instance, the red-glowed shape of a man, naked from the waist up and sweat-gleamed, a powerful arm rising and falling, bringing the hammer down on a glowing bar on the anvil.

It looked like Thor. I thought it was, but his face had high cheekbones, almond eyes like slits. A Finn. Was the Thunderer a Finn, then? No, not a Finn. A Volsung, who were all Odin's children, descended from him and able to shapechange as a result. I had forgotten that until now.

A shape changed the darkness beside me, too shadowed to make out, but I knew, somehow, that it was Einar, could see him standing beside me even without turning, the hanging wings of his hair like black smoke on either side of his head.

'I killed you,' I said and then:

'You deserved it, though.'

'I thought you were my doom,' he answered, 'and so it proved.'

'You killed my father,' I pointed out.

There was silence.

'Is it true that Valholl is made from battle shields and the roof from spears?' I asked.

'How would I know? I cannot cross Bifrost – I broke an Odin-oath, made on Gungnir,' he replied, and half turned, so that the shadow of his face was broken by the gleam of one eye. 'Until that is braided up anew, I am lost,' he added, in a voice that trailed off to a whisper.

I said nothing, for I had the notion he meant for me to fix it and I had no idea how.

The clanging went on without pause and he raised one hand – firm and strong, I saw, as it had once been. I even saw the scars on his knuckles, the marks all swordsmen get at play and practice.

'He did not make this for Starkad,' he said, pointing at the smith. In the dark, the serpent of runes curled along the sabre's blade, red-dyed in the forge glow.

'For Atil,' I said, confused that he should not know this, he of all people who now sat on that lord's throne.

'He is dead,' Einar replied. 'Your hand grips it now. You need to get it back.'

I felt him fade, the clanging of the hammer growing louder and louder.

'What is death like?' I wanted to know, almost desperately.

'Long,' he replied and was gone.

The thunderous clanging tore me back to the ruined room and the embers of the fire. Men were spilling up and out of the building, to where Hookeye, last man on watch for the night, rang a spearhead on a rusted iron wheel-rim. Those with byrnies struggled them over their heads.

'What the fuck—?' demanded Finn, a question chorused by everyone, bleary-eyed but weapons up and ready. Hookeye merely pointed.

On the hillside beyond, almost like the grey-green scrub they stood against, a dozen horsemen sat and watched us.

'They just appeared,' Hookeye said. 'At first light.'

'Form,' I told them and they obediently moved into a solid block, mailed men to the front, shields up. The horsemen moved down, fluid riders who took the wet scree slope with ease. In their lead, a black-turbaned man did it with his hands held out clear of his sides, to show he was unarmed and wanted to talk.

The horsemen were well mounted and a chill went through me at the sight of them as they came closer still, until Black Turban was no more than a few paces away.

The horse was large and powerful and he sat it easily. He had a cased bow, wickedly curved. A quiver was strapped to his left hip, angled backwards and cut deep to show the shafts of the arrows, which would, I saw, make it faster to get them out.

He had a sword on the other side – not a curved sabre, but one that was almost straight. From the saddle hung an axe and a mace with a strange animal head and, dangling from the strap, a conical helm with a mail aventail tucked neatly inside it.

He wore mail and had proper padding beneath it, but no protection other than fat trousers of some fine black linen on his legs – so slash at their knees, I noted. He had a shield, small and round and metal-fronted, and the horse was barded in leather made to look like leaves and covered in fat tassels of coloured wool and gilded medallions. A black cloak hung almost all the way over his back and the horse's rump.

And they were all like this, save that the others also had long lances.

We stood in silence, each weighing the other. He had the

dark skin of the Blue Men from the southern deserts, a close-cropped, neatly trimmed black beard and eyes like chips of jet. I called out to the Goat Boy to translate this Arab's tongue to Greek, for Brother John confessed he actually knew only a few words of it – which got him hard looks from me after all his boasting.

The Goat Boy stood, trembling like a whipped dog under my hand on his shoulder as the Arab spoke.

'I am Faysal ibn Sadiq,' he announced. 'Who trespasses on the lands of the Emir Farouk?'

'I am Orm Ruriksson,' I replied, hoping my voice was not pitched too high or trembled. 'I was told these lands belong to the Emperor in the Great City.'

The Goat Boy said it all and Faysal's eyes widened a little.

'You are a beardless boy.'

I rubbed my chin, which had some fine hairs on it – but inclined my head in acknowledgement and smiled ingratiatingly. Does no harm . . .

Faysal made a dismissive gesture. 'We were masters here before the Greeklings,' he declared haughtily. 'And know no others above us. Why are you here?'

'We seek the temple of the Archangel Michael in Kato Lefkara,' I told him. 'To worship there and speak with the holy men.'

He looked us up and down and then said something that the Goat Boy hesitated over. I nudged him and he looked miserably up at me.

'He says he has heard of the men from the northlands and that they are not followers of the Christ but are idol-worshipping sons of dogs,' the Goat Boy blurted. 'He says that—' He stopped, licking his lips.

I nudged him again, feeling cold fear creep into my belly and curl up there.

'He says that you and your pig-eating friends can go somewhere else and fuck boys, but not to defile the lands of the great Emir, Protector of the Faithful . . . forgive me, Lord Orm, but that is what he says . . .'

I squeezed his shoulder to shut him up, then looked into Faysal's black eyes. Behind me, there were mutters and growls from the eavesdropping Danes, who had learned good Greek in five years of breaking rocks.

'Tell him,' I said, 'that we are the Oathsworn, bringers of a sword age, an axe age, a fire age to his miserable life. Tell him that we will go to where we intend and if he stands in our way I will kill all his men and then make him walk round a pole fastened to his entrails until he winds himself to death.'

The Goat Boy, his eyes wide, stammered his way through all that while I tried to stop my legs from shaking and offered a wry thanks to Starkad, who had brought that terror to my attention.

The black eyes flashed and Faysal stiffened in the saddle. Then he rattled off a fierce stream at the Goat Boy, who turned to me. Before he could translate, I raised my hands and silenced him.

'Tell this goat-humping dog rider to piss off. I have no more time to waste on him. Either he fights, or shows us how he squats like a woman. His choice.'

I waited long enough for the Goat Boy to say all this, then spun him by the shoulder and walked back to the grim-faced shieldwall, where men growled their appreciation and banged weapons on their shields.

'What happened? What did he say? What did you say?' Finn was chewing his shield edge with frustration.

Beside him, Sighvat chuckled and said: 'You should have learned more Greek than how to get a hump and a drink.'

I gave my orders, for I knew the dozen we had seen were not all of them. I was right. As we trotted back from the buildings and cut into the neat groves of stunted trees, the hillside sprouted more horsemen. And more.

I cursed our Odin luck and the Greeks. A hundred or so,

Balantes had said. What he had not said was that they had heavy horse, leaving me to imagine some bunch of robed rag-breeks with spears and shields and not much else.

We formed up in the grove while the horsemen piled up and began shrilling out cries, which sounded like 'illa-la-la-akba'.

'Trader,' Finn growled, 'we are too open here and these trees are in neat lines they can gallop straight down. We should have stayed by the buildings. They might not charge then.'

But I wanted them to charge. I wanted them angry and confident against a boy who had picked what seemed a bad position. I wanted Faysal to ride us down like the dogs we were, rather than be cautious and use bows.

I said as much to Finn while sending men out with the heavy sacks they had carried and my instructions. He hissed through his teeth when it was all unveiled for him.

'Heya. Deep Thinker. If we live through this, it will make you famous.'

'I am famous,' I said loudly enough for them all to hear. 'I am the Bear Slayer.'

This was the price of the jarl torc – boasts and standing in the middle of the front rank of the Lost. It had the effect, of course. The Oathsworn pounded their shields and hoomed deep in their throats, which even made the horsemen stop their la-las for a moment. Then they began again and there was a surge of movement, like a landslip down the hill.

'Form!' I yelled and ducked into the front rank. 'Shieldwall. Form.'

The shields came up, ragged but solid, a ripple of sound as they interlocked and weapons thumped. Behind me, the tip of a spear slid, winking in the dawn light, one on either side of my head. At the last moment, they would thrust forward, so that we in front sheltered under a hedge of points, protecting the unarmoured men with our ringmail bodies.

The ground trembled. Little stones in front of us danced

101

like peas on a drumskin and the shrill screams grew louder. I needed to piss and my legs trembled, but I hoped that was just the ground shaking.

'Hold,' roared Finn. 'Stand hard as a dyke . . .'

They hit the claw-like trees, filtering into the neat lanes between them. White mulberry trees, I learned later, for feeding the silkworms this farm had made for the nearby church-factory.

They were thundering up the lanes now, no more than two or three abreast, holding their great lances two-handed over their heads, or low at the hip. I saw Faysal, helmeted now and in the lead, knew he was trying to single me out, but he was two lanes down and would have to crash through the stiff-branched trees and across his own charging men to do it.

They were almost on us. I heard men behind me roaring defiance, felt them brace, saw the spears slide out . . . then the leading horsemen hit the raven claws, a deadly sowing.

The whole formation cracked apart. Horses shrilled, broke stride, tripped and crashed to the ground, bringing others behind crashing over. An entire horse and rider ploughed forward, the animal flailing and screaming in a bow wave of stones and dirt, into the hedge of spears to my left, which stabbed viciously at the rider. He died in gurgles and had to be shaken off like lamb from a skewer.

Mulberry trees splintered; men struggled and fought to free themselves from those piling into them from behind. The rear ranks – pitifully few now – managed to wheel round and turn back, where they circled in confusion.

I led the front ranks of the Oathsworn forward in a steady walk, where they stabbed and hacked at the horsemen, shields up, leaving most of the killing to the ones behind. One of our men yelped, having stood on one of the three-pronged raven feet, which was a timely reminder to everyone else. I saw someone spear a man and then work the weapon free, a foot on the corpse's chest.

Hooves smacked my shield, knocking me sideways, and someone axed the fallen animal's skull to stop it kicking. Another scrambled up, screaming, tripping on its blue-pink entrails and a man heaved from the pile, coughing blood. He had time to look up and see my watered blade steal his life with a stroke.

Most were already dead, crushed in a great pile of men and horses so high we had to climb up it to get to the ones beyond.

Arrows whicked now, for the survivors had sorted themselves out and had thought what to do, but there was no fight in them – half their number were dead or struggling in the heap. I had the front rank shield those behind while they slaughtered the ones left alive in that pile.

Eventually, the *Sarakenoi* rode off, no longer shrilling their la-las. The crew gave a great cheer and beat on their shields and the Goat Boy was dancing up and down, pausing now and then to fit a stone in his sling and fling it at the retreating backs. If he hit one, it made no difference.

Finn came up, wiping sweat and blood from his face, and clapped me on the back. 'That showed the goat-humpers – and only two of ours dead and a few more scratched. Odin's hairy balls, young Orm, you are a deep thinker for war right enough.'

The rest of them agreed, after they had looted the dead. Horses still kicked and screeched, a high, thin sound that bothered us more than the moans of men. Those animals we killed, fast and hard, and the few which had surfaced from the carnage and stood, trembling and shaking, we gathered up and soothed, for we could use them.

There were thirty-four dead cavalrymen and almost as many horses – I offered silent thanks to Tyr One Hand, the old god of war, for the idea of bringing those raven talons from Patmos.

Brother John tended the wounded, none serious – and

only two dead. One was a Dane whose name I did not know. The other was Arnor. One of those dying, sliding horsemen had held on to his lance and it had skewered Arnor through the bridge of his butchered nose, for he had hammered up the nasal of his helmet to keep it from rubbing on the wound.

'He never had any luck with that smeller,' Sighvat said gloomily.

They found Faysal for me, six down in a heap, the life flung from him and the shock of it left on his face in a snarl and a thin trail of blood from the corner of his mouth. His neck was snapped and his head was turned so that it seemed he looked over his own shoulder at what had been his life to that point. The Goat Boy spat on him and then gave him a kick.

I let them loot for a while, but they were experienced raiders and knew the value of speed and that it was pointless trying to strip heavy armour and weapons to carry. While they searched for coin and ornaments, Brother John and I began stacking wood from the ruined buildings round the deepest heap of corpses until others noticed and were shamed into helping.

Then we placed Arnor and the Dane on top of the pile, his harpoon clutched to his breast, and burned them all, which was the old way, the East Norse way and, some said, better than a boat-grave. I found a mulberry leaf in Arnor's mouth when I sorted him out for burial and could not bear to throw it away. I have it still.

We left the place shortly afterwards, putting the wounded who could not walk on three horses, the two remaining heavy sacks of raven feet slung on another. We moved faster now, almost trotting towards where the Goat Boy said the village of Kato Lefkara was, until only that greasy plume of pyre smoke marked where we had been.

That and the treacherous, swooping Loki kites. I shivered,

104

almost believing that Sighvat was right about them having arranged this feast.

The Goat Boy sat and watched me the way a cat does, unblinking, so that you can feel the eyes on you even when you are not looking.

We were all crouched in the lee of a slope, sheltered by a stand of pines. Water slid over stones in a quiet chuckle and everyone chewed cold mutton and flatbread and spoke in grunts if they spoke at all.

'Brother John says you believe in strange gods,' said the Goat Boy in his stream-clear voice. 'Are you a heathen, then?'

I looked at him and felt immeasurably old. Two years ago I had been much as he was now, knowing nothing and priding myself on the courage to cull bird eggs from sheer cliffs, or sit cross-legged on the rump of my foster-father Gudleif's sparkiest fighting stallion in its stall.

Now here I was, on a bare, damp hillside somewhere on an island somewhere in the Middle Sea, the jarl torc dragging at my neck, dead men's faces filling my dreams, chasing a runed blade and the secret of a hoard of silver.

'Are you?' I countered.

'No! I am a good Christian,' he said indignantly. 'I believe in God.' Nearby, Brother John nodded appreciatively. Encouraged, the Goat Boy added: 'But you believe in lots of false gods, Brother John says.'

'*Fere libenter homines id quod volunt credunt,*' I said and Brother John coughed and grinned, though the Goat Boy did not understand.

'Men are nearly always willing to believe what they wish,' I translated. I did not know who had first said it, but he had a Norse head on his shoulders. The Goat Boy was none the wiser. 'Anyway,' I added, 'once the Greeks had lots of gods, too.'

'The monks in Larnaca said we lived in fear of them until we saw the light,' the boy said sombrely.

Brother John chuckled. 'The truth is, young John, that those gods feared us, envied us, for they could not die. Without the threat of death, how can you feel the joy of life?'

'Unlike our gods,' I added, 'who know they will all die one day, to make a greater life for all afterwards. That's why All-Father Odin is so grim.'

The Goat Boy looked from me to Brother John and back. 'But isn't that what the church teaches us about Christ, Brother John?'

'Just so,' Brother John agreed and the Goat Boy's brow wrinkled with confusion, until Finn slid over in a scrabble of stones and shoved goat cheese and bread at him.

'Give it up, *biarki*,' he growled, scowling at the pair of us. 'Talking about gods just makes your head hurt.'

They sidled away together and Brother John laughed softly again. 'I don't think we enlightened that little bear,' he offered, then looked at me sideways. 'All the same, I thought you had found God, young Orm.'

'I have heard many rumours,' I replied flatly, 'but I have never met the man.'

Brother John pursed his lips. 'You are growing darker,' he said seriously. 'And your dreams are blacker still. Careful you do not fall into the Abyss, Orm, for you will be lost there.'

I was saved a reply by the return of Hedin Flayer and Halfred Hookeye, who had been scouting over the other side of the ridge, looking at the huddle of houses that was Kato Lefkara.

'There are armed men there,' Hedin reported, 'maybe fifty, with shields and spears and blades, too, but no armour and only black turbans on their heads. But they have bows, Bear Slayer, and can pick us off as we cross the open ground.'

'Horsemen?'

Hookeye shook his head. 'Nor any sign. The ones who fought us did not come here.'

I did not think they would. They would have ridden straight

106

to Farouk, to tell him what had happened and now he would be riding here, for some of those riders would have heard me say this was our destination. I looked at the darkening sky.

'There are people there, too,' Hedin said, sucking shreds of goat to try and soften it enough to chew.

'Of course there are. It is a village,' Finn growled, but Hedin shook his head.

'Children and women, with cloths covering their faces. That's not Greek, is it?'

No, it was a Serkland thing. Of course this Farouk wasn't a simple robber, he was one of the lords who had been told by the Miklagard Emperor to quit Cyprus and had decided to stay and fight, and had all his people with him. Now he had a town and a couple of villages and was a real threat.

'We will hit them at last light,' I said, 'so that they will find it hard to use their bows. All we have to do is get to the church and find this thing Balantes wants. Then we get out and away.'

'Are we stealing it then?' Hookeye asked and even some of his own oarmates chuckled.

'That's what we do, you arse,' answered Hedin Flayer, punching him on the arm.

I left them to chew on it, for I had another problem – what to do with the badly wounded. One was already shaking with wound-fever and the other was hamstrung, would never walk properly again, though he could still sit a horse.

The fevered one was an old oarmate called Ofeig, the one who had stepped on the raven claw, I realised. Such a simple little wound, a nithing cut that had come to this in half a day, no more. There was, then, some poison there and I made a mental note to warn the men who scattered them to take more care, then felt ashamed for reeling with future plans while a good man lay dying.

Brother John sat with him, placing damp cloths on his fore-head and muttering his healing chants, crossing himself and

107

clasping his hands. 'I pray to Earth and High Heaven, the sun and St Mary and Lord God himself, that he grant me medicinal hands and healing tongue to heal Ofeig of the shivering disease. From back and from breast, from body and from limb, from eyes and from ears, from wherever evil can enter him . . .'

It wasn't about to make a hacksilver of difference. Finn knelt on the other side and Ofeig opened his eyes and grinned weakly, while the sweat oozed from him like water from a ripe cheese.

'I had expected a prettier Valkyrie,' he said, knowing well what was coming.

Finn nodded soberly. No Valkyries were pretty, we knew. They came riding wolves to heave the chosen dead away, savage and merciless – but there was a time for gentle lying.

'There is one waiting,' he said in a voice as soft as any new lamb. 'She has hair the colour of red-gold, breasts like pillows, eyes only for you and wonders what is taking you so long.'

His great, calloused hand closed over the brow of Ofeig, who stiffened – then a fresh spasm of shivering took him.

'Fair journey, Ofeig,' said Finn and his other hand stroked the razor edge across Ofeig's throat, then held him down, the blood spreading slowly over his chest, bubbling in spurts like a hot spring as he choked and died, congealing like thick gruel.

After a while, Finn straightened, wiping first his hands, then the blade – the one I had given him, that he had called the Priest – on Ofeig's breeks. He looked at me over the dead eyes. 'Next time, you do it,' he said and I was ashamed, remembering how Einar had done it when he lived. It was a jarl-task right enough.

'You can piss off coming for me,' growled Sumarlidi, the one with the cut hamstring, hauling himself to a sitting posture and jerking out his scramseax. 'I have one good leg left and after that I can still crawl.'

'Then crawl to your horse and get on it,' I snapped at him, 'and get ready to ride hard.'

'Hop to it,' added Finn and wheezed with laughter.

We huddled just under the brow of the ridge, so that if I raised my head only a little, I could see the silhouette of buildings, the dominating dome of the church of the Archangel Michael and the yellow glow of lights and fires, which only made the chill of the night wind colder and the dark blacker than ever.

When the leprous moon started to cast a shadow in between the shrouds of dark cloud, I gave a signal and the men rose up to a crouch and started to filter down the hill, scuttling like beetles. The scuff and clink of them made me wince, certain someone would hear it, but no alarm was sounded, and then we were crossing the first of the rickety fences, into the garden plots behind some houses.

Finn turned to grin at me and I saw he had his Roman nail in his teeth, one of the metal spikes he had used to mark out the *holmgang*, which he gnawed like a dog with a bone. His teeth ground down on it, preventing him from bursting into full-throated roar until I gave the signal. Slaver dripped from it as I nodded.

He spat the nail into his hand and threw back his head, howling like a mad wolf. The cry went up from all our throats, then we lurched forward into the houses.

I trotted forward, heading for the church, hearing the panicked screams and shrieks as the Oathsworn ripped through the village. I passed some huts and houses, heard doors crack under axes, the thump of booted feet and screams. A robed figure skidded round the side of a building, slammed into a mud wall, looking back over his shoulder. Then he turned, saw me and ran back the way he had come, straight into a skewering spear.

A woman screamed and, through the door, I saw her flung to the ground, two men frantically fumbling down their breeches and I cursed. It would be the Danes, who hadn't tasted that sweetness in five years. I should have planned for that.

I trotted across the square, saw Finn and yelled to him. Sighvat burst out of a building, saw me and ran across, laughing. Hookeye appeared, an arrow nocked and his bow straining. He grinned in a wolfish way and looked like he had been caught with his hand in my purse for a moment, then shrugged. The four of us headed for the dark entrance to the church, a narrow way only one man wide.

It was far too late, for the smart ones had already gone in and barred the door and the church had been designed as a refuge. The narrow entrance was a passage, which sloped down, then up to a stout door, making a ram impossible to use. On the roof above, I saw holes and barely jumped aside as a spearhead thrust down, then back, like the tongue of a snake.

Keeping to the sides, we slid up, studied the door, then slithered our backs down the wall to the entrance and out. I wandered to the middle of the village square, to a well surrounded by a series of water troughs, stopped and sat down, resting my shield on my knees and my sword on one shoulder, listening to the shrieks and screams, seeing the figures flit like dark bats. Then there was the bright flare of flame and a roof collapsed.

Finn growled and I wearily nodded. He trotted off, dragging Hookeye with him, who seemed inclined to stay near me, yelling at them to put the fire out or he would tear their arms off and beat out the flames with the wet ends.

'It's a fortress, that gods-cursed Christ dome,' Sighvat said. 'We'll have to burn them out.'

'No,' I said. 'Same problem as last time . . . what we want is in there and will burn with them.'

'We can burn the door, same as last time,' he answered and rose, cupped water in his hands and splashed his face. Shaking himself like a dog, he wandered off, looking to drag a few others into fetching dry wood and anything that would burn.

Two figures, laughing and yelling, chased a shrieking woman from a house and Sighvat polearmed one of them to the ground; he was Arnfinn, an old hand, I saw. His friend skidded to a halt, confused.

'I need you pair,' he said and Arnfinn's companion, seeing the woman shrieking round a corner and gone, snarled at Sighvat for the loss.

'Who made you a chief?' he growled, hefting a bloody axe.

'He did,' said Sighvat amiably, jerking a thumb at me. I waved. 'And this did,' he added, slamming the flat of his blade into the man's mouth. He went over spitting teeth and blood. Arnfinn got to his feet and grinned, shamed now at behaving like a raw beginner.

'Didn't expect that when you said to grab the woman, eh, Lambi?' he chuckled, hauling the bloody-mouthed man to his feet. 'What is it that you are wanting us for, Sighvat?'

While Sighvat explained, I heard hoofs and nearly wet myself, then I saw Brother John and the Goat Boy leading in the horses, the wounded Sumarlidi waving a spear while holding a shield and trying to keep his balance, for he was no good rider.

'Help me down, help me down,' he snarled. 'It's too far off the ground up here.'

Brother John and I dragged him down and the Goat Boy gawped at what was going on round him.

'You should have kept him away from sights like this,' grumbled Sumarlidi to Brother John as he dragged himself to the edge of the well. That leg of his, I saw, was ruined completely, a useless thing that might as well not be there at all, for it served no purpose for him now and was a dead weight he'd drag about for the rest of his life.

'I think he is well used to them already,' Brother John declared. '*Pede pes et cuspide cuspis, arma sonant armis, vir*

111

petiturque viro – it is the way of things round here, I am thinking.'

'If I knew what it meant, I would know more,' answered Sumarlidi. There was a pause as the burning house fell in with a roar and a cloud of flying embers. Finn yelled and cuffed left and right.

'It means people are always fighting in these lands,' I told Sumarlidi. 'How's the leg?'

'Useless,' he grunted and eyed me warily. 'But stay a blade length from me, Bear Slayer – I want no Valkyrie visits just yet.'

'Nor am I planning any such thing,' I snapped, angry with him now. Was I some butcher here?

'You'll beg for the Priest before long, One Leg,' growled Finn, coming up in time to hear the last of this exchange. His face was smeared with soot.

It took an hour to sort out the chaos and collect a sorry, panting bunch, two of whom were already drunk, three dripping blood and one with claw marks down the side of his face.

'I had her skirts up,' he was telling the man next to him, 'and getting no protests. Then I thought to see what I was getting, so I took the cover from her face. She went crazed at that, kicking and bucking and screaming. Clawed my face. Best hump I've had . . .'

'Stow it,' ordered Finn and the man's mouth closed with a click.

I told them what I thought and laid it on thick as a slab of week-old porridge. I warned them that if anyone disobeyed me again I would let them walk their entrails round the pole.

I was beginning to enjoy Starkad's vision now, for it was a good one and much better than the hoary old blood-eagle. Old beards like these would laugh at that threat, since it was more boast than fact, though there was a nut of truth in it, for Hedin Flayer hinted he had his name for having done it

112

once, raiding the Liv lands along the Baltic. Or so he said. Others said it was because his craft was hunting wolves for the pelts, which I thought more likely.

At the end of my rant, they shuffled off silently, knowing that they had made a mistake, for only a handful of the robed Saracens were dead and, though the rest had fled, a good two handfuls were locked up in the domed church and it would be a harder fight now to get them out.

So we sat in the square while men scuttled in the narrow doorway, braving the spears to stack wood and start burning through the door, while I fretted about Farouk and his horsemen. I posted watchers and sent Hookeye and Hedin out into the darkness to listen, but there was nothing to do but wait, while the smoke billowed out of the narrow church door-passage.

Now that there was time for it, the men were reluctant to go plundering and humping, fearing the arrival of more *Sarakenoi* – though Sumarlidi pestered them to go and find a woman for him, since he wasn't so nimble on his feet. After long minutes of his whining, two men went off and dragged back a whimpering woman, whom he perched on the edge of the trough and grunted over while the Goat Boy watched with interest. No one else cared.

Eventually, Sighvat reported that the fire was out, had done some damage, but the defenders had soaked the door and were even pouring wine down through the murder holes in the roof to try and soak the place.

'Which means they have used all the water,' Brother John pointed out.

'Which means they are not planning on a long stay,' I finished for him. 'Farouk and his horsemen are expected.'

That sprang the crew into action, for they knew that a second encounter with those would be a hard fight not in our favour. They would use bows this time, standing off and snicking us one by one, like loose threads off the cuff of a tunic.

That passageway was a tricky opening, for it allowed only one at a time, though it widened at the actual door to three. The wood was charred, but still solid, so we piled in and formed shields over our heads to keep off the stabbing spears from above. Under this crept Finn and others armed with axes to chop at the door.

It was sweaty, noisy work, fetid with the stink of men afraid and, after half an hour, Finn gave a bellow of triumph, for the upper left corner had splintered into a small hole. Frenzied, he hacked and hacked, spraying wood chips everywhere, while the men behind closed up, down on one knee under the roof of shields and ready to spring forward.

Without warning, a spear thrust through the hole, fast as an eye blinking. Finn was on a downstroke, which was Odin luck for him, for the weapon scored across his shoulder and into the throat of the man behind, who gurgled out a scream and fell backwards.

There was chaos then, for the felled man screamed and kicked and had to be dragged out. In the end, everyone abandoned the work and staggered out into the chill night air, gasping and spitting. The man – Lambi, the one whose teeth had been dunted by Sighvat's sword, I saw – was already dead, leaking a slow pulse of blood, which finally stopped.

We all looked at one another and no one spoke their thoughts, which were darker than the night.

'What we need is a battering ram,' I said.

'With a bend in the middle,' Finn pointed out wryly.

'We could use your tozzle,' Sighvat pointed out to Finn, who chuckled harshly.

'Too few men around to carry that,' he answered, but his eyes had no laugh in them when he looked back at that narrow doorway.

Then the Goat Boy came up, his eyes wide, pointing behind him while he fixed me with his dark-cat gaze.

'One Leg has gone in the well,' he declared.

114

Odin's arse – could this night get any worse?

'The Norns weave in threes, Trader,' Finn said wearily when I yelled this out. Everyone trooped across to the well, where Brother John was holding the shivering woman by one wrist and peering into the dark of it.

'She pushed him off,' Brother John explained, 'while he was trying to . . . never mind. But he fell in and hasn't made a sound since.'

Finn shrugged and grabbed the bucket rope, took up the slack and his eyes widened when he felt resistance. He got three others to help and, slowly, the bucket was inched up until Sumarlidi's legs flopped over the edge and they hauled him out.

His neck was broken and his wide-eyed face still looked surprised about it. Nearby, the Arab woman huddled, moaning softly.

'There's no more for him, then,' sighed Brother John sadly and Finn agreed with a sound deep in his throat, part sympathy, part disgust.

'A straw death, right enough,' he said and shivered.

I saw it differently, through the ring of that jarl torc. It seemed to me that if you fastened a good steel helm on him, he would make a battering ram with a bend in the middle.

Sumarlidi was better use in death than he had been in life, but by the time the door was broken open, even his mother would have missed him at his own corpse-washing. The helmet was rimmed into the flesh of his brow, so that it was never coming off, so we burned him with it jammed down to his eyebrows and Finn killed the Arab woman and put her at his feet, in the hope that this in some way made up for the death he had died.

Brother John didn't like any of this much, but the others glowered at him and he knew the worship of Christ was too new on them to argue. To me, who did not even try to interfere, he gave a hard look and said: 'The Abyss grows darker the longer you stare down into it.'

That was after the defenders tried to give in, which was as soon as the door broke. They were shouting frantically in their gabble, throwing down bows and spears and holding out their hands and clasping them. The crew were past caring and cut them down for having put them to all this trouble.

'They had courage,' argued Brother John, trying to get me to stop the slaughter, which was stupid since there was no way I could do that and the fact of it made me sick and angry.

'A cornered rat has that courage,' I snarled back at him, the thick iron tang of blood clogging my nose, then I went to find what we had come for. The container was where it was supposed to be, under the stone base for a brazier in what had been the monk chief's room, and I grabbed it up, stuffed it inside my tunic and ordered everyone out and away.

We paused only long enough to lay Sumarlidi and the dead, toothless Lambi out with the bloody enemy dead at their feet, then fired the church and scampered into the safety of the darkness.

Another god place burned and more men killed. In the dark, with the damp wind cooling my face, the sickness rose up in me and I boked and spat it out. I felt a gentle hand on my back and, though I wanted no one to see this, had no strength to do anything but retch.

Brother John patted my shoulder and I heard his low voice say, '*Facilis descensus Averno.*'

The descent to hell is easy.

Fuck him, what did he know? He wasn't the one in the lead.

SIX

I held him and he felt like a bird, the racking sobs shaking him so that it seemed his thundering heart must burst out of his rib cage. I wanted to hold him tighter, but it was an awkward thing with others looking and I had no words for him; none of us had. So Brother John peeled the Goat Boy off me and took him to the swift-flowing stream to wash the snot and tears away.

The rest of us stood, cold and tired, uneasy in the dawn light, with the tendrils of haar like a witch-woman's hair slithering round the farm and the mulberry trees and the old corpses, still blackened and charred. Crows sat hunched and sour in those trees, rasping out a protest at a meal interrupted.

A fresh meal, on a small corpse. The smallest one in that field of death, dark curls clotted with old blood, the eyes already pecked into dark holes, which still managed to accuse us all. The wound that killed him was a back-to-breast skewer and Halfred tracked the tale of it.

The horsemen had ridden to the silk farm from the town of Lefkara, which meant I had judged Farouk right – he had come straight to the plumes of pyre smoke, found nothing and headed for the village after that. Now he was probably finding more dead and a burned church and we had a start on him, but not much of one. It was good Odin luck for us, since it meant we had missed each other in the dark – but for such luck One Eye takes a high price in sacrifice.

So he took little Vlasios into their path just as they saw what we had done to their friends. Like startled game, the Goat Boy's little brother had probably made a run for it, leaping on those wiry legs, twisting and turning, but no match for horsemen with lances.

They had spitted him, said Hookeye, pointing it out – quietly, so the Goat Boy could not hear – and carried him back to the charred remains of the pyre, stinking and wet from rain. Probably still on the spear-point, Hookeye thought.

And they would be laughing about it in a grim way, I thought to myself, as they tossed the corpse on to the ash, like an offering to their own dead. It came to me that we might well have done something similar, in another place, at another time, and the thought did nothing to help the sick feeling in my belly.

Then they had ridden off, leaving one more small, bewildered little fetch in a clearing, wondering why the world had grown cold and empty and shadowed.

We had found him after a couple of hard hours' travel, moving as swiftly as we could in the dark. My plan had been finely worked, everyone agreed, but the dead boy was a stone thrown in the pool of my deep thinking and not because the Goat Boy was melting to tears over it.

No, it was the little stick in Vlasios's belt, which the *Sarakenoi* had not even bothered with. The one that said, in badly cut runes: 'Starkad. Go west. Dragon.'

It was from Kvasir and I knew what it meant. Starkad had arrived like a pinch of salt in clear water. Now Balantes and everyone else would know they had handed the prize to the wrong wolf and we would have all the Greeks on Cyprus after us, as well as the *Sarakenoi* and Starkad's men.

As Finn said, with a harsh chuckle, if you measured a jarl

by the number of his enemies, then Orm Bear Slayer was mighty indeed. The others had joined in, the fierce laugh of men with steel to their front and fire at their back, showing a lot of teeth but little mirth.

At least Kvasir and the others had had warning, time enough to plan swiftly and send the Goat Boy's brother with the gist of it.

I knew what Dragon meant. On the way here, less than a day from Larnaca and perched bare-arsed over the lee side in friendly conversation while we emptied our bowels, Kvasir had pointed out the headland like a dragon-prow. We had argued whether it looked more like the fine antlered one on the old *Fjord Elk*, or the snarling serpent on Starkad's stolen *drakkar*, which had replaced it.

That was where Kvasir was heading, but I did not know if he had one ship or two – or if he would make it at all.

I laid it all out for them, while Brother John brought the scrubbed-faced Goat Boy back. Finn was all for hurtling back the way we had come, to take Starkad on and get the runesword back. No one else looked eager for that, however, and I was cold-sick in my insides at the way my crafted plans had unravelled so completely. I was no Einar.

'What do we do, Orm?' asked Kvasir and I felt a mad moment rise in me, a great storm sea that made me want to agree with Finn, to shriek out that we would take on Starkad and every Greek, get the runesword back, fight back to our ship and then away . . .

Instead, I looked at them, one by one, battened down my pride and admitted the truth of it. 'Now we run, brothers. Now we run.'

We did, a jogging lope that burst the sweat on us, despite the chill. Across the bare slopes we went like startled game, from gully to rock, to stand of trees, heading hard west and south. Eventually, when I called a rest-halt, I could taste the brine on a breeze from the sea on parched lips and sucked it

119

into fiery lungs. There was another village – ahead and west, if I remembered Radoslav's chart – whose name sounded like air being let out of a dead sheep's belly. Paphos, it was called, but I wanted no part of that and planned to come out to the sea short of it by some safe miles.

The men were on one knee, panting, mouths open, tossing a flopping waterskin from one to the other and I saw the Goat Boy sit with his knees at his chin, his dark eyes big and round and fixed on me. I had worried about him keeping up, but that had been foolish – this was the boy's country and he had young legs that had chased all over it since he could toddle.

I grinned and raised a hand to him and he raised one back, though he did not smile. After a moment, he snatched the waterskin deftly up before anyone could stop him and brought it to me. As I drank, he squatted beside me, silent and staring at nothing.

'It was a hard thing, what happened to your brother,' I offered, handing him the skin. He stoppered it and sighed.

'My mother—' he began and then stopped. He wanted to be a man, but his lip betrayed him.

'You should go back to her,' I said, clasping one shoulder, but the look he turned on me was suddenly cat-fierce from a streaked face.

'I want to be one of you. I will take the Oath. I will fight the infidels.'

Finn overheard and chuckled grimly. 'Join another army, *biarki*, for this one is leaving, never to return.'

He looked alarmed and I caught the flash of disbelief and then his shoulders collapsed.

'Every hand is against us,' I pointed out, 'from the Kephale to the General as well as the *Sarakenoi*. We stole something valuable.'

'That's what we do,' added Hookeye, his voice thick with sarcasm. When I looked at him he looked challengingly back at me. At least, I thought he did, though it was hard to feel challenged when his left eye was seemingly staring over my right shoulder.

The boy was silent and someone called for the waterskin, so he got up and passed it. Brother John slid up to me and whispered: 'To leave the boy behind will be death for him. Balantes will not believe he does not know anything about this prize. Even if he does not, there is Starkad.'

The prize. I had forgotten it, still slung by its strap on my back. Now I took it and had a hard look at the outside. Interested, since this was what had caused all the trouble, the men crept closer and craned to look.

Plain leather, with a carefully fastened cap, which I opened. There was a musky smell and I tipped the contents cautiously into the palm of my hand.

Dried twigs and a leaf, browned at the edges though it had once been brilliant, glossy dark green. With it came some dark little specks, smaller than peas and hard as beads.

'Is that it?' demanded Finn huffily. 'Does not scale up well to our runesword, I am thinking.'

'Not much to look at, Trader,' said a voice.

'What is it?' said another.

I knew, even though I had never seen any of it before. The whole thing of it unwrapped like a folded cloak to reveal the pattern. I shrugged to the men, poured the whole lot back in and fastened the leather top. I had promised them treasure, brought them to a den of wolves where men had died and could not begin to explain what had been found. They wanted treasure, so I gave it to them.

'Pearls,' I said knowingly, ignoring the shame the word flooded me with. 'Special ones.'

That made them nod and smile. Pearls they understood. Pearls could be bartered for a sword with a rune serpent curled on it – Einar would have been proud of me.

But Brother John's eyes narrowed, for he knew I was lying.

I didn't want to tell anyone the truth of it, though – that the collection of leaves and little beads were mulberry leaves and shoots and the eggs, I was thinking, from silkworms. Silk was so precious you had to have permission to buy it. It had been stolen by two daring monks from the strange people who made it in a far-off land and now the church jealously controlled it.

If a high-placed Christ priest and a truculent general were handing what was a church monopoly to the likes of Choniates on the sly, there was more here than simple theft and money-making. There was the sharp stink of treachery, the sort where kings slip knives in the ribs of rivals of a dark night, and I had been in Miklagard long enough to know that Roman emperors sat on precarious giftthrones. Small wonder Choniates had handed over a runed sword to Starkad for a task such as this.

Stealing this had been a mistake and a bad one, such a bad one that my balls drew up, tight and scared. Leo Balantes made no secret of being the man of General Red Boots and Balantes was the one who had whipped up the riots in the Great City last year. If Red Boots was also behind this then the Basileus himself was the target. This was no bargain counter for a runesword. It was a death sentence.

Blood-feuds I knew about, as every Norseman did, but the feuds of the great in Miklagard were another thing entirely. Balantes would snuff us out like pinching a candle if he thought we knew too much – and the only one who could help, the Basileus Autocrator himself, was so far away as to make the sun easier to reach.

Only two winters ago, I thought wearily, my only worry was how much worm was in the keel of our little *faering* in Bjornshafen. Now I was wrestling with whether the gods were laughing at me for having the pride to become jarl of the Oathsworn and that this, my first serious raid, would be my doom.

Worse than that, I was hiding the truth from the others. I could almost hear Einar laughing as we ran on into a dappled day with trees like sentries on the hills behind us, so that every time I turned to look back, my heart surged, thinking they were horsemen.

But this was bad country for horsemen. I knew that when one of the three we had foundered and we turned him loose, doubling the wounded up on another. The slopes, however, were smoothing down to the sea and, suddenly, Hookeye gave a loud shout and pointed.

There, rolling gently in the swell in a curve of golden beach, was the *Fjord Elk* and my heart gave a jolt in my ribs.

There was a brief moment of capering and back-slapping, quickly lost as we realised the *Volchok* wasn't anywhere in sight. That, as Finn gloomily pointed out, meant that the cargo was lost.

'Ah,' said Hedin Flayer cheerfully, 'turn the coin over, Finn Horsehead. Perhaps the cargo has been rescued. Perhaps your *knarr* is sailing still, just out of sight.'

Perhaps. We trotted on, filled with fresh strength and eager to quit the land for the sea. We slithered out of the steep hills and on to a flat stretch leading to the tussocked grass and then the sand. Gulls wheeled, shrieking out their calls, sometimes like the laugh of some mad hag, other times like the cries of a lost child. Many a gull was the fetch of those drowned and uneasy in the silt-kingdom of Ran, Mother of the Waves, according to Sighvat.

We stumbled across a stubbled field, saw the thread of smoke from a chimney and the shadow that straightened from work, spotted us and sprinted away. We stopped to rest, for even the horses were blowing.

A cock crowed and Sighvat grunted.

'That's bad,' he said.

Finn spat. 'Is there one of your animal signs that is ever a good omen?' he asked.

123

Sighvat considered it carefully before shrugging. 'Depends,' he said. 'They warn and seldom praise. Roosters are Odin birds, for they crow to herald the sun, which Odin and his brothers, Vili and Ve, threw into the sky as embers from Muspell. Fjalar is the red cock, who will raise the giants to war at Ragnarok and Gullinkambi the golden one who will wake the gods for that fight. And let's not forget the One with No Name who crows to raise the dead in Helheim on that day.'

'Duly remembered,' muttered Finn. 'Now . . .'

'When a cock crows at midnight a fetch is passing and if it crows three times between sunset and midnight it is a death omen,' Sighvat went on mildly. 'Crowing in the day, as now, is often a warning against misfortune. Can you see if it is perched on a gate? If it is, it means tomorrow will have rain.'

'Odin's balls,' muttered Finn, rubbing the sweat from his face. 'Remind me only to keep hens.'

'Ah, well,' said Sighvat, 'a hen that crows is unlucky, as is one with tail feathers like a rooster. You would do well to kill them at once. And a hen which roosts in the morning foretells a death—'

'Thor's hairy arse!' shouted Finn in annoyance. 'Enough cackle about hens, Sighvat, in the name of all the gods.'

'You'd do well to listen, though,' offered Gardi, pointing behind us. 'Look.'

This time there was no mistaking the shape of horsemen, high on the ridge, picking a careful way down the scrub and scree slope. Once they hit the flat . . .

'Run,' said Finn, the sweat pearling his face. 'Run like the wolf son of Loki has its teeth in your breeks.'

We ran, stumbling and cursing. One of the wounded fell off the back of the horse and the other one checked, turned, saw the horsemen fanning out down the slope, riding hard and shrilling out those 'illa-la-la' cries. He galloped for it and the fallen man cursed, got up on to his good leg and started hobbling.

No one helped him, for the hooves were drumming harder now. There was a familiar bird's wing whirr and the hobbling man screamed and pitched forward in mid-run, an arrow in his lower back.

Finn cursed and whirled. 'Trader . . .'

I knew what he wanted and screamed: 'Form!'

They slithered and skidded to a halt, swept together like a flock of sparrows while the arrows came in again with the sound of knives shearing linen. A man yelped as one whacked his thigh and he started to drag himself down to the beach.

We slammed shields and faced them, no sound but the sob and rasp of our breath. Arrows hissed and shunked into wood; another man cursed and writhed, the shaft through his ankle.

'*Borg*,' roared Finn and the men behind swept their shields up so that there was a higher wall, angled back. The men in front, me among them, half crouched. Out of the corner of my eye, I saw Hookeye splashing through the water to the side of the *Elk*. His eyes might be squint, but his feet were sure and fast.

'Back,' I said into the gasping, sweating mass. 'We have to move back.'

We were a roofed fort, but only from the front, so had to shuffle, painfully slowly, away from the horsemen, who were sitting nocking arrows and shooting. They seemed content to do that and I saw there were only twenty or thirty of them and none that looked like an Emir – so he had split his forces to look for us.

One staggering Dane, trying hard to reach us, took about six arrows, one after the other, sounding like wet meat thrown at a wall as they hit him. He went down, one hand still clawing sand and stiff grass to try and get to us.

We backed off, while the arrows spat and hissed and slammed into shields. I hoped whoever commanded was too wary to work out that, as long as we were moving, we were not safe behind the raven claws that had done for them last

125

time. Without those claws, we'd be hard put to stand against lance-armed heavy horsemen and arrows at the same time.

Sand slithered beneath our feet, spattered with stiff-leaved grass. Then coarse sand alone and still we moved back, shedding another two bodies, passing two riderless horses.

One of the cavalry horses suddenly reared up and threw the rider and the rest wheeled round and galloped back, just as someone yelled: 'Water.'

It surged round my boots and I almost sobbed to hear it. Behind me, peeling off one by one, men slung their shields on their backs and splashed out towards the boats, while those on board, using the few short bows we had, plunked arrows enough to keep the horsemen cautious.

Something spanged off my helmet and my head rang like a bell. There was a hiss-shunk and an arrow whacked itself on my shield – on the inside. I snapped the shaft off with my sword and yelled at those in the *Elk* to watch their shooting, then turned and ran back into the surf, shield over my back.

I heaved myself over the rail of the *Fjord Elk*, hearing forlorn splashes as the last arrows missed. On the beach, the horsemen waved bows in triumph and screamed their la-la cries, as well as 'pig-eaters' in Greek.

Kvasir, beaming, dragged me upright and banged me heartily on one shoulder. 'Aye, a good steady defence right enough, Trader.'

'How many?' I managed to gasp as, around me, men groaned and sat, heads hanging and lips wet with drool.

'Four dead,' Finn answered, scooping water over his head. He spat towards the horsemen. 'Another six wounded, the boy among them.'

'Boy?' I asked, confused. Not the Goat Boy . . .

It was. He had taken an arrow smack in the side and Brother John was kneeling beside the little figure, poking carefully round the wound. The shaft had been trimmed off down to the flesh and the Goat Boy was limp and lolling and pale as milk.

126

Brother John muttered a prayer and looked at me, his face hard and sweat-gleamed.

Gizur came up and said, 'We have a west wind, Trader. Do we run with it?'

I nodded, then turned back to Brother John, who was examining the wound again. The Goat Boy moaned.

'Odin's arse, priest,' snarled Finn, 'do you know what you are about?'

'I am about this close to smacking you in the mouth, Finn Horsehead. Fetch some water and shut your hole.'

Finn stamped off, roaring, and I felt the *Fjord Elk* heel over, heard Kvasir chivvying tired men into hauling the sail full up.

'Do you really know what you are about?' I asked and Brother John shot me such a look I thought he was about to snarl at me, too. Then he wiped dry lips and I saw the fear and uncertainty there.

'It is in deep and barbed. I can't push it through, for I think it is near his vitals. If I try to get it out I will make more of the wound than his body can take, perhaps.'

'If you leave it?'

'*Coniecturalem artem esse medicinam.*'

Medicine is the art of guessing. I looked at the figure, shrunken even now; I wanted no more little corpses and said so. Brother John, agitated and fretting, nodded and licked his lips, then started to pray even more.

I stood, feeling the wind in my face, turned to the prow and saw Radoslav.

'Timely message,' I said, then told him what had happened and that the boy they had sent it with was dead. Radoslav shook his silver-bound braids, then looked at the little figure on the deck, Brother John hunched over him like some ragged crow.

'His mother will be cursing the day we sailed into the harbour, I am thinking,' Radoslav said, then spat. 'Not that we can go back. Your Starkad threw a fox in that hen coop right enough.'

He told it swiftly and simply. They'd seen the ship arrive and were puzzled, because it was a big Greek *knarr*, but coming in from the east and labouring against an offshore wind. Then, as it came round the headland, they saw it was full of Norse and Kvasir put it together fast enough for them to raise sail and catch the same wind out that made hard work for Starkad to get in.

Radoslav was still furious that the *Volchok* had been left, with Arinbjorn and Ogmund on board, who would have no chance. Worse, in his eyes, was that most of the cargo was on board, too.

'I am sorry for that,' I said.

Radoslav shrugged. 'No matter. The treasure will pay for it when we get it.'

I said nothing, for I knew now that Radoslav was still convinced we were off to find the hoard – that, after all, was what this chase to get the runesword was about. Yet there was a storm in me, tossing my resolve like a leaky *knarr*. Driven by oath to get the sword, I had no wish to go back to Atil's howe. Eventually, I would have to decide and matters would get uglier than Short Eldgrim.

'Where too, Trader?' demanded Gizur. I had long since worked this out and only the starting point was changed.

'North and then east, round the island and set a course to Seleucia,' I said. I had listened to all the gossip and knew that Antioch was in the hands of the Miklagard army. It wasn't the first time they had taken the city and, like all the other times, they'd probably have to give it up and fall back on Tarsus. I just hoped they still held it when we got to Seleucia, Antioch's port, which was a safer haven than some lonely beach in Serkland.

Short Eldgrim hefted my shield and fingered the stub of the arrow, visible on the inside, up near the grip. He looked at me and lifted what remained of one of his eyebrows.

'Aye, just so,' I offered wryly. 'An inch to the left and I'd be picking the back of my teeth with the point of it. Anyone would think you did not like me, wee man.'

Short Eldgrim fetched his tin-snips later and worried the point out of the wood, but there was no way of telling who had loosed it – for which Radoslav and Short Eldgrim and a couple of others were greatly relieved. I pitched it over the side and laughed.

We swept on, looking backwards for signs of Greeks and rubbed raw with the frustration of it, for Starkad was also there. I prayed that Balantes would not release his own ships to the north, that he would think we were scudding back to Miklagard with our prize, perhaps that we were even in the pay of the Basileus and about to expose him. I knew Starkad would not think so. I knew he would come our way alone and it was starting to irritate me that, every time we got close to him, our chances of making red war on him seemed to be furthest away.

Of course, I was heading straight into the arms of Red Boots, who commanded the Great City's army in the east, but I hoped to have slipped away from him before Balantes sent word to watch for Orm Bear Slayer. If Odin held true to us, Starkad would follow and then we could trade – or fight; at the moment, either way was fine with me.

We turned east with no wind and crept like a water insect along the Anatolian coast, rowing until the snot and drool ran in our beards.

It was a good *hafskip*, this new *Fjord Elk*, and Gizur was well pleased, though the mast had checked in the heat of five untended summers and sprung cracks and some of the planks were a little less tight than was safe. As long as there wasn't a blow and we had men bailing, he thought we'd make Antioch.

Brother John had worried and teased the arrowhead out of the Goat Boy without sign of fat on the end, then fed him a broth of leeks and found no smell when he sniffed the wound, both of which were good signs.

I came on him while he was looking at Ivar, whom we called Gautr for his wit and Loki tricks. Ivar had taken an arrow through the cheek, which was a clean enough wound, but it had nicked his gum and a tooth as well, which bothered him.

'How is the boy?'

'Alive,' Brother John said, clapping Ivar on one shoulder and straightening. 'I cannot be after saying how long that will last, all the same. I have cleaned it with vinegar and sewn it with fishing line and poulticed it with malva and wheat bran wrapped in a vellum strip of my best prayer.'

'What else can we do?'

Brother John shrugged. 'Pray he lives to reach Antioch and pray that the Greeks have not slaughtered all the *Sarakenoi* and pray that the ones they left alive include a doctor. The *Sarakenoi* have the best doctors, as any will tell you.'

'That's a lot of praying,' I pointed out and he nodded and smiled wanly.

'I have them to spare for him, all the same,' he said.

I went to the Goat Boy, who was barely awake, with a voice like the whisper of a distant wind.

'You should have let me die,' I heard him say.

'Your mother would have killed me,' I managed. 'Anyway, Finn Horsehead needs a helper at the cookfire and you have been selected. When you have finished lolling here, that is.'

He managed a smile, then a small tear, pearl-bright and fat, squeezed from the corner of one eye. His skin was so pale the blue-purple veins stood out like the scars on Short Eldgrim's face. 'Will I ever see my mother again?' came the whisper.

I nodded, unable to speak now, for his *heimthra* was choking me.

Short Eldgrim saved the day, shoving his scarred face into the tremble between us, offering the Goat Boy what was supposed to be a friendly grin but looked like a bad carving left too long in the rain. 'I'll take you back after this little trip is over,' he growled, 'for I have left my washing. Don't worry, little bear, enjoy a ship journey and an adventure in a strange place, some sweet things to eat and then home.'

The Goat Boy smiled at that, then his eyelids closed and he slept, his breath a rattle in the tiny cage of his chest. I sat and brooded on it, alone in the prow, while men went to their sea-chest benches and hauled us away.

Away from Balantes – and also away from Starkad and the sword we needed, though I knew he would follow and made the mistake of saying so when Radoslav pointed out that Starkad did not know where we had gone.

I told them, feeling the sick taste of the jarl torc in my mouth, hearing Einar chuckle.

'He knows,' I said flatly, 'because I told Arinbjorn.'

Radoslav's eyes widened slightly, then he nodded, quiet and thoughtful. I knew he had a new weight to add to his scales: Arinbjorn had been given command of the *Volchok* and I had told him my plans in case we were separated on the journey.

Now Starkad would make Arinbjorn tell all he knew – and I was sure he would keep that knowledge to himself. Starkad had come from the east, so he must have ploughed all the way to Jaffa, the Serkland harbour most used by Christ pilgrims heading for Jorsalir, and found I had lied, for a Christ priest like Martin could not have arrived without comment there. Now he wanted me alive long enough to tell him what he still believed I knew: where Martin was.

In the hiss and gurgle from the water creaming away from the bow, I heard Einar's laughter and drove it out with sweat and grunting, taking my place at a bench and hard-rowing all the thoughts out of me. We pulled in shifts for half a day until the wind swung round to a useful quarter, by which time my arse and back and thighs ached.

When a man took my place, I stood to the watch like everyone else, taking the prow and pulling on the new mail I had taken as my share from Patmos. It was snug. My old mail, which I had sold to help get us down the Dark Sea to Miklagard, would now have been too tight round the bunched muscle of my shoulders and it had been made for a grown man in Strathclyde. For a moment, quick as a flick of light, I saw the rain pooling in the dead eyes of the boy I had killed in that fight.

A lifetime ago.

Then, after a long ache of time, Sighvat called out a sighting of land ahead and, not long afterwards, a ship. By the time I reached him, he had changed that to ships, so that everyone, clenched and anxious, craned to see.

'Greek ships,' he said, pointing, and, sure enough, there were the great curled sterns you could not mistake. Three of them. Then four. Behind them, land bulked up and there was a smear of smoke, so that Gizur, frowning and shading his eyes with one hand, shook his head.

'This is where we should be,' he growled. 'Seleucia, for sure.'

'Well, we are in trouble now,' Kvasir growled, thinking these were the Greeks who pursued us.

I did not think so, for it could not be ships from Cyprus. I thought it more likely they were ships from Miklagard supporting the army – which meant the Greeks were still in Antioch.

Short Eldgrim grinned and bet Finn an ounce in hacksilver that I had the right of it and Horsehead, who would lay money on anything, took it, spat on his hand and sealed the event. A minute later he scowled, having realised that if he won he would be hard put to get a dead man to pay up.

Short Eldgrim was still grinning when the *dromon* washed up to us, backed water neatly and hailed us. He stuck out a hand, waggling the fingers delightedly until Finn, grumbling, started fishing his purse out from under his armpit.

On the Greek ship, a man waved at us with a golden stick. He wore a simple white tunic, but had a splendid helmet with a great fountain of horsehair maned across it.

'I am *quaestor* of the port,' he yelled across the gap between us. 'I did not know your Curopalates Nabites had any ships here. Where have you been?'

That made me blink. My who? I told him we had come from the Great City and did not know any Nabites, at which the *quaestor* indicated he would come aboard. We slithered our ships together in a soft swell, Gizur wincing and roaring at each dunt on the fingerwidth-thick pine strakes, and the Greek clambered aboard, clutching his golden stick.

It then turned out that Curopalates wasn't a name but a title worth three pounds of gold to whoever had it, but the Nabites confused us all, for it seemed this *quaestor* spoke of a Norseman. It was not a name anyone knew, either in the decent tongue of the West Norse, or the crippled way they spoke to the east of Norway.

But the *quaestor* said this Nabites was favoured by the Strategos John, commander of the Basileus's armies here, and had some six hundred men, plus all his women and even his dogs, brought down from the north.

'It's a mystery right enough,' said Brother John, coming from attending the Goat Boy, who lay bundled in warm cloaks, his hair like night against the pale skin. But he breathed, ragged and laboured though it was.

The *quaestor* handed us a stamped bronze medallion which would give us passage to the harbour, and we chewed on the strange name of Nabites, scratching heads all the way into safe anchorage.

That was in the curve of a bay, where the little white houses of the fair-sized town of Seleucia straggled up from a rough harbour and, confusingly, there seemed to be a forest right down at the water's edge. It was a puzzle to us all – until we realised that the trees were ships' masts.

I had never seen so many ships in one place and neither had anyone else. We gawped until Gizur roared and banged a pine-tarred rope's end on the deck to get all our attention fixed on not running into the massive fleet anchored there.

We flitted in like a chip of driftwood, dwarfed by huge supply ships and even bigger warships, dodging the smaller galleys and fat-bellied little Greek merchant ships – for they would not miss a chance like this – which were as like our own *knarrer* as to be brothers misplaced at birth. Finn stood in the prow, waving the bronze medallion at any guard ships and cursing them in the few Greek words he knew when they came too close.

Ours was the only *hafskip*, though, which made it easy to find a good spot near the village – none of the other ships could go as shallow. I wanted it run up on the beach, since I knew we'd be gone from her for a while, but Gizur baulked at putting five years of neglected timbers to that sort of test.

The *hafskip* had one other effect, which happened as we took it as close to the breaking waves as Gizur cared to go, then splashed ashore to cable it to the land. I was halfway over the side when Short Eldgrim gripped my shoulder and, when I looked at him, he nodded towards a group moving down to us.

There were men and women in it, children and dogs, all chattering excitedly – and all in a good West Norse, so that my heart ached for the sound of it. They had seen a sight they had not seen for some time – a Norse ship, prows decently removed – and had come running.

They stopped some distance off, which was both polite and sensible, then one stepped forward to hail us, a tall man in a fine linen tunic and breeks, with a good seax strapped round his waist. He had blond hair in two thick braids and a neatly trimmed beard, altogether the very way a fine Norse farmer should look. Which made it as strange a sight in this land as a calf with a head at each end.

134

'I am Olvar Skartisson,' he announced. 'Who leads this welcome band to us?'

I told him as the crew splashed ashore and began chattering and grinning with the girls and older women. In the end, everyone dropped into the water and came ashore, grinning and talking.

'Have you come to join us, then?' asked Olvar Skartisson and that set the whole saga tale of it out, as we pitched down on the rocks and sand and got more comfortable. Ale and bread came out and we started in to share our tales.

It turned out that this Nabites was what the Greeks took from *nabitr*, which means corpse-biter in Norse and was a nickname given to Jarl Toki Skarpheddin, a name that means sharp-toothed – another north joke the Romans did not understand. I didn't know this jarl, but Sighvat said he was a well-known and powerful man who fought for Harald Greycloak once, he who claimed to be a king in Norway.

Olvar said he had the right of it, and that when the good Christ-follower Harald Greycloak went under the treacherous swords of that heathen Haakon of Hladir, who was Bluetooth's man in Norway, Skarpheddin had to take his men and flee.

Since they would scarcely leave their families behind, he had to take them, too, and all the ships they sailed in were now in Aldeigjuborg. They had left them there to come by riverboats down all the rivers of the Rus to Miklagard at the expense of little Prince Vladimir, where the Great City's Basileus duly offered the jarl three pounds of gold annually to serve him in his wars.

Which, I thought to myself as this was laid out, showed how young Vladimir, sent to rule Novgorod at four years old by his father, Sviatoslav, was blossoming into a deep-minded prince before his first decade was out, even allowing for his clever Uncle Dobrynya at his side.

His dealing with Skarpheddin was as cheap a way of ridding yourself of a thousand unwanted mouths as you could find, as well as getting yourself a nice fleet of decent Norse ships. Now the landless, luckless Skarpheddin and his whole people were here, at the sharp edge of the Roman frontier, fighting the *Sarakenoi*, with no home to go back to.

At least it made the light brighter on my own problems.

I told him as many vague lies as I thought I would get away with when my men became loose-mouthed. At the end of it, he dabbed the ale from his moustaches, accepted a refill with a nod and a smile and said: 'Well, perhaps Skarpheddin can help you and you him.'

'And why would that be?' I asked, then paused as someone tapped my shoulder. I looked up to see a girl with an ale flask, looking to refill my own. She was red-lipped and pale, with the skin flush and thick white-blonde plaits that spoke of someone who should never sit long in the heat.

She offered up a smile like a new sun and eyes shaped like almonds and I gawped until the girl grew impatient and said: 'If your mouth hangs open so much, you clearly cannot hold ale in it.' And with that she was gone.

Olvar frowned. 'A *fostri* of the jarl is Svala, from foreign parts. She is young yet and too clever and favoured for her own good.'

Nothing more was said, but now that I looked, other women were circulating, pouring ale, offering bread from huge baskets of them: Norse women, in fine embroidery and headsquares, hung about with keys and scissors. There were girls, too, like Svala, with their hair in braids.

I saw the Oathsworn smile and blush and hang their heads at being chided for needing their hair and beards trimmed, or their clothes cleaned and mended. The same men, I remembered, who had tripped screaming, veiled women in the dust of Kato Lefkara and tupped them, drooling, only days before.

Olvar then went on to say that Skarpheddin needed new men, for there had been losses in the fighting against the Arabs. He would broach it with his jarl and take us to him.

I saw Brother John hovering. When he caught my eye, he came across and sat down.

'We have injured,' he said to Olvar. 'Do you have someone who can help?'

Olvar smiled and nodded. 'Thorhalla's charms are second to none,' he declared, at which Brother John scowled and, realising suddenly that he was talking to a Christ priest, the good Christ-man Olvar blanched and backed water.

'Of course, there are priests of the *Romanoi*,' he added.

'I was thinking more of someone who can fix wounds,' said Brother John sternly.

Olvar shrugged. 'That we get from the Greeks, who have chirurgeons for it, though some of them are Mussulmen and, being decent Christians, most of us have nothing to do with them.'

Brother John rose and left, shaking his head. Olvar was bewildered and frowning, then he brightened and offered to take me to see Skarpheddin. I had Finn and Brother John organise getting the Goat Boy to proper help, then asked Radoslav and Sighvat to come with me. The others, I thought, would be better staying with the boat.

It had rained, but the day was already warm and growing warmer as we set off, a fair procession of women and girls and men carrying their big baskets, still brimming with round loaves. Olvar said they did this every day, which was their free ration for being part of the army.

He also told us about the Serklanders, which was useful to know.

'They worship the Prophet Mahomet,' he said, 'and every man in the land is allowed to have four wives if he has embraced that way.'

'Four women should just about be enough for me,' grunted Finn, 'after the journey I have had.'

'If you do become a Mahomet-follower,' Olvar pointed out, 'you can never drink wine or ale or mead again.'

Kvasir laughed with his head thrown back and others joined in, for the struggle on Finn's face over what was more important to him was fine entertainment for a long walk.

Olvar, laughing also, added: 'My own belief is that the old gods are weak in this land and the Serklanders and Christmen are stronger. The Serklanders only have one god and they call him Allah. The Christ-men and the Jews also only have one God, which is confusing.'

I felt I should point out – for him and all the others who could hear – that All-Father was a force no matter in what corner of the world his followers were and had the satisfaction of seeing Olvar flush.

The land swayed and dipped, as it always did after days at sea and I stumbled, bracing for swells that never came, across rock and scrub heavy with the scent of watered dust. Already I missed the salt breeze on my face. At the crest of the hill above the village, I turned back, to find the *Elk* lost in that litter of ships.

The heat grew, though the sun was just a glow, as if seen through brine, and we sweated in our leather boots and wool over the dusty green land, on a long walk along a road busy with donkeys and carts and oxen, robed men and soldiers in leather and iron.

The sun had moved towards the other horizon by the time we crested the last slope and saw Antioch for the first time. It was less a city than a jewelled reliquary in the late sun, a confection like the ones sold on trays in Miklagard, made of spun sugar and made more dazzling against the black-humped hills behind and the green and gold of crops and grazing land it sat in.

When we reached the bridge over the river at the main gate, though, the spun sugar vanished and the white walls showed black scorch marks I knew only too well. Ox-carts and donkey trains straggled in and out of the gate, while several mounds nearby showed where the massed dead – probably the enemy, since nothing marked it – had been buried.

The Norse had started a camp near the river, where once there had been a Mussulman temple, which they called a mosque. The Strategos had handed this over to Skarpheddin as his hov for the while, but Skarpheddin was no fool, I saw, for he had not entered it, but had pitched a great swathe of tents instead, made from the striped wadmal of his sails, to remind him of what he had lost.

He knew that not all Mussulmen were enemy and did not want to outrage those still in Antioch by defiling one of their holy places, yet you would not have guessed all this cunning from the sight of this jarl, once ruler of Raknehaugen in Norway.

I came on him in his tent-hov, where he sat on a good seat, with the snarling prows rescued from his best ship on either side. Once he had been a powerful man, but never tall. Now he was a thin-shanked ale barrel wearing fine cloth the colour of the sea on a clear day and his hair was streaked with more grey than red.

Gold glinted on his chest and arms, though, and on the rings at wrist and ankle, for his feet were bare as he leaned forward for Olvar to whisper in his ear.

Then he looked up, frowning slightly and stroking the considerable length of his frosted red-gold beard, which had been forked into many plaits and fastened with silver rings.

'You are young,' he declared, leaning an elbow on one knee and cupping his chin. 'Younger than I thought, for I have heard of both you and the Oathsworn, though I thought Einar the Black led them still and had a young Baldur-hero join him, the slayer of a white bear. Now, it seems, young Baldur is the leader.'

If he had heard all that, he had heard also tales of a hoard of silver and more and my heart lurched. I could smell the greed-sickness off him from here, but swallowed and inclined my head politely enough.

'I am that bear slayer,' I said 'though my name is Orm. This is Sighvat Deep-Minded and Radoslav, who is called Schchuka.'

From behind Skarpheddin, I heard a sibilant hiss and, for an unnerving moment, thought he had broken wind. Then I realised the sound came from a woman and Skarpheddin half turned as she came out of the twilight of the tent to where we all could see her.

My skin crawled at once. She was old, but had her hair unbound, falling in iron-grey straggle-tails to her shoulders. She wore a dress the colour of blue twilight in the far north, fastened at the waist with a belt looped like a man's and hung about with all manner of things: a couple of drawstring purses; the skull of a small animal; the tail bones of a snake. Round her neck was a circle of amber beads big as gull eggs.

But it was the catskin cloak thrown round her shoulders that let me know what she was: that and the seidr flowing off her so that the hairs on my arms stood up, as if a storm was coming. I had made a sign against evil before I'd thought of it and she gave a short laugh, like a dog barking.

'Do you fear this *volva*, then, Orm Bear Slayer?'

I found my tongue locked to the roof of my mouth, but it was Sighvat who spared me with a calm answer, as if he were greeting her politely as an ordinary woman.

'There is nothing to fear as long as I am here,' he said levelly and Skarpheddin chuckled at the woman's frown, while both of them eyed the pair of ravens that Sighvat now took everywhere perched on his shoulders. Used to them, I suddenly saw it from the other side and how it marked Sighvat as a full-cunning man, one of seidr power himself, which was why the rest of the crew both respected and looked sideways at him; for a man to dabble in seidr was considered strange and unmanly.

'Well, Thorhalla,' said Skarpheddin, finally. 'It seems the Bear Slayer is well served with his own seidr And that,' he added, pointing to Radoslav's tattoo, 'is a useful mark to have, I am thinking.'

Radoslav grinned. 'Your witch spells won't work on me,' he boasted. 'I am Perun's man and his hand is strong over me.'

140

Thorhalla hissed like the cats she wore and made a movement of her fingers.

'Now, now, old one,' Skarpheddin chided with false bravado, 'that's enough of that. These are guests.'

Then, as the woman slid back into the shadows, he spread his hands in apology. 'Forgive my mother. She clings to the old ways and too many of my people are considering Christ here.'

His mother. At once I felt pity for Skarpheddin doubled from before. Here he was, exiled and wasting away in a foreign land and, like bitter gall on the rotten meat of it, he had a mother like that, a real *spaekona*. As Sighvat laid it out later: 'If it had been me, I'd have killed her long since as the cause of all his grief.'

After that came the hard talk and I knew Skarpheddin wanted us, not only for what he had heard of our skills, but for what he had heard of the hoard. I told him we were new-sworn Christ-men, heading for Jorsalir with our own Christ priest and he nodded, frowning. I could feel his own greed-plans ooze from him like sweat.

'I am of the Aesir,' he added, with a mild smile, 'and though prime-signed for Christ I will offer my help, of course. If you were to place your hands in mine, naturally I would be oath-bound then to provide aid.'

I thanked him for that, but told him I did not want any more oaths than the one I had already taken to my sword-brothers, at which he frowned. I did not tell him it was an Odin-oath, but let him think it one made to the White Christ. I added that I would be pleased to accept his hospitality and, when our task was done, would return. If he were then to offer a fair price for our services for a season, as the Basileus in Miklagard had done with him, then that was another matter and closer to my heart.

He brightened at that: the idea of being like the Basileus in Miklagard appealed and so he did not quibble, which was a relief. This meant my men had the chance of free food and ale for the time it took to find out what was needed – where Starkad and our old oarmates were – and did not fasten us to this doomed jarl.

Skarpheddin then said my men could find warm beds and hospitality both in the tents of his own hov and those of others in his company. I saw that shoal and steered round it, saying my men preferred to stay with their own ship, which had been their hov for so long; I did not want the men split up and scattered in a strange camp. Einar would have been proud of me.

After that, we were horn-paired round two large firepits and feasted, while the abilities and far-sighted vision of Skarpheddin were hailed by a skald and his skill and bravery lauded by men with grease-glistening faces and hefty roast ribs in their hand. Red-faced and bellowing, they declared Jarl Skarpheddin the finest ring-giver who had stepped on the earth each time a glowing woman refilled the horns.

My horn partner was Torvald, one of Skarpheddin's chosen men, but he was dark and dour and I looked all night for the girl they called Svala, so we had little to say to each other.

Next day, bleary-eyed and hurting, I went down to the river with Radoslav and, shivering in the morning chill, we sloughed off the ale and grease. When I straightened, scattering water like a dog, she was standing there, a hip arched and a wry smile on her face. I was aware that I stood wearing nothing but drenched small-clothes.

'Odin's arse,' roared Radoslav, surfacing and blowing like a bull seal. 'But that feels better . . . Oh, I didn't see you there.'

Grinning, he sloshed naked out of the river and stood drying himself while Slava raised an eyebrow and managed not to turn a hair doing it. She was, I noted, older than I was by a year, perhaps two.

'You are smaller than you look,' she said tartly to Radoslav. 'Perhaps you should get the Helm of Awe tattooed on something lower.'

Radoslav chuckled. 'It's only the cold, girl. It will grow bolder, like a chick rescued from snow, in the warmth of a loving hand.'

She snorted. 'Your own, I am sure.'

I liked her and she saw me grinning.

'I came to tell you that your priest, Brother John, and the man with the face like a fresh-gelded horse are looking for you. They said to tell you the Goat Boy is in good hands. Is he the little one they carried to the Greek chirurgeons?'

I nodded, pulling on my breeks and wondering if she dared face Finn with her description of him. In the end, as she smiled sadly over the plight of the Goat Boy, I decided she probably would.

'Is he badly hurt?' she asked.

I told her what had happened to us on the Cyprus shore – missing out what had brought us to it – and her eyes widened. I thought I saw something new there towards me, but I was probably wrong.

'Thank you for letting me know,' I said politely. 'Do you know where Olvar is? I would like him to come with us into the city, for I am thinking a guide would be a good thing there.'

She wrinkled her nose. 'You don't need Olvar. I will take you.'

'Perhaps your mother would not like that,' Radoslav offered, 'seeing as how going off with two handsome men, dangerous in the loving as they are, would be seen as reckless.'

Svala eyed him up and down and smiled, a dimpled, impish smile. 'Sadly she is dead – but had she lived to see two such as you describe,' she returned, 'she would have been concerned. However, there is only a limp man with a stamp between his brows and a boy.'

While my hackles rose foolishly at that, Radoslav threw back his head and roared with laughter and, eventually, I saw

143

the humour of it and we all three went off, laughing, to meet Brother John and Finn and go into the city.

That, even with the sheen of past remembering on it, was the last truly good time of my life.

SEVEN

The Goat Boy lay under clean linen in a cot in a shady room whose doors were framed with vines. It was at the end of a wide avenue so quiet that we were half afraid to speak and the whirr of a pigeon wing was enough to startle us.

It had been, one of the red-tunicked staff said, a place where Arab potion-makers – the staff man called them *saydalani* – mixed up their elixirs, and the place was ripe with the smells of spices. Some of them we knew; others, like musk, tamarind, cloves and a sharp tang Brother John said was aconite, were new to most of us.

Now it was a place where chirurgeons from the army treated their wounded and one of these blood-letters eyed us up and down before, reluctantly, letting us in to see the Goat Boy, on condition that we did not touch him, his wound or anything else.

Brother John asked him what he had done to it and the man, a grizzle-haired individual with skin like old leather, said he had put in a drain to rid the wound of accumulating fluid and that the boy's lung would heal itself if he was given time and rest.

'That's laudable pus,' exclaimed the priest, outraged. 'You will kill him if you take it away. It is meant to be there.'

145

The chirurgeon looked Brother John up and down, taking in the ragged breeks and tunic, the unkempt hair and beard. 'I have read Galen's *Tegni* and the aphorisms of Hippocrates,' he said. 'I have studied the *Liber Febris* of Isaac Judaeus. Have you?'

Brother John blinked and scowled. 'I cut the arrowhead out of him,' he answered.

The chirurgeon nodded, then smiled. 'The surgery was smart work but heathen prayers and chants are not suitable for healing. Next time, clean the blade, or heat it. If you want your boy to survive, let me do what I do best.'

Muttering, Brother John let the leash of his annoyance fall slack and we went into the shaded, quiet place, where a few recovering soldiers sat and chatted. They looked up when we came in and a couple offered up salutes and cheers to Svala, who merely grinned back at them.

The Goat Boy was asleep, but the rasp of his breathing had gone and, though his closed eyes looked like two bruises, there was, I thought, more colour to him than before.

We chatted to the soldiers for a while, hoping he would wake, but he slept on. Instead, we learned how the Great City's army had come up against a great mass of Arab horse and foot determined to defend Antioch and the battle had been a vicious affair, though short.

An Armenian archer called Zifus, perched with his leg in a sling, said that this was the second time he had been to take Antioch and that this was something like the tenth war between the Great City and the Arabs. The Hamdanids from Mosul and Aleppo always managed to take Antioch back.

'Red Boots means to have it all this time,' Zifus observed, 'for he has heard that old Saif al-Dawla is failing in health and he is the leader of the Hamdanites and the man who has kept the Romans of the Great City at bay here for twenty years, fuck his mother.'

It was all news and I was glad to have it, but only took it

in with half an ear, as they say, while Brother John translated for Finn. Those silkworm eggs made the footing treacherous here and I planned to be gone just as soon as the Goat Boy was well enough – sooner, if I found out what we needed to know, though I would leave silver enough for him to be cared for.

If I wanted to make use of that silkworm stuff and save us all, I had to either trade it with Starkad or kill him and then get it to the Basileus of the Great City, the only one I could be sure was not part of any plot. Either way seemed like digging through a mountain with a horn spoon.

We sat and drank *nabidh*, which is made from dates and raisins soaked in water, and talked more, with Zifus adding 'fuck his mother' to the end of every other sentence he spoke.

The gist of what he revealed was that, after the Serkland army fled, the city gave up and the marks we'd seen on the walls came from stray pots of Greek Fire, shot from the great throwers the engineers called onagers, which means 'wild asses'. I had seen these machines at Sarkel, watched them leap in the air and kick at every released shot, while those tending them ran for cover. They were well named.

'We will look after the boy for you, friends,' said Zifus when it came time for us to leave the still-sleeping Goat Boy. 'He is a sorry soul now, but even so he shows courage. A curse on the one who shot him, fuck his mother.'

We left in silence and, outside, Finn smacked a fist into his other hand.

'One day I will come face to face with this Starkad,' he vowed. 'Then I will pay him back for all he has done.'

'Fuck his mother,' we chorused and, laughing, strolled on into the city.

The five of us wandered wide, stone-paved streets lined with tall columns, which supported vines to make a roof that sheltered walkers from the sun. It was cloudy and damp and hot as we strolled along the length of this street, past a basilica and a building Svala said had been a palace, made from yellow and pink marble. There were others here from Skarpheddin's force, mostly the younger men from his own house guard, swaggering along with hands on their sword hilts.

They did not impress us much. In fact, Finn had lost patience with a pair of them he caught at swordplay outside Skarpheddin's hov, leaping and dancing and clashing steel on steel until no one could stand it any longer. Finn had hurled his shield between them, so that it skittered ankle-dangerous along the dust and they had whirled angrily, then spotted him.

He had said nothing, but they knew what he had meant – no warrior places edge against edge, since a sword is too valuable a weapon to ruin in that way. Sword on shield is the way and only if you must do you block with a good edge. A warrior knows this.

'They are farmers, whose palms are calloused from ploughs, not swords,' growled Finn with disgust. 'They think they are snugged up in the meadows of home and that this is all a dream. They raise their horns and shout: "*Til àrs ok fridar!*" By Odin's hairy balls, what use is that to those out on the viking?'

Til àrs ok fridar. To the year's crops and peace. There was a flash of Gudleif, my foster-father, flushed and grinning, almost shining in the dark reek of the Bjornshafen hov, horn held high, triumphant with what had been achieved: a good harvest, winter hunger kept at bay and no deaths among us or the thralls or livestock. Gudleif, whose head had been left on a pole by the dulse-strewn beach when the Oathsworn sailed away with me, stuck there by his own brother.

Maybe Skarpheddin's men saw that in us, or felt it, for they altered course far round us, wisely leaving us alone to enjoy the sights and swaggering only when they thought themselves beyond reach.

Antioch had countless tall buildings, domed Christ churches and some more mosques with their fat-topped towers. Then

148

we came out into a great round place surrounded by what seemed a high stone wall and tiers of seats.

There were stalls everywhere, selling bread and vegetables and chickpeas and figs. Svala bought two red fruits with tufts at one end and tough skin, but she held it in both hands, gave a twist of her wrist and split it open to reveal hundreds of little seeds, glistening like the *lalami*, the rubies in Radoslav's earring.

He admired her skill and had her show him how to do it, while the rest of us marvelled at the tart sticky sweetness of the seeds in what she called a *rumman* fruit.

'What is this place?' asked Finn, wiping juice from his beard.

'An amphitheatre,' answered Brother John, 'where the old Romans used to have gladiator shows.'

'I have heard of them,' Radoslav said. 'They were fighting contests, sometimes men against wild beasts as well as other men.'

'That sounds like more fun than the chariot races in Miklagard,' Finn growled.

Brother John scowled at him. 'It was banned in the time of the Emperor Justinian. It is the death penalty for anyone staging such contests now.'

'They do it all the same,' Svala said and we all looked at her. 'There are contests held in secret and bets laid,' she told us. 'If you know someone, they will tell you where they are to be held that night and give you a ticket to get in.'

'Bets?' said Finn and then fell silent, thinking about it.

We strolled and gawped and finally I thought it was time we went back to the ship, which would take us all day. I had arranged for food and drink for the men there and knew they would have rigged the sail as a tent, but if I did not fix ways by which some could go to the city and some stay behind, they would all take it into their heads to abandon the *Elk* to the Norns and go humping and drinking.

149

So we sat in a shaded *taberna* near the amphitheatre for one last wine and my head swam from the night before, so that all I wanted was to close my eyes and listen to Radoslav flirt with Svala, while Brother John and Finn argued about who could spit olive seeds furthest.

I saw myself back on the *Elk*, rowing hard away from Cyprus and was not sure whether the harsh whistle of breathing was my own or the Goat Boy's. But someone, somewhere was beating time for the oarsmen and each blow was a question, over and over . . . where was Starkad? Where were our oarmates? Where was Starkad? Where were our oarmates?

Adrift on a black sea, I stood at the prow of a dead ship, with the sails flapping, ragged and torn, though there was no wind at all. Ahead, bergs had calved off a glacier and moved like ponderous white bears. Ahead, a pale face surrounded by rags of hair, eyes so sunken and dark they looked like the accusing pits of little Vlasios. Ahead, a face I knew and, in that dark place, bright as a tear, sharp as a sliver of moonlight, the curved sword she raised . . .

'Heya, Trader . . . enough.'

The voice snapped me back to the *taberna*, where concerned faces loomed, pale as butter and swimming until I managed to focus.

'Bad head right enough,' said Radoslav and Brother John offered me watered wine, which I drank, suddenly parched.

'Who is Hild?' asked Svala archly and my stomach heaved, so that I couldn't speak. She waited for an answer and, when it was clear none was forthcoming, shrugged, pouted and walked off. Even long gone, the mad woman who had led us first to Atil's treasure still managed to poison my life.

'The sun has boiled your head,' Brother John offered helpfully. 'We'd better return to the *Elk*.'

150

'And you can go and boil yours,' announced Finn cheerfully, striding back into the company, tossing something in his hand, 'for it would be a shame to leave now and miss seeing the fighting men.'

Then he showed us the carved wooden token he had been given and the information that, when a bell was sounded, all those with tokens would make for the main entrance to the amphitheatre.

'A bell?' scoffed Brother John. 'What bell?'

'Did you part with money for this, Finn Horsehead?' demanded Radoslav with a chuckle. 'I fancy the man that took it is now wearing out shoe leather heading for a drinking place on the other side of the city.'

'No, no,' said Svala. 'It will be the vespers bell he is speaking of.'

Radoslav had to be told that the vespers bell was the one calling the faithful to prayer. We had already heard the Mussulman wailings that called their faithful to prayer five times a day. That seemed excessive to us, who did not pray to our gods at all unless we needed to, an arrangement, I thought, that served both sides well.

'Surely they cannot mean to hold fights in the amphitheatre,' Brother John declared and Finn stroked his beard and pointed out that the market would probably close at night, leaving it empty.

'It is death to hold such fights,' Brother John retorted scornfully. 'This arena is not a secret place, is it? You can hardly avoid attracting the Watch soldiers with hundreds of cheering people and the clash of steel.'

Finn swore, for he saw Brother John had the right of it and it came to him then that he had been gulled. This made him all the more determined to wait and, knowing him well enough, I sighed and said I would wait with him. Radoslav announced he was willing, at which point Brother John said he would take Svala back to her hov and return, hopefully before vespers.

151

Naturally she protested and had to be huckled off, furious at me, though it had not been my idea. So we settled down and stayed near the market in the shadow of the Iron Gate until the day sank slowly behind the citadel mound they called Silpius in a strange, cloud-wisped glory of red and gold.

Brother John came back, as planned, and we ate a couple of roast fowl with greasy flatbread and olives, while Finn searched all the faces in case he saw the man who had sold him the token. We watched the stalls pack up and the people in the market trail off one by one, listened to the muezzin calling the Arabs to their god, talked quietly of this and that and nothing at all.

Then the bell rang out for vespers, echoed by all the others in the city and, almost at once, we saw people move, quiet and flitting as moths.

'Oh-ho,' said Finn, rubbing his hands with glee, 'perhaps I have not lost at all.'

We followed what looked like a good group, half a dozen Greeks who might have been off-duty soldiers or merchants, to the main entrance of the amphitheatre, where now two burly men stood, all scarred fists and neck-rolling, armed with clubs. In almost total darkness we stood in a line and shuffled to the arched gate, the excitement sneaking from one to another in that milling crowd.

The guards took the token and searched us for weapons, but we only had our eating knives thanks to Skarpheddin, for it was only polite to attend his feast without serious blades.

Under the arch, three more men, holding dim lanterns, directed us sideways to where a door was now open in the side wall of the arena. In there, where torches guttered, a short passage led to steps and then down, a spiral that spilled us into a huge underground chamber, dank and cold.

'Where are we?' Finn demanded and Brother John looked round.

'Under the arena,' he declared. 'Here is perhaps where the animals were prepared. This would have been sectioned off . . .'

I didn't think so, for I smelled old rot and damp and saw the huge, rust-streaked pipe and its wheel. When I pointed it out, Brother John gave a low whistle of amazement.

'You have it right, Orm. This was where they stored the water to turn the arena into a lake. If we looked around, we could probably find the old pumps.'

'Lake? What lake?' demanded Radoslav.

Brother John explained that sometimes the men fought sharks or whales, or from boats, and then the arena above could be flooded to make a lake, and drained away again afterwards. This left both Radoslav and Finn drop-jawed at the deep-minded cunning of the old Romans.

Then Finn spotted an odds-maker and I did not know how he did that, for the man looked like any scarred-armed, bent-nosed ugly I had ever seen. Finn spoke to him, hauled out some coins and handed them over, then took a new wooden token. It was then I saw the marked-off area and the buckets and brooms to wash away the blood.

The crowds were milling and had even gone up the stairs to what had been the gallery walkway where the pumps and inlet valves were worked. They sounded like bees in the echoing chamber. Then the humming grew louder and, as Finn strolled back, we could all hear the sound of dragging chains.

'Who did you bet on?' asked Radoslav, having to raise his voice over the sudden cheers of the crowd. A man stepped out and announced the first contest, a match between two swordsmen and . . . the Mighty Blade himself.

The walls bounced with cheers, blood-thick with lust. The chains dragged again and I saw the two swordsmen, ankles fastened together by short lengths of chain, then chained one to the other by about four feet of links fastened to bracelets round their wrists. They wore loincloths, old-fashioned Greek-style

153

helmets with horsehair plumes, short swords, round shields and the desperate eyes of the doomed.

A trainer wearing a short tunic and not much else, keeping to the old Greek look, hauled them in and someone yelled: 'Fight well, you bastards. I have a bundle on you fixing the Blade tonight.'

'Not if the Norns are weaving this wyrd, I am thinking,' chuckled Finn, 'for I have the Blade down to win. I fancy his chances, for the odds-maker said he was an axeman of some skill and was fighting two with short swords. A good axeman will always win that.'

Across the other side of the marked-off area, into the fug of reeking torches and sweat and stale breath, came the Mighty Blade, naked save for a loincloth, the chain round his ankles and a long-handled Dane axe.

His shoulders, draped in the great, uncut pelt of his own hair, were like living animals when he whirled the axe from hand to hand and his entire body writhed with the coiled snake muscle on him. It was as Kvasir had once noted: he had muscles on his eyelids.

'It's Botolf,' growled Finn, staring at me in horror. 'Big Botolf.'

We stared and gawped, looking one to the other, then back again. It *was* him. Last seen on the deck of the last *drakkar* to bear the name the *Fjord Elk*, snugged up in the harbour in Novgorod two years since. And if he was here . . . I looked frantically around for the rest of the missing crew, the ones we had sent messages to and waited for in Miklagard.

'Perhaps the *lanista* will sell him to us,' Brother John offered in a wavering voice.

'What's a *lanista*?' asked Radoslav and Brother John pointed to the man hauling the chains of the two swordsmen.

'Is it that Latin tongue, priest?' asked the ever-curious Radoslav. 'What's it mean?'

'It means "trainer",' Brother John answered.

154

'It means dead man,' grunted Finn. He rolled his neck once, twice, then headed straight towards the *lanista* and his charges.

'We only have eating knives,' I warned, seeing the way the sail was filling. Finn's grin belonged to Hati, the wolf who pursues the moon.

'They have steel,' he answered, nodding at the swordsmen and strolled towards the *lanista*, who saw the big man coming up and put out a warning hand.

'Stay back, friend.'

'I am thinking your two pets look fine but I have laid good silver on them and would like to look at their teeth a while,' said Finn, all smiles, but the *lanista* never blinked.

'You might also want to make sure of winning,' he answered. 'With a thumb of pepper in the eye, perhaps. Won't be the first time someone has tried to nobble one of my fighters, so piss off back into the crowd where you belong.'

'Good advice,' shouted someone from the crowd. 'You're getting in the way—'

Finn elbowed the shouter without even turning round and the man howled, falling away and holding his mashed nose. The *lanista* looked startled but then Finn booted him right up beyond the hem of his short kilt and the man folded with a strangled whoof of sound, dropping the chains.

The two swordsmen were bewildered at this, while Mashed Nose sprayed blood and curses and showed the damage to his friends, who shot looks at Finn that were uglier than giant Geirrod's grisly daughters.

Finn, however, leaned casually across and gripped the wrist of one of the swordsmen, then plucked the curved Saracen blade from his hand like a honeycomb from a child. He turned, laid the blade against the neck of the second one and Radoslav came up, grinning, and took his sword and the little shield, too.

A couple of the crowd nearest Mashed Nose took three steps forward, then Brother John stepped forward and slammed a fist into the nearest head, knocking the man sideways. The others shied away like flushed plovers but Mashed Nose whipped out a long dagger, blew out bloody snot like some mad, injured bull, then started forward, all hunched neck and scowls.

Brother John smiled at him and held up one hand, palm outward, which stopped Mashed Nose in his tracks. Then he made the cross sign in the air, which made the immediate crowd stare. Finally, he gripped Mashed Nose by the shoulders, as if in a friendly fashion, then drew back his head as if to look at the sky and pray, the way priests do. Everyone looked up.

Brother John raised himself on to his toes and brought his head forward with vicious force. There was a wet smacking sound and Mashed Nose collapsed in a heap, while Brother John rubbed the red mark on his brow and scooped up the dagger.

'*Pax vobiscum,*' he declared.

The shouts had brought heads round, a ripple from us outward until it finally reached the hard men who were supposed to keep order. It also reached Botolf and the man holding his chains, so that when Botolf looked up, he saw me heading across the open fighting area.

He blinked. I yelled at him. He blinked again and I cursed him for having the cunning of a tree stump. The *lanista* holding his chains hauled out a leather-covered cudgel, for he saw I was unarmed, while two of the hard men came forward, spilling right and left round big Botolf in a way that let me know they had worked together before. It also let me know that I only had an eating knife.

But Botolf had worked it all out now. As Finn and Radoslav moved to take on the hard men and their knives, Botolf cuffed the *lanista* almost casually, a blow that spilled him his full length. Then, because he was still holding on to the chain, he hauled the groaning man back again as if he was a hooked fish, pulled him up and cuffed him back to the ground again, grinning. Then he did it again as I trotted up. The *lanista* finally worked matters out and let the chain go.

More hard men appeared; the crowd were shouting. Some were in fact cheering, because they thought this was a novel opening fight, but it would be minutes only before they worked it out and decided to join in.

Radoslav and Finn wasted no time against the hard men: it was short swords and shields against long knives and the not-so-hard men, after a couple of clangs and half-hearted swipes, backed off. I reached Botolf, who had reeled in the *lanista* yet again.

'Orm . . . you said you would come. Skafhogg said you were as useful as hen shit on an axe handle but he was wrong, eh?'

'No . . .' whimpered the *lanista*, cowering under the shelter of his flapping hands as I reached for him. I took the keys while he sobbed and bled and bent to unshackle Botolf's ankles, hearing him growl as I did so. Actually, I felt him growl, such was the force of it. A half-glance over my shoulder told me the two swordsmen had recovered and were howling across the open space towards me, released from their own chains.

It was such a mistake: I wish I had waited to see Botolf fight them before we'd started in to free him, for there were rocks with more clever in them than those two. It was only when they were within a few steps of him that they suddenly realised that they had no weapons at all and here they were, about to take on a giant armed with a Dane axe.

Botolf popped the butt end between the eyes of one of them, which slammed him to the ground, where he flopped like a sack of cats. Then he slapped the flat of the axe on the fancy helmet of the other one, proving the lack of worth in that battle-gear, because the blade caught the ornamental crest, snapped the chinstrap and screwed the whole thing sideways, so that the cheek-flap was now over the owner's nose. Blinded and bloody, the man screamed and stumbled away into Finn, who had chased off his opponent and now stabbed this new one in the thigh.

'Stairs!' screamed Brother John, pointing, and we all sprinted for them, me bringing up the rear just as the howling crowd surged forward – which at least got them between us and the rest of the better-armed bruisers who were supposed to keep order.

'Keep going! The door,' I shouted, pointing upwards. A hand grabbed my tunic and I heard it tear, so I whirled and let him have Botolf's chains, ring-bracelets and all. He fell back, screaming and losing teeth, which made the rest of the crowd think twice about crowding up behind me.

Ahead, Botolf pitched someone off the gallery and his shriek only ended when he hit the floor below with a meaty smack. Finn hauled me up and past him, turning to threaten the crowds. Something whirled through the air and smashed: an empty wine flask. A coin tinkled on the iron railings and Radoslav grinned.

'We must be good – they're throwing money—' He ended in a yelp as another coin smacked his elbow with a vicious sound. 'Turds – who did that?'

We were stuck on the stair, I saw, unable to go ahead until Botolf dealt with the armed hard men keeping us from the door. He was too dangerous, with that Dane axe, for them to rush in and tackle but there were too many for Botolf to take on if he left the narrow gallery for the open area round the exit, where they could surround him.

The crowd below threw curses, jeers and anything they could find. Coins and cheap pottery bowls rained on us and it stopped being funny when Brother John went down with his head bleeding. I helped him up, to the poor shelter under the jut of the inlet valve and took a swift glance at the flap of skin, while the blood poured over his face.

'*Morituri te salutant*,' he gasped, which was apt and let me know he still had humour in him. Finn and Radoslav backed up the stairs, their little shields up – though we'd have more chance keeping dry under a fern, for all the use they were.

Then I heard Radoslav start muttering the chant that would set his Helm of Awe to working and I knew things were desperate but the clash and clatter were a cloud on my thinking. When I had to duck a missile and clonked my skull on the rusted inlet valve I roared with frustration and pain.

The inlet valve.

'Botolf!' I shrieked and he risked a half-look over one shoulder and saw me frantically waving for him to come to me.

'Finn . . . Radoslav . . .'

They lumbered off to take his place. Something smashed into fragments and the crowd, seeing the swords disappear, were cautiously coming up the stairs. More coins whirred and rang to the catcalls from the crowd.

Botolf, a cut on one massive bicep, loomed over me and I pointed to the rusting valve.

'Hit it.'

Brother John scrambled frantically from under it as Botolf spat on his hands, gripped the Dane axe and whirled it up. A wine bowl bounced off his shoulder and I doubt if he noticed. The axe came down, the boom of it echoing round the brick walls. It smashed the rusting valve open, the axehead snapped off and was whirled away in the great gouting stream of water that spat out, catching Brother John on one arm. It would have torn him away if I hadn't grabbed the other and the roar of it drowned out everything else.

The crowd baulked when they saw it arc out, as if Thor himself had decided to take a piss. Then they realised what it meant and went mad with panic.

Of course, we were first to the door and beat the rush. I found myself shooting out into the empty, cool night air of the amphitheatre, spilling from the dark entrance out into the middle of the dusty circle. Alongside me, one of the hard men, spat out in my wake and on his hands and knees, looked at me, thought better of it, scrambled to his feet and darted off.

Finn and Brother John came up, then Radoslav and then, ambling carelessly away, the splintered shaft of the Dane axe across both shoulders, came Botolf, grinning and leaking blood. Behind him, spewing from the doorway and shrieking, came the fans of gladiators.

'By Thor's arse, Orm,' Botolf declared, clapping me happily on the back, so that I was sure I had been driven into the ground, 'you are a jarl and no mistake. Even if Skafhogg never says it to you, I do, for sure.'

I doubted if Skafhogg, the old Oathsworn's grizzled shipwright, would ever count me jarl enough – but, for the moment, I had no care of it. Finn, on the other hand, had something to say.

'You can drown him in drink,' growled Finn, 'but somewhere else. You can drown us all in drink, for I lost money on you.'

I followed them out of the amphitheatre, limping on that old ankle wound, the sound of the chains I dropped behind me lost in the screams of those running from the arena.

'Does this mean I am not a slave?' I heard Boltolf ask and wished then I had held on to the chains, so I could hit him.

We came to Skarpheddin's camp and talked our way past the Watch and up to his great tented hall in the dark, which confused the door-thrall. We had some Odin luck, though, for he was an Irisher known to Brother John from the night before, so it was no trouble for us to pile into the hov with an extra giant and rummage for sleeping space amid the curses of Skarpheddin's disturbed household.

Most were snoring in the reek of smoke and meat and mead and sweat, but two were blearily shoving 'tafl pieces round the board and Skarpheddin's skald was muttering his way through some *draupa* verse. I looked for Skarpheddin but he was in his *lok-rekkja*, his curtained bed-space – as was his mother, for which we were all thankful.

We all sank down in a cleared space, whispering out of politeness and secrecy and all of us wanted to know the one thing right away: where Valgard and the others were.

Botolf, craning to examine the slash on his bicep, picked at loose flesh and shrugged. 'We were sitting in Holmgard, waiting for word that Einar and the rest of you were rich,' he told us. 'Then word came that the Rus had fought with the Khazars, who had been beaten, and Sarkel had fallen, so we wondered how you had fared, for no word came.'

'That is because we were not there for it,' Finn chuckled and Botolf scowled blackly at him.

'Just so – which was the cause of what happened next. Prince Yaropolk came back, with his father and brothers – and Starkad, who pointed us out as Einar's men. Since Einar had run off from Yaropolk's retinue and disgraced him, Starkad thought to get his *drakkar* back that way, but burned his fingers, for Yaropolk took us and the ship. Us he sold to Takoub, a slave-dealer I will one day meet and whose head I will tear off.'

'Did you not get our messages, then?' I asked and he nodded grimly.

'Starkad came to where we were shackled and told us, with some delight it seemed to me, that Einar and Ketil Crow and others had all died on the steppe – and that little Orm had been made jarl.' He paused then and glanced at me, a little shamed it seemed. 'This we thought a barefaced lie,' he added, 'since the likes of Finn Horsehead and Kvasir were still alive. Valgard said it was unlikely that the likes of Orm would be preferred to Finn. No offence, young Orm.'

'What happened then?' I asked, ignoring this, though my face burned. Botolf shrugged his massive shoulders.

'Starkad said it was true, all the same, at which Valgard spat and said we could now expect no rescue from . . . I mean no offence, here, young Orm . . . a nithing boy.'

'Skafhogg needs a slap,' Finn growled and Botolf, teeth

gleaming in the half-dark, nodded agreement. I signalled for him to go on and he pursed his lips and frowned, thinking.

'Starkad wanted to know where that Martin monk had gone, but Valgard told him to go away and that he could as well die, screaming in his own piss. After that, we were shipped south, all the way to Kherson, and sold to the goat-fucking Arabs. Takoub packed us, nose to feet, in a big ship and sailed us off to Serkland.'

He stopped and blinked, the closest Botolf came to fear, it seemed to me.

'We came off the boat together, which was itself considerable luck,' he rumbled, shaking his shaggy head at the memory. 'That was a grim trip right enough – others died, but none of the Oathsworn.'

'How is it you went one way and they another?' I asked.

'Someone saw me, I am thinking, and thought I would be better fighting than any of the others. All I know is that I was unshackled from them and shackled to another lot and we were taken away – north, I think. The others went their own way, towards Damascus, I heard.'

'Together?' I asked and he nodded.

'Even that little rat-faced Christ-man, Martin,' he said. The news rocked us all; I heard the rumble of One Eye laughing in my head.

'The monk?' gasped Finn and Botolf nodded, grinning.

'Aye, he was rounded up with us – Starkad did not see him and Valgard thought it a good joke that what he sought so avidly was feet away from him all the time.'

'Heya,' breathed Kvasir, looking at me. 'Odin's hand, right enough, Trader. There you are telling Starkad what you believe to be lies and it was the truth all along.'

'What of the icon?' demanded Brother John, dabbing his cut head and Botolf frowned with puzzlement, then remembered and brightened.

'That spear thing? Oh, Takoub took it with him.'

'Where are the others now?' I asked, shooting annoyance at Brother John's interruption.

Botolf shrugged.

'So we have lost them, then,' growled Finn.

'Not lost,' answered Botolf cheerfully, finishing examining his cut. 'They went to Fatty Breeks. I heard men say so.'

'Who in the name of Odin's hairy arse is Fatty Breeks?' shouted Finn and then rounded on all those who woke and told him to keep quiet, folk were trying to sleep.

'Easy, Horsehead,' I said, laying a calming hand on his arm. 'Let's sleep on it and see if we can find someone who knows about it when it is full daylight.'

Grumbling, Finn curled up, scowling. Botolf shrugged, then grasped my wrist.

'You did well, Orm,' he said. 'Valgard Skafhogg was sure it was our wyrd to die like nithings, for he did not think you had the balls for the task of saving us. It will be good to see his face when we shake his chains off.'

He lay down and started to snore almost at once. I envied him, for I still heard that thumping beat of my thoughts, a tern-whirl of confusion. Now we had our oarmates to consider, as well as the rune-serpent sword, and I dared not wonder what came next, for it is well known that the Norns weave in threes.

In the morning, after we had splashed water on our faces, we went around Skarpheddin's camp, asking about Fatty Breeks, which got us strange looks and a few scowls, which big Botolf deflected with a look of his own. We learned nothing.

The camp was a busy place, a village of wadmal cloth in fact, where folk carried on as if they were still in a toft set in hills soft and round as a breast, clothed with the tawny grass of spring and alive with gull and raven.

They worked the pole lathe, turned shoes, pumped bellows and forged, cooked solid fare against a Norway chill and tried to ignore the rising heat, a sky so pale blue it was near white, a sere roll of scrub-covered hills and the slaughtered-pig screech of the *norias* on the Orontes River, those huge water wheels that carried buckets up to the old arched aqueducts of the Romans and watered the fields around Antioch.

Into this bustle came the merchants, the spade-bearded Jewish Khazars whose brothers I had seen in Birka and fought at Sarkel, fat-bellied Arabs, plush Greeks and even a few Slavs and Rus, smelling trade and bringing bargains.

Since Skarpheddin had parted with some of the silver he owed us, we took the chance to repair our gear and I sent Finn back to the *Elk* eventually, with instructions to have men on six-strong watches for two days at a time, the rest to come up and camp here as one body.

I was frantic to be gone from here, to be on some sort of trail, but no trail presented itself, neither of Starkad, nor of this mystery place, Fatty Breeks.

Radoslav, Brother John and I then haggled for good wadmal to make tents with and I managed to get a new set of striped Rus breeks and a cloak with a fine pin to go with it.

Brother John took the chance to examine my knees and eventually straightened, scratching his head and then looked at the palms of my hands, all of which was alarming.

'What?' I asked, making more light of it than I felt. 'How long do I have, then?'

He frowned and shook his head. 'Longer than anyone else,' he replied and grabbed Radoslav by the hand. 'Look here.'

Radoslav's hand was calloused and scarred, old white ones, new red ones and a couple that looked yellow with pus.

'So?' I answered. 'Everyone gets them. Ropes. Sword nicks.'

'Yours are all old,' Brother John said. 'Healed long since. Your knees, which you skinned on Patmos, will have scarcely a sign of scar.' He sighed. 'It is an ill-served world, right enough. *Vitam regit fortuna non sapientia* – chance, not wisdom, governs human life. There is you, whose youth repels all ills, it appears. Then there is Ivar Gautr, who is turning yellow and shrinking, even though the arrow wound in his cheek is healed.'

I felt the chill of it, for I had an idea what repelled all ills – would this fail, in time, now that Rune Serpent was far from my hand? Then Svala came up and drove all thoughts from me, for she seemed to glow.

Ignoring Radoslav and his broad smiles and winks, she cocked her head at me and said: 'The whole city is buzzing with talk of how the amphitheatre under-galleries were flooded last night, though no one can be found who saw it done.'

'You say so?' I replied flatly. 'To think we missed all this.'

She raised an eyebrow. 'The Roman soldiers are stamping up and down asking people questions and the engineers are fixing a huge leak in the arena's old underground cistern. There is talk of a giant and an axe.'

At which point Botolf came up, brandishing a new comb and trailing two or three giggling girls who were, it seems, intent on using it on his mane of red-gold hair. Spotting Svala, they found other business more pressing and looked almost afraid, which was strange. Svala smiled winsomely up at Botolf.

'A giant,' she said, then looked at me. 'But no axe.'

'It broke,' Botolf said with a grin, 'but if Orm gives me hacksilver, I have seen another at a fair price.'

I poured money from my limp purse, conscious of her eyes on me. Radoslav, chuckling, found something else to do and, suddenly, I was alone with her and my mouth worked like a fresh-caught cod.

'You are not as honey-mouthed as I had been told,' Svala said, then smiled and slipped an arm into mine. 'But that is no bad thing, for there is much about you that is strange and grand in one so young.'

'Just so,' I managed to croak, dazzled. Her face darkened.

'Your dreams, for one thing.'

165

My body was a sea where my stomach and heart heaved on the swell. What did she know of my dreams?

She said nothing more, though, and we walked the camp in silence for a while, examining this and that. I saw Botolf again, stripped to the waist and showing off his skill and strength by spinning a Dane axe in one hand and a heft-seax in the other, which was a long, single-edged broad knife on a long pole. In the end, as the crowd applauded, the owner of the heft-seax had to allow he had won his bet and knocked down the price of both weapons.

Delighted, Botolf came and presented them to me for approval and I duly admired them. Behind, I saw the same giggling girls as before and, as he went off, they slid to his side. Svala snorted.

'That Thyra is always in rut, so she comes as no surprise – but Katla and Herdis have no right to be doing that,' she declared. 'Their mothers will be furious, to say nothing of their fathers. And Katla should know better, for she only has to look at a prick and her belly swells. She has two babes already and a stupid husband, though his brain is not so addled he'll assume another is his, too.'

It was the word 'prick' that did it. On her lips it would have made one of the Christ saints kick in the door of his own church. Dry-mouthed, I could only stare at her and she must have felt it, for she turned, saw my look . . . and looked down to where my new breeks, fat and striped as they were, could not hide what I was thinking.

A slow smile spread on her face and she looked me straight in the eye, put her head to one side and then laughed. 'As well you got some extra ells of material in the fork of those new breeks,' she said archly. 'Let us go into the city, for the walk will cool you, I am thinking.'

So we did that day. And the next. And the one after. We saw gold from Africa, leather from Spain, trinkets from Miklagard, linens and grain from the Fatamid lands, carpets from Armenia, glass and fruit from Syria, perfumes from the Abbasids, pearls from the sea in the south, rubies and silver from even further east.

On the fourth day, Brother John came with us, for we still searched for the strange Fatty Breeks and, though we again discovered nothing of that, I learned of the lands of Cathay, from which poured shiny-glazed pottery, the feathers of peacocks, excellent saddles, a thick, heavy cloth called *felt* and richer stuff worked with fine gold and silver wires. There was also a strange, purple-coloured stick with leaves known as *rhubarb* which was worth its weight in gold – though I did not know why, for it clapped your jaws with its tartness and made your belly gripe.

There was also the achingly familiar: the amber, wax, honey, ivory, iron and good furs from my homeland. Most painful of all, though, was the sight of speckled stone, the fine whet-stones of the north. I snuffled them like a pig in a trough, fancied I was drinking in the faint scent of a northern sea, a shingle strand, even snow on high mountain rocks.

It was that night, thick with evening mist, floating with songs from the firepits around my own wadmal hov, that I kissed her on soft lips, at a lonely spot near the river, keening with insect songs.

It was that night that she panted and gasped and writhed against me, while at the same time warning that nothing must happen – then gripping me in a strong hand, like she was about to chop wood, she gave three or four deft strokes, for all the world as if she milked an annoyed goat, and there I was, gasping, squint-eyed and bucking like a mad rabbit, emptied.

It had been a time since, I consoled myself, while she chuckled and said that it was for the best – yet while she spoke to me like a polite matron, her lower body had not stopped twisting and grinding against me, so that when I put my hand down, she guided it to a spot and gave a gasp.

After that, she became a moaning snake woman, until, suddenly, she subsided, panting and smiling at me from flame-red cheeks, her eyes bright, her face sheened with sweat. Then she blew a strand of hair off her face with a sharp little 'pfft' and heaved a sigh. 'Lovely,' she said brightly. 'That was good.'

'It could be better,' I said, lost in those eyes, desperate for what they could give, for what they promised. For love, which I felt once with the doomed Hild, for a moment as brief as the flick of a gnat's wing. My head drowned in a sea of dreams.

'So you think,' she said, 'but that's as good as it gets.'

'After we are married, I shall expect more,' I answered, astounded at myself. I don't know what reaction I expected, but the one I got made me blink. She laughed.

'No,' she said. 'Do not think of it. It will not be approved.'

'Why? Am I not good enough?'

She stuck the tip of her tongue between her teeth and grinned at me. 'You are a jarl-hero, are you not? That's good enough. But you may have to kill more than a white bear to get what you want.'

She mocked me and I was not so young as I had been when first I had boarded Einar's ship, that I would rise to it. Instead, I wondered why she made light of it, but nothing more was said, though it was plain that she was a treasure hoard as removed from me as any belonging to Attila.

Nothing more was said because she had recovered her breath and desire and was starting to guide my hand again. But for all that she was sticky as a *rumman* fruit, it would have taken Miklagard engineers to storm that citadel – and I was too easy to disarm.

Afterwards, as I lay listening to the squeal-clunk of the *norias*, feeling the night breeze drift her hair on my cheek, I counted that night one of the best times I ever had, for I did not dream at all, whereas afterwards, I did not spend one night where I slept without my head crowded with the dead.

I should have known then, of course, that Odin sleeps, as they say, with his one eye open, waiting for his chance to punish the smug. It was a harsh raven trick when it came – and heralded by the arrival of a banner with that black-omened bird on it.

Svala and I had parted with the first thin-milk smear of dawn and later, just as I was eating the day-meal by the firepit with the rest of the band, she walked up as if nothing had happened.

Radiant and smiling, she held out a swathe of folded white cloth, while I became conscious of the others looking at me looking at her. I saw Short Eldgrim nudge Sighvat and whisper something I was glad I couldn't hear.

'I have heard tales of this brave band,' she said, cool and clean as new snow, 'but saw that you lacked one thing. So I have made one for you.' And she unfurled a strip of dagged white cloth embroidered with a thick black raven.

'Heya,' said Finn admiringly and the others rose up, wiping their greased fingers on beards and tunics, to admire the stitching.

I managed to stammer my thanks and she smiled, even more sweetly than before.

'You need a good long pole for it,' she said archly, looking straight at me. 'Do you know where to find one? If not, I do.'

I was dry-mouthed at the cheek of her and felt the blood rush to my face, for her words had inspired exactly what she sought. I sat quickly before it became obvious. There was the taste of *rumman* fruit in my mouth when I managed to stammer my thanks.

She left, swishing the hem of her dress over the grass, and I felt Sighvat come up behind me. He fingered the new banner and nodded.

'Fine work,' he offered, then looked at me. On his shoulder, a raven fluffed and preened. 'That one is a danger,' he went on, which made me blink and almost spit back angrily at him to mind his own business, save that I had good respect for Sighvat and what he knew. He saw the questions and the anger in my face and stroked the head of the raven.

'Neither of the ravens will sit near her,' he went on. 'Now one is gone, for I set it to watching the jarl's witch-mother and have never seen it since. There is something Other at work here, Trader.'

Coldness crept into my belly and crouched there. I knew the Other well enough and the sudden vision-flash of Hild, black against black, that snake-hair blowing with no wind, almost made me drop the new banner in the firepit.

Big Botolf scooped it up and put it back in my lap, grinning. 'A fine banner. Do you want me to find a pole for it? I was thinking of putting a new shaft on this heft-seax and if I made it a long one, there would be a weapon at the end of the banner-pole, which would be useful.'

There and then, to his delight, I made him banner-bearer and he was still grinning when Kvasir trundled up, saw the raven flag hanging in Botolf's griddle-iron fists and grunted his appreciation.

'Just in time, Trader,' he said, 'for another jarl has arrived – a score of good *hafskipa* are now in the harbour and a thousand people, no less.'

This was news right enough and the tale of it bounced from head to head. Jarl Brand of Hovgarden, a Svear chieftain who had backed out of the fighting there for a while, had gone west and south, down past the lands of al-Hakam of Córdoba, through the narrows of Norvasund, which the Romans call the Pillars of Hercules and into the Middle Sea, with twenty ships and a thousand people, at least six hundred of them warriors.

Suddenly, in the middle of a distant, Muspell-hot country of the *Sarakenoi*, there were more good Norse than I had ever seen in one place in my life.

We stood with the throng and watched him and his hard

men come up the road from the port to the city of Antioch, he on a good horse, they striding out, despite the heat, in full helms and gilt-dagged mail and shields.

He was ice-headed, was the young Jarl Brand Olafsson, as white then as he would be later in life, when he had become one of the favoured men of Olof Skotkonung, King of the Svears and Geats both and called the Lap King, they say, because he sat in the lap of King Harald Bluetooth's son, Svein Forkbeard, and begged for a kingdom.

Brand's face was already sun-red, though he had wisely covered his arms and he wore a splendid helm worked with gold and silver. He was glittering, this silver jarl. Gold sparkled at his throat and wrists and seven bands of silver circled each arm of the bright red tunic he wore. I watched him and his men march up the road and over the bridge into the city, to be presented in all pomp to the Roman general who commanded everything here, which honour Skarpheddin had not been given.

I ate the dust of their passing and smiled wryly at how I was a jarl also, which was the old way, when anyone with their buttocks not hanging out their breeks and two men to call on could be a jarl. Now the jarls wanted to be like the Romans and make empires. There was, I was seeing, less and less place for the likes of the Oathsworn.

Then Finn gave a curse pungent enough to strip the gilding off Brand's fancy mail, staring into the swirl of yellow dust like a prow-man searching for shoals in a mist.

I followed where he looked and saw a man limping along in the wake of the Svear chieftain, eating even more dust than I was, leading a pack as lean and wolf-hungry as he seemed himself. I did not see what he wore, nor what battle-gear his men carried. I saw only the curve of the sabre at his side.

Starkad was here.

EIGHT

It was the final day of the Greeks' Paschal ceremonies, which had gone on for weeks, it seemed to us Norse, complete with banging bells and swinging gold ornaments reeking incense and priests wearing so much gold in their robes that we were tempted to storm them then and there.

There had been an image of the dead Christ in a wonderfully decorated coffin, taken in procession with chanting and the beating of a book, which Brother John – with a hawk and a spit to them – said was the Greek idea of Gospels. It was only two years since I had known what a book was.

There had been singing and a scattering of bay leaves. There had been vigils and fasts and feasts. Of course, we had to join in, being good Christ-men, but I saw offerings of budded boughs being floated down the Orontes in honour of Ostara when it was thought no one could see. Not all of those who did it were our own Odinsmenn.

Brother John didn't care, for he regarded the Greeks as heretics and they, who considered most western Christ-men to be misguided, looked on him as worse. Come to that, every Christ-man seemed to look on the likes of Brother John as no true follower of the Dead God, which is why we all liked the little priest and had let him prime-sign us Christians. The shackles of that signing, never tight, were now falling away, I saw, for the reason we had done it had clearly failed: the Odin-oath was as binding as ever.

So we stood in the hot spring sunshine in our finery and watched the Greek priests, sweating in gold-dripping robes heavier than mail, wobble round Antioch's streets with their ikons and their Christ in a box. Then, with Brother John, Finn, Radoslav and a couple of others as a fitting jarl-retinue, I went off to Skarpheddin's hov, for it would not have been polite to refuse to join in his feasting for Brand.

Also, we knew Starkad would be there. Since his coming, I had been as confused as a maelstrom about what to do. I needed to get the silkworm canister and Choniates' letter to the Basileus, for I couldn't trust anyone else. But the Great City was far away and Starkad was not.

The others, who still thought the leather case I had hidden on the *Elk* contained tiny pearls, were only concerned about Starkad being so close – Botolf especially. He wanted to kill Starkad for what he had done in enslaving him and the others, while Finn wanted to walk his entrails round a pole while waving the recovered runesword in his face.

It was a warming image, but Starkad was clearly part of the snow-headed Brand's retinue and that had been a clever move, for it made any attack on him a sure sentence of death. Yet again he was close enough to kill and too far removed to attack.

Finn fumed and bellowed and scowls were rife, but there was no walking round it and I was fretting as much as the rest. The Rune Serpent was here and we were here and yet it was as far away as ever.

'Easy, lads,' counselled Brother John. 'There are ways and ways of lifting something from a man and, as you know, I am no stranger to such a thing – in a godly fashion, all the same. God will show us a way, never fear.'

So we smiled wryly at one to another and settled to wait.

There were lots of guests at Skarpheddin's tented hov that warm night. Outside, his people baked flatbread and spitted whole oxen for a feast. Apples in honey, fish stewed in goat's milk and onions, fat cauldron snake, pork and lentils: it was good Norse food served in the swelter of a Serkland night, in the fug of a tented hov thick with fat candles and which soon reeked of smoke, blood, piss and vomit . . . the smell of home.

There was horseflesh, too, a neat trick by Jarl Brand. In later life, after Brand's lord, Eirik, whom they called Segersall – Victorious – became a king and made the Svears and Geats into Christ-men, Brand was baptised, but at this time he and his followers belonged to Odin and Thor. Since there were Christ-worshippers among Skarpheddin's people who would not eat horse, it being the mark of a pagan, it let Brand see easily enough which was which.

There was no ale, for no one had the means to make it here – this was Mussulman country and their god didn't drink. Right there, according to Finn, was why they were getting their arses kicked by the likes of the Roman-Greeks of Miklagard.

Instead, they were allowed *nabidh*, which the Christ monks of Antioch made and sold to the Jewish merchants, who sold it to the Mussulmen. It was made from raisins and dates fermented in water and, for the Mussulmen, the legal length was two days soaking in water only. Naturally, three- and four-day was a roaring trade among those Arabs who liked their drink – and both Finn and Radoslav discovered six-day was best, mixed with honey and wine, which made it taste almost like mead.

Skarpheddin was out to impress Brand, but he needed to invite the Jewish, Arab and Greek merchants he owed money to, as well as officers from the Strategos's army – but not the man himself, who had pressing business bringing more men from Tarsus.

'Which means that the army will be fighting soon,' Finn growled as we sweltered under the wadmal tent, raining with sweat now that so many were in it.

'Sooner we move off, the better,' I said, wishing now I had not worn the new cloak to show off the new pin. 'If we wait longer we will dissolve like butter on a griddle in this Odin-cursed forge of a country. Or end up standing in a Roman battle line.'

Which was so far from what we intended that we laughed. You should never do that while the gods are listening.

It was, then, a strange feasting, trying hard to be a hall in the north and yet somehow skewed, as if seen underwater.

The Jews and Mussulmen smiled politely and tried to make sure they had no pork on their eating knives and fashionable two-tined forks; the Christ-Norse sniffed meat warily to make sure it was not horse; and only the old gods' followers were careless and laughing, though a few of them tried the little two-tined eating things while drunk and ended up stabbing their own cheeks or tongues, which ruined their meal there-after.

Skarpheddin, thin-shanked and butt-bellied, stepped forward, raised his hands and summoned his skald before sitting down on his giftthrone, for he was too important even to speak for himself. The skald, gold-browed but with dark patches showing under his nice green tunic, announced that the great jarl planned an offering to the good gods of the North.

The Jews and Mussulmen and Christ-followers all stirred uneasily and Finn, sweltering, muttered something about Odin's armpit. Then he stiffened and stared. 'Starkad,' he said.

Leaning forward like a hunting dog on scent Starkad stared back. He wore the rune-serpented sabre – everyone was armed tonight – and one hand hovered near it like a white spider, though it seldom touched the hilt. His eyes, white-blue as old ice, were fixed on mine, as if he was trying to make me burst into flames with his hate.

175

So there we were, each aching for what the other had, each fettered by the threat of what would be unleashed if we simply sprang at each other's throats. Legs trembling, the sweat working its way down into the sheuch of my arse, I stood and wondered how safe that little container was, tucked on board the *Elk* in my sea-chest. Skarpheddin's skald droned to a halt. The exhaled breath of relief from his audience threatened to blow out the fat candles.

Matters were not over yet and Brother John grunted as if he had been hit, then made the sign against the evil eye.

Not even Skarpheddin dared oppose his mother in this and so she shuffled out, swallowed by the catskin cloak, dangled about with all her wards and amulets. There was a noise like a flock of startled birds as the good Christ-followers made the sign of the cross and Jarl Brand's men signed wards against the evil eye.

But it was not Thorhalla that struck me a blow like Thor's hammer, even though she looked like Hel's ugliest daughter. It was the Skarpheddin *fostri*, the one Thorhalla was training to take her place and who now followed in her wake, majestic and seal-sleek.

She wore a dress the colour of a lowering sky, with glass beads lying on the front of it. A black lambskin hood lined with white catskin covered her blond hair and she had a staff in her hand with a brass knob, set above with a spray of raven's feathers. I heard Sighvat suck in his breath at the sight of them.

She had a belt of touch-wood, sewn with slivers of hazel, which is Freyja's tree, and on it was a large skin purse which I knew held her talismans. She had shaggy calfskin shoes and catskin gloves and not a slick of sweat anywhere on her. Even as she made a hulk of all my hope, I thought that Svala had never looked more beautiful.

'She has taken your raven,' I heard myself say to Sighvat and he grunted, the pain of it thick in his voice.

'Worse,' he said, laying a hand on my arm to draw me away. 'I am thinking she has taken your heart.'

There was a roaring now and my voice seemed distant to me, though I was rock-sure of what I said, sick with the certainty now that it was not my wyrd to find true love, only the seidr shadow of it.

'It will not end up crowning her *volva* staff.'

Honeyed Six-Day is a vicious were-beast, by night filling you with all the power of the gods and, in the cold light of day, sprawling like a day-old corpse in the pit of your stomach, having shat in your mouth and started a fire in your skull.

I woke, though sleep is a sad word for what had eventually happened to me, into a stranger's body. My legs would not bear me upright and my fingers felt like fat rolls of felt. Brother John squatted beside me, grim as black rock, nodded into my squinting eyes and then swam away again before I could focus properly.

Then the world exploded into the sea, sucking the breath out of me, shattering the veil that kept me from seeing what I lay in or feeling the glare of the rising sun. I surfaced, shook my head, whimpered with what that did, then sat up, wiping water from my eyes and coughing.

The Goat Boy stood, pale and grinning, holding a wooden bucket upside down. Brother John held another, brought from the nearby river, and hefted it, but I held up a weak hand and managed to gasp at him to stop.

'You are the last,' he said. 'Finn and Radoslav, you will be pleased to hear, are as bad as you are, Kvasir Spittle and Hedin Flayer less so. But Ivar Gautr is dead.'

I was wiping my streaming face and slicking my hair away from it, so I missed what he said. Then it hit me and I looked at him, eyes wide. How could Ivar be dead? He had been with the crowd of us, helping me dive into goatskins of six-day *nabidh*, his swollen face as flushed as those of the rest

177

of us and, though that swelling mushed his speech like a mouthful of bread, he made us laugh still with his wit.

Brother John saw my look and sighed. The Goat Boy dropped the bucket and threw my own cloak at me to dry myself with.

'My fault,' said the little priest mournfully. 'I should have made him go to the Greek chirurgeons with that tooth.'

'They would have healed him,' the Goat Boy declared, hauling his tunic up to show me the great purple-red welt of his scar. 'They can raise the dead.'

'Blaspheming imp of Satan,' growled Brother John fondly. 'Go and find Sighvat. Do not try and run, as I have warned you, or you will burst something.' He turned to me as the Goat Boy hirpled slowly away. 'He should not even be up, but he is leather-tough, that boy.'

'I know the *nabidh* was strong,' I managed at last, 'but it only makes you feel like you have died. It can't kill you . . . can it?'

Brother John passed me the bucket to drink from, which I did even though the thirst would not be slaked.

'Ivar's tooth killed him. There was something festering there in all that swelling. You saw him. He would not have it seen by the Greeks, though it was clear there was much wrong. Poison from that tooth must have been filling him every day since the arrow wound he took on Cyprus.'

I remembered his face, bulging on one side, so that the scar on his cheek where the arrow went in looked stretched and puckered. The other side was hollow and yellowed and he looked like a wormed cheese, collapsing from the inside out.

'His tooth ate him,' I marvelled and Brother John straightened with a grunt.

'He will be the first of many deaths, I am thinking,' he said. 'Word has come: the Strategos, Red Boots, will be here in two days and the army is marching. Starkad has been telling everyone who will listen that the Oathsworn sacked churches on Cyprus and killed good Christ-men.'

I got up and slung my cloak round my shoulders, wishing my head was clear. 'Is anyone listening?'

Brother John shrugged. 'Skarpheddin is. The Greeks who command the army here are. Jarl Brand, I have been told, laughed when he heard, which made the Greeks back water a little, for Brand raided his way all along the Middle Sea and I would be surprised if churches had not been included. The Greeks, it seems, need Brand and his men. All the same, Brand is bound to assist Starkad, since that dog has placed his hands in the jarl's fists and taken oath.'

'Doesn't church-sacking bother you, Brother John?' I asked, surprised at the ease he spoke of it.

'It would if they were good monasteries of the old way,' he replied, 'but they are eggshells of faith stuffed with the sour meat of bad teaching. *Lucri bonus est odor ex re qualibet*, as Jarl Brand would say if he knew Juvenal.'

I had never met Juvenal either, but 'sweet is the smell of money obtained from any source' certainly made him sound like a good vik-jarl to me and I said as much. Brother John helped me up and back to our wadmal camp, my head spinning with fumes and thoughts of how we could safely get away from here before all our enemies closed the trap on us.

We burned Ivar Gautr in the East Norse way, for the heat was already making him ripe. The Goat Boy stood beside me, pale and still laboured in his breathing, trembling as men from Brand and Skarpheddin, who had also liked Ivar's wit, stacked what wood they could scavenge.

The Greek priests were suitably annoyed that someone prime-signed as a Christ-man should be burned like a pagan – and we all agreed, for we wanted to howe him up decently, with his armour and his weapons. But those camel-herding grave-robbers would come in the night, since those weapons were worth a fortune, even if we broke them in three.

So we stood at an oil-soaked pyre and sent Ivar to Hel's hall in a wind of sparks.

'I was almost there,' the Goat Boy whispered and I squeezed his shoulder, feeling the terror rise and choke him. I could feel the heart in his chest flutter like a bird in a cage.

'You are not, so thank the gods.'

He looked up at me. 'How do you find the courage to face death, Trader?'

What a question. The answer to it was simple enough: when I do, I will let you know. But the Goat Boy needed a shield and I gave him one. I took the Thor hammer from round my neck, the one which had been round my father's neck until I raised his bloodied head from the mud-gore it lay in and took it off before the scavengers got to his body, under the walls of Sarkel.

'This is the best courage-finder,' I said, slipping the leather thong over his head. He fingered the amulet, as near to a Christ-cross as made no difference, and frowned.

'I cannot. What would you do if you gave it me?'

I half drew my fine, watered blade. 'This is even more powerful, but too heavy for you to carry. You take the amulet.'

He gripped it in his little fist and grinned, all fear gone. I felt a surge then, something seidr. Perhaps Redbeard was in the amulet after all.

Finn and others had wanted to raise a stone to Ivar, but there were none suitable and no master-carver of runes within a thousand miles – in fact, in all my days I met only one such myself and I doubt whether there were a hundred in all the world then. Fewer now.

In the end, they dragged off Short Eldgrim, who made the least mistakes with runes, took him into Antioch and had him mark Ivar's name on the door pillars of one of the churches, while the priests wagged their beards and threatened to call the Watch.

As Finn said, the least the Christ-men could do for Ivar,

who had been dipped in water with the rest of us and died a straw death, was mark his name on one of their god houses. They had enough of them, after all.

I reminded them that if the Christ wouldn't take him, Hel would and her hall was like herself, half foul, half fair. Those who died of sickness or age ended up on the brightly bedecked benches of Helheim.

It was at the pyre that we faced up to Starkad again, when he and his men came, supposedly to give polite honour to the dead Ivar. We stared at each other across the oil-slick wood, two packs of wolfhounds barely leashed by the presence of Ivar's fetch and the trouble a fight would cause.

'Another one gone,' Starkad observed, caressing the hilt of the sabre as if it was a woman's thigh. 'If this goes on, there won't be enough of you left to bother anyone.'

'You seem a little diminished yourself, Starkad,' I launched back at him, trying not to look at his fingers tracing the runes I had scratched on the hilt. 'But we gave your dead on Patmos a decent send-off, in the old style, with the *Sarakenoi* who killed them at their feet. Of course, we took all they had as well.'

Starkad twitched a smile. 'Soon the Strategos will have word from Leo Balantes on Cyprus,' he snarled. 'Then it may be that we will have it all back and more.'

'Perhaps the Basileus will have word before that,' I answered sweetly. 'I am sure he knows Choniates' finest hand in a letter that mentions your name and a package that will have your eyes out, you and all your crew.'

There was muttering behind him at that, but he ignored it and forced a smile. 'There is no need for this,' he said. 'My quarrel is not with you and Jarl Brand could be persuaded to help deflect any blow at you from Cyprus. We should be oarmates, for I understand you have as little regard for the Hammaburg monk as I do. I did not know this before, so perhaps we were pulling oars on the wrong stroke. I am prepared to overlook the lie you told about the monk coming to Serkland, for I have since discovered it was true – though you did not know that.'

I tried not to blink at that one; he had a deal of clever, had Starkad, and ways of weaselling out the truth that knocked you off balance.

'Hand back that sword you stole,' I said, which was all I could think of.

He cocked his head like a curious bird. 'You put great store by this blade,' he mused thoughtfully. 'A good blade and valuable, but still . . .'

'Will you trade?' I asked and he did not need to ask for what. He laughed instead.

'Why should I? Before long I will have what you took on Cyprus – and if the Greeks don't gather you up and blind you for it, then I will come for you myself. I have the protection of Jarl Brand, remember; you have no one.'

'Does Jarl Brand know you are King Harald's man?' I asked him and saw the blood in his eye at that. 'What will Bluetooth think of you swearing also to Jarl Brand? You take an oath too lightly to be now swearing peace to us.'

'For all that,' he answered thickly, 'peace is what I offer.'

I could not turn round, but I knew the eyes were skewering me and two of the deepest daggers in my shoulder blades belonged to Botolf. Deeper still were the eyes of those who could not see, kept in the dark and shackled. The weight of the invisible jarl torc, that other rune serpent round my neck, was crushing.

'Peace?' I replied sharply and paused. 'Why? Some of you are still alive.'

There were rumbling chuckles at that from behind me and Starkad whirled in a flare of red cloak and stalked off while the ranks of his men closed round him, looking darkly at us as they went.

The Oathsworn came round me, banging my shoulders and laughing. Botolf, rumbling with pleasure like some giant's cat, announced that he had seldom heard as gold-browed an exchange as that and others agreed. I did, too, when my knees stopped twitching. I thanked the gods for baggy Rus breeks.

'Well,' growled Finn, 'that settles matters. He will not trade, so we will have to take it from him.'

Back at the wadmal camp, hunkered round the pitfire and watching the black feathers of Ivar's fire thread the sky, Kvasir and Finn, whom I had appointed battle captains, agreed that the only thing left to do was seek out Starkad and fight him. What no one had an answer to was the problem of what to do with the container, for Starkad was right in that: as soon as he arrived, Red Boots would swoop on us.

'We could find out where Starkad sleeps and take him at night. That way we will offset his numbers a little,' Radoslav declared.

Finn curled a lip at him. 'At night? That would mean it was murder and not red war.'

I explained it to Radoslav. Any killing done in the night was considered murder, even if we decently covered the body and immediately reported the matter.

'Hardly matters,' muttered Kvasir. 'Jarl Brand will have our heads, even if we win. Even if only one man is left standing, he will have his head.'

I was sure that man would be either Finn or Kvasir, but was equally sure that it would not be a Dane. The Danes knew the sabre was valuable and why and had sworn our Oath, same as everyone else, but I still did not feel they would charge into a sure-death fight over it. The chance for unimaginable wealth was lure enough to keep them with me – that and the Oath they swore – but this? This was something else entirely.

There was other talk, too, as Finn prepared *mahshi*, an Arab pot with lamb, onion, pepper, coriander, cinnamon, saffron and other things, including *murri naqi*, a seasoning oil made from fermented barley. And this from a man who had learned the names of those spices only a few weeks ago.

While we watched with interest and drooled, we spoke of Red Boots and the Roman army he was bringing. Few of us could understand what riches or benefit could be got from conquering a land as dun-coloured as this – especially as this was the latest of many wars between the Great City and the *Sarakenoi*.

'I spoke with that soldier, Zifus,' Brother John declared, sniffing Finn's pot appreciatively. 'He told me that the Basileus has promised God to bring His Word to the heathens. This is a Holy War.'

I knew all our wars were blessed by the gods of the North, who supported one side or the other depending on how well disposed they were to your offerings. I did not know what the Greeks meant by Holy War, but wanted no part of it. I learned – too late – that it meant a land-ravager war, where everyone was killed and everything burned. Since the *Sarakenoi* preached the same, it meant a wasteland, where even hope was murdered.

We were drooling at the smell of Finn's cooking when up strolled Svala, as silencing to the talk as a hand on your mouth. She looked round us all, almost sadly, and I was the only one who met her eye, though I was sweating as I did so.

Kleggi the Dane opened his mouth to offer something witty, but she looked at him and he snapped it shut. Short Eldgrim glared at her, but while his scarred face carried no fears for the likes of her, no one dared even move to ward against evil as she crossed and hunkered down beside me, dressed simply now, her hair in coiled braids. I had never seen these hard men so cowed.

'Now you know,' she said, 'and I am sad for it, since you seem afraid of me.'

'You are the third *volva* I have met,' I said, which widened her eyes, since most men steered a clear course away from even one. 'Only one of them did me any good and even that was a blade that cut both ways.'

She pursed her lips at that. 'What harm have I done you?'

'None,' I told her. 'Yet. Nor have you done me any good. Nor should you have killed the raven.'

'He should not have set it to spy,' she answered sharply.

'Odin will not be pleased,' I pointed out, 'but you have more to fear now from Sighvat, I am thinking.'

'Freyja will keep One Eye away,' Svala said confidently, 'and your Sighvat as a worker of seidr cannot match two women such as us.'

I sighed, for talking to her was like feeling a storm cloud rise when you are in an open boat. The pitch and toss of it was made all the worse for what had been before.

'I want no quarrels between Skarpheddin's mother, you, me or Sighvat,' I replied. 'But you should stay away from all of us.'

'You?'

'Especially me,' I snapped.

She straightened, dusting her knees, then looked at me, long and slow. 'This Hild,' she said, while ice crept down my veins. 'I have seen her, dark and fetched in the night. She has a sword and you had its twin, once.'

I was frozen, tongue-cloven. Had she seen this, out there in the Other – or heard me mutter this while I dreamed?

She smiled. 'I have gifts. Listen, then I will trouble you no more. The first thing to say is that Skarpheddin trusts his mother's power – and so he should. Thorhalla has promised him that you will reveal the secret of your treasure hoard and it would go easier if you just spoke it to him with no trouble. Otherwise, he may do something . . . ill.

'The second is that you should get the sword from Starkad, for it is yours by right.'

I swallowed the clump of dry dust in my throat, but I was

angry with her, this slip of a girl who thought she could make cows out of the Oathsworn.

'Witch gifts come in threes,' I croaked, which was daring, but I was young and not so convinced that her powers were more to do with keen watching than anything Other.

Her smile, though, was sweet as *rumman* fruit.

'I know the secret of Fatty Breeks,' she said.

NINE

The heat of the day was leaching out of the dusty scrub, but the sky was dying in flame to the west where the hills rolled, grey-blue. Olive trees were pale purple in the twilight, their leaves black, while the air was arid with a dusty, woody smell, the ash-bite of fires springing up like a field of red blossoms.

Cloaked over it all was the great, crushing stink of an army, a throat-catcher made of leather, iron, horses, an acrid pinch of sweat and the thin, high smell of fear.

I had never seen anything like this, nor ever would again. I had thought Red Boots was bringing up a few more hundreds of men, no more, but this was Miklagard, the Great City, and the army around Antioch was a *knarr* on the ocean of men who came up from Tarsus.

We saw them first as a cloud to the north, rising up like a pale brown cloak over Antioch, and Brother John started to order us to lash down the wadmal tents, for he had seen such sweeping sandstorms further south, in the desert around the Sea of the Dead. But I had seen one, too, out on the steppe, and knew it was no sandstorm. It was the dust kicked up by the army of the Strategos John the Armenian, favourite of the Basileus and nicknamed Tzimisces – Red Boots.

As with Sarkel's siege, the scholars of the Great City sought

187

me out later, when I was a trader of note. One was Leo, who was close to my own age, but while I stood in the ranks at Antioch, he hunkered on his knees back in Constantinople learning the ways of the Christ religion. In later days, as he scratched out his saga tales – as monks do – they knew him as Leo the Deacon.

By then, all that we had done had been lost and John Tzimisces' battle at Aleppo was a hero-tale to the Romans of the Great City. Leo, sleekit as a fox though he was, once went with Basil the second of that name and the army when it was cut to pieces by the Bulgars years after these events and barely escaped with his life, so he knew a thing or two about armies.

He wanted me to tell what I knew of the fight at Aleppo, to add to the accounts he had from others, and I did so, as far as I was able. I liked Leo, so I did not tell him he had no understanding of us Norsemen at all – he called us 'Tauroskythians', as if we'd all come from the steppes north of the Dark Sea.

I told him what I knew, which was little enough and shrouded in a golden haze of dust, but he didn't want to hear that. In the end, he told me more than I gave him and we agreed it was the confusion between the Miklagard Handshake and how Norsemen fight bear that had cost us the victory. The first wanted to clasp the enemy with one hand and stab them with the dagger they could not see, while the second wanted to rush in and kill the beast before being crushed in a deadly embrace.

Forty-seven thousand men marched from Antioch a week after Red Boots arrived – and there were more, sweeping through the land known as the Jezira, all the way across the Euphrates and Tigris rivers in the north, before turning south and then west again, to come up behind Aleppo. It was a great raid, to drag off the Hamdanids and their allies, so that Red Boots could crush Aleppo and take all that part of Serkland known as Syria.

When we eventually met the *Sarakenoi* our army was formed up 2,700 yards long and in two lines. The jarl-men were in the front line, which was all *scutatoi*, the Great City's foot-soldiers with their huge shields. The Norse were on the right and on the right of the right the Oathsworn. The end of the line.

I did not tell Leo the Deacon that we had come there reluctantly, that we had been too fastened by the chance to kill and loot Starkad to get away before the storm of war swept us up.

Not so Starkad, who broke his oath to Jarl Brand and vanished into the dust haze. By the time we discovered this, it was too late for us to leave without drawing to ourselves attention of the worst sort. So we joined Red Boots's ranks for the battle we knew was planned and cursed both ourselves and Starkad for being so snared in a fight none of us wanted.

The *Sarakenoi* came with horsemen heavy with mail and banded leather, the ragged-arsed foot they called Dailami, desert horsemen called Bedu, who swooped like swallows in and out of the dust, and the Hamdanid horsemen, who still flew the black banners of the Abbasids even though they had rebelled against them. There were even Turks from Baghdad, where the generals permitted the Abbasids to rule in name only.

They overlapped our lines by a mile either side – which was why it all went wrong, of course. The Great City's army was used to this, had a second line to take care of it, but we didn't know that. All we saw were too many enemies.

Skarpheddin had already decided on our fighting plan, which was the one we usually used. We would bang loudly on our shields and pour scorn on the size of their balls, then we would run at them, howling like wolves. Not that Finn or I, or any of the Oathsworn, knew much of even this grand plan. The army marched, with all 47,000 soldiers, 15,000 mules, camels and oxen and 1,000 carts with the bits and pieces of the artillery engines, the two jarls and all their men – and the Oathsworn, scowling and angry about it, for this was no fight we wanted to be in.

The women and children stayed in their camps around Antioch, save those few who would not abandon their men, and Gizur and four of my men, the Goat Boy with them, went back to the *Elk* to watch it.

Radoslav had volunteered to stay, too, at which Finn had said nothing, though his look was an entire saga poem on its own. The big Slav, seeing the scorn, had shrugged and come with us, but if Surt, the Norn-sister of What May Be, had kindly drawn it all out for us in the sand, we would probably have agreed with Radoslav and all of us would have quit the army then and there and gone to Fatty Breeks.

Fateh Baariq. Which meant Shining Conqueror in the Saracen tongue. But Svala only told me that as we clattered out in the ranks of Skarpheddin's men, too late to slip away unnoticed. Her smile was malicious and I turned my back on it and tramped into the dust; it only came to me later that she had also told Starkad this earlier, which had made him start after Martin.

'Well,' argued Botolf, scowling, when, at the end of that first day's march, we told him what we had found. 'I don't speak their cat-yowl of a tongue. It sounded different to me. And I was being dragged in chains at the time.'

I had soothed him over it, for we knew now where our oarmates were: in the Fateh Baariq mine, east and north of Aleppo, in a place called Afrin. That left us with a new problem: how to get there. It was miles from the shield of the army, in country we did not know and seething like a maggoty corpse with *Sarakenoi*.

I felt the weight of the jarl torc, anvil-heavy. It was a long way and in the lands of the enemy.

'It is a long way and in the lands of the enemy,' Radoslav then declared moodily, making me twitch and wonder if he could read minds, too. 'We would need our own army,' he added pointedly. 'If we had a hoard of silver we could afford one.'

Kvasir and Finn grunted and said nothing, so Radoslav, seeing he was gaining nothing, rose and went elsewhere.

'He is greed-sick, that one,' growled Finn.

'He has lost his boat,' Kvasir pointed out, but Finn hawked and spat into the fire. That night, Radoslav vanished from our ranks, which everyone thought was a nithing thing for him to do.

'He has all that a warrior needs . . .' Kvasir growled wryly next day, 'except the balls.'

I wondered more on it, but was not sure what Radoslav was doing. Perhaps he was just ducking out of the fight, though I did not think much of that explanation. Perhaps he had gone back to steal the container from my sea-chest: Odin luck to him if he crept on board past the men I had left to guard it. Nor did it matter much if he succeeded; the contents were not pearls and, since Starkad would not trade, worthless now. Worse than worthless, since they still marked us all for blinding and death by the conspirators.

Still, it nagged me . . . and left me hollow, too, for I had liked the big, bluff Slav who had, after all, saved my life.

Sighvat came up into this and sat beside me, his raven as silent and brooding as my thoughts. 'I heard the girl came to you,' he said and I shot him a warning glance, for I wanted no one poking a finger in that wound.

He nodded, tickling the beak of the raven. 'She is Sami,' he added, 'from the Pite tribe in Halogaland. Her true name is Njávesheatne, which means Sun Daughter in their tongue.'

A Sami from the north of Norway. Kvasir made a warding sign, Finn spat in the fire and I felt my skin crawl. The Sami, the Reindeer People, were older than time, it was said, and full of stranger magic even than the seidr. They worshipped a troll goddess, Thorgerthr, who used seidr to call down thunder like Asa-Thor himself.

'How do you know this?' I asked.

Sighvat grinned. 'A bird told me,' he said. 'Or perhaps it was a bee.'

Finn rolled his eyes and snorted. 'A bee. Honeyed words, were they?'

Sighvat smiled quietly. 'Bees have many messages, Horsehead. If one flies into your hall it is a sign of great good luck, or of the arrival of a stranger; however, the luck will only hold if the bee is allowed to either stay or go of its own accord.

'A bee landing on your hand means money, on the head means a rise to greatness. They will sting those who curse in front of them and those who are adulterers or unchaste – so, if you want a good wife, have her walk through a swarm and if she is stung, she'll be no virgin.'

'I knew it was a mistake to ask,' mourned Finn, shaking his head.

'Did this singular bee tell you how we can rescue our oarmates?' I snarled, the Sami thing sick in my stomach. 'Or find Starkad and get the Rune Serpent back?'

A lie. She had been a lie. It was my curse – worse, a Loki joke – to end up snagged like a lip-caught fish by every seidr woman in the world. And Radoslav – I had thought more of him . . .

Sighvat smiled, unoffended, leaving me ashamed of my anger. 'No, Trader, but I will ask.' He rose and left, the raven clinging to his shoulder and fluttering.

Kvasir shook his head. 'Sometimes our Sighvat scares me more than any Sami witch,' he said.

We marched a second day and then sat surrounded by the low, growling hum of the army, a sweating beast in the red-flowered darkness. The tail of it still curled wearily in, tramping on into the night, where Finn and Kvasir waited for me to come up with a full-cunning way to get out of this mess. I sat silent and wished they'd bugger off and give me peace, for I was an empty hold of ideas.

After a night of formless, brooding dream-shapes, I was still as empty, sitting by the smouldering firepit, pitching twigs and dung-chips into it as the dawn smeared up the sky. It took me some time to realise that men were moving and talking excitedly, flowing like ants from a broken nest.

Then I heard the blare of trumpets and Finn lumbered up to me, chewing. He tossed me a scrap of flatbread and nodded at the commotion and dust.

'Red Boots is awake then,' he said.

Nearby, Brother John crossed himself '*Non semper erit aestas*,' he said and Finn looked from him to me, puzzled and scowling.

'Get ready for hard times,' I translated and he nodded, grim as old rock.

We were formed up the way the Great City's army was always formed up – so I learned later – with the foot in front, backed by archers, light horse on the wings and slightly pushed forward, so that the whole would look like a gently curving bay if you could fly above it like Sighvat's raven.

Behind that was a second line, all the prized heavy horsemen and the great metal slabs that were the pride of the Miklagard army.

We had seen them ride out of Antioch's St Paul Gate on horses draped with leather sewn with metal leaves. The archers had horses covered on the front, the others had their horses completely cloaked in these little metal leaves. Some carried lances and some had maces and swords only, for when these ones – so fearsomely costly even the Great City could afford only a thousand of them – formed up it was in a boar snout, with the bowmen in the middle, the lancers on the sides and the skull-crushers in front.

All you could see of them were their eyes. They even wore iron shoes and scorned shields for the most part. They were

193

draped in linen to try and keep the sun from broiling them, but we all pitied those splendid soldiers, the ones the Greeks called *klibanophoroi* – the Oven Wearers.

There were *numeri*, *bandae*, *turmae* and a score of other names for their units, some of them Latin, some Greek which was the way with these people, who could not make up their minds on who they were. Red Boots had come with two of the three *Hetaireiai*, the Guard companies. These were the *Mese* and the *Mikre*, the former being for non-Greeks who were Christ-worshippers, the latter for foreigners who scorned the Christ. This last was full of Pechenegs and Rus Slavs, though the *Mese* had Saxlanders, whom the Greeks call Germans. Though the Great City accepted Germans as chosen men, they did not like the nation of Otto, who occupied Old Rome and called himself Emperor.

They were almost as big as us, these Saxlanders, and they swaggered and snarled at each other like prize hounds. As Finn growled, they needed a sharp kick under their tails to show them who was better.

Most impressive of all were the Great City's chiefs, whom they called *comes*, or *tribunus*, or *dux* or *drungarios* and who, even though they had never met any of the men they led before, could get them moving as one, to the beat of ox-hide drums, with only a few words.

Truly, they were a marvel, these Romans, and, for the first time, we realised how they had ruled the world. We felt like gawping bairns.

We met our own commander then: Stefanos, who called himself Taxiarchos. He rode up with a guard of armoured horsemen and spoke with Skarpheddin and Jarl Brand.

This Stefanos, young and moon-faced, had charge of, it seemed to me at the time, the whole right of the army, a great swathe of *scutatoi* and the Norse and hordes of light horse archers, for it was always the way of the Romans to have their own men in command.

194

In fact he only ordered the last nub end of it, which was all of the Norse and some of the Greek archers and light troops. It is possible he never had command of anything ever again, thanks to us.

'We should have that sort of marking,' growled Kvasir, nodding at the coloured helmet-tufts and shields while we knelt, blowing dust out of our nostrils and trying to make sense of it all. I agreed, for even Jarl Brand's own chosen men, his *dreng*, had red-and-black wool braids hanging from their sheaths and shields all of one design – Odin's three drinking horns – in the same colours.

In the end, the best I could do was tear strips off the dirty-white linen surcoat I wore to stop my byrnie from heating up and get the Oathsworn to fasten them round their upper arms.

We leaned on our shields and sweated and I tried to work out where we were and what we were supposed to be doing.

It seemed the Norsemen were formed in one body, Brand and Skarpheddin side by side and three ranks deep, for that's what Skarpheddin had told us to do on his right flank – politely, since I was, nominally, as much of a jarl as he, even though I led only forty-four men. We formed in three ranks, mailed men in front – the ones we called the Lost – and spearmen in the second and third, save for a handful with some bows, and agreed to follow the signals given by Skarpheddin's banner.

Behind us, a few hundred paces, hazed in dust, were rank upon rank of the Great City's foot archers, sticking arrows in front of them like a sheaf of barley, for easy reach.

In front, the light troops flocked, raising most of the dust now as they trotted up, with their throwing spears cased in soft leather sheaths lined with beeswax. On our left, shouldering the last men in the left of our line, were the sweating Norse of Skarpheddin. Further out to our right were the light horsemen, archers and lancers, their horses foaming at the neck with sweat, the stink of their dung and piss choking us.

There was a flurry behind us, which made everyone crane to see until Finn cursed them back to facing front.

Sweating Greek thralls appeared, rolling a barrel on a two-wheeled cart and doling out water in cups, little sips and no more, but which men grabbed eagerly. There was a priest with them, swinging his little smoking brazier of perfume and chanting something long and sonorous, while he dipped a silver baton in the cups and scattered droplets on us.

Brother John, so dry he could scarcely spit his disgust, translated the Greek for us as we grabbed and swallowed. He did not drink, for all his thirst.

Behold that after drawing holy water from the immaculate and most sacred relics of the Passion of Christ our true God – from the precious wooden fragments of the True Cross and the undefiled lance, the precious titulus, the wonder-working reed, the life-giving blood which flowed from His precious rib, the most sacred tunic, the holy swaddling clothes, the God-bearing winding sheet and the other relics of His undefiled Passion – we have sent it to be sprinkled upon you, for you to be anointed by it and to garb yourself with the divine power from on high.

The Basileus's holy-water gift to the army against the infidel. Kvasir, gulping it down, made a face and said: 'After all that, you'd think it would taste like mead instead of freshly warm sheep piss.'

I hardly noticed, being too busy wondering what 'undefiled lance' they had used, for I was sure Martin had the true one – or by now, some slave-dealer called Takoub had it. Did that mean this holy water was only slightly holy? Not holy at all?

From far off came the rasping blare of trumpets and I heard the Greek chiefs from the light javelin men, the ones they called the Hares, yelling 'Foreskins', the command for these men to peel back the covers from their throwing spears, immaculate and trim-straight.

Drums thundered from further down our own lines and a huge cry went up, 'Tydeus! Tydeus!' and then, out of the dust, cantered a group of horsemen, all red cloaks and plumes and self-importance.

Two of them carried huge swords, far too big to fight with and clearly ikons of some sort, like the huge banner with a woman painted on it that Brother John said was Our Lady of Blachernae. Another carried a huge purple banner on which was sewn a white square called the Mandylion. It was, said Brother John, a shroud from the dead Christ and had his face imprinted on it.

Out in front was a huge horseman, carrying a flag as big as a bedsheet, which they called the Labarum and on it was the symbol of the Great City. Brother John told us it was a holy symbol, adopted by the Emperor Constantine, who had named the Great City after himself.

The symbol, it seemed, meant 'In This Sign Conquer', but it looked to us like the runes *Wunjo* and *Gebo*, which read as 'a gift of success' to us. Which was not the same thing, as Sighvat grimly pointed out, *Gebo* being an illusion rune that cannot be *merkstave*, or reversed, but may lie in opposition all the same and might mean success, but at heavy cost.

As a call to war it fell far short of Feeders of Eagles or Hewers of Men, but it had been blessed by the White Christ's best priests. As Kvasir said, we couldn't fail with all this holy help and the whole of the Pharos Chapel must have been emptied of Miklagard's relics.

Behind all this came a short, stocky man riding a huge white horse eaten by its own purple drapings. He waved a lot as men cheered and was the only one who wore bright red leather boots, Armenian-style, almost to his knees.

197

'Is that the Miklagard General? Why are they calling him Tydeus? I thought his name was John?' grunted Hedin Flayer, who was to my left.

'Not much to look at, the little short-arse,' growled Finn from the other side.

The man commanding the most powerful army in the world stopped, exchanged a few words with our *taxiarchos*, then reined round and rode off into the golden swirl of the day, the shouts of 'Tydeus!' swelling and ebbing like a tide as he passed the ranks.

'Who the fuck is Tydeus?' demanded Kvasir from down the line and Brother John leaned forward, his eyes red-rimmed with dust.

'An ancient Greek hero who killed fifty men in single combat, according to Homer.'

'Did this Homer say he was a short-arse, then?'

'That sort of loose mouth will lose you your other eye.'

At which point, Sighvat stepped forward a pace and held up his hand as the raven fluttered out of the great golden pearl we stood in and down on to his wrist. It smoothed a wing feather, opened its dark maw of a mouth and said, clear as a ringing bell: 'Look out.'

We gaped. It cocked a head and said it again. Then it added: 'Odin,' and flew up and away as Sighvat launched it back into the air.

'The enemy are on us,' Sighvat said and then saw all our gaping mouths and alarmed eyes. 'What? Didn't you know ravens speak?'

Its speaking had struck us all dumb, but we had no time to say anything anyway. Botolf, Brother John beside him in a too-large helmet, untied Svala's banner and it had barely started to flap in the lava breath that stirred the dust when, as Sighvat had promised, the enemy were upon us.

The horsemen to our right vanished in a huge billow of dust and after that we only saw shapes, shadows in the gloom that circled like a ring of wolves and I had no idea whether they belonged to us or the enemy.

'We'll know soon enough,' yelled Kvasir above the din, hawking dust from his throat. 'The enemy will be the ones who tear us a second bung hole without warning.'

We gripped shields and stood, sweat running from us, hilts and shafts slippery with it. We had been standing, that was all, yet we panted open-mouthed like dogs and I sent Brother John to get the waterskins we had stashed in the rear ranks. We sucked hot, brackish water as if it was *nabidh*.

Time passed and dust swirled. There was a constant low drone, broken by the shriek of the enemy horns and the thunder of drums from both sides. I was aware of Hedin Flayer's rank breath and the press of Finn's big shoulder. Behind us came the sound of a giant tearing his cloak in half: the archers, letting loose a volley on something we couldn't even see.

Out of the dust in front we saw the Hares skipping back like their namesakes, sprinting hard and clutching their empty spear-bags. Most broke round us, but some came dashing up, the dust spurting from their sandalled feet like water, skidding against our shields and hammering on them as if on a door.

When we wouldn't open up, they reeled frantically away, though a few hurled themselves down and wriggled between our feet, so we kicked them in the ribs for their pains.

Then, suddenly, there were robed men in the dust, a massive black banner, the glint of spears – and the Dailami foot came hurtling down on us.

They had crashed towards the centre, splattered by arrows and throwing spears from front and either flank, so that they moved like stumbling sleepwalkers now, a great black-robed beast trailing blood and slime and bodies, screaming: 'Illa-la-la-akba.'

We braced; they hit the shieldwall, but they were almost done by the time they stumbled up to our swords. A knot of five or six crashed in on us, thrusting spears and screaming. I slashed at a black-bearded face and felt the edge bite, heard him scream. I saw a spear-shaft stab past my cheek and the point went in under a turban, straight into the owner's ear, so that he shrilled and fell away, holding his head.

Then they were gone and, with a huge wolf-roar, the whole Norse shieldwall surged after them. I was shouldered to one side, watched Finn and Kvasir howling into the haze, saw Botolf lumbering past me, banner held high in one hand, red mane streaming.

Stefanos the *taxiarchos* flailed furiously, his angry screams lost in the bellows of the Norse, he and his little guard no more than a rickle of stones in a flood. Wearily, I trotted after them, stepping over the robed bodies that they had hacked down.

'Bring your men back,' Stefanos squealed at me, red-faced with fury. 'Now. At once!'

I didn't bother to answer him, but jog-trotted on, leaving him squeaking his fury until he disappeared into the swirling dust behind me.

No more than twenty paces later, sitting in the middle of a scatter of *Sarakenoi*, some still twitching and groaning, I came on Amund, the strip of white cloth that had marked him as one of the Oathsworn now tied round the stump of his wrist, one end gripped in his teeth as he strained to halt the black-red dribble from it. Black-robed bodies were everywhere, a few still moaning or writhing.

I stacked shield and sword and knelt to help him, snapping off a discarded arrow shaft to use as a lever in his binding to squeeze harder. The iron stink of blood was thick in the dust, so it seemed I breathed through linen.

'See if you can find the hand,' he said, calm as you please. 'I had a ring I liked.'

Then his eyes rolled and he fell backwards, shivering and

shaking. I put his sword in his good hand and stayed with him until his heels stopped kicking, while the screams and yells and drums and trumpets floated from the gold shroud of the battlefield. Then I found his severed hand, a white spider in the bloody slush nearby, and tucked it inside his tunic, so that we could bury him whole later.

I collected my shield and sword and moved on.

Four hundred paces later I came on the Oathsworn, where the air had cleared enough to show the great brassy glare of the sun in a sky pale and blue as Svala's eyes. I staggered over the stones and scrub bushes into a place of hummocks like burial mounds: black tents made from the hair of camel and goat, erected low to the ground to fool the heat.

There were shrieks and shouts and I saw someone I knew – Svarvar, the die-maker from Jorvik – stumbling along with his tunic full of brass lanterns and blue-stone talismans.

'What do you call this?' I shouted at him, thinking they had all been sucked into some dreadful battle and angry that they were not. He grinned, hugging the great mass of plunder to his tunic.

'Fun,' he yelled and plunged on into the haze.

The Oathsworn had hit the Saracen baggage camp, as if they had plotted a straight course to it using Gizur's little ivory reckoner. The few troops left to guard it were dead or scattered and the Oathsworn were enjoying themselves.

There were horses and women, arms in stacks like corn-stooks, mail suits, ewers and vases of gold and brass – and leather bags of money, for the Saracen soldiers insisted on regular pay, something we had all already learned from stripping the dead.

I stood in the middle of this maelstrom, watching men stagger and stumble and howl like dogs, wrecking good pottery and gutting the dead to make sure they had swallowed nothing of value. They ripped rings from corpses; they threw screaming women on the ground, or bent them over cart shafts.

201

I saw Hookeye, a black turban askew over his squint, a richly brocaded robe over one shoulder and a richer cloak over the other, pumping furiously at the naked buttocks of a screeching woman and waving a jewelled dagger in the air. For a head-swimming moment, it seemed that the spade-bearded high priests from Miklagard's cathedrals were here, baying with lust, and not the Oathsworn men at all.

I roared, I threatened, I even pleaded, but it was like herding cats. A hand gripped my arm and I found Brother John at my elbow, face grim as a crucifixion. 'Best let this fever run its course,' he said. 'Anyway, we have found something.'

I followed him to a black tent and ducked into it, blinking at the move from light to dark, from the realm of stark Helheim to a place cool and coloured bright as Bifrost. The light of fat candles bounced off the dazzling rugs lining the floor and the gilded drinking vessels and carvings teetering on low wooden tables. Botolf crouched, Dane axe butted in front of him and the raven banner laid out on the floor, grinning at the figure opposite.

Sitting on one of the many fat cushions, hawk-faced and dark-eyed, his skin a spiderweb stretched over his face, was Martin the monk. His eyes had a secret, secluded look, like a turf house seen between trees.

'He was caught by the *Sarakenoi* making for Jorsalir, which fact he let slip in the joy of his rescue by Botolf here,' Brother John said. 'Since he is an escaped slave, they were not planning to be lenient or merciful.'

Someone burst through the flap of the door and Botolf whirled and snarled at him like a dog. The figure yelped and backed out.

'Some of your hounds can still be leashed, it seems,' Martin said in that dry rasp.

'Be grateful for it,' I said. 'If Starkad comes, things will be different, I am thinking.'

Martin blinked a little and the harsh little lines round his mouth tightened so hard it looked like a cat's arse. 'So, is my life any happier in your hands, Orm Ruriksson?'

I sighed and picked up one of the drinking vessels, but it was empty. Botolf shoved an almost-flat waterskin at me and I drank the tepid stuff, straining the worst of what was in it through my teeth.

'I have no quarrel with you this day, monk,' I said. 'The world is washed in blood and I command no one, as you see. Tell me of my men, the ones who were with you, while we wait until this pack have looted and humped themselves to sleep.'

'Your men?' answered Martin, adding a twist of a smile. He massaged the manacle sores on his wrists. 'I hardly think that, Orm Bear Slayer. Their leader is Valgard Skafhogg and all of them take their lead from him and believe their gods have betrayed them.'

'Are they together still? Bound for the same place, this mine?'

Martin nodded. 'Yes. I escaped. Two men, good Christians, went with me. They were killed and I was taken.'

I did not wonder at this, for Martin had many talents, his best being the skill to wriggle like an eel out of any trouble. The other was convincing men that the White Christ could save them.

'What of the spear?' demanded Brother John and Martin, sensing the eagerness in his voice, twisted out a smile.

'That I still have to get. I will, do not fear. You have an interest?'

Brother John's hackles rose at the implication of greed. 'Don't presume to judge me, priest. The Great City also has a Holy Lance. For all I know what you have is a lump of wood and iron, no more.'

'But if it is not that?'

Martin's question hung in the air, unanswered. In the end, Brother John uncurled from the floor and ducked out of the tent.

203

I looked at the monk, remembering the blow I had given him once, turning blade to the flat and sparing his life at the last, which I had come to regret. Here he was again and once more I would let him live, for I was sick to my stomach of death this day.

I raised a hand to bring Botolf over from where he had been standing at the entrance. Martin saw it, saw my missing fingers and chuckled, raising his own, the one lacking the little finger. That had been lopped off by Einar, while Martin hung upside down from the *Elk*'s mast and told all he knew about everything, screaming and pissing himself. You could tell by the look in his eye that the memory was bright in him and would always be.

He looked at my own maimed hand, two fingers less than it should be, legacy of the fight with the man – gods, the boy – who had killed Rurik, the man I'd thought my father.

'An eye for an eye, a tooth for a tooth, a finger . . .'

He stopped when he saw my face and he was right to do so, for I was trembling with the idea of killing him, remembering how he had put that boy and his brother on our trail, an event which had ended in the death of Rurik, his own two nephews and the loss of my fingers. The memory of how I had come by those lost fingers came back to Martin and he blanched and clamped his lips shut, feral as a wildcat.

'Watch him,' I said to Botolf. 'Keep him unharmed, but keep him.'

Martin smiled and inclined his head as if accepting some gracious donation. 'A gift for a gift,' he said. 'Hurry to the rescue of your men, Bear Slayer. I escaped when I did because I know what will happen when your men reach the mine and, though I have foresworn the pleasures of the flesh on God's behalf, I still prefer not to pass water down a straw.'

Then I was outside in the howl and horror, with fear rising like morning haar off a fjord and a flood of anger that he should have thrown that at me. I wanted to kill him, but

204

needed him close; Starkad would come for him and we would be waiting.

For now, the men I was supposed to command, that rune-serpent torc round my neck, bayed and snarled like wolves. No one would hear that it was Hookeye who humped a Hamdanid princess to ruin, or that Kvasir cut the fingers from sixteen men and women for their rings, or that Finn poked bloody fingers in the bellies of the dead he had gutted open to find their swallowed wealth.

Instead, everyone would hear that these and all the other things done that day were done by the Oathsworn of Orm Bear Slayer, for my name was their name and theirs mine.

It was dawn before they could be rounded up, wincing in the molten light of day, a few of them sorry for what they had done, the rest sorry for what they felt and all of them so foundered by the event that they could only haul away the lightest part of the stuff they had plundered, stuffed down their boots and inside tunics. Furious and scowling, they could only watch others come up to steal what they had gained.

I marched them back to where the army had been, across a corpse-strewn field where the kites and crows rose in flocks and the flies in clouds. Entrails skeined a ground slippery with fluids, wounds gaped like lips and eyes, pecked sightless, implored us still for help. Though we looked for it, I could not find Amund's body. He was our only casualty and we could not even find him.

We had won, as it turned out – or so Red Boots claimed, though it was doubtful. The mad charge of the Norse had dragged most of the *scutatoi* with it, for all their boasted discipline. Once they had stopped hacking down the Dailami, were puking and gasping, open-mouthed and on their knees, the enemy's *ghulam* horsemen in their fish-scale armour and lopsided maces had splintered them apart and ridden down the screamers who fled.

It was only when the Oven Wearers were released that Red

Boots saved the day and claimed a victory – but he quit the field and took the army back to Antioch all the same and we straggled to the Orontes, where the air was thick with grief and funeral smoke and wailing women.

Jarl Brand's men were grim and licking wounds, but at least they had managed to bring back both their dead and wounded. Skarpheddin's men had fled and those who had made it back now had to return to that field of scavenging birds, cursed by the women who were hunting for their men. A battle drawn is worse than one lost, for it promises that it all has to be done again the next day.

We arrived at our own wadmal-tent camp dusty, bloody and sick at heart, the worst affected puking froth and snot down their beards by this time. Some of the Hares thought they had found a perfect billet, which almost came as a welcome release. Finn, blowing on his skinned knuckles and bellowing as they ran off, eventually threw himself down, too exhausted even to start a fire. Botolf flung down the monk who was leashed to him and sat in sullen, weary silence.

There, within an hour of us squatting, heads hanging and souls cut by the keening grief and the clouds of insects and the sick despair, came Gizur with Odin's latest twist to our beard.

'The Goat Boy is gone and Radoslav with him,' he said. 'That skald of Skarpheddin, Harek, came to tell us. The seidr women have them at some place called the Sumerian palace, north of the city.'

TEN

The sky began to lighten and we all waited in the narrow mouth between cliffs, where pillars of splintered stone, worn by weather into tall, thin mushrooms, stabbed a charcoal sky. There were men all around me, I knew, but it seemed as if I was as alone as I would ever be, standing in what could have been a pillared hov, where sand sparkled faintly as the moon rose. A Freyja dawn, a night as light as day.

The silver light cast crawling shadows on the jagged rocks, fingered into corners and slid into cracks, then swept over us, turning us all into blue fetch shadows and washing the riverbed with glow. Sighvat's raven fluttered silently from his shoulder and whirred away, playing hide and seek with the moon.

It was a trap, of course, but we had all known that. It was how you sprung it and got away that mattered, as Hedin Flayer said. Since he was our expert on traps, having been a wolf-hunter in his time, we listened politely, though all he had to offer that was useful involved how bad a trap it was.

'Too big,' he frowned. 'Like using a bear trap to catch a wolf because you don't care what happens to the pelt.'

We all nodded, for we knew what he meant. You hunted wolf with meat and a small sliver of green wood, sharpened at both ends and no longer than your finger. Tied with gut into a circle and placed in the heart of the meat, it would be gulped down and, when the gut eventually parted, the sliver would spring apart and, sooner or later, rip the wolf's innards to bloody shreds. You could track it by the bloody vomit and it would die sooner rather than later, with no damage at all to a valuable pelt.

That was deep thinking, but the seidr women's plot was not.

'If they sought the way to the hoard of Attila,' Finn growled, 'why could they not find it in the Other? Did they not go into the seidr trance and seek it, then?'

'If they did, they failed, which shows they are not very good,' answered Sighvat.

I remembered Svala's voice telling me of seeing Hild and it came to me then that they had done what seidr women do and found Hild there guarding that road, as terrible in death as she had been in life. I said as much and the ones who remembered her nodded.

Svala and Skarpheddin's mother were bad enough, though seidr was a subtle magic and a good edge, strongly swung, was a ward against all of it in the end. But there was Skarpheddin and his *dreng*, those men who clung to him by oath and gifted rings. His men had been torn to shreds in the battle and women were cleaning and burying them still, but he had these last thirty or so grim blades and the desperation of a man seeing his luck flow away from him.

So I went to Jarl Brand and laid it all out at his feet, even what it was Skarpheddin thought to get from me. Jarl Brand, like an old bone in the flickering torchlight, stroked his icicle moustaches and looked at me warily, while the light flung away from the silver on his arms.

'And can you tell him of this treasure hoard?' he asked mildly.

'Lord,' I answered, feeling the sweat trickle down my backbone. 'Of course not.' Which was no lie without the rune-serpent sword. 'Once, we followed the trail of it, but it led to death and despair in the Grass Sea,' I added, which was also true.

'So you say,' Brand answered, then grinned. 'I, too, had heard of Einar's hoard. A good saga tale. I took him for someone as crazed as a bag of frothing dogs and it seems I was right, for I heard he and most of his men died.'

I smiled, almost sagging with relief. Let him think so, Odin. Just this once, you one-eyed raven of treachery . . .

'I will help you,' Brand went on, 'but you must help me.'

A trade. Now trading I understood . . .

'I will help you root out Skarpheddin, for the sake of his people if nothing else,' he went on mildly. 'I am going back to claim my lands and help fight for a throne soon and will take them with me when he is dead.'

I blinked at that, for he delivered it with the same flat calm as if he announced he was taking Skarpheddin's old ox drinking horn. The truth was, of course, that Skarpheddin had finished himself in that battle and now Jarl Brand would step in and take everything the old man had, including the high regard of the Great City.

'I will also give your men the pick of battle-gear stripped from the dead, which you will need if you go in search of Starkad and lost comrades,' Brand added and then nodded sombrely. 'Worthy though I think that is, I am also thinking that your arse will end up roasting on a stake, but that is your affair.'

'Just so,' I offered, weak at the image he had made for me. If it had just been seeking out my comrades, I might have thought twice about it then – but, of course, I could not tell him I sought out the sabre and the secret of the path back to Atil's treasure.

'What you must do for me is hunt Starkad. Kill him. Bring me proof of it – his head, unless it stinks too much by then. His jarl torc otherwise. He has offended me and no man does that.'

'He is Harald Bluetooth's man,' I offered weakly, thinking it only fair to bring him visions of serious bloodprice, but he shrugged.

'Bluetooth knows when to cut his losses. Two *drakkar* and a couple of fistfuls of his chosen men and their battle-gear are enough, I am thinking, for I hear he has trouble with the Saxlanders of Otto now. He will not worry overly much about the loss of a chosen man two years missing.'

I left, swallowing my own sick fear, knowing that Jarl Brand was bound for greatness, for the gold rune serpent he wore round his neck hardly weighed on him at all. His men by-named him Ofegh and some of the Greeks had picked it up, thinking this was his proper name and were told it meant 'long-lived'. But *ofegh* is more subtle than that; it means 'one who has no doom on him' and no one was better named than Jarl Brand Ofegh.

He sent his own *dreng* battle captain, Ljot, a man as dark as his jarl was white and he brought sixty men with him, which was too many when we tried to flit moth-silent up this riverbed.

At the end of this crack between cliffs sat the palace, which wasn't a palace at all but a tomb to some old king of a people called Sumerians, long dusted to eternity. Still, what they had left was worrying enough in the blue moonlight: lion-headed lumps of stone, worn and twisted by age and weather into something that so much resembled trolls that it made us all grunt and grip our slippery hilts the harder.

They flanked a set of steps, leading down to darkness, and Finn looked at me, licking his lips. Kvasir, squinting his one eye into the darkness, squatted on one knee, as if to begin a Thing on the matter, but Botolf, growling, pushed on to the head of the steps, Sighvat with him. The raven had returned to his shoulder and said, in his voice: 'Odin.'

'A fine bird,' said Skarpheddin's skald, Harek, 'but I wish it was a tongueless breed.'

The skald's nickname was Gjallandi, so it was enough to raise a chuckle when a man called Boomer started wishing for silence. I was still wondering where his allegiance lay; though he had brought the message to us, as instructed by his lord, it seemed he was in no hurry to go back to Skarpheddin's side. Still, I had set Brother John to watch him.

Ljot pushed up, looked round us all, then at me. 'Well?'

I thought about it, frowning, then decided to sneak down with Short Eldgrim, Finn, Sighvat, Kvasir and big Botolf. I would take the skald and Brother John, too, to keep that verse-maker close. When we came to the need for blades, I would call on Ljot who should then, as I pointed out firmly to him, come at the run.

Which was a lot more calmly said than done, as I took the lead and moved down the steps into that maw of darkness. Perhaps it was the cold stone closing around me in a desert night chill, but I had to clamp my teeth hard to stop them chattering. When I turned to make sure I was not doing this alone, though, I saw Finn grinding froth round his Roman nail.

I fumbled down the steps, then froze at the sight of a faint yellow-red glow, enough for me to see that it was light bouncing off a wall. The steps led to a landing and a turn to the right led to more steps, where the light revealed two more lion-headed stones and a chamber.

The air was cold and smelled of old dust. The floor was littered with rubble and, as I came down the last steps, there was a slither of sound and shadows bounced on the walls as men took up arms round flickering torches.

Thorhalla stood with Skarpheddin and his men, while Svala held the Goat Boy, his face tight, his whole body clenched and trembling. The wink of light on the blade at his throat was blood-red.

Behind them, a great block rose from the floor and on it stood a statue of a powerful, haughty man. Once it had been

211

painted with gold, and the empty eye-sockets perhaps held gems, but that was long ago. It was now just the shape of a man and even the ancient carvings on it were worn to nothing.

'I said, I said,' Thorhalla cackled. 'I said he would. He comes, my son.'

'You did say,' Skarpheddin rumbled.

The others crept in, shields and weapons up. Skarpheddin's men stirred and the barrel-bellied jarl cleared his throat.

'Best if we lose the hard edges, I am thinking,' he said and jerked a head at the Goat Boy, sucked into Svala's embrace, the knife steady at a throat that wavered like a bird's heart. I caught her eye and she smiled, but only with her mouth.

'Drop them,' Skarpheddin said harshly.

I had seen Svala now; I knew where her heart lay. I signalled and the clatter of metal was loud and echoing. There was a sound like the desert wind – Skarpheddin's *dreng* letting out their held breath.

'Tell us,' Thorhalla said, shifting forward so that her face was half shrouded. It looked like something long dead and freshly dug up.

'Let the boy go,' I countered, knowing they would not.

'When you tell us where the hoard is that you found last year,' Skarpheddin answered, hitching thumbs in his straining belt.

'Tell,' cackled Thorhalla. 'Tell.'

I opened my mouth – and closed it again. I don't know why. I thought the Goat Boy a fair trade for a fortune in drowned, cursed silver and might have made up a lie easily enough. For a seidr moment, though, I saw that any answer would end the same way and the Goat Boy would die.

A voice curled into the silence, soft and reasonable and gentle as a liar's kiss. 'The boy is not precious enough for him,' said Radoslav, pushing from behind the *dreng* ranks. 'He is just a boy. I told you that already. Good enough to get him here, not good enough for him to give up a king-gift for.'

Radoslav. Unfettered and smiling like a cornered rat. All was clear as new rainwater. Finn growled, a low sound that raised the hackles on my neck.

Radoslav merely grinned at my stricken face and spread his arms, his voice reasonable. 'I gave you every chance. I gave you a ship, my time, my patience and yet still you persisted in the silly story of needing that silly sword to go after the silver you found. I would have been your man if you had, young Orm, but it seems you are too afraid. I am not. I will go, as soon as you tell us where it lies. So what will make you – *who* will make you, eh?'

I couldn't speak, the utter back-stabbing treachery of it robbing me of my tongue. I saw him pulling the dagger from the Dane's neck in the alley, ducking debris on the stairs under the amphitheatre. All that – and now this?

Finn, though, had voice for all of us. 'Can you crawl there, you nithing?' he spat. 'I will rip off your legs and beat out that tattoo on your head with the wet ends, you pig fart.'

I was still in that alley in Miklagard, hearing Radoslav say, calm as a stone: 'I heard him call you pig fart.' How could I have been so wrong about him? Had those seidr witches worked his mind over to them?

I had not, of course, been wrong, only blind. The silver-sickness was on him from the start and the likes of Thorhalla and Svala had not missed it. It was bright in his eyes now, thick in his voice as he looked Finn over. His smile was dazzling.

'Hmm . . . perhaps you, Horsehead?' he said, then shook his head and laughed. 'I am thinking not. Orm might even thank us for getting rid of your mouth.'

He studied, then grinned. 'Him,' he said, pointing to Botolf. 'We went to such trouble to get him, after all. Orm will talk if he is facing death.'

Skarpheddin signalled and some of his men moved forward, to be met with growls. They stopped and both sides tensed like rival dog packs. They were armed and our weapons were on the ground, but I knew Finn and the others would fight sooner than see Botolf dragged off. So did Botolf.

'Heya,' he rumbled cheerfully, stepping forward. He winked at me and moved into the lee of Skarpheddin's men, then turned to face us – and knelt. I swallowed as Skarpheddin took the hint.

'Well,' he said admiringly, 'a man who spits at death.' His sword coming out was a snake-slither of sound.

'Just so,' declared Botolf and winked at me again. What was he doing? I was shaking so much I could hear my ring-rivets jingle.

'I am thinking, though,' the giant rumbled on reasonably, 'that you may have to neck me, just to prove the point to young Orm here, who is a deep thinker and stubborn.'

'Are you so eager to die, then?' snarled Radoslav, bewildered by this. He was not alone – I looked round at all the grim, puzzled faces. Finn scrubbed his head in an agony of confusion, the sweat rolling off him in fat beads.

Botolf shrugged his massive shoulders. 'You chose me, Radoslav. I am just showing you the weave of it.'

Skarpheddin stroked his forked beard and then shrugged and raised the sword. 'So be it,' he said.

I wanted to shriek, but Botolf winked for the third time and held up a hand.

'Wait, wait,' he said and turned to grin at Radoslav. 'If this is my wyrd – and it looks like it is, for sure – then let me die as fair as I lived. I would hate to shear my hair off with my neck.'

Radoslav blinked, then laughed a nasty laugh, for he had seen – as we all had seen – how vain big Botolf was about his long red hair, now fixed in two massive braids.

'Do me the courtesy,' growled Botolf to Radoslav. 'Pull them free of my neck.'

Radoslav put his back to us as he moved to stand in front

of Botolf, gripped a braid in each fist and pulled them forward, so that the massive neck was exposed. I sweated. Did Botolf believe he really was the frost giant Ymir? That his muscled flesh could bounce edged iron like a berserker?

The sword swung up, a red-gold arc in the torchlight.

'Wait . . .' I started to say, then it hissed down, full force.

Botolf gave a bull bellow and his whole muscled torso heaved backwards. Radoslav shot forward, hands outstretched and shrieked with horror as Skarpheddin's blade sheared through his hands. One was severed completely at the wrist, the other lost all the fingers in a spray of flesh bits and blood.

Screaming, he reeled away, while Botolf rose like Ymir himself, the spider of Radoslav's left hand still gripping one braid, a grisly hair ornament that swung as he shoved fat-bellied Skarpheddin into Thorhalla, who cannoned into Svala and the Goat Boy.

Something black rasped: 'Odin,' and whirred across the room; men scrabbled for weapons; and Brother John roared: '*Fram! Fram!* Brandsmenn! Ljot!'

I scooped up my blade and started towards Svala, to free the Goat Boy. Botolf, roaring and beating with his fists, vanished into the middle of Skarpheddin's men and Short Eldgrim followed after, Kvasir on his heels. Finn lunged, snarling, towards Thorhalla, who shrieked and danced, her catskin cloak flying as she spat at Finn, shouting, 'Blunt, blunt.'

It was well-known that a seidr witch could take the edge off a weapon with such a look and chant, but Finn swung his sword anyway and cursed when the Godi bounced off her thick catskin cloak. Thorhalla cackled in triumph, but Finn, grim as a shoal in a storm, whipped up his Roman nail from between his boots and rammed it between her eyes. Later, he said it felt like pushing a knife into an old bird's nest.

A mailed figure loomed in front of me, bright light flashed on a blade and I struck at his shins as I ducked. They cracked

215

like twigs and he wailed and fell over, so that I moved past him to where Sighvat was collecting the Goat Boy from a shrieking Svala.

She was slumped and bloodied already, whimpering from the ruin of a face. A small puff of wet feathers lay at her feet, but Sighvat's raven had clawed and pecked her eyes and face before she had torn it to bloody pats, letting loose the Goat Boy to do it.

I hauled the Goat Boy away and he clung to me and looked up into my face, dry-eyed. 'I was not afraid, Trader,' he whispered, his voice winking on the brim of tears. 'I held your amulet and was not afraid.'

I dragged him to one side and hunkered down at the base of the great stern statue while the chamber filled with grunting, panting, howling men, hacking and slashing at each other in a fury of fear and frenzy.

They cursed and staggered and slipped in gore and lashed out at each other. Shadows danced madly in the guttering torches but Sighvat knelt nearby as if he was the only one in that place, gently gathering up the body of the raven, every last bloody shred and pinfeather, cupping it in his hands while Svala lay, face leaking blood between her fingers as she rocked and moaned.

The raven. Had it said 'Odin' because Sighvat had trained it to speak, as Kvasir had scoffed when we had first marvelled at it? Had he trained it also to kill, or was that the hand of One Eye? There was so much skin-crawling seidr in this hov, though, that even Sighvat's raven seemed the least of it.

The fight did not last long, though it seemed so. The last of Skarpheddin's *dreng* flung down their weapons when they saw Brand enter the chamber, magnificently mailed and chill as snow. Skarpheddin himself, beaten flat by Botolf, could not even rise or speak, for his ribs were smashed and his jaw broken.

Botolf sat, panting and scowling and running with blood

from a dozen cuts as everyone sorted themselves out and realised that no one was hurt save for a few bruises and slices. We all crowded round, demanding to know where he was cut worst and Botolf sighed, holding out a hand, from which dangled one limp braid, sliced off in the fight.

'Now I will have to get it all shorn,' he scowled.

We were laughing like girls from the sheer relief of it, echoing loud in that chamber. The Goat Boy danced and shrilled.

Then the whimpers and moans and blood sobered us.

'Help me, for the love of all the gods,' yelped Radoslav, his stump jammed under his armpit where it soaked his shirt. His other, fingerless hand he had stuffed between his thighs to try and stem the bleeding and he begged Finn to tie off his arms and save him.

It came to me again that he had not, after all, been immune to the women's seidr magic and that the thoughts in his head had not, perhaps, been all his own. I pitied him – but I was alone in this, as it turned out.

'You need a Greek chirurgeon,' Brother John pointed out and Radoslav whimpered agreement.

'You need a priest,' corrected Finn in a low, rasping snarl and raised his named sword.

Radoslav shrieked once as the blade – not blunt now, I saw – sliced him through the throat, then gurgled his way to meet his Slav gods.

Finn, grinning madly, leaned over and tore Radoslav's ruby earring out, then searched him for more spoil. Once, Radoslav had been an oarmate, a sword-brother; now he was pillage and it came to me then that he had managed to avoid taking our Oath and that I had missed that sign, too. I thanked him for it now, all the same; the Oath had not been broken by his treachery and death.

'He thought you were lying about the runesword,' said Brother John softly, looking down at the ruin that had been Radoslav. '*Libenter homines et id quod volunt credunt.*'

217

What men wish, they like to believe. It did not seem much to mark the passing of a man who had once saved my life.

Jarl Brand, his hair and eyes picking up all the red torch-light, stepped over to the groaning Skarpheddin and his dead mother. His sword was one befitting a great jarl, for it took only two strokes – deep, wet sounds – and their heads were off. Then he turned to Svala.

'Take her and bind her. Cask those two up,' he said to Ljot, 'and place the heads on the thighs.'

Which was the correct way, of course, to lay any witch-fetch vengeance to rest, for they cannot walk abroad as undead if they cannot see. Svala would not be killed; no one sensible killed a witch and it was not good that Finn had killed Thorhalla, but I trusted to Odin to watch over him for that. I watched Brand's men haul Svala by the armpits and take her up the worn steps, her calfskin shoes bumping as they dragged her, blood dripping, fat and red.

Brand turned to me and smiled. 'A good service,' he declared. 'I shall keep my word. Come to me in the daylight and we will see your men well fitted out.'

We left that old tomb, stinking with fresh blood and new fetches to haunt it down the ages, scampering away from it down the moonlit crack between high rocks and out to where the river flowed. There we stopped and splashed water and told Botolf what a saga tale he had made, though all he could think of was his lost hair.

It did make such a tale, too, for that skald Harek – who had stayed true enough to us – took the bones of it and fleshed it into a saga. Though when I heard it, years later, it was part of another tale entirely, about the *jomsvikings* from Wolin, and nearly all lies.

As we trooped back to the wadmal-camp, the Goat Boy striding beside me, fist clenched tight in the hem of my mail, all I could see were Svala's red cheeks, lips pursed to blow a strand of hair off her face with a little 'pfft' of sound.

218

'Lovely,' she had said.

I could not get the stink of *rumman* fruit out of my nose all night – and the gods revealed the price to be paid for killing a witch when we stumbled back to our mean camp. The man I had set to watch Martin confessed he had ducked from the tent for a moment – a moment only – to take a piss, for the prisoner had been bound.

When he came back, the monk had gone.

ELEVEN

The click of wooden goat bells and the bleat of camel calves snatched me from a dream which smoked away like prow-spray into the morning, where shadows already grew fat beyond the sheltered overhang of rock where we were camped.

Men yawned and unrolled from cloaks and stretched, farting. Two fires were already lit and Aliabu, our guide, was slapping wet dough backwards and forwards in his hands, expertly making it into thin bread for the hot stones. He grinned, all white teeth and eyes. Nearby, Finn ducked the smoke from his own fire, moving to the lee as he stirred oats and water in a pot, a good Norse day-meal.

Short Eldgrim strolled up as I rolled out from my own cloak and finally found the gods-cursed stone that had stuck in my ribs for most of the night.

'You look like a camel's arse, Trader,' he grunted amiably, hunkering down awkwardly in his robes and mail. Finn threatened him with the wooden spoon as he craned to look in the pot.

'Fine talk from the likes of you,' I gave him back, 'with a face like a bad chart.'

The Goat Boy brought me some of the Arab flatbread and hot goat's milk, at which a few of the men chuckled. The

Goat Boy, still pale and weak, had refused to be left behind with Gizur and the six we had sent to guard the *Fjord Elk* and the Oathsworn admired his bravery – and enjoyed poking fun at me for his doglike devotion. I had to spit out flies drinking his hot milk, though; even this early they swarmed on any food.

Most of the band were awake and had been since first light, slithering into leather and mail. After that, they shrouded it all in the flowing robes of the Bedu tribes, leaving helmets dangling like pots from the waists and wearing cloth wrapped round their heads in a strange way, which Aliabu and his brothers, Asil and Delim, had to do for the band every day.

That had been Aliabu's idea, that and the handful of goats and camels which carried our gear, since it made us look more like *Sarakenoi* in the country that we travelled through. Not that, so far, we had seen many others and those we did find sprinted for it. Ruined farms, shattered houses, broken lives – the armies of both sides were ravaging those who always suffer: the weak.

Now, eight days out from Antioch, we had gone beyond even the Miklagard army scout patrols and the two ravaged steadings we had come across had been destroyed by the *Sarakenoi* themselves, who were fighting each other now. I thanked the gods we were more battle-ready than we had ever been.

Jarl Brand had been a ring-giver of note to us, for sure. In front of the assembled ranks of his own men and us – and what was left of the sullen, wailing company of Skarpheddin – he had offered his aid to each and every one of the Oathsworn, who had then picked spears, axes, helmets shields and prized ring-coats from a heap gathered up from the battle-field.

There were a few swords, too, but he gave them to me to hand out, which was a fine jarl-gesture and not lost on all there, so that the women who wailed at the sight of familiar

221

battle-gear being lifted by strangers were made easier. That, of course, and the fact that Jarl Brand had swept them into his own hov, which at least gave them a future and made it harder to protest.

He also provided a feast, with heaped platters of food and fat jugs of *nabidh*, consumed under the stars down by the Orontes, with clever jugglers and fire-eaters and all in honour of the Oathsworn and their leader, Orm Bear Slayer.

Harek, who had now become court-skald to Brand as he had been to Skarpheddin, composed as complicated a *draupa* as he could manage on the greatness of Orm Bear Slayer while half-drunk, but the 'hooms' and 'heyas' that made my face flame simply made his tongue more wild.

Of course, as Brand confided to me, his face so close to mine that I could see the light sparkle on his silver lashes, it was what the Oathsworn deserved for having such Odin luck as to have attacked the main baggage camp of the enemy just as it looked as if the *Sarakenoi* might win.

Instead, they had panicked and tried to get back to defend it, at which point Red Boots and his horsemen fell on them, rescuing something from a bad day. Which was double luck for us: if the *Sarakenoi* had got back to their camp, we'd have been skewered and considered ourselves fortunate to die so quickly after what we had done there.

'General Red Boots now commends me,' Brand went on, 'which is only right and proper. He has made me Curopalates in Skarpheddin's stead.'

I smiled and nodded, though I did not think he would have the enjoyment of it for long – Red Boots had not beaten the wily old Hamdanid ruler and, as long as he threatened from Aleppo, Antioch would have to be abandoned yet again. The army would be reduced once more, until next year, or the year after. As seemed usual, neither the Great City nor the *Sarakenoi* had gained anything for all the blood spilled.

Perhaps Skarpheddin chuckled at that from Helheim where

he surely was, for he and his mother were both carefully casked in a Christ coffin lined with lead stripped from Antioch's outraged churches. This was so that they wouldn't leak until they were howed, with due solemn ceremony, four days after we were gone. Of Svala there was no word at all.

'So you did me a good turn there, too, young Orm,' Brand was saying, stroking his grease-stiffened moustaches, so that they looked more like frozen eaves-water than before. 'Which is why I equip you well, as promised. I will also give you some good Arabs, the ones they call Bedu from hereabouts, three brothers and their women led by one Aliabu . . . something. He will make you look more like his people and, if you travel with the camels I will give him, there is a better chance of avoiding that stake up the arse.'

It was a good plan and I simply nodded, thinking more about how I might just miss getting arrested by Red Boots, who was now galloping off back to Tarsus. I did not hold out much hope of it, all the same – now that he had time to think on it, Red Boots would want that silly container and the lives of all connected with it.

There wasn't much else to do, I was thinking, except brood on it and watch Kleggi and Svarvar arm-wrestle while Hookeye and Arnfinn raced each other to swallow whole ox-horns at one go. Hookeye finished, dripping and triumphant, while Finn bellowed that he had won only if the bet had been to try and drown himself in *nabidh* instead of swallow it. Hedin Flayer interrupted to excuse Hookeye on the grounds that his squint made it hard for him to get horn to meet mouth first time out.

I remembered Hookeye, draped like a Miklagard priest and arse going like a washerwoman's elbow, while the Hamdanid chief's woman under him shrieked and squealed. She had not been a pretty *Sarakenoi* princess afterwards.

None of that, though, drove the certainty of what I had to do out of me. So, swallowing the spear in my throat, I did it: I told Brand what we had done on Cyprus, for he was the only one who could, I was thinking, protect us from Red Boots and get the secret to the Basileus of the Great City. I did not tell him we had lifted the prize to trade for the sword Starkad had, all the same. I just told him what we had lifted and what I thought it meant.

He sat and frowned on it for a long time, while the din of feasting roared and flowed like a river in spate round us. So long, in fact, that I grew more wary and began to consider a way out of that place. Then he stirred, stroking his icicle moustaches.

'Here's the way of it,' he said, bent close to speak in my ear. I could see Finn watching and it came to me that it did no harm for my reputation to be seen touching heads and planning at the high seat of a jarl such as Brand.

'I am pledged for a season to the Basileus Nikephoras,' he went on. 'This, of course, also means his commander, John Red Boots.'

My eyes must have narrowed too much, for he waved a soothing hand.

'It comes to me that the business of thrones in the Great City is nothing much to do with either you or me, young Orm,' he went on. 'After my season is up, why should I care what happens in their blood-feuds? It comes to me also that keeping this a secret until I see the Basileus – a costly and long-drawn out affair of bribes, I might add – will be difficult. Red Boots, I understand, is already made aware of your name and will certainly want you dead.'

I was more afraid than ever and he saw that and chuckled.

'I can help you, but you must place your hands in mine over this. I shall take these twigs and eggs to Red Boots and say that you were my man when you did this offence and that you did it for gain and no more and thought it richer than it turned out to be. I will tell him you are a fool who does not understand what was lifted, only that it was not as

224

golden a prize as you thought – which is no lie, after all. Nothing bad has come of it and he will have my pledge on your silence.

'It is as well no Romans were killed in getting this prize,' he went on, taking a swig from his *nabidh*, then passing it to me as if we were horn-paired at this feast, another thing that did not go unnoticed and gave me even more standing. I also saw that he had done it deliberately for that effect.

'As it is, of course,' he went on, wiping his lips and talking as if he was discussing a winter cull of livestock, 'Red Boots will still try and have you killed in the dark, for it is the Great City's way of things and another reason to be off smartly. He would like to do the same to me, but he needs me. He cannot hold Antioch unless the whole army stays and that isn't something that can be afforded for long. He will march off and leave a garrison behind to be besieged by the camel-humpers. That garrison will be me and most of my men.'

I blinked at that and again Brand chuckled.

'Of course, my ships will lay off around Cyprus, which is where you can find me, providing you are back by the end of the year. After that, I will be off up to Kiev and then home and if you want to be with me, as a chosen man, you had better make it in time. Then both of us will be beyond Red Boots and he can do what he likes.'

'What happens if you get besieged in Antioch?' I blurted and he smiled like a bear trap being set.

'No "if" about it. I will, of course. Red Boots knows it. I will also negotiate the surrender of Antioch to the Hamdanids – at a price and amicably. Red Boots knows that, too. The Hamdanids will prefer that to fighting several hundred well-armed men from the viks, having seen how we do it. Naturally, I will wait for the safe withdrawal of the Great City's armies to Tarsus, which is all Red Boots wants. Next year, or the year after, he will be back and the business will start again.'

There are those who say Brand got his jarldom by rolling

on his back and having his belly tickled by his King, Eirik, and, after him, his son, Olof. They say Olof only got to be King of the Svears and Geats because he climbed into the lap of Svein Forkbeard like a little dog and that made Brand the lapdog of a lapdog.

That's not the right of it. They called Olof the Lap King – Skotkonung – because he took what his father Eirik had made of the Svears and Geats and made them pour a handful of dirt from their tofts into his lap, a ritual that admitted he owned the earth they walked on and would pay him in silver to keep those tofts. Taxes, in other words.

Olof, like all the jarl-kings, made those easterners who couldn't even speak decent Norse into a kingdom called Greater Sweden – and Brand was at his shieldless side through all of it and his father's before that. The rune-serpent torc sat round Brand's neck lighter than swansdown.

I knew what he offered was the perfect solution. It saved me from the Great City and offered protection from Sviatoslav and his hawk-fierce sons, allowing us to take the shorter route back to the North. It went a long way to lifting the weight of that jarl torc pressing on my shoulders, the ends of it forged with the runesword on one side and my thralled oathsworn oarmates on the other. The swaying balance-rod of it, hauling me this way, then the other, was crushing.

But all I could think of at that moment was her and I said her name aloud, a question.

'What of Svala?' I asked and Brand studied me.

'You don't even ask about this Aliabu,' he frowned. 'A jarl needs to think of such things.'

I saw my mistake and managed to grin and dance lightly on my tongue. 'I would say, if I had a gold-brow, that any choice of the jarl is sound,' I replied and he chuckled, acknowledging that.

'But I am also knowing you have taken this Aliabu's two children to care until he returns, always within reach, as it were,' I went on. 'What you offer is good and I will find Starkad on your behalf. It may be that I can put my hands in yours when we put a keel on good Baltic water. Then again, it may not.

'I would also say,' I went on, the *nabidh* numbing my lips, 'that my men watch you and I closely and it would be better for us both if some token changed hands here when this leather container is handed over, as if it held a treasure worth having. A bag that chimes softly, as they say, makes the loudest sound.'

Brand smiled and nodded, stroking his fine moustaches. 'It is no good-luck thing to kill a *volva* woman,' he said after a while, surprising me by picking up on a subject I'd thought deliberately ignored. Somewhere, a bench went over and a knot of men roared and fought good-humouredly. Brand watched them, stroking his ice-moustaches, then continued speaking to me and looking at them. 'I am hoping your man Finn has the grace of the other gods, so that they can calm Frejya for the loss of Skarpheddin's mother. A spike of Roman iron – heya, she could not blunt that. I wish I could have known what went through her mind at that moment.'

'A spike of Roman iron,' I answered wryly and he chuckled. In the next breath he was stone grim.

'This Svala, who is really a Sami witch with an outlandish name, I will keep until she is healed,' he said flatly. 'After that, I will thrall her to some Mussulman or Jew, who will not be affected by her seidr and once she has been broken into, the strength of her will be diminished.'

I was silent for a moment. It wasn't that a Mussulman or a Jew couldn't be affected by seidr just that it didn't much matter to us if they were driven mad by it. I was sure she could work her magic on a stone Christ saint, but I did not like the idea of her being 'broken into', like a locked temple. It spoke of pain and blood. In his way, Jarl Brand was being generous-handed and lenient with her – yet, still, there was that lingering scent of *rumman* fruit.

227

'Will you sell her to me?' I asked, surprising both Brand and myself with those words.

Frowning, he thought about it. 'She is dangerous, I am thinking. Odin's arse, young Orm, she has a face like a chewed fig thanks to that raven and is a well of hatred for us all, yet still she weaves her seidr and makes you come to her rescue. What more warning do you need on this?'

'Will you sell her?'

He thought for a little longer and shook his head, so that my heart dipped.

'It would be your doom, I am thinking,' he said. 'But it is also your wyrd and no one flaunts the Norns' weave without price. I am reluctant to sell a Sami witch to a good man from the Vik, but here is what I will do. Return with proof that Starkad is dead. That, surely, will be a sign that you are gods-lucky and you will also have had time to consider whether you are favoured enough to take this woman.'

I knew this was as much as he would do on it, so I nodded. Brand nodded back and the bargain was struck. I expected a purse of hacksilver when I handed over the container there and then, but Brand was a jarl of different stock than that and surprised me. He stood and thumped on the bench until people fell silent, then peeled off the fine silver torc from around his neck and presented it to me.

He did not have to say anything, for the Norse knew what it meant and those Jews, Arabs and Greeks would have it explained to them later. The roar and bench-thumping went on a long time as I took the twelve ounces of braided silver from him and placed it round my own neck. For all the night was leprous with sweat, the silver was cold on my skin for a long time.

Now, in the desert heat of the early day, I fingered it, the snarling wyrm-head ends and the runes skeined on it and wondered if all the blood was off it, for it was only later that I realised it had belonged to Skarpheddin and preferred not

228

to tell of that. There were those who would think it a bad move to be wearing the rune-serpent jarl torc of one who had been so luck-cursed.

Of course, I did feel a moment of guilt over the container and its secret, but that was not for more than a year, when I heard how Red Boots, Leo Balantes and others had crept into the palace bedroom of the Basileus of the Great City and stabbed him to shreds while he slept, Red Boots walking out and on to the throne. Red Boots, I heard, had even smashed the Basileus's teeth from his head with the butt end of his sword and kicked in his head, which was a sorry way for the most powerful man in the world to end up.

But blood-feuds in the Great City were no business of mine, as Brand had said, and, in this gods-abandoned waste of heat and dust, I considered the trade worth it at the time. The Oathsworn, I was thinking as I sat there blowing flies off porridge, were under Odin's best smile, for many problems had been fixed and money and battle-gear gained.

Aliabu's woman, Nura, crossed to the camels with a milking bowl they called an *ader* and stood by one of the camels. Sixteen of the beasts, I had learned, were she-camels and five had calves, so that those who were not suckling were heavy with milk.

While Delim gathered in the four males from where they had been hobbled and turned them loose to graze the sparse shrub, Nura unfastened the covers on the udders of one she-camel and encouraged her with sucking sounds. Standing on one leg, the other balanced against her knee, she took the fat teats in her hand and started squirting expertly into the bowls.

I sat and watched while the morning grew to glory and started to sing and hum with strange life. She saw me and smiled with her eyes, which was all that could be seen.

She had a blue cloth wrapped round her in a single piece, which they called *mehlafa*, and it covered her from her silver-ringed feet to her braided hair, though, unlike other Saracen women, she did not seem to mind exposing her face.

She unloaded milk into a fat pottery pot and, from there, Aliabu's other woman, Rauda, poured it carefully into goatskins. Even with just her eyes visible, this Rauda was a rare beauty, it seemed, for her full name, Aliabu had told me proudly, meant the Pool that Gathers after the Rain.

Not a pool others drank from, even among his own. None of his brothers had women, but Aliabu had two and his brothers did not seem to mind this, nor ever demand their use. Neither, of course, did we, though a few thought of it.

But Aliabu had a long and wickedly curved knife hidden in his robes and had made it clear he would use it on any *afrangi* who caused him offence. We needed his skills and goodwill more than we needed a hump, as I told the Oathsworn.

Aliabu had told me his full name and those of this brothers, but the most any of us could remember of it was the first part and that 'Abu' meant 'father', which title you take in Serkland when you have sons.

Short Eldgrim sat back with a sigh, waiting for Finn's morning gruel, listening to the wooden goat bells and savouring the water he had dug up. Aliabu had taught us to bury the waterskins each evening: after a night buried in the chill, they were cold as a winter fjord first thing in the morning, which made that the best part of the day.

Usually, we should have been up and away, with a few hours' walk under our belts before we stopped for the day-meal, but we were travelling in the cooler part of the day – practically evening – and for a good part of the night, so would lie up in the shade of the rocks which overhung this crack in the ground all that day.

'It is a nice sound, the goat bells,' Short Eldgrim mused, then shook his head. 'But I wish it was on a wether in a meadow under hills which had snow on them.'

'Aye, blowing a snell wind that promises a winter digging it and all the other sheep out of drifts,' grunted Kvasir, crunching through the stony desert to squat beside him. He took a wooden bowl from Finn with a grunt of thanks and fished his horn spoon out from the depths of his tunic. He ate, waving at the flies and spitting out those he could. Most he ate along with the gruel.

If Short Eldgrim had been meant to thank his luck that he wasn't digging sheep out of snowdrifts, it didn't work. He nodded, wistful-sad, his *heimthra* made the worse for the view Finn had seidr-magicked up for him.

'Don't worry,' growled Finn, passing him the porridge while it was too hot for flies to land on. 'One day you'll be back with the snow wind blowing up your backside and then you'll look back on the days you spent lolling in the warmth of Serkland.'

One day. There were forty of us left now and four were already sick. I was cursing myself and all the gods that we had stayed for Brand's feasting – not that we had much choice in it. Brother John had warned us, right enough, looming grim-eyed out of the dark a day after we had come back from killing Skarpheddin and his seidr women.

'They are wrapping red-rashed corpses down by the river,' he had told me and needed to say nothing more, for I had seen all this before at the siege of Sarkel. Sure enough, the next day, four of our men started to shiver and water flowed from them in fat drops.

The day after that was the feasting and the day after that was when we left and three were dead by then, put in the great howed pit Brand was digging to cope with the numbers. The fourth we left with the Greek doctors in Antioch, while we ran into the desert's heat and Gizur and the *Elk* crew ran to the sea winds. I offered prayers to Odin that all of us had escaped the sickness and that I had made the correct choice – to go after our oarmates first, then chase Starkad down.

Now we lay and thought of green hills and slate-blue seas capped with white and the snow whipping off the tall mountains like Sleipnir's mane. It was better with your eyes closed, for then you did not see this strange land, nor the massive winding ribbon of stones we lay in, whose walls rose like tongues of orange flames to a washed blue sky.

Here were no sheep, but little scaled lizards that popped out and scuttled down the blind turnings that led only to holes where little birds lived. It was a world of brown and pale green, of strange boulders shaped like mushrooms and swirling patterns of sand, which seemed to be all the colours of Bifrost. I supposed Aliabu and his people had as many names for sand as the Sami have for snow.

I lay and thought of her, too, all through the day until it was my time to stand watch and even then. Always the same, too: the laugh; and the day she and I and Radoslav had enjoyed in the city of Antioch on the Orontes, a day as perfect as a *rumman* fruit – yet one whose heart had already rotted unseen. A cracked bell of friendship and love, even then. One such betrayal would have been enough, Odin. Two was larding it thick.

Finn and Brother John came to me as Aliabu and the others were packing the groaning camels to start the day's journey, taking a knee where I sat and eyeing me grimly. I eyed them back and jerked my chin for them to speak.

'Three were felled by heat,' Brother John said. 'They will recover if they are fed water and kept shaded for a day.'

'Good news,' I said, knowing with a sick dread what came next.

'There is a fourth down, but he does not have the red pox,' Brother John said. 'He has the squits, or the sweating sickness, or both. He will die, for sure, just the same. His vomit has blood in it. *Dabit deus his quoque finem.*'

God would, indeed, grant an end to these troubles. I remembered the sweats from Sarkel. Old oarmates, Bersi had it one day and was dead of it the next and Skarti, whose lumpen face told how he had survived the red pox, would probably

232

have died of the sweats if an arrow hadn't killed him first. The squits were better, in that you could recover from them after some days of misery and mess – but when the blood streaks showed, you were finished.

'He needs the Priest,' said Finn, looking at me. I remembered that look from the last time, across the body of Ofeig. Next time, Bear Slayer, he had said, you do it.

I held out my hand and he slid the hilt of the sword into it.

It was Svarvar, the coin-stamper from Jorvik, lying on a pallet of scrub and his own cloak and soaking his life away, so that you could see him shrink to a hollow man by the minute, while he shook and trembled and his eyes rolled. The stink of him filled the air, thick enough to cut.

I called his name, but if he heard it he gave no sign, simply lay and muttered through chattering teeth, shaking and streaming with water. Brother John knelt and prayed; Finn hefted a seax hilt between Svarvar's hands and I could not swallow. The Priest, when I guided the blade of it to his neck, felt cold as ice.

His eyes flickered open then and, just for a moment, I knew he knew.

'When you get across Bifrost,' I said to him, 'tell the others about us. Say, "Not yet, but soon". Good journeying, Svarvar.'

It didn't take much pressure, for Finn had spent the day putting an edge on the Priest, a rasp that had irritated us all at the time. The neck-flesh parted like fruit skin and he jerked and thrashed only a little while the blood poured out with an iron-stink that brought flies in greedy droves almost at once.

'Heya,' Finn said approvingly, and I rose, wiping clean the blade and handed it back to him, hoping my hand did not tremble as much as my legs did.

Then Sighvat and Brother John and others gathered rocks and stones and used them and a shallow scoop in the stony sand to howe up the coin-maker from Jorvik. Five years he had spent digging stones, only to be freed to end under a pile of them. Odin's jokes were never funny, but sometimes you could not even grin for the clench of your teeth.

It was not a good omen and made the long journey through the shivering night a bleak, moon-glowed tramp. When the sun trembled up, a great, golden droplet on the lip of the world, we squatted and panted and licked our own salt-sweat into stinging, mucus-crusted mouths until it died again and gave us the mercy of cooling night and the right to drink.

Some began to shiver with the change and hoped that was all it was, checking each other for sign of sweating sickness or red pox. The three who had been heat-afflicted were showing signs of recovery, though they were calf-weak when they tried to walk.

Aliabu and his people silently got ready to move on. In the last light of day, at the ridge that had sheltered our little camp, he turned and looked back, as if searching the twilight for his unseen sons. For a moment, his ragged robes hidden and silhouetted against the sky, he looked as jarl-noble as any man I have seen.

There grew in me then the respect of a whale-road rider who sees another of his kind and marks him even though there is no sign on him other than the stare which has searched far horizons.

Until now, the *Sarakenoi* had been screaming Grendels with weapons, or flyblown savages who squatted in their own filth, ate using one hand, wiped themselves with the other and worshipped one god, though they had blood-feuds with each other over how best to do it.

But the Bedu navigated their own sea out here, as skilfully as any raiders in a *drakkar* two weeks out of sight of land, and found sustenance here as we would from the waves. Eaters of lizards and rats and raw livers, they took the jelly from camel humps, squirted it with the gall-bladder juice and sucked

234

the lot down, smacking their lips as we would over a good bowl of oats and milk.

'By Odin's sweaty balls,' Finn growled when I mentioned this, 'just because they can eat shit and ride a horse with a hunched back doesn't make them worth anything, Trader.'

'They are proud and noble, for all that,' I answered. 'They are masters of this land and survive on it. Could you?'

Finn spat, shouldering along in the blue dark. 'Take them to a cold winter in Iceland, see how well they fare. They are masters of this land, Trader, because no one fucking wants it and are left in peace because they haven't a hole to piss in, nothing anyone would want to steal, not even their sorry lives. They are the colour of folk two weeks dead and that short-arsed little lizard-chewer Aliabu thinks the best name he can give his favourite woman is Puddle, by Odin's arse. That tells you all you need to know.'

He stumbled, cursed and recovered his walking rhythm. 'I never had the ken of why the Irishers liked Blue Men as slaves. They always die on you when the snows come and Dyfflin's a long way to cart the buggers while trying to keep them alive on a *hafskip*.'

I grunted, which was all that was needed. Finn looked at the world down the blade of his sword, measuring its worth in what he could take. But, even travelling along Odin's edge as I was, I still saw these Bedu as *knarrer* in this ocean of sand and stone, charting ways less travelled and always open when others were shut. One day that would be of more use to me than plundering them – if Odin spared me.

Aliabu's shout shook me back into the now, where the sweat stung my eyes and the desert grit rasped in every fold and crack. I stopped, panting, dropped to one knee like all the others, pushing up the little tent of robe with the stick I carried.

One of my boot soles flapped; the thong that had fixed it in place had snapped and been lost on the trail and I fumbled

235

to find one of the few I had left. We all had flapping seaboots, cracked and split in the heat, the soles held on by thongs and whose bone-toggle fastenings had long since vanished.

Hookeye moved up, his bow out and strung, so I knew it was serious. In this heat, he kept both wrapped and greased with camel fat to stop them drying out.

'Another group of camels,' he reported. 'There are men there, armed and ready.'

I climbed to my feet and gave my orders. Botolf, the only one not wearing padded leather and mail, since none large enough had been found to fit him, unravelled the raven banner, but it flopped like a hanged man on the pole.

The Goat Boy and Aliabu came up as we formed into a loose shieldwall. Aliabu waved his hands and rattled off a stream of words and I knew I was getting better at things, for I made out a word in six.

'These are outcast men,' the Goat Boy translated, 'men from weak tribes who have fled their masters and make a life here. Aliabu knows them, but they are not *shawi*. He asks if you understand?'

I did. *Shawi* meant something about grilling and was a term the Bedu proudly used, since it meant they offered such shelter and hov-rest that they would slaughter and roast a prized animal for a guest. If these were not *shawi*, they could not be trusted.

Between the three of us, we worked out a plan. Camps would be made, the Oathsworn would show their strength and Aliabu and his sons would smile and talk to these outcasts. With luck, we would get news, perhaps some water and supplies and no blood would be shed.

'No different from meeting ships in a strange fjord,' growled Finn, hunched under his loop of robe.

'Save for the heat,' muttered Kvasir.

'And the absolute lack of water,' noted Brother John wryly.

'Sod off,' grunted Finn, too hot to argue. 'Shouldn't you be there, Trader?'

236

He was right, but Aliabu had pointedly not invited me, so I stayed on the course he had set and sweltered through another hour while the outcasts put up their tents. We had no tents.

In the end, Delim and two of the strange Bedu came back and, effusively, invited me down to the shade of the awning where everyone sat. I went, conscious of the envious, seared eyes of the rest of the band.

The leader of these outcast Bedu was called Thuhayba, which I was told means 'small bar of gold', a man shrunk like a dried-out goatskin, with bristles of grey hair on his chin and more gap than teeth. But he had eyes like something seen at night through the bushes.

There then followed a conversation like a game of 'tafl, a three-handed affair where I was a goose chased by foxes. Eventually, though, the tale of it was squeezed out like curd from cheese.

The Goat Boy told me: 'Ahead, a day away, lies the village of Aindara, which these ones used to visit now and then, but will not do so now. The last time they did, which was recently, they found it deserted and the people fled – those who had not been killed. It was there they found the *afrangi*, whom they now wish to sell to us.'

I knew that *afrangi* meant 'Frank', which name the Arabs called us, having got it from ignorant Greeks.

'Like us?' I asked.

They talked to each other like pine logs popping in a good blaze, then the Goat Boy turned and said: 'No, Trader, not big and fair-haired like you. Dark. A Greek, I think. They say they found him after the fight which the yellow-haired man won.'

My hackles rose at that and it took a flurry of sharp questions to tease the weft of it out and even then only one part was clear. Starkad had come this way and had men with him still.

In the end, when they saw I was interested, they hauled

237

their prisoner out, a shivering individual called Evangelos – either that or he was praying, for his mind was so far gone he could not stop drooling and babbling. Getting answers from him was like holding water in your fingers.

At first it had been my thought that he was a runaway from the Miklagard army, but he had shackle-marks on his legs, old sores that still wept.

'Fateh Baariq?' I said to him and his head came round at that name. I said it again and a shiver ran through him. If he'd been a dog, his tail would have curled between his legs.

'Pelekanos,' he said softly. Then louder. Then he screamed it, so that everyone was startled and men from both sides got to their feet and had to be placated with hand gestures.

'Who is Pelekanos?' I asked the Goat Boy and he shrugged.

'Or what. It means carpenter. Perhaps it is his craft, Trader?'

The Greek heard the word again and nodded, rolling head and eyes. Then he hunched himself deeper, almost a ball, and whimpered: 'Qulb al-Kuhl.'

There was a movement, a rustle of robes and indrawn breath from Aliabu, while the wizened old Bedu muttered some sort of charm against evil.

The Goat Boy looked at me and shrugged. 'I think he said something about "the one with a dark heart", but these Bedu talk like true Arabs only some of the time, so it is hard to follow.'

That was all the Greek managed that made sense and, when it became clear I did not want him, he was dragged off and more profitable trading began, for water and food. Of course, the outcasts wanted our shiny weapons and gave us so much water and food I was convinced they'd starve or parch. I hoped the single axe they took for it was worth it.

Brother John was angry that I had left a good Christ-man to rot, but everyone else agreed with me that dragging a useless mouth along would make us as daft in the head as the Greek in question.

'There was a time, Orm Bear Slayer, when you would not have done this,' Brother John said, almost sadly, and the truth of it made me bark back at him.

'There was a time, priest, when I did not wear a jarl torc.'

And, as ever, I heard Einar's death-husked whisper about discovering the price of that rune-serpent neck ring. Now, of course, there was another rune serpent slithering round my life; the one snake-knotted down that cursed sabre which I had to retrieve.

We put some distance between ourselves and the outcasts, for I did not want them trying out that axe in any of our skulls. We had travelled only a little way into the cool of the night when Aliabu came up beside me where I walked with Brother John, both of us trying to find a way back to friendship. In the twilight, robed and bearded as he was, Aliabu looked like one of those seers Brother John talked of in his Gospels.

'I will not go nearer to Aindara than this,' Aliabu said through the Goat Boy. 'Not far from that village is a temple to the old Hittites and beyond that, in the hills, is where the mine lies. I am going no closer than this, but will wait for you seven nights, no more.'

'Why? Are you afraid?' I taunted and should have known better, for he nodded with no shame of it, which is the Bedu way, I learned.

He told us, in that quiet, insect-singing twilight: 'Those outcasts told tales that all was not well here. Friends of friends, they say, have told that some of the soldiers at the mine ran off, for they had not been paid and no supplies came from Aleppo, because the silver was gone and there is so much fighting that the mine has been forgotten. Some say the ones who remained started to raid and they have grown strong indeed if Aindara is no more.'

Camels were being hobbled, tents pitched, fires lit and it was clear his mind would not be changed. The Oathsworn, confused, sat and waited and watched.

I saw the Goat Boy's face as he translated all this and knew there was more, tilted my head in a silent question. The Goat Boy shrugged. 'He is afraid of more than soldiers. I heard him talk with his brothers and could not hear it all, but they are terrified, Trader.'

'Ask him,' I said and so he did. Aliabu waved his hands as if he did not want to discuss it at all, but he saw the blood in my eye and knew that I would go on anyway. He was torn between his fear and his pride in Bedu hospitality, which would not let a man who had sheltered in his hov walk into unwarned danger.

His eyes were all that could be seen now, though the fire that flared up cast his shadow, wavering and long.

'*Ghul*,' he said and the other Bedu heard it and stopped, as if frozen. Then they went about their work again, almost frenzied, as if to try and drive out fear by being busy. Aliabu spoke swiftly, spitting the words out as if it hurt him to talk, wanting to get them out of his mouth as fast as possible.

The Goat Boy, when he turned to me, was a pale oval of a face in the darkness. 'He hears they have become eaters of their own at the mine, Trader. He says it happens now and then, when there is a drought and hunger drives people to it. He himself has been reduced to eating the shrivelled remains found in camel dung – but not yet to eating other beings.'

The others, when this was laid out for them, made wardings against evil and there was a lot of amulet-touching and prayers from Brother John.

We Norse are half afraid of the dead-eaters, half disgusted, and will shun any such who are found, no matter that they have been snowed in and forced to it. Almost all had a tale, heard from some hall round a comfortable fire, and many of these stories were children-scarers, no more.

But there was worse than all that in this tale, as Kvasir and Sighvat both pointed out. If no food had been sent to the mine and all that had been in the village was consumed, so that rumours of dead-eating were now abroad, then things were desperate for those guarding the mine.

So whom were they eating?

'We have to move fast, Bear Slayer,' Finn growled in a voice thick and black as the wheel of night, 'before our oarmates are stew.'

TWELVE

The *Sarakenoi* say that their god, Allah, has one hundred names and that ninety-nine of them are written in their holy book. The camel, it seems, is the only living thing that knows the one-hundredth name of God, which accounts for the way he looks down at you, curling his lip like a prince with a dead rat shoved under his nose.

They have little else to be haughty about. True, they can carry a pack which weighs the same as two big battle-geared prow-men and will outlast a horse on a walk – but a man on two legs can walk faster than a camel with four.

Riding one is not something I would do twice, for it sways like a badly trimmed ship side-on to a swell and while I never get sick on a deck, I felt like hoiking up my guts the one time I climbed on the back of a camel.

Even getting on one is harder than boarding one *knarr* from another in a two-foot sea. Because they tire if you get on while they kneel, you mount by pulling on a cord attached to the beast's nostrils, which makes it lower that snake neck and head. Then you stick one foot in the crook of the neck and let go of the cord, at which it will raise its neck and swing you up.

If you are steady, you can settle yourself on the hump; if not, you end up falling off and having to do it all over again.

Aliabu gave us three of the four male camels, since we could not milk the she-camels (for all that a couple of the band tried, being good husbandmen once). Well, that had been years before and a camel is not a cow or a goat. When a raging Botolf fisted teeth from one for spitting at him, Delim and the others, scowling, took their camels out from our reach. That one beast then kept trying to get at Botolf and bite him with her remaining teeth, yellowed as boar tusks, which at least kept us smiling at something in that place.

However, we knew how to manage three male camels and moved off with them in the cool of early morning, making for Aindara and hoping to get to it before it grew too hot.

The flat plain, fox-red and weathered ochre, sprouted a white ribbon of road and then, almost an ache to the eye, a great swathe of olive groves and vegetable plots splashed the land with dusty green. Ahead lay rounded hills; below them a dash of whitewashed mud-brick and stands of palms. Clouds were gathering in a sky that had been washed blue and tiny red birds sang in the stunted trees along the road.

'See anything?'

Hookeye, shading his eyes with one hand, looked a moment longer then shook his head. His face was the colour of old leather and his tunic, which had once been red, was now a washed-out pink. I realised we must all look the same, seared by the sun. My hair, when I saw it flutter loose round my face, had paled from red to yellow-gold.

Hookeye and Gardi loped ahead, having shed their heavy tunics and kept their robes and head-coverings. Gardi had also stowed his boots, since the soles had vanished completely and he was now barefoot.

We followed them at camel-pace and soon a wind soughed out of the hills, driving a fine spray of grit and dust against us. I leaned into it, the white robe, now rusted with dust, wrapped tight around my head and shoulders. Gravel, whipped by the wind, stung at my legs through my breeks as we ploughed on, the camels grumbling, heads lowered.

The green fields surrounding the town were hazed with dust now; beyond them only rocky hills and an endless plain of stone and scrub and broad dry streambeds.

'This is a bad storm coming,' Brother John said, having to raise his voice against the wind and the hiss of grit. 'We must get to shelter.'

Hookeye and Gardi sat hunched and waiting for us, wrapped tight against the driving sting. Together, we moved into the village of Aindara, where only the sound of a batting shutter welcomed us.

The centre of the village was a square of bare earth fronting a sad mosque of brick, whose great arched horseshoe of an entrance had two huge doors flung wide. Slats of wood, painted to look like marble, flanked this entrance, which led to a courtyard of bare earth, stamped hard and smooth as stone.

In the middle of the village square was a raised stone trough with a well on one side where women had once drawn water and beaten clothes clean. The water in the trough was ruffled slightly by the wind and a fine layer of dust sifted down on it, so I knew the villagers had long since gone; the Mussulmen think all water has to flow and standing water is unclean. Other buildings crowded round, their doors dark and empty and a garden wall jutted out from a house, ornamented by a trailing tendril of green, fluttering with little blue and white flowers.

The mosque was the biggest building to hand, so we went there, taking the camels in through the courtyard to an enclosed space, barn-large and pillared. High up on the walls were arched windows, some of the shutters banging loose and letting dust sift on to the flagged floor and a short stairway that led up the wall . . . to nowhere.

I was too relieved to be out of the wind and grit to chew

the problem of the stairway, or the large arched recess flanked by stone pillars that looked like a door but also led nowhere.

Among the forest of pillars, we quickly tethered camels, unpacked them and shoved armfuls of their rough fodder at them. A camp was made, watches posted on the door leading to the courtyard, the only way in or out, it seemed.

The doors were thick and studded and it took three of us to close them, for it didn't seem ever to have been done and the hinges squealed like stuck pigs. There was a smaller postern door in one, which was easier to guard.

Finn and Gardi scouted around and found lanterns with oil in them and Kvasir managed to spark up a fire using some of the camel-fodder shrubs. Hookeye and Botolf discovered the stair that led nowhere was made of painted wood and cheerfully began breaking it up to feed the cookfires.

Then Kleggi and his oarmate Harek Gunnarsson, who was called Town Dog, found a doorway at the back, which led to a narrow, winding stair up to the top of the tower we had seen attached to the mosque.

We had seen Saracen priests up these narrow little towers in Antioch, wailing out to call their worshippers to prayer. Now I sent Gardi up it as a lookout, though he had to come part-way down after a while, as the sand was scouring his eyeballs from his head even through the shroud of a robe.

The Goat Boy was uneasy at all this, saying it was a bad thing to defile a mosque, but that made everyone laugh. We had raided, burned and broken god temples from here to Gotland and back – what was one more to us?

Brother John patted the Goat Boy gently on his sand-matted curls and said, '*Salus populi suprema lex esto* – which is to say, young man, that our need is greater than that of the infidel's god.'

Sighvat, passing with some of the wood broken from the stair that led nowhere, chuckled and added: 'Don't fret, little bear, this Allah doesn't seem to have thunderbolts, from what I hear.'

So we settled down to wait out the storm, while the wind hissed and sighed like the sea on shingle, a sound that ached in all our hearts through that long night.

Of course, you should never mock the gods, even those of other people, since they have a nasty way with them. In the cool of next morning, with the storm blown out, we found out how much we had pissed this Allah off.

'Trader . . . we have company.'

A dream smoked away like spume off a gale-torn wave, a dream where Starkad and I fought and he hacked off my arm – but it turned out to be Finn, smacking me on it to wake me up. I scrambled up into the mill of men collecting their leather and mail and weapons.

Behind Finn, hovering and anxious, was Runolf Skarthi, whose watch it had been in the tower and, though the harelip that gave him his nickname warped his speech, he gave it clear enough: men were coming from the temple on the hill nearby. A lot of men, moving in one body.

'How many?'

'A hundred,' he mushed. 'More, maybe.'

'Armed?'

'I sent Town Dog and Hookeye to have a look,' growled Kvasir, tossing my ringmail at me. I caught it with fumbling fingers, then slid myelf into the cold byrnie. My sword rasped from the wool-lined wooden sheath and sand grains dribbled. Finn made an annoyed noise in his throat at the sight of such neglect.

Fastening the stiff thongs of my helmet round my chin, I collected my shield and looked round at the men, faces red-brown, all snarling smiles and grim lips. There was that familiar smell of sweat-soaked leather and fear, the tang of iron and savage eagerness.

246

A better jarl would have come up with gold-browed words, calling them Widow Makers, Sword Breakers, Hewers of Men, promising them rivers of gold and silver and more glory than Thor. Instead, I could only turn to the Goat Boy and tell him to start a fire, for once we were finished we'd want our day-meal. At which they all hoomed and beat their shields and grinned those fox-in-the-coop grins.

Hookeye and Town Dog lurched back through the door, panting. 'A good hundred, I would say,' gasped Town Dog. 'But armed with nothing much: a few bows, spears that are no better than sharpened sticks, clubs. Hardly an axe or a sword to be seen.'

'If it is the villagers of this place,' Brother John said, his unfastened helmet tilted ludicrously over one eye, 'then we should treat with them. Maybe—'

'Not after what we have done to this mosque,' the Goat Boy piped and Brother John shot him a savage look, made harsher by his own anger at having ignored the boy's warnings.

Anyway, I was thinking, wide awake now, where had they all been to leave every home deserted?

Hookeye, too, was shaking his head and stringing his bow. 'Not villagers, I am thinking,' he growled. 'And not from here. All men, no women or bairns. They dress like thrall scum, but they have weapons.'

He was right. They were as ragged-arsed a band of thieves as ever disgraced the ground they walked on, slouching their way through the streets into the square, clutching skin bags and clearly making for the water trough and the well. A cool breeze sifted last night's sand in skeins across the square and it lay in drifts against the trough, where the water was scummed with it.

When they saw us lope up, shieldwall stretching from wall to wall across the other side of the square, they stopped and milled about, confused. I heard some shouts of '*Varangii*', which let me know some of them knew Greek. Deserters, I was thinking, from the Great City's army.

They circled and looked at each other and I waited, for soon the one who led them would appear. Finn, though, was chewing on his Roman nail and slavering round it that we should hit them now, while they were thinking about things.

Then the leader appeared, a Greek or a Jew by the look of his oiled black curls and beard, waving a curved sword but wearing a Norse ring-coat – you could see the thick, riveted ringwork in the byrnie he wore from here and the Saracen ones were thinner, because they liked them light in the heat. That closed the door on these men as far as I was concerned, for there was only one way Black Beard could have got his paws on such an item.

'Now,' I said quietly and Finn bawled out for us to form the shieldwall while the raven banner snapped out in the cool early morning breeze, which hissed like a snake suddenly and raised dancing whorls of dust and grit, settling them into a new pattern. It looked like a face with one eye, I noticed, and wondered if it was an omen.

They should have run for it then, but the leader saw how few we were compared to the mob he had with him and that, with the fact that they needed the water, made him bold. He snarled, waved his little curved Saracen sword once or twice in the air, then thrust it towards us and charged. Howling, his men followed. Of course, by the time they reached us, Black Beard had managed to drop back a rank or two.

I didn't have time to think of much else before they were on us, a spear rushing at me, behind it a red-mouthed, mad-eyed face in a tangle of hair and beard, like a wild animal plunging from a forest. I knocked the spear-point away with the flat of my blade, then bulled in, slashing overhand. The man was scrawny, hesitant, and he jumped back. His movements seemed slow, though it was clear he knew something of spear-work.

A soldier once, I was thinking, even as I moved in, slapping the spear away with my shield, moving up the shaft before he could recover, then chopping hard at the knee. He tripped over someone else's foot and my edge slashed his thigh open in a red crescent that split apart even as he fell back with a high, wailing scream.

He was done for, so I left him. Our shieldwall had dragged apart, though the Oathsworn were still working in teams of two or three.

To my left, some of the brigands were hopping into buildings, shooting their little bows, and I saw Kvasir, with a handful of others, rush through the doorway. A figure loomed, screeching, and I blocked and struck, all in the one movement that was now second nature.

The watered blade blurred in the haze of dust and grit, took the man in the neck, cutting upwards so that his jaw flew off. He tried to cry out, but the sound was choked off in a gurgle and I kicked the body away with one flapping boot. Still sharp, I thought, for all I had neglected the blade.

There was a yell; I spun, blocking the snake-tongue strike of a spear with my shield. Another man rushed me, shouting wildly, but mad-eyed Town Dog skewered him, then swung the man furiously to one side to shake him off his spear.

They broke then, running wildly everywhere while the Oathsworn hunted them down. Arrows whicked and clicked on the stones and hard-packed bare earth, and at the point the houses slithered down to fields of melons and beans, I killed my last man of the fight, a series of desperate, weary strokes that carved out his ribs from his backbone as he stumbled and fell and scrabbled, wailing, away from me.

I had to follow it up by breaking his skull like an egg, for he was still alive, leaking blood and whimpering, trying to crawl to safety. Afterwards, I sat beside him while the flies droned greedily in, feeling sick and wondering who he had been, what he had thought that day would bring when he woke up and went with everyone else to fetch water.

When I came back to the square, the bodies were being dragged away and Finn, seeing me, blew out with relief.

'Thought you'd run into trouble, Trader,' he said. I shook my head, scooped water from the well and doused my head in it, surfacing with muddy runnels coursing down face and beard.

'Here's some fresh,' said the Goat Boy, hefting a bucket, and I drank. 'There is food cooking,' he added and the men cheered him. Those who could cheer, that is.

We had six wounded, none badly enough to have to drink from Brother John's onion-water flask. One was dead, though: Town Dog had taken an arrow in the armpit, having unpicked the rings of a too-tight byrnie so that it would fit better.

'I told him to keep his arms by his sides,' mourned Kvasir moodily, shaking his head. 'But he waved that silly spear in the air and that's what happened.'

'At least he *had* such a coat,' Botolf growled pointedly, cleaning the blood off the heft-seax. He had unfastened the raven banner and was washing the blood off it as best he could, though the end result simply made it even more streaked and grisly.

'Who were they, do we know?' demanded Brother John, standing hipshot like a man four times his size, spear held tall and proud in one hand. Sometimes I wondered if he really was marked by his Christ-god for a priest, for he was like no robed monk we had ever seen.

Who were they? I had no answer for Brother John, but had sat and looked at the man I'd killed for long enough to see that he was too thin, dirty and had the old sores of manacles at wrists and ankles.

When we had laid out Town Dog as best we could, I took a dozen men down the white road, between the irrigation ditches and the fields of plundered beans and herbs, past the abandoned olive presses and out on to the stony desert plain, back along the route the brigands had come.

As we came up the hill to the columns of the Hittite temple, dust marked where the remnants of the band were fleeing towards the hills, Black Beard with them.

I did not know what a Hittite was – another people turned to dust – but they built well, for this was a flat area flagged with great square stones and studded with the remains of pillars, some toppled like trees. There was an altar and low, square buildings and several stairs that led down to underground places.

This was where the brigand band had been staying, that was clear, for it had been made into a fort, after a fashion, with dug-up flagstones and earth. They had been here a while, too, judging by the firepits and gear.

'Quite a jarl-hall,' Finn noted admiringly, nodding towards the village. 'Water to hand, too, when they needed it – though they'd have done better to leave men to guard it and prevent the likes of us wandering in.'

'Water,' I said. 'But only melons and beans, if any are left. Small wonder they were scrawny. Escaped men from the mines, I am thinking.'

Finn shook his head. 'Not the one I killed. He was sword-calloused, for sure – a Greek or a Bulgar by the way he cursed. Strong, too, for a man on melons and beans.'

Then Brother John turned over the bones in the midden-pit and came up with a skull that was no animal and the sickening rush of it came over me. Not just melons and beans. Meat. In a land where we had seen not so much as a lizard.

We found the larder where you'd expect to find it . . . underground, in the cool. They could have wrapped the cuts better, in linen to keep the flies off, for some of the meat we came across was already too far blown to eat.

Not that they needed to. They had come across a way of keeping their meat fresher, longer: they cut off what they needed from the living, then tied off the wounds to prevent them bleeding to death. When we came across four men, with arms and legs missing, hung up on hooks through their shoulder blades, I was near to hoiking and Finn wanted to hunt down the ones we had seen fleeing to the hills.

Three of the four were dead. The fourth was barely alive – and was known to us. Finn knew him as Godwin, a Christ-sworn Saxon from the Danelaw, and called him by the name everyone had used: Puttoc, a Saxon word which, it seemed, meant 'buzzard', on account of his great beaked nose. We knew him because he was one of Starkad's men, had stood and scowled darkly at his master's back when we had exchanged words over Ivar's pyre.

After we'd cut him out of the hanging hooks – more meat off him, not that it mattered, since he would not live more than a day – he lay in the cool dark of that stinking place and clawed his one remaining hand on Sighvat's sleeve. The other arm was off just below the shoulder and tied with blood-crusted thongs.

'Help me,' he hissed and Sighvat leaped up and backward as if he had been stabbed, which caused us some concern. Brother John moved in, knelt and began the low, ritual drone that would call Godwin to his Christ-god and we gathered in that throat-catching gloom and listened to his confession, as harsh a sagatale as any Skallagrimsson himself came up with.

Sighvat, after a moment of sitting, silent and clasped and rocking, got up and went outside. I did not notice at the time, too engrossed in what spilled from Godwin's crusted mouth.

Godwin was one of Starkad's crew, so that relentless hound had been here. That probably meant Martin the monk had come this way and the wyrd of it rocked me back on my heels, for it seemed the Norns wove our threads in and out like a cat's cradle. For all we wanted Starkad dead, we gener-ally agreed that he was a grim and questing hound, every bit as good as his reputation. I hoped the monk was stew, but I doubted it; he could wriggle out of a closed cauldron, that one.

The mine guards, Godwin said, in a voice like the whisper of a moth wing, had run off, in groups and singly, until the prisoners had broken their shackles and freed themselves – by which time, of course, they were already starving. Godwin thought that some of the slaves were former soldiers from the Great City and they had taken over, raiding out to this Aindara for food, chasing off the villagers in the process. Then that source had run out, too, and the ex-slaves had turned on their own.

At this point, Godwin had arrived with Starkad and his men, hungry and thirsting. The leader of the freed prisoners, the one the Greeks called Pelekanos and the *Sarakenoi* called Qalb al-Kuhl, had attacked at once, so that many on both sides were killed and Starkad had been forced to flee with what remained of his men. It was here that Godwin had been taken prisoner and kept for weeks eating beans before they had started to carve him up.

'Well, I'm sorry we missed killing Pelekanos today,' growled Short Eldgrim. 'I would thank him for giving Starkad a fair dunt – and then cut the liver from him and force him to eat it as a lesson.'

Godwin's laugh was a dust-dry rasp of sound. 'You didn't fight Pelekanos today. That was Giorgos the Armenian. He did not want to go with Pelekanos, who is mad and seems to want to kill Starkad. They parted and not as friends. Pelekanos took some people with him, chasing Starkad, some as soldiers, some as fodder. The others went with Giorgos and came here.'

'The mine is empty then?'

'No one . . . there. Gone.'

His head lolled and Brother John poked and peered and shrugged. 'Alive and deep asleep. That tie round his arm will need loosening or else it will fester and he will die. If we loosen it, though, he will lose more blood than is good for him and will die.'

I hardly heard him, but reached out and cut the crusted leather thongs out of mercy. While I watched the blood ooze out of the half-formed scabs, my mind was crashing like surf on a shoal.

Valgard and the crew we'd come to rescue were gone and we were too late. I had thought of that, that they might all already be dead, had even prepared for it in my head. But not this. Dragged off by dead-eaters? Not even Svala and her seidr magic could have foreseen this.

Odin, it seems, was not easing up on his revenge for oath-breaking at all.

THIRTEEN

Brother John wanted us to go after the Greek Giorgios and, as he said 'end his affront to God'. I told him we would go south as fast as possible, because I thought soldiers would arrive. Aliabu, when we got back to him, proved that I had the right, scratching out the warp and weft of it in the sand.

Around Aleppo, he told us, marking it out in stones while we gathered round, were the Hamdanids, who had led the fight against the Great City's army at Antioch. Many of the ones we had fought had been made up from the Kitab tribe of Bedu.

To the east were the Buyyids, latest in a long line of such who held the Abbasids caliphs of Baghdad hostage. They had joined the Hamdanids to fight us, but were no real friends to them, while the Qarmatians of Damascus seemed to be the same sort of Mussulmen as the Fatimids, but the Fatimids said the Qarmatians were no Mussulmen at all. The Qarmatians were, it was generally agreed by everyone, not ones to fall prisoner to.

To the south – busy celebrating victory in the newly-named Cairo – were the Fatimids of al-Muizz under his general, Jawhar, with their pink and green flags. They were no friends to anyone who did not believe as they.

And all around were the almost hidden Bedu, with their own allegiances and blood-feuds.

'Fuck,' said Kvasir, grim with disgust. 'There are so many camel-humpers fighting over this place you would think it worth something, but look at it. It's stones and dust. Now, soft green fields I can understand fighting over. But what does this place have? Even the silver mines are empty.'

For one thing, Aliabu told us, there were horses. The *asil*, he said, is the best horse in the world and people kill for them. It was this horse, Aliabu revealed, that had landed him in the clutches of Jarl Brand at Antioch.

In the Kitab tribe was a powerful clan called the Mirdasid and Aliabu had been sent to them by his own people, the Beni Saher from around the Pitch Sea, to find out the pedigree of the forty head of horses the Beni Saher had lifted from them months earlier, a great feat which the Kitab still mourned.

'Wait, wait,' demanded Finn, thrusting his chin out with disbelief. 'What does he mean? Is he trying to tell us he went to the camp of the people his people had just robbed and asked him the value of what they had taken?'

It was exactly so. It seems that Aliabu's presence was as sacred as that of any herald, because the first thing a Bedu who gets an *asil* horse wants to know is its descent.

However, now that he had that information, Aliabu did not want to overstay his welcome in Kitab country and was taking the fast route home when he stopped to trade with the army at Antioch – and had his sons taken in care by Jarl Brand.

He would get them back when he delivered us to the Pitch Sea, as the Greeks call it. The *Sarakenoi* call it the Dead Sea, though it wasn't true that it was dead. In fact, as we saw, it was greener than anywhere, though the shoreline of it was white with salt and the water undrinkable, even if you strained it through wadmal.

256

Finn heard out Aliabu's marvellous tale, shaking his head and marvelling at how someone could walk, unharmed, in and out of the camp of someone they had just raided. Everyone talked of that all day – save Sighvat, who sat apart, drawing runes in the sand and scrubbing them out.

Brother John, meanwhile, spent his time protesting that it was not right to leave dead-eaters like Giorgios behind. I soothed him by reminding him that we had soaked Godwin in oil and burned him and all the rest of that underground larder. Giorgios and his friends would have to eat each other now, which was only fitting.

'Maybe they will manage it before soldiers come and finish them off,' I offered.

Brother John, his face burned leather-brown so that the wrinkles at the edges of his eyes showed white, looked at me and shook his head. '*Malesuada fames*,' he said. 'And there is more than one kind of hunger.'

A hunger that persuades to evil. Perhaps he was right, looking back on it. We were all full-sail with it, driven across this sand sea, still hungry for the silver of Atil's hoard. Still on the whale road, yet not a whitecapped wave in sight.

Not all were happy with this. There were thirty-eight of us left, burst-lipped, sun-slapped, sweating and weary and only a handful were the old Oathsworn. Two or three Danes from Cyprus, led by a muttering Hookeye, were already growling about being no closer to this silver hoard and others were starting to listen. It did not help that Hookeye reminded me of myself when Einar led the Oathsworn; now I knew how he had felt.

Like him, I tried to ignore it and plough on, even if the furrow was stony. We staggered from shadow to shadow, the only safe way to travel in a land where the sun will kill you and even veils won't shield you from the glare that flashes up to your face.

Anyone who stopped – or worse, collapsed and lay on the

hot ground – was hauled up at once, because that sucked the water right out of your body. We learned to wrap our robes tight, which was better against the heat than having them flap loosely, and all our waterskins were coated with fat churned from camel milk to stop seepage.

Lie only in the shade, the Bedu told us. Maybe one of the lizards there will stand guard while you sleep – since they are twice the length of your forearm, they make formidable watch-dogs and only eat small animals. If you can't sleep, count the camel fleas, so big you can see them clearly.

We also learned a lot about food. The Bedu of the Beni Saher, for example, eat lean fox meat, which they say is good for sick bones. They also like rabbit, which they skin and gut like a goat, then cut the meat into pieces. Then they stuff the meat back into the skin and tie it up. A hole is dug in the sand and into that is put burning wood and two stones, one under with the wood and one over. The whole thing is then covered with embers and sand and left for three to four hours – perfect during the rest-up period of a long hot day, when no one wants to be near a fire. When it comes out, the meat looks like gold.

We ate it with the bread they made every day, taking wheat live with worms and mixing it with water and salt, the dough flattened and then covered in ash and cooked for five minutes on both sides, then removed. The black soot was easily knocked off and it was a good taste.

All of us now had great respect for Aliabu, his brothers and his wives – but we were surprised to find that they considered us worthy of the same.

'It's because you sail on the sea,' the Goat Boy told us. 'They call it Ocean and fear it.'

Ocean, it turned out, has many of the most dangerous *jinn*, which seem to be like fetches are to us. They are everywhere else, too, but never touch the earth and you can only see them when the wind of their passing whirls the sand into little circles.

The Bedu don't talk about them much, which is sensible, for neither do we like to speak of fetches and for the same reason. These *jinn* can inhabit the bodies of men and make them mad in the head and Aliabu remembered seeing one such, so crazy he ate sand and had to be held down and prayed over. Even so, it seems, he was never the same.

He told us this because he was concerned about Sighvat, who was showing all the signs this man had before he started eating sand.

I was, too, and could not work it out, but Sighvat remained apart and silent and brooding all through the long days down to another ancient city, nothing but fallen pillars and ruin and which, I learned later, had been called Palmyra. We were then heading further south, into the true desert, said Aliabu, before turning west to reach the head of the Pitch Sea and then to Jerusalem.

'True desert?' gasped Short Eldgrim, sand on his lips and not enough wet in his mouth to spit with digust. 'What can be worse than we have already come through?'

We found out, moving in the dark between the colonnaded ruins of the old city of Palmyra and the Saracen stronghold called al-Gharbi, like ghosts in the night, unseen and unheard.

We rested up, as usual, all that next day, in a heat like a bread oven, with the sky a washed and weary blue. The land wriggled and the horizon was sliced through with sheets of water that were not there, or hills whose summits were halfway between earth and sky.

In the cool of the evening we set off again and, when night fell, the land leached out most of the heat and grew chill as a summer fjord.

'Muspell,' growled Finn, exasperated. 'We are in Muspell.'

'What is Muspell?' the Goat Boy wanted to know, so Finn told him. Burning ice and biting flame, that was Muspell, the place where life began.

It seethed and shone here, too, and before we had been

on our way two hours, Thor unloaded his own fury and a great storm marched across our path just as we reached the remains of an old Silk Road stopping place, which was Odin luck for us.

We stopped and took shelter in this collection of ancient stones, huddled in a world gone dark, where blue-white sparks flickered in great masses of cloud, which we saw for the eyeblink of the flash.

The Thunderer spoke from them and then came a howl of sand-hail, until we were scourged and bent by a wind that scurried over the plain and took possession of the world. For all that fury, not one drop of moisture fell, which was strangest of all to us, who expected a soaking from a storm.

Even Brother John was cowed by all this, though he was more furious that we had travelled hard and fast by night, so that he had missed seeing the pillar near Aleppo where some Christ saint called Simon had perched like a bird for years, or the Street Called Straight in Damascus, or the old ruins of Palmyra.

'If this was a simple journey, one of those walks you *peregrinatores* take,' I snapped back at his latest brooding, 'I would be agreeing with you.' I paused to let the latest flash light up his scowl, then added: 'But this is no silly Christ walk. We are surrounded by enemies and only by sneaking along in the dark can we get to where we must go.'

'And where is that, young Orm?' Brother John answered bitterly. 'We pursue men, pursuing men, who pursue a priest into the bowels of Satan. If anything smacked of *jinn*-madness, this it it.'

It was not altogether wrong, I was thinking, and there were other faces flickering grimly in the darkness, other thoughts on the same subject.

'Our way home lies along the track Starkad leaves,' I said, loud enough for them to hear, I hoped. 'We came to get the rune-serpent sword and free our Oathsworn comrades. After that, I will be going back to the *Elk* and sailing away from this gods-cursed country and hope never to see it again. Those still oathbound can follow if they will.'

'On to a hoard of silver that will make you all kings,' Kvasir reminded them and there was silence while they drank in the rich mead of that and the sky grumbled.

'If our comrades are not already eaten,' growled Short Eldgrim, his eyes white in the darkness. Thunder rumbled, as if agreeing with him. 'What if we are too late and they have already lost their balls?'

'All the more reason for haste,' Finn said vehemently. 'If it were any of us . . . By the gods, think of it. Dragged along by dead-eaters, already having lost your balls? You would give up all hope, even of the Oathsworn.'

'At least, if they have lost their balls,' Kvasir pointed out moodily, 'it is one less thing for the dead-eaters to cook.'

There were grunts and growls of derision at this, while Kvasir spread his hands and demanded to know what was so bad about what he had just said.

I said nothing, for the fear and uncertainty was rich in the voices I had heard. I caught Botolf's eye and the look that passed between us let me know he was thinking the same.

'It isn't a disease,' said a voice into the sullen silence of this, in between the moody mumbling of the thunder. Sighvat.

'What say you? Woken up, have you? About time,' growled Finn.

Sighvat ignored him, shuffling closer as the wind screamed and Redbeard's unseen goat-chariot banged about the sky on iron-rimmed wheels. 'Eating the dead isn't a disease, nor are they fetch-haunted. It is hunger only, so bad that meat is meat no matter what it looks like.'

'Men are never the same after they have done it,' Brother John persisted. 'At best, they cannot be trusted.'

'None of us can be trusted then,' answered Sighvat

261

sonorously, 'for we are all as likely to turn to it, given the same circumstance.'

'You would be last on my list of fare,' I offered, trying to make lighter of all this. A few chuckled, but Sighvat, curse him, was not for bringing cheer into that Thor-raging night.

'I may be first available,' he said, flatly. 'For my doom is on me.'

'What's this?' demanded Botolf, alarmed. Doom was not a word anyone cared for and, for all his muscles, the giant was mortally afraid of the Norns and their weaving.

'That Godwin, the Saxon,' said Sighvat. 'He spoke to me first. My wyrd, as my mother has told me.'

The sky banged like a great flapping door and the blue-white seared my eyes. I felt the sick in my belly like a ballast stone, smooth and round and sinking, saw him look at the greyed sky on Cyprus and tell me how his mother had it from a *volva* in the next valley that her son would find his doom when the kite spoke to him.

Godwin's name, Puttoc, did not mean 'buzzard' – my *Englisc* was limited. It meant 'kite'.

Sighvat told them of it and everyone was silent. Those nearest to him touched a shoulder, or clasped his forearm in sympathy and none doubted the fact of his doom – save Brother John, of course, who was driven to a near frenzy of tongue-lashing over it.

He called us useless pagans, nithings, never to enjoy the fruits of the Christ heaven until we had stopped being stupid, hag-ridden barbarians and how a good dipping in holy water would be a waste of his and God's time.

I thought, at one point, that I would hear the meaty smack of someone hitting him, but none did. Instead, they hunched against his ravings as they did against the storm and, like it, he ran out of breath before long.

Then, burned away to the enduring husk, we staggered out of the desert. Which is easy to say and hard to do and, though it took us only a few days, it was through a world of sand, piled up in great waves like an ocean frozen in time. Rippled and ridged, it flowed round us like water, crawled as if alive into every crease and crevice.

Even here, in this absolute waste, I watched Aliabu dig in a certain place, insert a long reed and, like some seidr magic, there was water you could sip. Warm and filthy, but mead in that place.

It was our only comfort. Even Botolf's strength was fading by the time that great sand sea lapped on to firm rocks, but by then he was carrying the Goat Boy on his shoulders and the rasp of that little one's breathing, from the dust that lashed his barely healed lung, cut like an adze.

'He weighs about the same as the ring-coat I don't have,' Botolf muttered, which would have made us chuckle but for the fact our faces were fixed in masks of crusted sweat and dust.

Bergthor, who had been Kol Fish-hook's oarmate, had taken a cut in the fight at Aindara, a little slash on the forearm that had gone bad, spreading red lines and foul smells, despite Brother John wrapping it in a cloth marked with his most potent prayers.

Watery red pus oozed out of the wound, dripping on his breeks. It dried in the heat, but still managed to infect the air with a sickly sweet smell. Now Bergthor had turned green and staggered like a drunk when he walked and, as he saw the climb ahead, he sank to his knees and cried, though no sound came, only tears.

A strong man, who had survived everything the gods could throw at him, was crying because of a cut arm. Even as we marvelled that anyone had moisture left to waste, we looked away, because we were also strong men and knew we would weep when our time came. When we foundered, our eyes and minds struggling even as we lost control over our bodies, we would weep like this.

I should have used The Godi on him there and then, but wanted him to savour his last moments. Four of us carried him up to higher ground of rock and yellow-brown scrub, a sweating affair of groaning men and camels until, at the top, a breeze like balm took us and we saw the sparkle of water and the eye-aching sight of green.

'The Jordan,' Aliabu declared. 'My task is finished. I will lead you to where you can cross, then you will follow the road south to Jerusalem.'

'The Jordan,' Brother John said, blood seeping from lips too cracked to take his smile.

'Is it safe?' panted Short Eldgrim.

Aliabu shrugged. 'Jerusalem is held by a Turk, called Muhammad ibn Tugh,' he answered. 'He has taken the title of Ikshid but his rule is a fragile thing, though he holds to the view that the city is holy to all People of the Book. There are more Christ-men in Jerusalem than either Jews or men of the True Faith.

'There are mosques and Jewish temples and Christ churches there, but the Jews fare better than Christians, for Christ temples are sometimes molested, especially when the Great City makes war. A law prevents either new ones being built or old ones repaired; but the city is holy to all, so none are molested, according to the law.'

'*Mirabile visu*,' said Brother John and got down on his knees and started to pray. He would have wept had there been any moisture left in him – and, to be truthful, so would we all, for it was wonderful to behold, as the little priest said. I have never seen a green so green as that day.

Then Bergthor vomited and the juice of it ran sluggish at our feet, mixing with the dust on our boots and forming small clumps of sand. Lines of blood streaked it and the desert sucked it up. Pus, thick and yellow as cream, dripped from the black ruin of his arm.

Of course, we should have killed him, for it was clear he

264

wasn't going to make it, but I could not bring myself to it, not after what we had all done. I wanted him to live a little longer in the sight of the green and feel the breeze on his cheeks. When I said this, the others nodded and hunkered down, understanding it at once.

The Goat Boy made him a shelter and we sat and listened to him vomit into the dry desert sand. We gave him our water to drink, but he threw that up, too, and the desert lapped it up.

Towards the end, Finn shoved the handle of his seax into Bergthor's good hand, but he was too far gone to hold it, so I sat with it, holding his hand in mine, both wrapped round the hilt. It felt like a bird's wing. Others stirred themselves wearily, began collecting stones and scuffing out a hole.

'This is how we will all end up,' muttered Hookeye and a few others growled their agreement. I said nothing, but saw where the lines were being drawn, saw that the weld between the old Oathsworn and the Danes from Cyprus was fracturing now.

Bergthor started coughing, as if the sand was in his dry lungs, as if it had come to claim him. I saw it then, while my mind swam as if I were underwater, the desert snaking round him, consuming and absorbing him.

It wrapped itself around him, sticking to the water droplets on his face, painting him grey, minute by minute, clinging to his beard. He gasped for air, yet breathed only grit, seemed to decay in that spot, collapsing into nothing more substantial than sand.

Wearily, we howed him up under rocks when he died in the dark, then moved off, leaving him to the desert, that feeding animal which grows ever larger and will eat all who dwell in it, one day or the day after.

We came down into Jorsalir like sleepwalkers, drunk on the bustle and the green of it all, forcing the four camels Aliabu

265

had given us for our gear along a road choked with beggars and cripples, pilgrims and thieves, merchants and soldiers.

None spared us more than a glance, not even when they saw our wild hair, blue eyes and weapons. *Afrangi*, we heard them say, then offer whatever they offered to Allah to spare them from evil.

The guards on the gate looked us over warily and we did likewise to them, for these were *Sarakenoi* and we had been fighting them only recently. But such was the strange way of things here that they shrugged and passed us through the Bab al-Sahairad, the gate named after the Mussulman burial howes nearby and which means 'Gate of those who do not sleep at night'.

As we went, a guard said something which the Goat Boy, puzzled, told me was to do with 'the peace of Umar', which just bewildered us all.

It was fitting, when I looked back on this and other omens, that we should have come into this holy city of the Christ-men through a gate meant for dead men and later spat out of it through the Dung Gate, used to dump their shit.

The stink and the heat was a hammer blow and we stopped in a teeming square, the first one we saw with water, then had to bat the camels aside for a chance at it. I surfaced, blowing water and luxuriating in the feel of it coursing down my back. There were cries of outrage as we muddied the trough and the surrounding area, but we put hands to hilts and scowled.

My ring-coat was rolled up on a camel, but I still sweated in stinking wool and had gone through too much to be cursed at by a pack of Saracen goat-fuckers.

'Shame on you, Orm Ruriksson, in this holiest of holy cities,' growled Brother John when I voiced this same opinion out loud – and provoked laughter from the others, enough for me to think that all it took to fasten us together again was a little water and a common foe.

'The Trader's right,' Finn agreed. 'Let them mutter. I have skulked and crawled through their festering desert until even my prick is full of sand. Enough. If these shits want to kill me, here I stand.'

And he did, wet hair straggling, flying round his shoulders as he spread his arms wide and spun in a circle. 'Here I am, you goat-fucking eaters of dogs,' he bellowed at the top of his voice, thumping his chest with both fists. 'Finn Bardisson from Skani, whom they call Horsehead, is ready for you. Are there any takers?'

There was a moment when everything stopped and was still, a marvellous thing in that teeming place. Then the noise crashed in again and people moved on their way and into their own talk, leaving Finn standing with his wild-bearded chin out and his arms flung high. Few looked at us now and none made growls in our direction.

'Ah, shit,' said Kvasir suddenly, seeing two spear-armed guards come up. 'Well done, Finn Bardisson from Skani, whom they call Horsearse, we are not two minutes in the city and you have brought trouble on us, I am thinking.'

The guards stopped and rattled off in their tongue, which I had picked up enough of to know they wanted to talk to the leader. Me. The Goat Boy, pale but still standing, closed in beside me like a shadow and we fell into the three-handed conversation we had grown skilled at.

The exchange was brief and sharp and polite. We were in the wrong quarter and would be more at home moving to the foreign side of the city, for most *afrangi* and others usually entered through the Jaffa Gate, which was west. Unless we were Jews or Armenians, in which case we should go south.

Either way, we'd better do it quick, for the Peace of Umar was a pact which *Sarakenoi* had with the Christ-men, forbidding the latter to wear Arab clothing or carry weapons, among other silly things. We should comport ourselves more seemly, too, for there was bad feeling for Greeks and Christ-followers in the city, who outnumbered everyone else, but had no power.

'We aren't Christ-men,' snorted Finn, truculently, then caught Brother John's eye and shrugged. 'Well, just new ones and not like the puling bairns they usually see.'

We went west, pushing down the narrow, crowded streets, the Goat Boy in front to call out warnings and Finn, Kvasir and Short Eldgrim swaggering behind him, hands on sword hilts to make the point a little more firmly. On the way, I saw the marks of old fires, charred black buildings and ruins, so it was clear there had been trouble.

It took a long time in the swelter of early afternoon and we were practically at the Jaffa Gate when we spotted camels and what appeared to be mud-brick hovs for travellers. At the same time, we were swamped by those who wanted our custom.

I picked an evil, scar-faced individual and negotiated a price. The Oathsworn straggled in and started unloading their gear, in a street where cookstalls elbowed each other for space and the braziers and ovens belched out even more heat.

The smell of hot oil and cooking meat was heady enough to send most of us lumbering over for cubes of lamb on olive-wood skewers, or vine leaves stuffed with shredded goat, or flakes of fish, pungent cheese, figs, those *limon* fruits we loved. The desert had kicked out all our dreams of smiling naked virgins with bags of silver and a horn of ale and replaced them with ones of such food, washed down with fountains of crystal-clear water.

They wandered back, beards greasy, chewing and smiling and blowing burned fingers. They sat cross-legged in the shade and, within the space of an hour, were sorting through gear and starting to fix what they could.

'They seem quieter now,' muttered Kvasir, handing me two skewers of lamb. 'It would be better if we had some hope of plunder at the end of this, though, Trader.'

'We have had gods'-luck so far,' I pointed out, 'for these Mussulmen could just as easily have caused us grief. If we go robbing them, I am thinking their goodwill will be shortened.'

Kvasir nodded reluctantly. 'In that case, we had better find Starkad and get this over with in a hurry. After that, I am thinking it would be a good idea to go back and raid Cyprus on the way to our silver hoard. That way we will not only get loot, but the Danes will have had some revenge on those who held them prisoner.'

This was alarming, for Leo Balantes' promises still rang in my ears and getting past his ships would take more gods'-luck than I thought we had. Still, it came to me that it was no bad thing to tell the Danes, which thought I shared with Kvasir.

He chuckled and nodded. 'Now you are thinking, Trader. Einar could not do better.'

He meant well of it, but the fact that he was right chilled me on that searing afternoon, so that my smile back at him was sickly.

As he turned to spread this, casual as a rumour, I was at least glad Brother John was out of earshot, for one more knowing look from him would put an end to our friendship. The fetch of Einar hung about the rest of that day and into the yellow-lit night, where the smell of frying meat seemed to grow even stronger, the cries of vendors even more shrill.

We had scared everyone else off from this hov, much to Scar Face's scowling annoyance. He had twice tried to up his price and twice been sent packing, the second time with the threat of Finn's boot up the arse if he came back a third time. Since our purses were thinner than the wind, this was all he would get.

Those same thin purses kept most of the men sitting morosely round the fire, hugging dreams of Cyprus plunder and revenge to themselves as if they were naked women. Those with money juggled the sense of new boots with the hook of drink and women; I was wrestling with this myself, in the middle of this Street of Poor Cooking, when Brother John bustled up, bird-bright and wearing the brown robe of a Christ priest, which he had never done before.

'I had it from the monks of the Holy Sepulchre, no less,' he told me cheerfully. 'Though they are unrequited heathen Greeks, they have such vestments for pilgrims.'

'The holy what?' I demanded, bemused by the sheer, shining ferocity of the little Irish priest.

'The Church of the Holy Sepulchre. The new one, since the original was broken down some three hundred years ago by the heathens, may God have mercy on their benighted souls.'

'Whisper that in this place,' I told him, shaking my head that anyone could think a three-hundred-year-old building was new. 'I am glad you found some friendly Christ-men, Brother John, for it seems to have lightened your spirits and renewed your clothing.'

'Renewed my spirit, boy,' Brother John corrected sonorously. 'I have stood on the spot where our Lord Jesus Christ was crucified and I have now achieved my dream. Now I can go home to Ireland.'

I blinked at that. Though the little priest could be a pain in the arse, I did not want to lose him quite as sharply as this. He saw my look and grinned, shaking his head.

'I am hoping you will get me some of the way, young Orm, for I still do not swim well.'

'Just so,' I replied, then winced as a vendor bawled out a long string of words, of which I recognised only 'fish' and 'Lake Galilee'.

'I was not merely renewing my spirit and my clothing,' Brother John went on, falling into step with me. I sighed and went with it, taking it as a sign from the gods that the priest was with me, thus preventing me from heading for the lure of women and drink. New boots and sense, then.

'What else?'

'News. The burnings we saw came about only a few weeks

270

before, because the chief Greek priest here, the Patriarch John, publicly urged the Basileus to reconquer Jerusalem, the stupid man. So the Mussulmen and Jews attacked the Anastasias, set fire to the roof of the Martyrium and looted the Basilica of Holy Sion.

'They found the Patriarch hiding in an oil vat and dragged him out. Maybe a torch got too close to him, for he ended up burning. The Ikshid, this Turk, is very sorry for it and peace has been restored – but the *Sarakenoi* want no more trouble here.'

That was timely news; we would keep our heads down and our tongues between our teeth then.

'Just so,' agreed John, hugging himself with the glee of more news, which he finally threw out just as I was getting irritated. 'I know where Martin the monk went and so where Starkad is.'

Now that was news that stopped me in my tracks and, grinning at his cleverness, Brother John laid it all out.

He had worked out that, like him, Martin would head for one of the holiest places this holy city had to offer if he had reached it and there was none more Christ-kissed than this Church of the Holy Sepulchre, where visits from *afrangi* were few enough for the Greek priests to remember them all.

Sure enough, five or six days before, a hawk-nosed western priest carrying a bundle on his back had come to pray and had then asked the way to the tomb of Aaron. A day after that had come the limping man with golden hair, asking after the hawk-nosed priest. And now us.

Brother John beamed and stood, his arms folded, hands thrust inside the sleeves of his new robes.

'Fine work, right enough,' I said to him and his smile threatened to split his face, shining bright in the dying twilight. 'Where and what is the tomb of Aaron?'

'A church where it is said the brother of Moses is buried,' answered Brother John. 'And staffed with western priests.

Though still not good Celts, they at least cross themselves in the right way and so are better than Greeks, I am thinking. It comes as no surprise this Martin would go there, for he would be assured of rest and food.'

'Good work,' I said to him and watched him beam. 'No mention of Valgard Skafhogg, all the same.'

'Even that,' grinned Brother John. A woman flitted silently behind him, paused, looked at me from over a veil, her liquid, dark eyes smiling. I swallowed, wondering if I was mistaken.

Oblivious, Brother John went on: 'The Greek priests are furious at rumours that some deserters from the Great City's army have come this far south on a raid. Caravans to the east, from Baghdad, have been attacked. The situation is delicate and they don't want any excuse to let the Mussulmen and Jews loose . . . are you listening, boy?'

I blinked, but he had caught where I was looking. By the time he had turned, the woman had drifted into an alley out of sight.

'Of course I am listening,' I snapped. 'I was thinking, that was all. It sounds like the ones who have our comrades in thrall. Did they say how many?'

Brother John shook his head. 'Hundreds. Even allowing for rumour, there must be a fair few. No caravan would come from Baghdad these days without armed guards.'

Hundreds. Our comrades, perhaps growing fewer by the day out there in the desert with these dead-eaters, who were growing madder than the full moon's ghost. I saw this Dark-hearted One, crouched like a wolf in a pack, gnawing on the gods knew what and the shiver lurched along my spine so that the priest saw it.

'Just so,' said Brother John, grimly. Then he asked me brightly what I was doing now. So I told him a lie – buying boots – while thinking of the woman and if she was still in the alley.

'I'll come with you then,' he said.

'No. Buying boots is a solitary thing, priest. Go and tell Finn and Kvasir what you know.'

He looked at me, shrugged and then moved off, seeming to glide now that he had robes that went all the way down to cover his feet. I watched him disappear round a corner, then moved slowly up the alley.

She was there, I could see, for the alley had a strong yellow lantern hung at the end of it and, if I had been thinking at all, that would have warned me, for there was nothing there save some steps up on to the first level of the tangled roofs and why would a whore want to hump in lantern light?

I had no experience of Mussulmen women, so moved cautiously, knowing only that to lower their veils was a sin, though the Bedu women did this with no shame, which was confusing. Then she shrugged her shoulders, slipped the dress off and I looked at the most beautiful breasts I had ever seen, it seemed to me. They glowed in that yellow-lit alley, tipped with dark berries and trembling. Dry-mouthed, I took a step and heard another behind me.

'Ha!' shouted Brother John. 'Boots is it, then?' He darted in front of me and raised one hand to make the sign of the cross at the woman. He started to speak as, annoyed, I was moving to thrust him aside with a curse. 'Begone,' he growled at her. '*Apage Satanas.*'

I was about to roar at him when the arrow struck, a dull thump of sound that pitched him forward, leaving me to gape at this strange feathered sapling which had suddenly sprouted between his shoulder blades. The woman screamed.

I knew I was next and sprang forward, smacking the lantern off its hook, so that it clattered and rolled and went one way, while I went another, into the now darkened lee of the stairs. A second arrow whirred and the woman screamed again, then I heard her fall.

Black silence and the stink of smoking fish oil from the lantern. The woman gave a gurgling moan, but Brother John was still and quiet and the surging of blood in my ears was almost as loud as my breathing. Strain as I might I could not hear anything around me.

Then there was a scuff, from above, from the rooftop the stairs led up to.

I saw a flicker of shadow. I wanted to get back to Brother John, pictured him bleeding to death, or lung-shot and gasping like a landed fish, able to be saved if help was at hand. But the killer lurked yet and I did a desperate, foolish thing: I charged up the stairs.

It took him by surprise and the arrow he had nocked hissed so close to my face that the flights flicked my cheek. I hit him then and heard him whoof out air, heard the bow clatter to the ground and then I was over and rolling, confused, across the flat roof. My elbow banged pain through me.

A shadow sprang up and leaped up a little way to another roof and I scrambled up and after him, grateful to all the gods that, as I only saw now, he had been alone. To my shame, I left Brother John, all thought of last-minute doctoring blasted away in the heat of the chase.

A dark shape – no cloak, I noted – vaulting over the lip of mud-brick to another roof. A pot clattered and he cursed, though he mangled it, as East Norse often do. One of Starkad's Danes, then, left to kill me in the dark.

The dark shape plunged down three short steps, fell over and cursed again. Voices yelled and figures sprang up; people, sleeping on their roofs for the cool of it, scattered as he hurled through them, cursing. I saw steel glint and so did they and they pulled apart, jabbering and yowling.

I went through them as if they were reeds and he saw me coming, though I still could not make out who he was. He slashed at someone with the knife, then ran on, leaped a fair gap and landed, stumbling, on a new roof.

I went after, landing better for I had the advantage of seeing what he had done. There were lights now, yellow flares in the darkness, as he raced down tiered rooftops. The smell of cooking hit me and I knew we were stumbling across the roofs above the Street of Poor Cooking.

He skidded to a halt, teetered for a moment, then went over the edge with a sharp cry. I got there a second later and saw him crash into the street, hit a vendor's charcoal brazier in a spill of coals and hot oil, then sprawl in the middle of the road with a gasp and a grunt.

The vendor and his neighbours went wild, flailing the air with their arms and shrill words. They redoubled this when I landed in the middle of them, went over on my old ankle injury and crashed down in a pool of hot oil. Flames licked dangerously as the oil sludged into the dusty street, washing over spilled embers. Other screamers anxiously sprinted to scatter dust, or beat them with wet cloths.

They dragged up Brother John's killer, then recoiled as he flashed his knife at them. One, slower than the others, staggered back, put one hand to his side and then looked at the blood on it, before screaming and staggering away, showing this horror to everyone else around. They backed away from him, too, as if he had leprosy.

Hands grabbed me, hauled me up. A black-bearded face screamed into mine, spittle lashing me. I wanted to get round him to the killer, had to find out who he was, but Black Beard belted me one in the ribs, which made me wince. I hit him back and, suddenly, they were all on me, kicking and slapping and trying to tear my clothes, so I went down and curled into a tight ball.

There was one, a fat man in a ragged robe smelling of onions, who bent over me, his legs slightly apart, trying to grab my hair and beat my head in the dust while I slapped his hands away as if they were flies.

Then a booted foot shot up between his parted legs and the man screamed and flew through the air, arse over tip.

275

There was no way he was getting up again; he was blind with the agony of it and probably maimed for life.

Another man went sideways and bounced off a wall with a puff of dust. The others split apart and Finn stood there, Kvasir beside him; Botolf, who had kicked Onions to moaning ruin, stood next to him and others were coming up fast.

I saw the killer, knife still in his hand, start to get up, but there was something wrong with his leg. 'Grab him,' I gasped, pointing. 'He shot Brother John . . . the alley.'

The killer was hirpling away, but Botolf's meaty hand took him by the collar and Short Eldgrim snicked the knife out of his hand as if a baby were holding it.

'Heya, you arse, stop struggling or I'll throttle you,' Botolf said amiably, holding the killer up with one hand so that his toes scrabbled an inch above the ground.

I uncurled and got up slowly, testing bits to see if they still worked. Botolf turned and brought the struggling, snarling killer with him, so that light finally fell on his face. When it did, when he knew it was all up with him, he stopped writhing and hung there, grim and jaw-clenched.

I knew the woman had been hired to lure me into the light of a neatly placed lantern and that Brother John had taken the arrow meant for me. The killer had silenced the woman when it had gone wrong, a ruthless move all done in the blink of an eye.

I had recognised that as deep thinking even as I had chased him across the roofs. I had thought Starkad had left one of his best men behind to make this mischief.

But hanging like a caught shark in Botolf's fist was Hookeye.

FOURTEEN

The church of the tomb of Aaron was a huddle of white buildings on a high plateau reached by a winding path from barren
tablelands and sparse vegetation. I stood and brooded over
the land, as if I were adrift in a hostile sea where something
dark and intent shark-slid under the surface.

The sun was heavy as Thor's hammer, fields were dusty
plantings and ragged fences leaned drunkenly, broken teeth
in the raw red gums of the earth. The world was a pool of
despair, collected among the scattered bricks of this place.

Finn and Kvasir appeared, flanking a robed figure, his hands
stuck inside his sleeves, even in this heat. He was a tonsured
monk and what was left of his hair was the colour of a wolf
pelt, but his eyes were keen and gentle and his name, he said,
was Abbot Dudo.

'Well,' said Finn, 'that's Brother John delivered up then,
Trader. I am sorry to see this day.'

'He was a stone in the shoe,' agreed Kvasir, nodding sorrowfully, 'but he was our stone in the shoe.'

'I am sorrowed to hear of your loss,' Dudo said. 'Doubly
so, since it was a brother in Christ and so cruelly slain.'

He spoke Norse with a strange lilting accent, for he was
from Bayeux in Valland and had once gone with William

Longsword's son when the boy had been sent to Bayeux from Rouen to learn the language of his ancestors, for even then the Norse of that place – they called it Normannsland these days – were growing less Norse and more Frank.

Still, in the thirty years since, Dudo had held on to the *donsk tunga* well and only stumbled a little with it, like a drunk leaving his bench for a piss.

'Slain by one of our own,' Finn growled. 'And in the back. And weaponless. Do you need extra candles lit to get him to his god's hall for having died such a straw death?'

Dudo smiled and shook his head. 'There are no straw deaths in the sight of the Lord,' he said and managed not to make it pious. 'After all, this is the church of Aaron, who was stripped of his priestly regalia by his own brother, Moses, on orders from God and died of shame and sorrow for it. Even so, he was gathered into the bosom of Christ.'

I didn't know whether the brother of Moses was really howed up here or not and it did not matter much. We had come here for two reasons, the first being that Brother John would not rest easy in any Greek church of the Patriarchate of Jerusalem and, apart from mean little Nestorian and Jacobite places, there wasn't a decent Christ temple to howe him up in that city.

The second was Ibn al-Bakilani al-Dauda, governor of the city of Jersualem in the name of the Ikshid, Muhammad ibn Tugh, ruler of Egypt, Syria and Palestine – or so he claimed.

I knew enough of al-Dauda's position to know it was precarious, for he had not enough troops and his Ikshid was too busy fighting a losing war against the Fatimids of al-Muizz. Not to mention all the other little jarl-dreaming dynasties that were springing up like maggots on the sickening body of the Abbasid empire.

We had been ringed by guards in our hov in the Foreign Quarter, men with studded armour and spears and helmets with mail that covered all of their face but for their eyes. They were there as much to keep the rest of the street from tearing us to bits as arrest us.

They had swept up Hookeye and me, all the same, and kept us in separate stone rooms in one of the towers of the Jaffa Gate.

Towards dawn, as I shivered in the dank chill of that place, hearing the straw rustle with vermin, I was hauled out and, blinking in the light, stumbled up spiralling stairs to a similar room at the top of the tower, though this one had rugs on a polished wooden floor and rich wall hangings.

There was a man there, a figure in green and white clothes that flowed like water, with a jewel-hilted dagger thrust through the braided cord round his waist and a soft, folded cloth hat with a green stone in it which, if it really was an emerald, was the price of a farm in the Vik.

Abdul-Hassan ibn al-Bakilani al-Dauda, as he introduced himself in flawless Greek.

'Orm Ruriksson,' I answered, but he waved one dismissing hand.

'I know who you are. You are trouble.'

Not the best of openings, I was thinking, remembering Jarl Brand's remarks about ending up roasting with a stake up my arse. Sensibly, I kept my teeth touching and waited as he flipped open a small box on the table with his ringed hand and drew out my Thor hammer, one finger hooked distastefully in the sweat-dark leather of the thong.

'You are not, it seems, followers of Jesus,' he said, bringing the amulet up to eye level and studying it as it swung. 'Yet you travel with a Christian priest – and not a Roman one from Constantinople. One from the uttermost west. Such monks are rare in these parts in these times.'

'We are Christ-men,' I answered carefully, 'dipped in holy water, as is the custom. That is a Christ sign you hold.'

'I often think,' he replied flatly, 'that we True Believers deny ourselves much grace and pleasure by not allowing artisans to form figures. This, for example, is a masterpiece of ambiguity. If this little mannikin is your god, then the Christian Jesus seems to have lost his cross and gained some sort of hammer.'

'Thor,' I answered, giving in. 'God of Thunder, son of Odin and guardian of men.'

'As I thought. You are not People of the Book, though this little *jinni* seems more powerful than the Christian god,' replied al-Dauda, dropping the amulet distastefully into the palm of my hand. 'He spared you, whereas the infidel priest's god seems to have failed him.'

Strangely, I found that irritating, dangerously so.

'And the woman? Did Allah fail her?' I prompted.

His face never flickered, but he cocked his head to one side with interest that I should know the name of his own god. 'She was an Armenian, a whore and was as much an infidel as you or the Christians. Obviously the defiling goddess she worshipped failed her, as all false deities will,' he answered crisply. 'What I am more interested in is why she and the priest died at the hands of one of your own followers.'

'When you know, please tell me.'

He sighed at that, lacing his ringed hands. His eyes were chips of jet. 'I have two dead infidels and several injured followers of the True Faith, not to mention property damaged. There was almost a riot. You have not been more than a few hours in the city and came across the desert, or down from Damascus. I ask again: why was the priest killed?'

Sweat trickled down my back, for his tone was steel-cold now. I spread my hands and smiled. 'You must ask him. His name is Halfred and, until I saw his face after chasing him over the roofs and – unfortunately – into the street traders, I did not even know it was him. Until then, I also thought him a friend.'

His gaze was dark, stooping like a hawk. 'He has been asked. At length. He does not deny culpability, but I can make no sense of his reasons for it. Something about a Greek, by name Balantes.'

Even though he made mush of the name, there was enough in it to bring my head up and he saw it.

'You know that name, then?'

I nodded. 'A Roman lord who doesn't like me. He has, I am thinking, used this Halfred for his own ends and the first arrow was meant for me. Brother John simply got in the way. The woman, I believe, was paid to lure me to where Halfred could shoot. He killed her to silence her tongue.'

He nodded, his bearded mouth pursed like a cat's arse. 'More or less as he says it and I had deduced,' he replied evenly. 'Which makes you a victim rather than a suspect.'

'Am I free to go?'

'Scarcely that,' he replied flatly, with no sign of amusement. 'I want no more trouble and so the sooner you leave the city the happier I will be for it. You will be returned to your men and then escorted from the city when it is dark. The body of the priest will be returned to you, so you may deal with it decently as you see fit. A useful gesture would be to contribute to the damage caused – I suggest the price of two of those camels you have.'

I bowed. Bloodprice I knew – the Norse were no strangers to it and we were lucky to have got off so lightly – but the sick loss of Brother John robbed me of any sense of triumph, lay coiled round my heart like Nidhogg in the roots of the World Tree.

'I have, however, a commission for you.'

I could not have been more surprised if he had suddenly lifted his robes and danced a jig. At first I thought I had misheard him and simply opened and closed my mouth like a stranded fish, which cracked the first smile on him that I had seen. Having seen it, I did not wish for a repeat.

'Out in the desert are a band of brigands,' he said. 'At first I thought you were part of them. But these have been described

281

to me as Greeks and runaway slaves from one of the mines further north and you look neither like slaves, nor runaways, nor Greeks.'

'Just so,' I managed weakly.

'I thought also that you were these Mamluks that the Abbasid unbelievers are so fond of, for they are no decent men but Turks and Slavs and worse. But they have embraced Allah, albeit on the wrong path, which you clearly have not.'

'Good Odinsmenn, all of us,' I agreed, swallowing. 'In a Christly fashion, of course.'

'So,' he said. 'You are those *rusiyyah* I have heard of, swords for hire – is that not so?'

'Well,' I began, caught his look and drifted off into eloquent silence and a weak, ingratiating smile.

'So, I will give you provisions and letters, which will state you to be in my employ, as retainers. You will seek out and destroy these brigands for me. I need my soldiers in the city.' He paused and stroked his beard with the price of a good farm in rings on his fingers. 'When I have heard – and I will – that they are scattered or dead and their leader dealt with, you may return to me for reward. Should you decide otherwise, I will, reluctantly, be forced to deal with you as with them. Since this will cause me considerable trouble and expense, you need not look for mercy at the end of it.'

I thought about it. No fee had been mentioned and, when I looked at him, I realised none would be and if anything came by way of reward, I would take it and back out from his presence, my arse in the air and my life in his hands.

But that letter would be useful in the lands south of Jorsalir. He knew I had seen that, too, and nodded. 'Good. It is settled.'

'And Halfred?'

He looked surprised that I had even asked. 'He is guilty of murder. We will hang him in a cage from the walls for all the People of the Book to stone him until he dies. So justice is seen to be done, by the will of Allah.'

They let me see Halfred before they turned me out of the tower, escorting me to a small, heat-drenched room where he lay on a cot, rolling with sweat yet in no real discomfort, for they had expertly treated his broken leg and even given him something for the pain – after they had inflicted enough for him to tell all he knew.

'So,' I said to him as he turned his face, pallid beneath the wind-blast and tan, the eyes flat and grey as a summer sea, one still looking over my shoulder while the other looked at my face.

'Indeed so,' he answered and sighed. 'It seems my luck has flowed away from me. Loki luck, mine. I had hopes of going home with something to show.'

'What did Balantes promise you and why?' I asked, hunkering down beside him, for there was no other furniture in that place.

'A hundred ounces of silver,' he answered. About the price of thirty milch cows. He saw the look on my face and rasped a bitter chuckle. 'I know, not much to think on now. But then I had just spent five years in a stone quarry, so it seemed a good price for killing someone. Anyway, it was only to be done when you showed that you would double-deal the Greeks and steal that leather pouch rather than deliver it as arranged.'

An age away. I remembered us on the beach, backing under cover of shields towards the *Elk* and the arrows smacking my shield from behind. Now I knew where they had come from and shivered at how close he had come to succeeding. Odin, it seems, prized me still, if only to keep around to taunt.

'You took your time over it,' I said.

He shrugged. 'I tried once or twice,' he grunted with a twisted smile and I remembered him at Kato Lefkara, his bow strung, arrow nocked and a look on his face like a boy caught in the winter store with honey round his mouth.

'Once we had escaped Balantes I actually thought it a good

thing and that you would lead us all to this treasure hoard we heard about,' he went on. 'So I decided to let you live.'

'Generous,' I replied. 'Should I thank you now?'

He ignored it and went on. 'I was even prepared to stick by you in that fight we had near Aleppo. I did quite well out of it, though that Saracen woman was either not the princess claimed, or one who had less than regal habits, for my balls itched ever afterwards.'

We both grinned at the memory, though my throat was gripped with the waste of it all.

'Then it was clear you were not going after treasure and it seemed to me we were all wyrded to die in this oven of a country,' he sighed. 'People in Red Boots's camp wanted you dead, even after you had handed back that leather container. I agreed that it was a good idea, but even so . . . the tales of all that silver were good ones. In the end, though, I thought them just that: tales. I was to go back to Cyprus and Balantes for payment once you were dead and thought that a much better arrangement.'

More than likely, I thought to myself, you'd have ended up back in the stone quarry, but blind this time. It came to me also that to do all this would have taken more than him alone but when I put it to him, he shook his head.

'No names from me. I will take that to the grave.'

'You will,' I answered, more bitter than I had intended to show, 'for I can't help you. Are there any at home you wish to know of your death?'

He shook his head. 'If this is my wyrd, that's what the Norns weave, but it is not a good saga to leave to loved ones,' he replied. 'I am sorry about the priest though.'

I nodded, feeling a wave of desperate sympathy, remembering all the better times. Then he scattered that to the winds with his next words.

'Not because I liked the little arse,' he said moodily, 'but I have broken my oath to Odin and suspect the only gold I

284

will see will be the coating on the Gjallar bridge on my way to Helheim. Since I have also killed this priest, I won't get into the Christ halls, either.'

That was too much and I got up and stepped away from him in disgust. 'I shall remind the jarl of this place to put your head on your thigh, then,' I answered harshly from the door. 'He isn't going to want your fetch hanging round like a bad smell any more than I want it hagging me until I quit this country.'

'Fuck you, boy. I wish I had killed you instead.'

'You should have shut that squint eye when aiming,' I said and left him – but the black dog of it followed after me all the way back to the others: the dark despair of knowing he had broken his oath and that others with him had done the same, and the emptiness where Brother John had been.

Now the Oathsworn were fractured and what was left no more real than a painting of marble done on wood.

That same black dog padded out of the gate in the south wall of Jerusalem with us, the one they call the Dung Gate since it is where they cart out the city's shit and the joke wasn't lost on us and fed the dog more bile.

It slouched along with us for two days, to this huddle of white buildings served by a handful of priests, who took the ripe body of Brother John with reverence.

Now Abbot Dudo, his homilies spent, moved quietly off and left Finn and Kvasir and me to move into the shade and squat. Our one camel and the couple of mules I had bought were listlessly chewing fodder, standing hipshot under an awning. Even the flies were quiet, slow and lazy, hardly bothering Kvasir as he ate a fruit the monks called golden apples, putting the peel in his helmet.

Like me, he had never tasted one until yesterday and now he could not get enough of them. According to Dudo, the Old Romans believed they were brought to Italy by the daughter of a god called Atlas, who crossed the sea from the land of the Blue Men in a giant shell.

Another strange thing in this strange land. From where I sat, I could see over the long white scar of the road across the wash of green and gold fields south of Jorsalir to the ochre and tan wastes where, it seemed, we would have to go. Kvasir finished peeling the fruit and stuffed a section into his beard, where only he knew his mouth lurked.

'They want a Thing of it,' Finn said, stirring the dust with one finger. 'For the Hookeye matter.'

'Who wants a Thing of it?' I demanded sullenly. 'The ones who shared the secret with him?'

Kvasir frowned at that and Finn looked awkward.

'It is only right, after all,' he said. 'Short Eldgrim thinks so. And Thorstein Blaserk – he is one of our lot, Orm, and he thinks so.'

'Thorstein Blue Shirt is a droop-lipped coal-eater,' observed Kvasir and we all nodded at that. Not the sharpest seax in the sheath was Thorstein.

So if even he saw the right of it, argued Finn . . .

I sighed, for there was no going back from what happened. The Oathsworn were shattered. Those who weren't being eaten or gelded were lurching along with oarmates they could no longer trust because they had broken their oaths and were too nithing to admit it.

Inside, I was feeling a rising excitement that perhaps, at last, Odin had broken us and, tired of the affair, had gone off to annoy the new dead, or taunt bound Loki. All that remained was to survive.

Sighvat came over to us, having been in deep conversation with the priests. I had thought he was trying to find ways of avoiding his wyrd by using the Christ, for he had been braiding his eyebrows over the matter for long enough.

Now he loped over the sun-seared earth between the white buildings and squatted in the shade next to us. Finn offered him a grubby slice of fruit and he took it, which was an encouraging sign, for he had been listless over his feed of late.

'Martin the monk was here and gone, only four days ago,' Sighvat said. 'Starkad came with about fifteen men. Dudo remembers him well, says our Starkad was deeply troubled and cannot sleep at night for dreams. He left here two days ago heading south after Martin. No one knows where the monk is going, but even Dudo was impressed by our Martin and says he has the look of a very holy man, probably destined to be a hermit, or a pole-sitter.'

No one said anything, for the way south stretched like a Muspell nightmare and I knew we all thought the same thing: who would follow me down that road from here?

The sun wheeled on. Birds flared up, flashing black and white, from the complicated network of irrigation canals, hunting insects before night fell. The air seemed brittle and thin, oddness flickered at the edge of my vision, half-seen whorls of dust and half-heard voices from the empty spaces of the desert.

The Oathsworn came, lighting torches for the bigger insects to sizzle into, gathering silently and slowly like the grim dead round the pitfire Finn had made. It was chill on top of this hill, but the fire seemed excessive to me and I wondered what he thought he was going to cook on it. We were eating boiled vegetables and gritty flatbread and unlikely to get meat from these lean monks.

It turned out to be Kleggi and Hrolf the Dane carpenter who had something to say, urged forward by Kvasir to stand in front of me, twisting the ends of their belts like boys caught with tunics full of stolen apples.

'It is this way,' said Kleggi, apologetically. 'Halfred Hookeye was kin, you see, and we are thinking that compensation is in order.'

'Why?' I asked, sullen and unwilling to make the road smooth for them.

Hrolf looked at Kleggi and then at me. 'Well, he is surely dead, because you left him with the *Sarakenoi* to be hung in a cage and stoned, which is a straw death and so twice as bad.'

'He killed Brother John,' I pointed out, astonished at this. 'And a woman. And wanted to kill me.'

'Murder, as it was,' Finn pointed out, 'since it was dark and unannounced. Nor did he cover the body.'

There was general agreement over this, but Kleggi and Hrolf were still unwilling to let it go, arguing that there was no proof Hookeye had done it, even if I had chased him off the roof, where he might have been innocently taking the night air, or chasing the real culprit. And anyway, the woman was a whore, probably a thrall, and so did not count. They wanted to say that Brother John was only a Christ priest and so did not count either, but even they knew how the old Oathsworn had revered the priest and did not dare go that far.

Most of the others shifted uncomfortably at what they did say, which was a step too far for most – even Kvasir who, it was clear to me, was unhappy that Hookeye had been left with the *Sarakenoi*, though he seemed to think it was their fault and not mine.

'So you think it was not murder? If a thing looks like a duck, makes a noise like a duck and walks like a duck, chances are it is not a chicken,' I told them. 'Besides, he confessed it.'

I looked them over hard as I told them this and that he had planned to return to Balantes on Cyprus and what he had been promised for it all. 'Nor was he alone in this,' I ended and watched the alarm crawl over their faces.

I had an idea they were the ones Hookeye had dragged into his scheme, but thought it unlikely he had told them much about what he would do, so that these events were a nasty shock to them. Now they heard the ice they walked on creaking.

'This means that he and those he spoke with broke their

oath,' I pointed out and they now stood there feeling the lance-eyes of all the others, who sat behind them.

Then I shrugged. 'If he has kin who will not see it this way, I would rather have the matter settled, but we have no Law Speaker or summoning days or jury panel here, so it is a rough Thing at best. However, if you will allow Sighvat to justify on this, we can fix it all this night.'

Trapped, they could only nod, for Sighvat, everyone agreed later, was a deep-thinking choice, not only because he was clearly a full-cunning man, a *volva* of some strength, but his doom was on him, so there was no point in him grinding any new axes, as they say.

I had reasoned all this out and thought myself double-clever for it. As they say: if you want to hear the sound of gods laughing, all you need do is tell them your plans.

'Having reduced himself to a nithing by killing a Christ priest and breaking an Odin-oath,' Sighvat said, 'then Hookeye is worth no more than a new thrall, it seems to me. I set his death at twelve ounces of silver.'

Twelve ounces: the weight of a jarl torc. I wondered if there was more in that than there seemed, but faces were bland when I studied them.

The price was even better than I'd hoped, for Kleggi and Hrolf were too aware of what continued refusal would signify to the others – that they had been in the plot with Hookeye. I had no idea whether they were or not, but if it healed this widening breach I'd be happy. That way, I was thinking, we could all part, if not as friends, at least not as enemies.

'Just so,' added Sighvat. 'This must now be ratified and sanctioned by the gods, so a sacrifice must be made to Odin by Orm, who is godi here. I say a mule, which is as close to a good horse as we will get here.'

I bit my lip at that, for we needed the mule, but I nodded. So did Kleggi and Hrolf.

'Then we can all swear our Oath anew,' Sighvat said

cheerfully, 'in case Orm is right and Hookeye managed to induce others to tempt Odin's anger.'

Then I saw Short Eldgrim, Finn and Kvasir nodding and smiling and suddenly realised why the long firepit had been dug and what they had planned to cook on it.

They had conspired this on their own and it was cunning, right enough. As Finn said later, mild as summer, I would have done it myself had I not been grieving for Brother John. That made me ashamed, for I was not grieving – I was blinded by the lamb-leaping idea that, at last, the Oath was broken and I was free of them all.

Now I had to sit and smile while Finn winked at me and rubbed his hands with glee at how their little scheme had saved the day.

The mule was duly dragged out and I, as godi, said suitable dedication words. The monks were outraged and started to demand that we quit the place but a few growls and waved weapons sent them scurrying. Finn had the mule's head off, neat as snipping an ear of corn, and, in the red-glowed dark, with the stink of fresh blood in our nostrils, we all intoned the Odin-oath once again.

We swear to be brothers to each other, bone, blood and steel. On Gungnir, Odin's spear, we swear, may he curse us to the Nine Realms and beyond if we break this faith, one to another.

Every word was a great Roman nail driven into me.

Hedin Flayer butchered the beast and Finn started to cook it while the rest of us trooped over, in packs and singly, to the church. The torchlight flickered on the little coloured tiles that made a picture of some robed, winged man with a bright sword and one of those gold circles round his head and I marvelled at all that work for something you walked on.

We let Dudo intone the Christ words, while Brother John lay on a stone table, wrapped in linen strips so that he was just a bundle with candles at his head and feet. At the end of it, when Dudo made the cross-sign in the air and said, '*Pax vobiscum*,' I heard a sob and found the Goat Boy, wiping tears into a damp sleeve.

'He is in heaven now,' he hiccuped. I hoped so, but it was the *pax vobiscum* that had crashed the whole thing on me. Somehow, the thought of never hearing Brother John spout Latin made him more dead than before. Botolf laid one of his ham-hock hands on the boy's head and patted it with surprising gentleness.

What with that and the weight of the rune serpents – both round my jarl torc and down that cursed sabre – curling tight on my throat and twice as heavy, it seemed, to me, I could not choke much of the mule down. I was surprised to see others were as off their feed as I was; the death of Brother John had affected us all more than anyone had thought it would.

In the end, we passed platters of it to the monks and, for all they wrinkled their noses at the 'pagan rites', they were too drool-mouthed to turn down meat after a long diet of boiled vegetables. They had a long discussion about whether a mule was a horse or not and the smell made them vote in favour of not, so they fell on it as the insects whined and fluttered.

But Kvasir kept the mule's head and spent the night huddled with Short Eldgrim, who knew his runes, carving great serpent skeins of them on a spear-shaft, winding from spearhead to butt, squinting into the fading embers of the pitfire. I watched him uneasily until my eyes slowly drooped to sleep.

In a charcoal land split by a ribbon of water blacker than old iron, black as a blind man's eyes, I saw the dust of that place whirl like a jinni *of raven feathers and there was no noise to it. I stood while the river flowed without sound and, on the other side, gathering silent as a murder of crows, came dark figures with pale faces: all the dead I had known.*

There was Eyvind and Einar and Skapti Halftroll, still with his mouthful of spear. There was Pinleg and I felt a pang at that for we had always said that, because we did not actually see him die, perhaps he had not been hacked down, surrounded and outnumbered and berserking.

Then Hookeye appeared at my side, climbing into a boat which had not been there before. He looked at me, his head canted to one side so that I could see the great blue bruise round his neck. I knew – and didn't know how I knew – that he had shoved his head between the bars of his cage and broken his own neck.

'Did it hurt?' I asked.

'Not as much as it will,' he answered, sitting down in the boat. It moved off, spray rising from it and soaking my face, blinding me as if with tears, so that I could not be sure I saw someone limp to the front of that throng on the other side of the river and stare at me with a face I knew.

A pale face on a pale man with pale hair. And no runesword.

I woke to see the Goat Boy and Botolf standing over me, the boy with one hand still dripping from where he had sprinkled me with water.

'You were dreaming of Starkad,' Botolf growled. 'Still, makes a change from that Hild creature.'

I struggled up, feeling the sweat cool on me. Odin's balls, did everyone know my dreams? Did they form above my head, then, like reflections in a still pool?

'That would be interesting,' chuckled Kvasir when I grumbled this out, 'but the truth is simpler: dream silently.'

It was dark, with a moon too like one of those pale faces from the dream for my comfort and a great wheel of stars, so vast a frosting that it shrank everyone beneath it.

'If that should fall . . .' Kvasir mused, looking up from where he was wrapping the head of the mule in sacking. I knew what he meant; it was like crawling through a tunnel and feeling the weight of the rock press on you. After the dream, the whole world seemed skittish and hair-raising with strangeness.

The one camel and the last mule were packed, the latter uneasy with the smell of blood from its late partner, whose wrapped head Kvasir swung over his shoulder, though I thought at the time it would be poor eating. We filed down from the Church of Aaron's Tomb and, at the foot of the hill, the men assembled.

I looked at them, stepping back a little in my head, that ability Einar had prized so much.

They were built like huge oxen, with muscled shoulders and broad chests, giants in a land of small men. They had a wild tangle of bleached hair, beards that hung halfway to their chests and faces and forearms reddened by the sun. Their boots flapped, their tunics were ragged and almost all the same colour now, and their shields were scarred and battered – but they held axes and spears with sweat-oiled shafts and sharpened edges, their ring-coats were carefully rolled and stowed and helmets swung from tunic belts on firm leather fastenings.

They were grim as an edge, with eyes like pale stone in the blue dark before morning.

I knew what to say. I pointed south, beyond the dusty, moon-washed fields and the huddled town and told them how that was the way home. I reminded them of what Starkad had done to us and to our comrades. I reminded them of the reward for disposing of the dead-eating brigands and hinted that even more plunder might be had there. I reminded them we were here to fulfil our oath to our oarmates, even if most of us had never seen them.

After all that, into the silence of their indifference, I spoke with Einar's voice. 'We are sworn one to another,' I said.

'There are other *varjazi* and we have heard recent saga tales of the men from Wolin, whom they call Jomsvikings and who are bright with fame. They say these live all together in one house and no women are allowed.' I let that drift like an insect in the night air, then shrugged. 'Well, that's a fame I could do without myself. If they take turns on the ninth night to be used as a woman that's their own affair.'

There were heyas and some sharp intakes at this, for this was strong stuff; that particular insult, to accuse a man of behaving like a woman every ninth night, was so bad it was forbidden by law in Iceland and other parts. I had heard it from old Wryneck once, who had died at Atil's howe, and thanked him for it now.

'Our fame will be brighter still after this,' I said. 'In winter halls from now until Ragnarok, they will sing of Botolf's hair, Finn Horsehead and the mighty Godi, the gold-browed wit of Kleggi.'

'And Kvasir One Eye's shame pole,' Kvasir said into the pause I took. He unwrapped the mule head and stuck it on the spear with the runemarked shaft, then drove the whole thing into a cleft in the rocks, turning the head to point towards Jerusalem. I said nothing, for only something momentous would have forced Kvasir to interrupt his jarl in mid-speech.

'I set up this shame pole and turn this shame against Jorsaland and the guardian spirits who inhabit this land, so that they shall go astray, unable to detect or discover their dwellings, showering discord on this land until every person in it comes to the true gods of the Aesir and Vanir.'

He raised both hands and spread them. 'I say further and now that, though I was prime-signed a Christ-follower by Brother John, it was a mistake on my part, for if the Christ-god refuses even to save his own priests, what use is he to me? I say here that I am of the gods of the Aesir and the Vanir, and that I will honour the Disir, my hearth-gods, from now until my end and will not be turned from them again.

294

Now I promise that I owe them many sacrifice-deaths in payment for my lapse and shall fulfil my bargain.'

This was powerful stuff and, taken with all else, ran a stir through the rest of the Oathsworn, like a breeze ruffling dust. Shoulders went back, heads came up, hands went to hilts and, like a pack of wolves scenting blood, they growled in the backs of their throats.

They wanted riches, fame and the favour of the gods – as we all did – and I knew I had them with me then, though the way of it left me sickening. This jarl business was, in the end, like sucking silver – it seems as if something so prized would be sweeter, but it is always just a foul taste of metal in the mouth. The same taste as blood.

We moved off into the darkness and on to the unknown, Oathsworn still.

FIFTEEN

Out of dust thick as gruel the rabble army spilled down the road, all rags and weathered, wary looks, darting this way and that, looking for fruit or roots, flowers and dung chips. The flies followed them, heavy with blood.

They washed up to us, broke like water round a stone and then milled in a confusion of fear, backing out of swinging range. Those dull-eyed children who had the energy to try and beg from us were grabbed by their sunken-eyed mothers and dragged back. They had fled their homes and the peace they had known and their god, it seemed, had turned his back on them.

'About two hundred or so,' Gardi said, sitting down to inspect the ruin of his bare feet. He had run in from scouting and where he had stood was spotted with fresh blood.

'Where from?'

Gardi jerked his head in the general direction of south and shrugged. 'About half a day away, no more. It seems this Black-hearted One attacked and they fled.'

Two hundred villagers, about a third of them men. These brigands were growing in number and boldness if they could attack a village of that size and win.

A figure pushed through the throng, which was beginning

296

to sink down and wail like a pack of anxious cats. He walked with a staff, his robes were ragged and stained with dust, his beard matted and he stopped in front of us and looked at us with mournful olive eyes in a long, sunken-cheeked face. Then he bowed and greeted us in Arabic and looked surprised when a half-dozen sun-blasted foreigners with faces like slapped arses gave the formal response.

He gabbled out a fresh stream, of which I understood something about us finishing them off, for they had no weapons and it was the will of Allah. The Goat Boy nodded and smiled and soothed him with soft hand movements.

'He thinks we are part of the brigands, though he has hope since we have not yet fallen on them and killed them all,' said the Goat Boy. 'His name is Ahmad, which means Most Praiseworthy, and he is the leader of these people, who are all from the town of Tekoa, which lies under the Cliff of Ziz.'

'Talkative, isn't he?' growled Kvasir.

'Shitting himself,' noted Finn, then squinted at me. 'What do you think, Trader?'

What I thought was that we were short of water and food and far too far away from where the sun sparkled on water and gulls chuckled for the joy of it. What I thought was that two men had been left with the monks on Aaron's hill, with faces the colour of straw and their lives leaking in stinking dribbles down their legs. What I thought was that they were the first of many.

That's what I thought. What I said was to the Goat Boy, to ask this village elder about Martin and Starkad and any other sightings of wild *afrangi* men like us, not expecting anything from it.

The Goat Boy gabbled and then Ahmad gabbled and the Goat Boy grew excited and the gabbling got faster until, suddenly, the Goat Boy whirled to me, his thin, brown body trembling, his arms waving like leather thongs in a breeze.

'There is a Roman church in Ahmad's village, an old ruin,'

he told us. 'A Christ monk is there, not a Greek one, but one like those from the Church of Aaron. And there were other *afrangi* there, who stayed to fight the brigands, who were led by a man with scarlet hair. Ahmad fears the monk and the *afrangi* who stayed must be dead, for there were too many brigands for them to fight and their red-haired leader was a powerful warrior. He says the brigands are *jinn*-mad, but are afraid to stay long, for fear the garrison at En Gedi will find them.'

'Well,' said Finn at the end of all this. He ruffled dust from the Goat Boy's beaming head and, dropping his pack, began undoing leather thongs so that the mail shirt unrolled with a soft shink of sound. 'Time for battle-gear, eh, Trader?'

'Who is this red-haired man?' demanded Sighvat. 'He sounds like one of us.'

'It will be Inger,' Kvasir decided.

'Inger? Who's Inger?' asked Sighvat.

'Short,' Finn grunted, struggling into his mail. 'Bow-legged. From the Hedemark.'

'That was Sturla and he was more brown than red,' Kvasir answered scornfully. 'Inger was the big Slav we took on in Aldeigjuborg.'

'Fancied himself as a wrestler?' Botolf asked.

Kvasir nodded. 'That's the one. Had hair the colour of old blood. Almost as nice as yours was once, Ymir.'

'Pig-humper.' growled Botolf amiably. 'Why do you think it is him, then?'

Kvasir shrugged. 'He has the reddest hair I know, he was one of the crew so I know he is around this place and he was part Hallander and so cannot be trusted.'

Botolf scowled. 'I am from Halland.'

Kvasir spread his hands, smiling like a shark. 'Exactly. I give you two for one that Inger is the treacherous, camel-humping turd that old *Sarakenos* is speaking of.'

'Done,' declared Botolf. 'I have an ounce in hacksilver that says you are a mush-mouthed chicken-fucker.'

298

Finn looked at me and I met his flat, sea-grey gaze. He didn't have to say anything; if it was Inger, it meant he had turned his back on his oarmates, had broken the Oath.

While that hung overhead like the dust and wails made by the villagers, we slid into mail and leather and checked straps and argued and grumbled, falling into the old, familiar pattern that was our lives, the only one we had.

Gardi climbed back to his feet and I saw he was wearing new footwear, no more than a sole with thongs, which he had just bartered for. A villager gnawed a horse bone and contemplated his naked feet while Gardi, grinning, unshipped his bow and knuckled me a farewell before shoving through the crowd and flapping out on to the road. Hedin Flayer joined him and the pair of them loped off like hunting dogs.

Ahmad gabbled at the Goat Boy, who gabbled back.

'He asks if we are going to fight the brigands.'

'Tell him we are,' I said. 'And we will expect food and water as payment for returning his village to him and his people.'

'Fuck him and his people,' growled Thorstein Blaserk in passing, his underlip thrust out petulantly. 'We take what we need – that's what we do.'

'We have to come back this way once all is done,' I pointed out. 'Do you want to find them friendly or angry?'

He subsided, muttering, and Short Eldgrim chuckled savagely at him, the network of scars making his face look like tree bark.

'He's a rare one for the thinking is the Trader,' he noted. 'You, on the other hand, have nothing in that head worth protecting with a good helmet.'

I listened to them squabble and growl while I put on my own mail, grease-slick and cold even in that heat, checked straps and the edge of my sword and all the time wondered about the red-haired man and if it was indeed Inger the Slav, one of the ones we'd come to rescue.

If so, what was he doing leading the people who were holding his oarmates prisoner? Were the rest of them already dead and eaten? Was the monk really Martin? And who were the men who had defended the village? Valgard and the others, who had escaped, perhaps?

The questions circled and flocked like the birds whirling out of the fields as we moved on, leaving the wailing behind. Black and white, they swooped low and one circled and landed on a fence post as we came up to it, cocking its head and looking at us.

Sighvat stopped dead and the rest of us, anxious and wary, fell into fighting crouches, looking this way and that, shields up.

'What?' I hissed at him.

'Magpie,' he declared morosely.

'Odin's balls,' growled Kvasir. 'If it isn't bees it's birds. What now, Sighvat?'

I saw the Goat Boy cross himself and he caught me looking and clutched his Thor amulet. 'Very bad. Magpie is the only bird who did not wear mourning for Christ. One means sorrow.'

Finn spat with disgust. 'Now even the boy is at it.'

Sighvat shrugged. 'I don't know what the Christ-men believe, though it is interesting to hear of it. This is the bird of Hel, Loki's daughter, made like her face, half black ruin, half pale flesh. It is her *fylgia*, come to take those who can never make Valholl.'

The men made signs and the fear rose in them, like stink from a swamp.

'We are all doomed, then?' demanded a voice from the pack and I knew then what I had to do, the sour taste of jarl silver in my mouth as I spoke.

'No, not all,' I said. 'Only one is marked, by his own admission.'

Sighvat looked at me, closed his eyes briefly and then

nodded. I could almost hear Einar chuckle his appreciation as the others sighed out loud with relief.

'Move,' I said, harsh as winter, and they trotted on. Sighvat, with a twisted grin at me, followed after them and the magpie preened and fluttered across the road, tail bobbing. Botolf watched it, half turning as he jogged after the others.

'Will he die?'

The voice was a soft pipe of sound from the Goat Boy, looking up at me, fingering the Thor amulet.

> *'Cattle die and kinsmen die,*
> *Yourself will soon die,*
> *Only fair fame never fades . . .'*

I gave him the words as I remembered Einar saying them on that hill in Karelia another world ago, just before he had fought Starkad and given him his limp. Whether the Goat Boy understood any of it was another matter, but he nodded with a wisdom beyond his small years.

Then he tilted his head to one side and said: 'The villagers are starving. There isn't a goat or a chicken to be seen, so how will they feed us if they cannot feed themselves?'

He was clever and I remembered Einar looking at me as I supposed I looked at the Goat Boy now, one eyebrow up, squinting thoughtfully.

'Most men think in a straight line,' I said, hearing the echo of the words as Einar had said them to me in Birka before we burned it. 'They see only their own actions, like a single thread in the Norns' loom, knotted only when they thrust their life on others. They see through one set of eyes, hear through one set of ears, all their life. To look at things through someone else's eyes is a rare thing, which cannot be learned.'

He nodded as if he understood and I waited, while he frowned and thought. He had recovered well from his wound

301

and only winced now and then at the pain from his healing lung.

'You lied to them?' he suggested. 'You knew these villagers could not feed us, but you made the bargain anyway, to get our men to fight. You did the same with Sighvat because he says he will die anyway.'

I said nothing, for his saying it stripped it bare and revealed it for what it was and I was ashamed and trying not to show it. He just smiled and nodded happily, as if he had uncovered a great secret, then trotted off on legs like knotted thread.

I looked at Hel's bird and it looked back at me with its bright, unblinking eye, black as the Abyss Brother John had always warned of, until I broke the gaze and jogged after the others.

The town had the strangeness of a stone circle, which made you walk soft and speak hushed. No birds fluttered and sang here. There were no goats, dogs, cats or any living thing that walked and only the insects and soft plash of water from a fountain split the stillness.

When I arrived, past a crust of white, flat-roofed houses on the earth, under palms like feathers on sticks, the Oathsworn were moving, silent and awkward, wary as cats, poking in doorways and turning in half-circles.

The only sign of life was the insects, humming and thrumming from hanging basket to pot, from blood trail to gutted corpse. There were a lot of gutted corpses.

I went to the fountain, a simple affair of basin and spout, peeled off my helmet and dipped my hand in to cup cool water on my face. My other hand rested on soft moss and, beneath it, an outcrop of stone had a perfect, round dip in it. As I watched, a drip formed above and trembled and fell with a spiderweb splash, moving one more grain of stone.

Years it had been here, this fountain, this place, watching the likes of us come and go, flitting like moths through the world. I felt like a spark, whirling on the wind, and had to grip the edge of the mossy lip to keep from falling.

'Signs of a struggle, Trader,' growled Kvasir, his voice booming. 'Blood. Bodies stripped; some opened. Look here.'

He scooped water into his helmet, then I walked with him to where the fish-white corpse lay, sightless eyes filmed with dust. A fly crawled, bloated, from one nostril.

'See here. Gutted neatly and the liver removed.'

He did not have to say more. Raw liver was good eating when you were in a hurry and hungry and I had eaten it myself, warm from a fresh-killed deer.

I fought back to the now, blinking into his tilt-headed concern.

'The church?' I managed.

'Finn's off to find it. You should soak your head a bit, Trader. You look heat-felled to me.'

'Where are Gardi and the Flayer?' I asked, ignoring him.

Kvasir rubbed his bearded face with water, blowing it off his moustache. He shrugged. 'Scouting, I suppose. That's what they do.'

The Goat Boy came up on his thin legs, massaging his side where the lung punished him for his running, and announced that Finn had found the church and that I was to come at once. I went.

It was as typical a Roman church as any we had burned: solid walls, a dome, a stout door flung wide, narrow entrance, a floor of coloured tiles, some of them smashed away. It had long been abandoned to the spiders and rats but, as Finn said, stern as a whetstone, it had worshippers now and I had better see.

I slid in through the door, blinking at the sharp change from light to dark, heat to cool. The place seemed as empty as the inside of a bell, thick with shadows, and my feet crunched on the spill of little floor tiles from what had once been some holy picture from the Christ sagas.

Gradually, the shadows slid into the shapes of two people, one sitting cross-legged and facing me, the other kneeling, facing him, his head on the floor as if in obeisance, a magnificent rust-red cloak draped over his shoulders and back and a carpet of the same for him to kneel on. There was a dull droning, as if unseen priests muttered in the dark corners.

The cross-legged one looked up as I crunched forward, one slow, bewildered step after another. His spiderwebbed face was harsh as a sun-cracked plain, stretched tight over cheeks in which black, haunted eyes peered familiarly at me.

'Orm,' said Martin in a tired voice. 'Welcome to the house of God, idolatrous though it may be. Here also is one other you know: Starkad. Forgive him if he does not get up. I fear he is past that.'

I moved closer and sideways slightly. The kneeling figure was Starkad right enough, and he wasn't wearing a red cloak on his back, he was wearing his lungs; I hunkered down, tremble-legged and dry-mouthed at the sight of a real blood-eagling.

They had cut his ribs free from his backbone moved them forward so that they could lift his lungs out and drape them on his back, like wings. He was caked in old blood, knelt in a crusted-over pool of it and the priest-droning sound was every blood-gorging insect in the land enjoying a feast.

'I hid,' Martin said flatly. 'When Starkad and his men caught up with me here, I hid. They were looking for me – politely, so as not to annoy the locals – when they were attacked. Hundreds of them. Screams and death, young Orm.'

He shifted slightly and the insects rose in a puff, like smoke, then settled again.

'When I came out, everyone had gone – save him. So I sat with him and offered him the peace of God until he died.'

'He was . . . alive?'

'Oh yes,' Martin said calmly. 'He lived for a good hour, did Starkad, though he didn't say much. I sprinkled water on his lungs to keep them from drying out, but even that touch was pain to him.'

I wiped dry lips and batted insects away, trying to suck in the enormity of it. This was . . . vicious and meaningless. It had to have been done by a Norseman – no renegade Arab or Greek would even know of this – and such a thing was done to strike fear, or as a warning. Which meant this Red Head knew who we were and did not like it much. He was as dark-hearted as he was red-haired.

Martin looked at me across Starkad's corpse, hazed by the insect flutter. 'Starkad was a hound from Satan,' he declared harshly, 'who hunted me all the way from Birka to here – two long years of running, curse him. I found a place to hide here, but I could not take the Holy Lance in it. He had won, I thought – then this.' Savage as a fanged grin, he was trembling with the triumph of it. 'If you did not believe in God before, Orm, look on this and tremble. He smites His enemies with a terrible Hand.'

I blinked the stinging sweat from my eyes; the air was thick with death and blood and flies and I wanted out of that place. I looked at Starkad and saw only a man, stripped naked and blood-eagled. No helm, no mail, no holy spear.

And no rune-serpent sword.

Martin smiled. A fly crawled at the edges of it, but if he felt it at all he gave no sign. 'Indeed,' he said. 'The spear is gone. Your famous sword is gone. Whoever killed him has it now. We must find them—'

There were shouts from outside and the slither of feet. The Goat Boy hurled into the church, his voice echoing and shrill. 'Trader . . . men are coming. Hundreds of them. And a man with red hair.'

I looked at Martin as I rose. 'We do not need to find them, priest,' I answered. 'I would run back to your little hole. They have found us.'

By the time I had hauled out my sword and unshipped my

shield, they were on us, spilling over the dusty fields where they had been hiding, darting among the houses, a tide of screaming, rag-arsed men, desperate with outlaw fear and well armed.

The Goat Boy skittered back from the entrance as a figure hurled in, panting and grunting. I saw a mass of matted black hair and beard, a ragged, stained tunic and a long spear. His feet slapped and skidded on the ruined mosaic tiles and he crouched, snarling Greek curses and blinking in the transition from light to dark.

I stepped forward; he spotted the movement and hurled himself at me like a mad dog, the fat spearhead slamming hard enough into the shield to stagger me backwards. He tugged; it stuck. I shook the shield free and the weight of it falling dragged the spear down. While he was trying to put out a foot and pull it free, I spun round, up the shaft of the spear in a half-turn, my sword whirring in a killing arc.

The bite juddered me to my teeth and he shrieked and fell over as ribs crunched. When I spun the rest of the way round he was sprawled out, writhing like a landed fish and gasping and moaning. I saw he was barefoot, the soles black as ash.

The Goat Boy darted in then, a little knife flashing as he cut Black Hair's throat and looked up at me, panting with effort, teeth bared like a savage little dog. Another for his dead brother.

I took four steps to the narrow entrance, to where I could see the street outside: a madness of men, flashing axes and spears and swords, where figures slid and screamed like vengeful ghosts in the shrouding dust.

The flash of flame hair was beacon-bright in it and I saw Kvasir had won his bet. Inger came crashing through the wolf pack of his own ragged men, heavy with ringmail and carrying, I saw with a shock that puckered my arse, a byrnie-biter, a three-foot long, three-edged spear-blade, with only a foot of wooden shaft to wield it with. It was a vicious stabbing spear that could carve through three thicknesses of ringmail if a man of strength used it. And Inger fancied himself as a wrestler.

He saw me, knew me. His mouth opened in an O, framed by matted red beard, a roar of challenge I couldn't hear above the din and he hauled out a seax, slinging his shield on his back. Now with a weapon in either fist, he hurled himself at me from behind the mass of men, all hacking and cursing and slipping and dying in the dirt and blood of the street.

Botolf was trying to get to him, roaring spittle, but Inger dropped a shoulder and slammed him sideways, which staggered him off-balance, so that Sighvat thought he had a chance and leaped in, slashing.

I saw it framed neatly in the narrow doorway like an ikon painting. Inger took the blow on that byrnie-biter spear of his, half turned on the run and sliced with the seax, so that I saw the spray of blood arc out from Sighvat's throat as his head was flung back.

I shrieked then, howled like a dog as Sighvat vanished into the maw of the fighting, tumbling backwards.

Inger was still running as I headed for the narrow entrance, but he was faster and stronger and I was dead, for sure, against that vicious byrnie-biter spear. The thought of it melted my bowels and I skidded to a halt, frozen, shieldless. Doomed.

He knew it, was screeching his triumph as he pounded through the doorway, the byrnie-biter up like a cavalry lance, aimed right at my chest and looking like a ship's mast as it hurtled down on me.

Then the shield on his back slammed into the doorposts, too wide to pass.

Even as the strap fastening it to his back snapped his legs flew out from underneath him, dumping him hard on his arse. The byrnie-biter flew in the air, turning end over end, right over my head and clattered to the mosaic floor, bouncing and scattering blood-fat flies into the air.

I stepped forward, raised my sword and swung. Just the

last three or four inches caught him on the forehead, above the right eye, splitting his skull like a *rumman* fruit, even as he blinked away the dust and whirling stars and realised what had happened to him.

He had time, I was thinking afterwards, to see the edge of that wave-patterned blade come down on him, the new oil on it running with the colours of Bifrost. I did not care what he felt, only that he was dead. He wore Starkad's gilt-edged dagged mail, so I knew who had done the blood-eagling.

'I got your message,' I said to his splintered face, then stepped over him and out into the hazed dust and the bodies and dark shapes, looming like ships in fog. Steel flashed; there was the wet sound of edge on flesh.

Botolf loomed like the Cliff of Ziz, holding up one hand as he saw me drop into fighting stance. I relaxed; the fight seemed over.

'We would not be standing if they had not arrived,' panted Botolf, jerking his beard in the general direction of the Dead Sea. I looked up in time to see, through a swirl of red-gold dust, a magnificent figure on a white horse that was all arched neck and proud tail. One hand held a riding whip, the other peeled off a plumed helmet – the only armour he wore – to reveal a shaved head, and a young, sweat-streaked, bearded face, smiling with dazzling teeth.

He wore a white *jubba* over a long full tunic and the trader in me recognised satin from the Great City and that his cloak was hemmed with golden Arabic squiggle-writing and he smelled of aloes, even through the stink of shit and dust and death.

'I am the Bilal al-Jamīl ibn Nidal ibn Abdulaziz al-Miṣrī,' he declared. 'If you do not have a letter I have been told of, make your peace with whatever gods you worship.'

I fumbled like a sleepwalker in my pouch and fished out the governor's crumpled, stained letter, then bowed, which seemed only right in the circumstances. He plucked it, smoothed it, read it, then handed it back to me with a small smile, raised the whip in salute, wheeled that magnificent horse round and pranced off the way he had come.

'What the fuck was that?' demanded Finn, lumbering up, sword out and shield scarred with fresh marks.

'Our saviour,' I said, still bewildered.

'So be nice,' added Botolf with a grim chuckle. Finn laughed back, just as savagely, and ruffled the Goat Boy's dust-matted hair. His young laugh was high and shrill and ended on a rack of coughing. Everyone joined in the laughter, even me. The mad relief of survivors.

Then Kvasir stuck his one eye into it and brought us back to the now. 'Ten dead, six wounded,' he said to me, flat and grim as an altar stone. 'Sighvat is one of the dead. We found Gardi and Hedin Flayer out in the bean fields, gutted and stripped.'

Botolf let out a long, weary groan and Finn flung his head back and howled like a sick dog until Kvasir shook him out of it.

'It would have been more if those *Sarakenoi* had not come up,' he said, taking Finn's bowed head on one shoulder. 'Old Ahmad here says their leader is commander of the garrison at En Gedi.'

I saw the haunted-cheeked leader of the community hovering in the background and he inclined his head in a stiff little bow, then went off as his people flooded back in to reclaim their village.

Sighvat lay on his back with two grins, one a wistful affair from cheek to cheek, the second a lipless grimace from ear to ear. The blood had pooled to muddy slush under his head.

'That magpie had the right of it after all,' said Short Eldgrim morosely. 'His doom was on him.'

'At least that Inger was killed for it,' Botolf growled, coming out from the ruined church and hefting the byrnie-biter in one massive fist. 'We can put him at the feet of Sighvat and the others.'

Which we did, making a good boat-grave a little way outside the village, helped by the villagers themselves. We howed Sighvat up with Gardi and Hedin Flayer, Oski, Arnfinn, Thorstein Blue Shirt, Thord, Otkel, Karlsefni and Hrolf the Dane woodworker, all washed and laid out neat and clean, with their weapons and mail and Inger at their feet, as was right.

We added Starkad and what was left of his men, picking our way through the ravaged fields and irrigation ditches to find them.

Kleggi, black-browed at the death of Hrolf the woodworker, was sure these men would be dug up as soon as we had left, for we had buried them with their mail and swords, but Ahmad looked so astounded and shocked when the Goat Boy told him this that I believed they would rest quietly.

We slumped down in the lee of the ruined church for the night – no one wanted to go in it, for it still stank of blood and death, even after the weary villagers had collected the dead brigands and buried them somewhere else.

For all that they were going hungry themselves, Ahmad and the others did their best, bringing what had been scavenged from the fields, but it was poor stuff. However, that and our own meagre provisions allowed us to eat and we tried to ignore the cooking smells from the *Sarakenoi* camp nearby.

'We took a sore dunt today,' Kvasir said and everyone hunkered round the fire, morose as crows in the red glow, growled agreement.

'Sorer for some than others,' grumbled Botolf, two ounces of hacksilver lighter after his bet with Kvasir – but even Kvasir was not grinning at his win.

'There is worse to come,' I said and that fell on stony silence, so I closed my teeth on it and stared into the flames, brooding on what had happened to Martin – vanished during the fighting – and his holy spear and the serpent sabre. Neither had been found on Inger or anywhere nearby and the only prize taken was from Inger: he wore Starkad's jarl neckring as well as his dagged mail and so I had what Jarl Brand wanted. Whether it was worth all the dead was another matter.

Two *sarkenoi* loomed out of the dark, fully armed and armoured, to invite me to speak with Bilal al-Jamil ibn Nidal ibn Abdulaziz al-Miṣrī. I almost sprang up with the relief of getting away from the fire and the despair that hunkered at it, signalling the Goat Boy to come with me; on the way he told me that this Bilal al-Jamil's name meant 'Father of Salim, Bilal the beautiful, son of Nidal, son of Abdul the Magnificent, the Egyptian'.

'But you may call him Lord,' he added pointedly, when I grumbled about constantly filling my mouth with so much name.

This Bilal al-Jamil had a brilliant gold and white tent, blazing with lanterns and carpets and tables and cushions. He ushered me and the Goat Boy to sit and, aware of the dust and blood and worse that stained me, I almost refused.

'You are Orm,' said Bilal al-Jamil, in Greek and almost without accent. 'Al-Quds sent word you were pursuing brigands who have been a plague for some weeks now. At least we were able to dispatch some – about thirty in the end, including kinsman of yours, I understand.'

'No kinsman,' I answered hastily. 'From the north like us, but not a kinsman. We thought him a prisoner of these brigands, but it seems he was leading them.'

Bilal al-Jamil frowned while a silent, padding slave offered suitable *nabidh* in silver cups and sugared nuts, which the Goat Boy crammed until his cheeks bulged.

'Not the leader,' he said with a dismissive wave. 'A captain, not a general. Not the Dark Hearted One. That one has taken all the foodstuffs he has raided from here back to his lair with the bulk of his forces, some three hundred men.'

He made a grimace of distaste. 'They are eaters of their own dead,' he confided, as if it had been a mystery to me.

311

Then he smiled, that dazzling, open, happy smile you see on madmen and drunks 'But we will beard him in his lair, this Qualb al-Kuhl, you and I.'

I choked on my *nabidh*. I had thought the affair done with and now this. As far as I could see, this Amir had a small unit of horsemen, what the *sarakenoi* call a *saqa*, plus some foot soldiers. Together, he had a hundred men at best and there were a handful of Oathsworn left, no more. I wanted to tell him to go fuck a goat, that I would be lucky to get the Oathsworn to stay together until tomorrow, never mind march off to the gods knew where and take on too many enemies.

Instead, I wiped my lips and managed to ask where the Dark-Hearted One had his lair.

Bilal al-Jamil smiled happily. 'Masada,' he declared airily, 'not far from En Gedi.'

SIXTEEN

It was, as Finn said, Hel's privy and a suitable place for a baby-killer like old Herod. His grasp of the Christ Gospel sagas was loose, but he had the right of it for all that.

A flat-topped camel-dropping, the mountain of Masada was a dung-coloured horror slashed with the white of Old Roman camps and the great spillway of the ramp they had made to get to the top was a waterfall of scree.

The ramparts were crumbling, but it was a sheer cliff, high enough to be seen from En Gedi, so they didn't have to be in good repair. Even climbing that old ramp would take half an hour and, in the merciless sun and under a hail of arrows and rocks, it would be a bloody killing ground.

'Then we will attack at night,' declared al-Miṣrī. I wiped sweat from my face and looked at his troops: Bathili from Egypt, the blue-black Masmoudi, some local Bedu. Only the Masmoudi were footsoldiers, wearing robes and turbans, armed with shield, spear and bow, and they couldn't find their own pricks in daylight, never mind climb a mountain at night.

There was another way up, for I had asked that. It was called the Serpent Path – and there was Odin's hand, right there – round to the north and east of that great ship-prowed fortress-mountain. Bad enough in daylight, it was a narrow place where one good man could hold off hundreds. At night it would be easier to close with any guards, but treacherous to climb – worse still, the defenders had blocked off the last part of it, according to scouts al-Miṣrī had sent out.

'The only way up is climbing a cliff the height of ten men,' they had reported.

Finn looked at me and I looked at Kvasir and my heart shrank as my bowels twisted.

'Piece of piss to a boy who hunted gull eggs in Bjornshafen,' Finn growled cheerfully, clapping me on the back.

'If you see that child, let me know,' I answered bitterly. 'Perhaps you may like to ask him if he has ever done such a thing in the dark, on a strange cliff in a foreign country.'

But I already knew it had to be done, had suspected my wyrd was on me from the moment the Goat Boy had come to the quiet fire beside me in En Gedi and, with one simple question, ripped the veil from the face of truth.

En Gedi, when we came to it, was a Dead Sea jewel in that land of wasted folds of tan and salt-white hills, a place of feathered palms and – wonder of wonder – waterfalls. We simply stood, faces raised like dying plants to have the mirr on our cheeks and dreams of ships and sea and wrack-strewn strand circling in our heads like gulls.

We were honoured guests of al-Kunis, but settled in cool tents outside the towers and fortress built to protect the balsam fields, whose plants soaked the air with scent. Our host was too wise a commander to allow the likes of us inside his walls.

We lit fires and soft-footed thralls brought food in bowls – such food. Mutton and lamb and young doves, cooked in saffron and *limon* and coriander, with rosewater and *murri naqi*. We ate with fingers, stuffed ourselves and belched through greasy beards.

For two days we lived like this, repairing gear and sharpening edges, braiding ourselves back together like a frayed ship's line.

We swam in the waterfall pool, while the black-shawled women who came with jars for water shrieked at our nakedness and scuttled away, hiding their faces in their hands – and peeping, giggling, through their fingers. There were even women we could touch, sent by al-Miṣrī, whom everyone agreed was as fine a jarl as any open-handed Northman. If any had worked out that it was because he needed us to kill ourselves on his behalf, no one spoke it aloud.

On the night before we were to march to Masada, while the insects whirred and flicked round the fire, I sat and listened, half lost and yet – Einar would have been proud – feeling out the Oathsworn's mood.

Someone was playing a pipe, going through the notes rather than playing a tune. Finn was trying to make *scripilita* out of the local flatbread, arguing with Botolf about when he was going to get the rest of his money for being right about Inger. Kvasir and Hlenni, whom they called Brimill – Seal – because he slicked back his hair with scented oil, were playing 'tafl and arguing because it was really too dark to see.

And Kleggi was sitting with the Goat Boy near the prone figure of Short Eldgrim, who had taken a sword hilt to his temple and was one of the six wounded we had and the worst of them, too.

At first it had seemed just a blow to the head and he had got up from it, staggering and rubbing the blood away, grinning. He had hoiked up his belly an hour later and an hour after that had folded up like an old tent and stayed that way, his breathing so hard I could hear the snore of it from where I sat.

I would leave him here, together with Red Njal and Thorstein Cod Biter, the one with his thigh laid open, the other missing two toes off his left foot. I hoped they would keep Short Eldgrim alive for us to find on the way back. If we came back.

Then the Goat Boy loped over and plunked down beside me, greasy-grinned and chewing Finn's efforts. Goat Boy, as everyone agreed, was the perfect name for him, for he ate anything and everything and all the time.

'How is it?' I asked and he nodded, cheek bulging, frantically chewed and swallowed so he could speak.

'Good. Almost as good as the ones in Larnaca.'

'Ah, wait until you taste it in Miklagard,' I said to him and he grinned brightly and chewed for a moment.

Then he said: 'Will Short Eldgrim die?'

I shrugged. 'Odin knows. By that snoring, though, he is sleeping only. He will be awake by the time we get back.'

More chewing. Then he said: 'If he does die, can we wash him? Not the women?'

I blinked at that and agreed we could. His smile was relieved.

'Why?' I asked. 'I should think Short Eldgrim, even dead, would like to be washed by women.'

The Goat Boy wrinkled his nose. He knew what I spoke of, but girls were creatures who got in the way and women were worse, always wanting to comb his tangled hair.

'They laugh,' he said. 'I heard them when they washed the red-haired man.'

'Well,' I offered, only half listening, 'he was their enemy.' He had, I thought, probably sent them screaming and running and had maybe thrown at least one on her back.

The Goat Boy knew what I meant; he knew us well by now. He shook his head, swallowed the last of his *scripilita* and looked at me with those dark, cat-stare eyes. 'They laughed because he had no . . . no . . . nothing,' he said and grabbed his crotch. 'Does Short Eldgrim have a pisser, Trader?'

The night air was suddenly blade cold, enough to creep my flesh. 'What?'

He heard the change in my tone and grew uneasy at it, wary and silent.

'What about Inger?' I demanded, more fiercely than I had intended, and he blinked and shrank. I took a breath and smiled. Asked him again, gently.

316

'When they stripped him, he had no pisser. The women laughed and said he was no man. Had no balls, nor pizzle.'

I was dry-mouthed and silent, thoughts tumbling like water down the falls. No balls. No pisser. Cut.

And then the other thought that had nagged me crept in and grinned with wolf teeth, making a mockery of all, leaving me stunned and silent and lost.

I was still lost when we were standing under the dawn-smeared night at the top of the Serpent Path, rope coiled round me and the rest of the Oathsworn hunkered down, watching, pale and grim in the blue shadows.

'Easy as shinning up a mast,' growled Finn, mistaking my silence for worry about the climb. He looked even more worried when I didn't tell him to go fuck his mother or something like it, but he clapped a hand on my shoulder after a moment and both of us looked up at the wall of it, which seemed to tower into the dawn.

It wasn't the climb that bothered me but what I would find at the top. What I could not – dare not – tell the others, though they would have to know soon.

The first four feet went well enough and the night wind hissed puffs of dust from under my handholds, which was a sign I did not miss. This was no black sea-rock, slick with spray and gull shit, where terns screamed at you and puffins whirred out of their secret holes into your face – that I knew well enough. This was dry and crumbling and treacherous with dust.

I went on, fumbling in the half-dark for small folds and fissures that didn't even deserve the name of handhold, feeling the weight of the rope drag at me, feeling the wind bite with the chill of night, yet the sweat on me was slick as oil.

Halfway and I rested, looked down, saw only a black fleece of shadows. Out on the horizon, the smear of light was larger, brighter, and I knew I had little time left.

Two feet further up and my foot slipped, pulling loose my

left hand, the one with the fingers missing. I swung, held only by my right arm, dangling like a hanged man, feet flailing. I would have screamed if I hadn't bitten my lips until they bled; the sinews in my arm were doing all the shrieking for me anyway.

I heard my grunts, loud in my ear. My feet kicked rocks loose and, from below, I heard a faint hiss that might have been curse or query.

Panting, I curled at the waist, as far as the rope would let me, scrabbled, caught one foot, lost it, caught it again. Swung against the rock, slapped my ruined hand back on rock and clawed into a niche.

Sagging a little, I felt the sweat run in my eyes and tasted salt in my mouth. My arms and thighs and calves all creaked with pain, trembling against the rock.

I reached up, my hand fluttering like a lost moth, found another handhold, clamped fingers on it and brought a foot up, hearing the leather seaboots rasp, knowing they would be finally wrecked, shredded on these rocks. Strange what bothers you at the oddest times.

The top came as a surprise and I heaved myself over the last of it, panting and gasping. The Serpent Path was lost in darkness away to my left and there were no ramparts here. The bulk of Herod's tiered palace slouched to my right and the wind hissed and moaned over the plateau, studded with strange shadows and the red flowers of fires. Somewhere, goats bleated.

I moved up slowly, trying hard to listen and not scrabble like a mad chicken on the rock and loose scree. There was a nub of stone, the last of a fat pillar that had once held up a shaded walkway. Now it took a loop of the rope and the rest of it slithered over the edge in a rustle of stones and dust.

I waited, crouched and watching, while the milk-smear on the horizon grew wider and more honey-stained and the wind mumbled through the ruins like a hot breath. Yet I shivered.

318

Kvasir was first up, panting and grunting, hand over hand. I helped him over and he collapsed, breathing like a fighting bull. 'Odin's. Arse. Tough . . .'

Finn swarmed up as if he were climbing the rigging of a large mast. Barely out of breath, he handed me my shield and sword, which he had brought up with his own, and his grin was feral-yellow.

'Well done, Trader. You are the one for the climbing, right enough.'

They came up one by one, rasping with hard breathing, clinking and clanking in mail and shields and weapons. I winced at every noise, never considering the feat of it until afterwards. Even with a rope that had been a hard climb for men in mail – and Botolf brought my own up, wrapped neatly and slung over one shoulder.

Last up was the Goat Boy, struggling, with the slight strength of his knot-muscled arms almost gone, and my belly was in the back of my throat – until I saw him fastened to Botolf by tunic belts.

Botolf, grinning, got to the top, reached down and plucked the Goat Boy up as if he were picking an ear of wheat. I swallowed drily, for I had not wanted the Goat Boy on this one but that had got me sideways looks from everyone else, since he had been in every other hard place with us.

I measured the distance to the nearest building, which was a grand affair, once two storeys, now partially collapsed into ruins. It was a long run across the open plateau and I didn't like the look of it much . . . The Arabs were set to attack when the sun was up, which meant we were here for too long a time, squatting like stupid ewes in fast-vanishing shadows.

'What do you reckon, Trader? Make a run for it?' breathed Finn in my ear.

Truth was, I didn't know. Either way seemed to mean discovery and even if most of the brigands were close round those fires, someone would go for a piss and the Serpent Path

319

Gate was a hawk and spit away. There was almost certainly a guard on that who could not fail to see us as the light grew and I could not rely on him being as blind as he clearly was deaf and stupid.

As if he heard me thinking, there was a query from the darkness, neither Greek nor Arab, but West Norse.

We froze. The query came again, harsher this time, and I heard the shink-chink sound, saw the spark of flint and steel as the guard tried to light a torch. Folk looked at each other, bewildered eyes white in the dark, and Finn growled. He peeled the slavered Roman nail from his mouth, so that I knew he was about to reply – but then the Goat Boy bleated.

It was as perfect a bleat as any pathetic goat I had heard and he did it twice more. I stilled Finn with a hand on his arm, felt rather than saw his unease in the darkness. A Norseman on guard? Not friend, but foe . . .

There was a muttered curse of annoyance and the guard moved back. Silently, Botolf ruffled the Goat Boy's hair and his grin was white in the darkness.

I looked at the sky, trying to judge how much time we had, but could make no sense of it. The whole horizon was an ugly yellow and the wind had died to nothing.

Odin is the All-Father, the Great God. He is a shapechanger when he is seen at all, but if you want to feel the presence of One Eye, go into a lonely place and wait and listen. I have done it and felt the passing of him through a forest, in the thousands of mysterious sounds and breaths, in the soft sough of wind that blows through the leaves and branches, in the storm-wind that racks trees and shows where the All-Father passes on the Wild Hunt.

But most of all, you'll feel him in the strange and awful stillness that settles sometimes on sea and hill and wood.

It is easy to feel One Eye in a land of mirrored fjords, tumbling ice water, bare, granite cliffs and the hot, heavy pine forests of summer – but that night, on the bare waste of a flattened mountain in Serkland, we all felt One Eye descend in a silence that seemed to suck the air.

Eyes gleamed, looking one to the other, aware in the hackles and creeping of arm flesh that something was happening. Something smacked my bare arm and I jumped, touched it, felt wetness and grit.

Another time, another place. On a rock stairway outside a Hun chief's tomb near Kiev I had been splashed by gritty water from a sky yellow as a wolf's eye.

'Dengizik,' I said in Finn's ear and saw his wide-eyed look, saw him remember the Hun chief's name and what had happened there, even as the wind rushed in, flattening the distant flower-fires to the ground.

'Run.'

We sprinted as the world turned to darkness.

The sandstorm had roared in under cover of night from the parched Nabatean hills bloated with heat from the wastes of Zin, flexing muscles all the way from Aqaba.

It seared everything in its path in the long Wadi Araba, shrieking with dancing dust *jinn* and blurted itself into the Valley of Salt. Then it crushed its massive shoulders between the rusted stones of the Moab and the folds of the Judean hills round the Dead Sea, so that it reared up like a screaming stallion and fell on Masada with hooves of wind and scouring dust.

It sucked the air from lungs, shoving us with huge blows this way and that and howled like Fenris released, while the sun was stillborn and dawn never came.

We staggered like drunks, clung to each other, were bowled over as the wind caught shields like sails. Scrabbling on all fours like dogs, we clawed to the shelter of the ruined building, scurrying ratlike into the gaping holes in the back walls, hurling down behind anything that was shelter. Anything to get away from that sand-studded wind that drew blood like a lash.

There was light and heat – lanterns and a fire, throwing

long, strange shadows on the men round it, who rose up as we crashed in, panting and gasping, stumbling over the rubble litter.

They gabbled in surprise and I heard Greek and Arabic, but all they heard were grunts and hissing steel and it was only when their worst nightmare snarled down on them that they realised these men who had staggered in were not friends.

It was a struggle as short and vicious as most of them were. In the end, eight men lay dead and no one cared how loudly they screamed, for no sound would be heard above the vengeful shrieking wind outside. Only one had actually managed to get a hand on the hilt of a weapon and that was as he died.

Slack-jawed and heaving, the Oathsworn sank down, heads drooping. I looked round, kicking scattered embers back to the fire. We were in one large room with a huge square of stone in it – an altar, I recognised, to the Roman Christ.

There was one door in and out and it was still shut, though it fluttered and battered against its lintel as the wind hammered it. Sand filtered in from the ruined room we had just come from and the fire guttered, making huge shadows dance strangely on the walls.

'Thor's wind,' muttered Kvasir, then grinned. 'Our Orm weaves his own wyrd, it seems. Perhaps we have found favour with old One Eye at last and he called in a marker with the Thunderer for us.'

Men made warding signs and held amulets to their own gods for protection, for on this night, when it seemed the membrane between worlds was thinner than before, it was not wise to talk of such things.

It was widely known that a man's wyrd – his Norn-weaving – was not set, but could be unravelled. Einar had believed it and, for a while, it seemed he had succeeded, but boasting of it tempted those three sisters to weave something worse – especially Skuld, mistress of That Which Might Be.

Anyway, I had my own thoughts on the matter. Odin, unless

I had misjudged One Eye as a kindly old uncle, had made his purpose clear to me, if not everyone else. I knew what we yet had to face and could not bring myself to tell the others.

Now that we were squatted in this blood-reeked place, looking around at the shadows and the strangeness, men licked their lips and wondered at it.

'The Great City's men made the Christ altar, but before that this was where this Herod kept his thralls,' Finn told them knowingly. 'He was King of the Jews.'

'And he stayed here?' demanded Hlenni Brimill. 'Anyway, I thought the Christ was King of the Jews.'

Finn shrugged. 'Maybe this was another one. Anyway, nine hundred Jewish warriors were once besieged here by the Old Romans, who built that ramp to get to them.'

There was silence, for we had all seen and marvelled at the ramp. As Finn said, it was as if Bagnose had leaned his neb against the mountain, but there were few left who remembered old Geir Bagnose, so his joke fell flat.

'Did they win?' asked Botolf.

'Who?'

'The Old Romans. Did they beat the Jewish warriors?'

'Of course,' answered Finn, but Kvasir hawked and spat.

'No warriors died here,' he growled. 'That Syrian whore in En Gedi, the one with the wen, told me of this place when she learned that was where we were going. When the Old Romans attacked they discovered no one to fight. All the Jews had killed themselves: men, women and children.'

There was a deeper silence and men tried not to look over their shoulders at the fetches haunting this place.

I climbed into my mail and we waited, watching through the hole in the back wall as the storm thrashed and the dust whirled in and flared like embers in the fire.

It was as dark as I remembered it, gleaming still with those great, age-blackened piles of silver and the throne he sat

323

*on was massive. The shackles that had once held Ildico to
it dangled from one arm, but of her bones – or Hild – there
was no sign.*

*There was only Einar, sitting on Atil's throne as I had
first seen him sitting in Gudleif's at Bjornshafen, bulked by
a great fur-collared cloak, one hand resting on the hilt of
a straight-bladed sword, turning it gently on its point, the
other stroking his moustaches.*

*Framed by the crow wings of his hair, his face was how
I remembered it last in this howe, milk-pale, with yellow-
cream cheeks and eyes so sunk they had disappeared into
black pits. I had shoved my sword through him at the last,
a bloodprice blow for his murder of my father.*

*'Will you tell them what you know – or let them find
out?'*

And when my silence was the answer, he lowered it again.

*'Now you know the price of a rune serpent,' he whis-
pered and the light caught the blade of that turning sword,
flash on flash on flash, blinding me . . .*

The sun was up, shining in my eyes and Finn was standing
over me, kicking my tattered boots to wake me. Stiff from
sleeping in a coat of iron rings, I stumbled upright into the
day and we waited, watching the sun arrive through the hole
in the back wall.

When the first warmth of it touched my face, spearing into
the room and spilling us all with gold, I turned to see the last
of the Oathsworn, waiting and silent, faces hard as grind-
stones.

Then I knew, felt the Other-rush of it, the surety of it, and
I told them that we had been tested and that those who stood
here, in this room, were those Odin had deemed fit to have
his Oath in their hearts and on their lips. We were Odinsmenn
and the way home was one last battle. Einar's curse was lifted.

Kvasir gave a hoom in the back of his throat and I waited,

half hoping one of them would have enough clever to work out the part I had not told them. For a moment I thought Kvasir had, but then he shrugged. Finn's grin was tight and harsh and he spoke through his teeth when he turned to the rest of them.

'Hewers of Men, Feeders of Eagles: pray to Odin and take up your shield and weapons, for we are once more brothers of the blade and this will be a hard dunt of a day, I am thinking.'

Then Botolf, looking round, asked: 'Where is the Goat Boy?'

And al-Miṣrī sounded his horns and attacked up the ramp.

We were supposed to hold them for twenty minutes, no more. We fought them alone for twice that and, in the end, were in a shrinking ring of shields and dog-panting terror and bloody weapons, where those who had bare feet were better balanced than those sliding on the bloody slush in what was left of their boots.

There was a saga tale for a good skald in it, but like so many it went unsung. I have since tried to tell it, without success.

I can remember only splinters of it, like images in the shards from a broken mirror-glass – Kleggi, stumbling in circles, complaining that he had lost his shield, the blood arcing from the stump of his arm. The Arab falling back from me, his teeth flying from his mouth like the little tiles of a shattered mosaic.

And Finn, hacking and slashing and slamming shields until, suddenly, he stopped, gaping at the man he was about to kill, who snarled back at him and swung.

Finn lost a hank of hair and his ear because of his astonished hesitation, shrieked with the pain of that and the horror of the truth he had just discovered and hacked lumps off the man's shield until, finally, one carved through bone and ringmail and a second stroke took his enemy in the hedgehog of his face.

Haf Hroaldsson, whom we called Ordigskeggi, Bristle Beard, was dead. One of the Oathsworn we had come to rescue.

By the time the Masmoudi piled up over the lip of the ramp, scattering the brigands and hunting them down, we were on our knees in the bloody slush, drooling, bleeding, every breath a sob. It was as if I walked underwater then; I could see the pearl-string of bubbles stream from my mouth and feel my lungs burn with bad air. The ground and the sky lurched, changed places . . .

In the whole vault of the sky, only two crows moved, rich, black crosses on a translucent blue that was heavy with wavering heat, so that it seemed I lay on the bed of the ocean, looking up at the surface of the water.

Widdershins, the crows circled lazily. All crows are left-handed, according to Sighvat. Unless they were ravens. I thought they might be ravens, a sign from Odin.

I was on my back . . . how did that happen?

'Trader?'

The sky blotted out, a shape loomed, a silhouette with black streamers of hair in a wind that hissed over the plateau. For a moment, just a heart-ending moment, I thought of Hild crawling over me in the dark, hissing her warnings. But she was long gone, buried in Atil's howe.

'Trader, are you hurt? Have some water.'

The shape shrank, wavered, then rematerialised in front of me. A waterskin was shoved at me and I saw it was Kvasir who held it, grinning. He had lost his patch and the dead-white of his eye was like a pearl in the smeared blood of his face. Raw skin flapped loose on his bloody forehead and the iron stink of death was everywhere. Flies growled in search of it.

'You dropped like a felled tree, Trader, too much heat,' Kvasir said. 'But the fight is out of them now and we have water at last. Here, drink.'

It was warm and brackish, but the rush of it in my mouth

was mead. I struggled up. There were bodies nearby, already thick with flies, and I saw Hlenni Brimill happily fumbling corpses for the purses they carried.

'Eighteen of ours dead, Trader,' Kvasir said, sucking water from the wineskin. 'But those outlaw bastards are cut to pieces and fled. There.'

He pointed across the sere brown and ochre plain, past the rubbled buildings, into the water-waving heat that made Herod's hanging palace shiver. Figures, trembling and eldritch long in the haze, moved purposefully back and forth.

Of course. The last refuge, three huge steps of buildings down the prow of Masada, this fetch-haunted, Muspell-hot, gods-cursed mountain in the middle of a burning waste.

I struggled to my feet and leaned on Kvasir. Under the cotton robes we had put on, his ringmail seared my palm and I knew my own was just as hot. My legs shook.

'The Goat Boy?'

He shook his head. 'No sign, Trader. They must all be in that fancy hov.'

I shook my head to try to clear it, which simply made the pain ring it like a bell. I staggered a little and Kvasir steadied me, thrusting the waterskin into my hands.

'Drink some more. Not too much, though.'

I drank, felt better, grinned at him. 'No blood in it, I hope.'

He gave a lopsided, wry grin. 'Only Christ-followers care,' he answered, remembering Radoslav's story.

Blood in the water. Odin's cunning plan to get us to this place.

The way to the truth of it all was red-dyed in the blood of those we had come to save, most of them killed by a weeping, slashing Finn. The others in the band were not much better; all of them knew now what I had known before – our oath-brothers were the leaders of the brigands, the gelded eaters of the dead.

I came across Geirmund Solmundarson, who had helped

327

me back to have my ankle seen to after I had done it in chasing Vigfus Quite the Dandy across Novgorod roofs for Einar. I found him bleeding from half-a-dozen wounds and too dying even to speak.

Then there was Thrain, whom we'd called Fjorsvafnir, Life Taker, after he had won a contest for killing more lice than anyone else, running a brand down the seams of his clothes and popping them in the flame. Now the bubbles of his life broke pink and frothing on his lips.

And Sigurd Heppni, which was a bad joke on him, for he was not Sigurd Lucky at all. From his sprawled corpse I took a familiar stick: Martin's holy spear.

Them and others, all dead, all the ones we had come to rescue.

The last stood in the ruins of Herod's topmost tier, backed up to the balcony, the rune-serpent sword a savage grin in one fist, the Goat Boy struggling in the other. Finn, snarling and bleeding, the Godi dripping blood in fat splats of sound, faced him on one side; Botolf, the great byrnie-biter in his massive fist, glared at him on the other.

Not again. There was a flash of another time, another place, the bird-heart tic of the Goat Boy's throat under a blade, reddened in the torchlight and gripped in Svala's hand.

Like her, Valgard Skafhogg was not ready to give up. Skafhogg, the chippie. The closest Greeks could get to it was *pelekanos*, of course. And he was black-hearted now, for sure.

'Give up the boy,' Finn was yelling, trembling on the edge of a mad rush, like mead in an overfull horn. 'Give it up, Valgard, you nithing . . .'

'I may be cut,' Valgard said, 'but I still have enough balls for this, Horsearse.'

'We came for you,' howled Finn, almost weeping now. 'We came all the way from Miklagard for you. You were Oathsworn . . .'

'Oathsworn no more,' Valgard said with a shake of his

head. 'The first cut ended us all as men, the second ended us as Odinsmenn. He abandoned us – Einar's doom, right enough. What we have done since to survive would not get us a straight look from the ruined half of Hel's face.'

His voice was quiet and calm and more chilling than if he had snarled and slavered like a rabid wolf. He was burned dark as a Masmoudi, wore robes and the remains of a turban, was leached of fat and moisture, honed down to bone and desperation. Even his reason was thin, I saw, just as he spotted me.

'Well, well, young Baldur is here.'

It was a voice shorn of everything save weariness, but his eyes blazed when he met mine and he twitched the sabre meaningfully; a shaft of light caught the sinuous runes snaking down the blade.

'Starkad said this blade was yours once, boy,' he said. 'A rune blade. He said you got it from Atil's tomb.'

Starkad had said a lot, I was thinking, as you do when someone is carving your ribs from your backbone and you are looking for a reason for him to stop. Valgard blinked when I said all this to him, so I knew it was so exactly what had happened that he was wondering if I had been there, seidr-hovering and invisible, to witness it.

'I took it from him,' he replied, challenging, yet wary and uncertain, trying to convince himself that if I had any seidr-magic powers, the sword gave them to me – and now he had it. His fear-sodden hand worked fingers on the hilt, flexing and loosing; his sweat slid into the grooves that told where unimaginable riches lay.

'Now I will take it from you,' I told him mildly, aware of Botolf sidling further round, trying to work into Valgard's blind spot. The Goat Boy was still, his big round eyes fixed on me, his right hand clutching the Thor amulet round his neck. 'You have put your jarl to a deal of trouble and expense, Valgard Skafhogg, but I kept my Oath.'

'What?'

'I came for you. I am jarl of the Oathsworn, after all.'

He smiled then, one as warped as a dry bucket. I jerked my chin at the Goat Boy. 'What now, Valgard? Your men are fled and there is a Saracen jarl who wants to ram a stake up your arse.' I hoped I sounded smooth and easy, for the terror of the moment howled in me.

'And you will save me?'

'I am your jarl.'

His mouth twisted in a spasm of rawness and he could barely get the words out. 'No jarl. Of mine. You nithing boy.' His face was a bruise of madness and his eyes, sunk like wells of despair, now held only the faintest gleam, but his voice was harsh and edge-sharp. 'We have paid the price,' he went on. 'Us. The ones Einar left behind like a sacrifice.'

'Everyone paid the price for Einar,' I countered. 'But that is over. Odin smiles.'

I heard a crow-rasp laugh, rheum-thick and bitter with loss. 'Odin smiles? Are you godi also? If so, you know One Eye smiles only when the stink of sacrifice hits his nose.'

I knew that, of course. I had known it and had not shared it with the others before we fought. All the ones who had broken their Oath so badly had to die – and he the last of them. Finn knew it now and looked frantically from me to him and back.

I shrugged as languidly as I could manage and rubbed my beard, a gesture I had picked up from Rurik, shipmaster of the Oathsworn before he had died at Sarkel. I know Skafhogg saw it, with a flicker of recognition. They had been friends, the shipmaster and the shipwright, but I saw that things had gone past all friendships.

Botolf shifted and Valgard moved the sabre edge closer to the Goat Boy's neck and said: 'One more move, Giant Ymir, and I will have the head off this boy. I want to hear blades hitting the stones.'

330

Finn slumped wearily and flung the Godi down with a clang of disgust. I saw him look at Valgard and remember that they had been oarmates long before I had joined the *Elk*. I saw, too, that Valgard did not have the regard for it that Finn had and that Finn knew it, was drained by it so that he had to hunker down, all strength to stand gone.

Botolf's byrnie-biter clattered down and Valgard looked at me.

I dropped my sword and he eased a little, though stayed clenched as a curl on his little hostage. The Goat Boy's face was pale, but his eyes were steady and I cringed for him. To be like this once for our sake was bad enough, but twice . . . I vowed then that, if Odin spared him, the boy would never be put at risk again.

'It was a surprise when this little one ran in out of the storm,' Valgard said, caressing the Goat Boy's cheek with fingers from the hand that gripped him close. 'I knew then there were problems – and that he was an answer to them.'

'Give him up,' Finn managed to wrench out hoarsely.

Valgard said nothing and his eyes scoured Finn's face with scorn. He would not give up: not he who had done what he did to survive, who could chew on another man's warm liver, or order a blood-eagling on his hated enemy.

Botolf shifted. He caught my eye. And winked.

My mouth went dry and I forced my tongue from the roof of it. I knew I had to keep Valgard's fluttering madness focused on me.

'What will you do with the boy?' I asked, offering extravagant promises to Odin to keep my voice from trembling.

'Hold him close until promises are given and sherbet drunk,' he said and laughed. 'Oaths sworn, too, maybe.'

He knew what he was about, for sure. If he drank sherbet from Bilal al-Jamil, it meant he had been accepted as a guest and could not then be killed. If he got us to swear an Odin-oath for the same, he would actually Loki his way out of this.

331

But the Arab would offer no chilled cup in return for the life of a skinny Greek boy – Odin would make sure of that, for he wanted the life of Valgard the oath-breaker and not even the Norns would deny him. Not even Allah.

Botolf leaned and shifted slightly and I saw Valgard's head start to turn towards him, knew Botolf was poised for a desperate leap. Odin settled gold on my brow.

'You will never manage it, Skafhogg,' I said scornfully. 'You think this scrawny-arsed boy is a good exchange for letting you escape? Do what you will with him, Trimmer. But eat him quick, for it will be the last meal you have.'

The howl from Valgard had everything in it, from rage to shame and back. He flung back his head and wolfed it all out to the sky – and Botolf hurled himself forward.

I knew he would never make it. Valgard snarled and cut viciously. That snaking curve of blade should have snicked Botolf's great, stupid head clean off his shoulders; he knew it, too, and was roaring himself into Valholl.

It was then that the Goat Boy took his hand from his Thor amulet and elbowed Valgard in the groin. Afterwards, he said he had felt it hit just where he had thought it would after having seen Inger's naked body being washed: on the length of reed that allowed Valgard to piss.

It drove up into the soft depth of him, into the bladder. Valgard doubled up and screamed and the cut took Botolf in the left leg, a handsbreadth below the knee. The limb flew off in a lazy curve, slathering blood everywhere, and, even as he toppled like a mast-pine, Botolf's right hand came up and took Valgard by the throat, shook him left, then right, like a dog with a rat. Then he fell, howling and pushing Valgard backwards.

There was a sharp scream as Valgard hit the balcony and it crumbled like old bread. He went over like a flipped louse, flailing his limbs and with a short bark of sound that could have been laugh or curse, drowned out in the sound of the

332

rune-serpent blade scoring a shrill, grating screech all the way down the support pillar until he hit the cracked paving far below with a wet slap.

Finn hurled himself at Botolf as the giant sprawled, the pair of them almost spilling over the edge of the balcony. The Goat Boy hurled himself at me and I knelt and swept him up; the pair of us were trembling and I was closer to sobbing than he was.

'I was not afraid this time either, Trader,' he said, shaking so hard he could hardly get the lie between his teeth for chatter.

I couldn't reply for holding him and watching Finn drag Botolf back from the edge and strap his tunic belt round the bloody ruin of his leg.

Eventually, slick with the slime of it, he looked up as the blood trickled to a close. He grinned through the red mask of his face as Botolf groaned and told him to get his shoe, just before his eyes rolled into his head and he passed out.

Finn chuckled, blood outlining his teeth. 'The big idiot will live – but he'll be shorter by a foot after this.'

EPILOGUE

The most prized possession of a sea-raider isn't a good blade, or fine mail, or rings of silver. It's a sea-chest, slightly longer than a sword, a hand-span wide and deep as your arm up to the elbow.

It holds everything you have of worth and you should be able to leave everything that isn't in it behind you with merely a shrug of regret. It is your seat at an oar, your pillow when wrapped in a cloak, your first waking thought and your last dream of the night, for in it is your life.

Mine still has some of the silver coins we got from the *Sarakenoi*, who were true to their word and not only handed out fat bags of the stuff, but took us to the coast, where we sent word to Gizur. He sailed down to us in the *Elk* with a crew lent by Jarl Brand, for there were barely enough Oathsworn left by then to move it under oars when we had it to ourselves and all had hurts of some kind. Bar me, of course, and Kvasir fixed me with his one good eye and smiled, shaking his head at my foolishness for believing the rune serpent on that sabre held such powers.

The sabre. I climbed down and prised it from Skafhogg's dead grip and could not help but examine the blade, having heard it shriek like triumph down the stone as he fell. There was no mark on it. Even the sunlight stepped carefully along the gleaming length of it and the strange warped and twisted reflection of my own face slid down the long serpent of runes, curling and crooning their secret to the steel.

This had cost us pain and death. This sensuous curve, grinning like the smile on a skull, had led us to an Odin-forge of a country, where the One-eyed God hammered and folded us into what he desired, casting aside the dross.

And for what? To be given the gift of all the silver in the world? To be worthy of this rune-serpent blade? I wrapped it in a tattered Arab serk and snugged it up in my sea-chest, cheek by jowl with the equally cursed spear which had helped make it, both buried under a spare tunic, breeks and a folded cloak. Yet I could feel the seidr heat of them all the time, feel the scratches I had carved on the hilt, the secret to Atil's silver. After all that had happened, I still had no idea of Odin's purpose, only what it had cost.

In that chest also was a withered leaf, the one I took from Arnor's mouth after the battle by the mulberry trees. It reminded me of how we had lost him and Vlasios, the Goat Boy's brother, among others, and of the deaths I could have prevented, but did not. As Jarl Brand said, what were Roman blood-feuds to us? Still, I tasted the jarl-torc silver of it for a long time, that blood-metal tang that makes you want to spit.

It also held Starkad's silver torc until I handed it to Brand when we reached him, just as he was stowing a heap of dirhams for giving up Antioch and sailing for the Dark Sea, as he had planned. Svala was gone, sold to an Arab, and I would have been angry save for the relief – and the shame for feeling that. So we joined his ships as chosen men, as he had promised.

My sea-chest also held a short length of ship's rope from the *Fjord Elk*, tight-wrapped and stitched with cord, thickened with pine tar to stop it fraying. I have it still.

When I open the chest for a bone needle, or dry socks, the

335

smell of it brings back the sea and the *Elk* and all the Oathsworn of that time: the Goat Boy, serious, pale and thin, with limbs like knotted thread and the great white-mauve scar on his side; Finn's savage grin; Botolf, raving and locked in wound-fever while his leg-stump wept; Short Eldgrim, who woke up to find he could not remember anything much from one day to the next, the inside of his head scoured clean.

There, too, are the dead: Valgard Skafhogg and Bristle Beard, Thrain Life Taker and the others who had lost their manhood and their Odin faith and finally their lives, fetches drifting like *jinn* and forever lost in the Serkland sand.

Balancing that on One Eye's scales were those who survived: Finn, Gizur, Kvasir, Hlenni Brimill, Thorstein Cod Biter and the others, scarcely more than two handfuls, but all Odin-forged Oathsworn brothers now. They took the *Fjord Elk*'s oars in their calloused fists and rowed away with Jarl Brand to the promise of waters where the spray froze like silver beads.

The *Elk*'s prow turned north and they heaved up the sail, sure that the Bear Slayer, favoured of Odin, would steer them yet to that secret hoard now that he had his rune-serpent sword back. And if some wondered about their jarl, hunched and brooding over a silly nub-end of pine-tarred rope used to beat time for the rowing, they kept their teeth together on it. Orm Bear Slayer, they reminded themselves, had once killed a man in a *holmgang* with a single stroke.

The shipmasters, as ever, have their own name for even this stub of unattached line and the Loki joke of it was not lost on me, trying to weigh the deaths of Skafhogg and the others against Odin's cursed gift of silver.

They call it a bitter end.

HISTORICAL NOTE

Making sense of the Middle East of the late tenth century –
at any time period, it would seem – makes your head hurt.

The Sunni Abbasid Caliphate was slowly crumbling under
the weight of its own Mamluk armies, composed of Turks,
Slavs and Berbers, with a succession of trembling caliphs
appointed and then murdered by the Buyyid family in Baghdad.
At the same time, another dynasty, the Hamdanid, held Aleppo
as an independent fief, but still flew the black Abbasid flags,
vowing lip-service allegiance to the caliphs in Baghdad.

Meanwhile, the triumphant Fatimid Shias stormed across
North Africa, took Alexandria and renamed it Cairo
(Victorious), then pushed north, bringing an end and a measure
of stability to the chaos of little kingdoms in Syria and
Palestine, one of which was ruled by the self-styled Ikshid
Muhammad ibn Tugh from Jerusalem.

At the same time, a resurgent Byzantine Empire fought over
Antioch and Aleppo and a series of campaigns by Nicephoras
Phocas led to the taking of Tarsus and, in the year or so
covered by this book, a great raid which laid waste the Jezira.

Some two years later, Nicephoras Phocas was murdered by
John Tzimisces (Red Boots) and Leo Balantes – with the
connivance of the Empress Theophano – while he slept in his

palace. John became the new Emperor and there are those who believe this act actually saved the Byzantine Empire. Red Boots – and after him Basil II – finally took control of Antioch, as well as half of Syria, the Halab and most of Palestine all the way south to Nazareth, in a religious *reconquista* that anticipated the First Crusade by a century or more.

The Jarls Brand and Skarpheddin are based on several accounts of Norse chieftains ousted in various conflicts – mainly from the north of what is now Sweden – who went raiding in the Mediterranean with entire populations of men, women and children, mainly in Spain, which was ruled by al-Hakam II until 976 and afterwards by the legendary al-Mansur.

There is no record of a massive battle at Antioch involving the full panoply of the Byzantine forces at this time but there were almost certainly several large ones. Since I wanted Orm and the Oathsworn to take part in such a conflict, I engineered a great battle with no shame.

As ever, when anyone writes of this period, a debt is owed to Leo the Deacon (Leo Diaconus), born around the year 950. In his early youth he came to study at Constantinople and, in 986, took part in the war against the Bulgars under the Emperor Basil II, was present at the siege of Triaditza (Sofia), where the imperial army was defeated, and barely escaped with his life.

Around 992 he began to write a history of the empire, presumably at Constantinople, but he failed to finish before he died. The history, divided into ten books, covers the years from 976: that is, the reigns of Romanus II (959–63), Nicephorus Phocas (963–9) and John Tzimisces (969–76).

It describes the wars against the Arabs, including the recovery of Crete in 961, the conquest of Antioch and Northern Syria (968–9), the Bulgarian War (969) and the defeat of the Rus (971), one of the most brilliant periods of the later empire. For the reigns of Nicephorus Phocas and John Tzimisces, Leo the Deacon is the only contemporary source, from whom all later historians of this period have drawn their material.

The idea that, more than a hundred years before the Crusades, the Byzantines launched a religious war to retake Jerusalem is frequently overlooked. Jerusalem was considered a city of three faiths – Jew, Christian and Muslim – and defended as such by the Arabs, regardless of who warred beyond its walls.

This allowed Christians to pilgrimage to the Holy Land, visit the sites mentioned in the scriptures and do so in reasonable certainty of protection. More of a surprise still is that many of them were freshly converted Norsemen, or Norse/Slavs of the Rus lands, unfazed by far-travel and foreigners and ready to swim the Jordan to prove their new faith.

It seems right, then, that those who believed in the old Norse gods should also find a renewal of faith in a country called the Holy Land.

As ever, this is a saga to be told round a fire in the long dark reaches of the night. Any errors or omissions are my own and should not spoil the tale.

ACKNOWLEDGEMENTS

This book – and its predecessor – would never have been written without a huge team of willing people. Top of the list – my wife, Catherine, who puts up with a deal of neglect with good grace, until she decides enough is enough and that her husband's damned book can take second place to a social life. My respect and love for her is undimmed by years.

None of what you read could have been achieved without the co-operation of the Vikings themselves, particularly both of the Glasgow longships, who provided characters and events which they accepted with good grace and even excitement. My thanks especially, to Helen, Gail and Jill, who provided praise and correction by ploughing through *The Wolf Sea* when it was a rough voyage of a manuscript.

Finally – my thanks to my agent, James Gill, who pushed the Viking ship out to sea with his enthusiasm and insight for the whole project, and Susan Watt, my editor, and all the team at HarperCollins who kept me from getting in a guddle once I was afloat.

Largs 2007